Praise for *USA TODAY* bestselling author Delores Fossen

"Clear off space on your keeper shelf, Fossen has arrived."
— *New York Times* bestselling author Lori Wilde

"Delores Fossen takes you on a wild Texas ride with a hot cowboy."
— *New York Times* bestselling author B.J. Daniels

"You will be sold!"
— *RT Book Reviews* on *Blame It on the Cowboy*

"In the first McCord Brothers contemporary, bestseller Fossen strikes a patriotic chord that makes this story stand out."
— *Publishers Weekly* on *Texas on My Mind*

"Fossen delivers an entertaining romance between two people with real-life issues."
— *RT Book Reviews* on *Texas on My Mind*

"Fossen's stories are known for non-stop, explosive action with nail-biting close calls."
— *RT Book Reviews* on *The Deputy's Redemption*

**Also available from Delores Fossen
and HQN Books**

A Wrangler's Creek Novel

Lone Star Cowboy (ebook novella)
Those Texas Nights
One Good Cowboy (ebook novella)
No Getting Over a Cowboy
Just Like a Cowboy (ebook novella)

The McCord Brothers

What Happens on the Ranch (ebook novella)
Texas on My Mind
Cowboy Trouble (ebook novella)
Lone Star Nights
Cowboy Underneath It All (ebook novella)
Blame It on the Cowboy

To see the complete list of titles available from
Delores Fossen, please visit www.deloresfossen.com.

DELORES FOSSEN

BRANDED AS TROUBLE

HQN™

ISBN-13: 978-0-373-80228-9

Recycling programs for this product may not exist in your area.

Branded as Trouble

CONTENTS

BRANDED
AS TROUBLE

CHAPTER ONE

ROMAN GRANGER KNEW there were few advantages to being a badass over the age of thirty. Especially when you had a thirteen-year-old son. But this was one of those times when he could put his bad-assery skill set to good use.

"No," he told the naked woman standing in his living room. "I don't want whipped cream sprayed in my boxer shorts."

Roman added "the look." The slight sneer, chin down, the stare that he hoped conveyed that this whole whipped cream thing stood no chance whatsoever of happening.

The naked woman—Tiffany Ann Baker—stuck out her bottom lip in what he supposed was meant to be a playful pout, and she crooked her index finger, also playfully, for him to come to her. Roman wanted to tell her that if seeing her stark naked hadn't already caused him to move in her direction, then a crooked finger sure wasn't going to do the trick.

"How'd you get in my house?" he asked.

She smiled as if that was a good response to his snarled question. "Your housekeeper let me in before she left to do some errands. Oh, and she said to tell you that the upstairs toilet is making a gurgling sound. She jiggled the handle, but that didn't work."

Then he needed to have a chat with his live-in housekeeper, Anita, about allowing in women with whipped cream cans. Apparently, he also needed to call a plumber.

"You can't stay," Roman spelled out to Tiffany Ann. "My son, Tate, will be home from school soon."

Plus, even if Tate hadn't been on his way, Roman would have passed on the whipped cream sex. He'd just walked in from an overnight business trip where he'd gotten kicked by a rodeo bronco that he'd been in the process of buying. He was in pain, tired and hungry. Tiffany Ann would have stood a better chance of enticing him into having sex if she'd brought him a cheeseburger and some extra-strength ibuprofen.

"Oh, you devil, you," Tiffany Ann purred. Using the nozzle of the whipped cream like a wand, she waved it over her body. "You can't make me believe that you don't want more of this."

Believe it.

Since the badass look wasn't working, Roman tried a different approach. He picked up her clothes that she'd tossed on the back of his sofa and handed them to her. "Get dressed and leave. Sorry, but I don't want to have to explain a Brazilian strip wax and nipple piercings to my son when he comes through that door."

Of course, Tate probably knew all about it. He was thirteen, after all—almost fourteen—but Roman didn't want him to have a visual of the woman his dad had hooked up with twice.

Tiffany Ann stared as if waiting for him to change his mind. When she realized that wasn't going to happen, she huffed, threw the whipped cream and started dressing. The can smacked into the fireplace and started spewing. Tiffany Ann was spewing in her own way, too, because her eyes narrowed, and she jerked on her clothes as if she'd declared war on them.

"I thought we had a connection, Roman," she grumbled.

"We had sex," he corrected. "Remember, we discussed it before we got naked, and I told you that I wasn't looking for a relationship?"

It was easy for Roman to recall that because he had that same chat with all his potential lovers. Between his job as a rodeo promoter and being a single dad, he didn't have time for anything more than just casual sex. And hell in a big-assed handbasket, it wasn't as if he was the relationship type, anyway.

That's why he had a three-fuck rule.

Three times or less was just casual sex, but anything more than that strayed into commitment territory. He'd spelled out that rule to Tiffany Ann.

Despite that spelling-out, Roman could tell from Tiffany Ann's body language and expression that she hadn't bought it. He could almost predict what she was going to say: *I thought I could change your mind. I didn't believe you were serious when you said that.* Or, *I was certain that I was different from every other woman and that you really cared about me.*

He did care.

Just not in the way that Tiffany Ann or any other woman would ever want. That ship had sailed a long time ago.

But Tiffany Ann didn't say any of those things or even a variation of them. "I hope your toilet explodes and dumps pee-water all over your stupid head."

With that grade-school remark, she snapped back

her shoulders and walked out as if she'd been the one to put an end to this tryst. It was a good spin on things for her and meant she'd likely move on fast.

Despite his badass label, he really didn't want her hurt.

Definitely didn't want her shedding any tears over him.

That was another reason Roman had told her the truth right from the start. Of course, he was learning that the truth didn't always keep things as uncomplicated as he wanted. Celibacy didn't, either. For some reason, women took that as a challenge to test his commitment to it.

He doubted Tiffany Ann would come back, but he locked the door just in case. Tate could use his key to get in when he got home, which should be in less than fifteen minutes. The reason Roman had bought this particular house was because it was just up the street from the middle school. Tate had insisted he'd rather walk than have a sitter drive him to and from school while Roman was at work. His son hated the idea of a sitter.

Actually, Tate hated a lot of things these days.

Roman included.

He took his suitcase to his bedroom, wincing with each move, and he headed straight for the bathroom so he could locate some pain meds. He downed them with water he drank straight from the faucet, stripped and got in the shower.

Hell, he had a fist-size bruise on his lower right stomach and another on his chest. He hoped he didn't have a cracked rib to go along with it. If he did, it served him right. He'd ridden broncos for years and knew better than to get too close to one named Shit-kicker.

His phone was ringing when Roman stepped out of the shower, and he saw his sister's name on the screen.

Sophie ran the family business, Granger Western, which Roman wanted no part of. That applied to a lot of things when it came to his family. He didn't want the Granger Ranch, either, even though he legally owned it. And he definitely didn't want to deal with his mother.

Since Sophie's call was likely about one of those things—mother, ranch, business—he let it go to voice mail. He'd talk to her later, after the pain meds had kicked in and he'd gotten something to eat.

Roman made his way to the kitchen, located some leftover chili in the fridge and went through the mail on the island while he zapped the chili in the microwave. Junk mail, electric bill, junk mail. And his stomach tightened when he spotted the return address on the next envelope that had been sent to his son.

Valerie Banchini.

His old high school girlfriend.

But more importantly, Tate's mom.

It'd been over six months since she'd communicated with Tate in any way. That had been a birthday card that was four months late. Hell, it hadn't even been a real birthday card. Valerie had scratched out "Be My Valentine" and scrawled "Happy B'day, Baby" instead. On the inside, she'd lined through "Love, Doug" and written "Mommy loves you!!!!"

Maybe this was an early card to celebrate his fourteenth birthday, which was still weeks away. Or it could be just a "thinking of you" note.

Either way, it would send Tate into a tailspin.

Anything from his mother always did. His son had never come out and said it, but Roman suspected that the meager contact was a reminder for Tate that the only part his mom had had in his life was regifted cards and an occasional phone call. It sucked. And Roman despised her for it.

But not nearly as much as he despised himself.

He should have done better by his son. Should have been able to rewrite the past and give the kid a mother he deserved. Instead, he'd started out Tate's life in a tangled mess.

Roman had been just eighteen when he'd gotten Valerie pregnant. No three-fuck rule back then. They'd been going out for a couple of months, had had sex too many times to count, and one of those times the condom had failed. Hard to curse the condom company, though, because he'd gotten Tate.

Of course, he'd also gotten "Valerie baggage" since she'd skipped out on both of them shortly after Tate was born. Too bad that baggage wasn't just his and only his, but this crap always got on his son.

His phone rang again as the microwave dinged. Not Sophie this time but his brother, Garrett. This would be about ranching business, so he also let it go to voice mail. Apparently, though, his brother wasn't taking no-answer for an answer because Roman's phone rang again right away.

But it wasn't Garrett. It was Tate's school.

Everything inside Roman went still, and he hit the answer button. "Mr. Granger?" a woman said after Roman greeted the caller. "This is Principal Wilson."

Yeah, Roman recognized her voice. That was because he'd been called in for chats with the woman about Tate's sullen behavior and slipping grades. "Is Tate all right?" Roman immediately asked.

He heard something he didn't want to hear. The principal's heavy sigh. "I'm sorry to tell you this, but Tate got in a fight at school. He got a cut on his lip. He's fine physically. The nurse is treating it now."

"I'll be right there." Roman grabbed his keys and headed for the door.

"Good. I was afraid you wouldn't be able to come. Tate said you were away on business again."

Roman didn't miss the *again*, and he couldn't argue with it. He was gone a lot. That's why he'd hired Anita, but a live-in housekeeper couldn't fix something like this.

He tried to tamp down the emotions that bubbled up inside him. And failed. His boy was hurt. "Who gave him that busted lip?"

"A classmate. But you should know that Tate punched him first. The other student has a cut lip and a bruised face. Since we weren't sure if anything was broken, that student's being sent to the hospital."

Roman bit back the profanity, barely, and he hurried out the door. Not walking, but rather running, which wasn't exactly easy in cowboy boots and with his side throbbing like a bad tooth. He got in his truck and took off, heading for the school.

"Why did this happen?" Roman asked her. "How did the fight start?"

"Neither boy will say, but Tate might talk to you about it."

Roman doubted it. He wasn't his son's go-to person for any form of communication.

"You should know that this is very serious," the principal went on. "Tate will be expelled for this."

Now Roman cursed, and judging from the sound

of disapproval the principal made, she was convinced
that Tate's cursing, badass, black-sheep father was the
reason for this mess he was in.

And the principal was probably right.

"Expelled?" Roman questioned. "That seems pretty
extreme for a schoolyard fight."

"We have a zero tolerance policy for this sort of thing
when injuries are involved. Mr. Granger, you'll need to
find Tate another school. I also think you should get him
some counseling. We can talk about that when you get
here." And the principal ended the call.

He'd tried to coax Tate into counseling, and hadn't
succeeded in doing that, either, but Roman would try
it again. He would also somehow convince Principal
Wilson into nixing the expulsion so Tate could stay in
school. Tate had several friends there, and Roman didn't
want the kid to have to re-create his life.

Roman pulled into the school parking lot, took the
first spot he could find and hurried into the building.
The principal's office was just off the main hall so he
headed there and immediately spotted Ms. Wilson
standing next to another woman.

Both turned to him when he came through the door.

Roman instantly knew something was wrong. Something more than the obvious.

"Mr. Granger," Principal Wilson said. "This is
Mandy Rodriguez, the school nurse." The two women
exchanged glances.

Uneasy glances.

This was where Roman's experience created some
very bad scenarios in his head. He'd been in bar fights.
Had had his face punched and his lip busted. But not

once had those injuries been serious enough to send him to the hospital.

"Is Tate okay?" Roman asked.

The nurse nodded but then shook her head. "I left him alone for only a couple of minutes when I went to get some cotton swabs to clean his lip." She paused, swallowed hard. "When I came back, Tate was gone. Mr. Granger, I think your son ran away."

CHAPTER TWO

MILA BANCHINI KNEW there were few advantages to being a virgin over the age of thirty. Especially not in a small ranching town like Wrangler's Creek.

One of those nonadvantages was waiting for her when she stepped outside her bookstore to close up for the day.

Ian Busby.

He was in his early twenties, as skinny as a zipper, and his pinched, flushed face reminded her of a rooster. He also had *horny* written all over him. Literally. Well, it was printed on his T-shirt, anyway.

Me So Horny was emblazoned above a picture of a rhino.

She doubted the shirt was a bad gift from a friend. Or that he'd lost a bet and been forced to wear it. No, he'd probably picked it out himself and was proud of not only the sentiment but also the butchered grammar.

Mila didn't acknowledge he was there. She locked up and started walking home. Normally, she drove the quarter of a mile or so to her house, but the spring weather had been so nice that morning that she'd decided to walk. Bad idea. Because now she had to walk back, and with each step Ian was trailing along beside her.

"Did you give any more thought to going out with me?" Ian asked.

"No. Because I told you when you asked that it wasn't going to happen." She didn't try to sound even remotely pleasant because Mila had learned the hard way that pleasantness only encouraged Ian and the rest of his brothers. Of course, ignoring them seemed to encourage them, as well. Her breathing did, too.

The Busby boys, and apparently every other eligible male in town, were on some kind of quest to rid her of her virginal condition. Maybe because they thought that since she was thirty-one she was desperate. And that she had therefore lowered her standards to rock bottom.

She hadn't.

Just the opposite. It was those high standards that had left her in this condition in the first place, and if she were to loosen those standards, it wouldn't be with somebody like Ian.

"But I really like you," he went on. "And you're one of the prettiest women in town."

If that was true, which it wasn't, then she could have pointed out then that her beauty gave her far better options than his gene pool. The Busby brothers' claims to fame were cow-tipping, peeing on electric fences and wearing T-shirts with *horny* written on them.

"I won't go out with you," Mila stated, and kept walking. She couldn't get home fast enough. Then she could change into yoga pants and watch one of her favorite movies. She was in a *Titanic* sort of mood, but she only watched the romantic parts.

Ah, Jack.

Now, why hadn't he survived, moved to Wrangler's Creek and frozen time so she could meet him?

Of course, time had frozen in a different kind of way. Not just because it was taking forever for her to get home, but because she was walking down Main Street, which looked almost identical to the way it had over three decades ago when Mila was born. No big-box stores here. In fact, no chain stores of any kind. This was the mom-and-pop business model where everybody knew everybody and bought local as much as possible. That was good for her bookstore, but there were times when Mila dreamed about ditching everything and starting fresh.

"I wish you'd change your mind about going out with me," Ian went on. "I got a real nice date planned. Friday is two-for-one corn dogs at the Longhorn Bar. Two-for-one beers, too, if we get there early enough. Then I could take you to that pretty spot out by the creek where we could look at UFOs."

She mentally stumbled over that last word. He probably thought he was being cute by not saying something expected like stars or moonlight on the water. Then again, UFO could be code for his penis. Maybe Uncovered F-ing Object or Unzipped Firehose Organ.

Mila huffed. "I don't eat corn dogs, don't drink beer and I have a phobia about UFOs."

He nodded as if he got all of that. Which should have stopped him and caused him to turn around. It didn't. He just kept on walking. Talking, too.

"Say, you're not still into that pretend stuff, are you?" he asked.

Mila made sure she didn't hesitate a step. In fact, she sped up. And she didn't dignify his insult with an answer.

"Because I heard about it," Ian went on. "Somebody

said you dress up like people in the movies. Like *Dirty Dancing* kind of dress up. But that you don't do the nasty with any of those fellas, that you just do the dancing parts. Well, if you want, I could dress up like somebody from the movies and dance with you."

She wanted to say she had a phobia about dancing with him, but they both knew this wasn't about dancing. It was about his wanting to get in her pants.

"I don't do that *pretend stuff* anymore," she assured him.

That was a lie. But she was taking a minibreak from it because the previous night's enactment hadn't played out so well. Apparently, her fantasy partner had a different interpretation of Buttercup and Wesley rolling down the hill. He thought it should involve clothing removal while he yelled, "As you wish."

"Guess you're still hung up on Roman Granger, huh?" Ian asked several moments later.

Mila hadn't thought there was anything to get her to slow her lightning-fast pace, but that did it. "Roman?" she repeated as if that were impossible.

Of course, Ian knew it was more than possible. Everyone in town did, just as they knew about her fantasy role-play. She'd had a crush on Roman since she was old enough to realize that boys and girls had different parts.

Or "secret places" as her mother called them.

And speaking of her mother, Mila saw Vita sitting on her front porch as she approached her house.

"Oh, I gotta go," Ian said. He pretended to check his watch, no doubt to make her believe that he had somewhere else to be.

Which wasn't that far off the mark.

When it came to her mother, most people wanted to be anywhere else. Vita was the ultimate person-repellant, and while that had caused Mila plenty of problems in her life, she was thankful for it now because it sent Ian scurrying away.

Vita wasn't your ordinary mother. Nope. She had her freaky flag flying with her Bohemian clothes—a long brown shirt, peasant blouse and dozens of cheap bead necklaces and bracelets. When she walked, she sounded like a chained Jacob Marley from *A Christmas Carol*.

But it wasn't just the clothes that made her odd. Vita claimed to come from a long line of Romanian fortune-tellers. Even though Mila had never met any of her kin, the story that Vita liked to tell was that her family had stowed away on a pirate ship from Romania when Vita was just a baby. Mila doubted the story, mainly because her mother was only in her fifties, and that mode of transportation probably wasn't possible in modern times.

Of course, there was nothing modern about her mother.

Or normal.

Vita did charms, exorcised spirits, blessed houses and read palms. Surprisingly, people paid her for those things, which only proved that some residents of Wrangler's Creek weren't normal, either. Even those people, though, thought her mother was weird.

And that meant Mila was weird by genetic association.

It didn't matter that Mila owned her own business and never chanted, exorcised spirits or read palms. She would always be her mother's daughter. It didn't help, either, that Mila's father had died in a car accident when she was just a kid, only five. He might have added some normalcy to her life if he were still alive.

Or at least that's what she liked to tell herself.

It was just as possible that he would have only added another level of weirdness. After all, he'd married Vita.

Still, Mila had some incredible memories of Frankie Michael Banchini. He'd done funny faces to make her laugh, had secretly eaten those much-hated Brussels sprouts that Vita had insisted on serving her. And he'd never turned her away when she wanted him to read her a story. Mila was certain that's where her love of books had started, and being around them was a way of keeping her father close.

She had loved him. Always would. And she loved her mother, too. Sometimes, though, Vita didn't always make loving her that easy.

"There's an ill wind blowing," her mother greeted her. She lifted her head, looked at the cloudless sky. There wasn't so much as a wisp of a breeze. "Bad juju. That might help."

Vita tipped her head to a small white box on Mila's doorstep. The kind of box that someone might use to gift a small piece of jewelry.

Since the porch wasn't that big, Mila leaned in and had a look. Not jewelry. It appeared to be a blob of some kind of animal poop. Chicken, probably, since her mother raised them.

"Sometimes, you have to fight caca with caca," her mother added.

Mila could only sigh, and she sank down on the step next to her mother. She considered asking her if she wanted to go inside, but she'd left her Buttercup clothes on the sofa and didn't want to have to explain it.

"So, what bad juju should I expect?" Mila asked.

"I had a vision. Within thirty days, your life will be turned upside down."

Oh, this was such a cheery conversation. Mila hadn't lied to Ian when she had told him she didn't drink beer, but there was a bottle of wine in her fridge that she'd need after this visit.

It wasn't fun to encourage this conversation thread, but her mother wasn't going to leave until she had said whatever it was she'd come to say. Best to get that "say" started.

"Are we talking a tornado here?" Mila asked. "Or something more personal, like me tripping and falling?"

Vita lifted her shoulder. "The vision doesn't always dot the *i*'s or cross the *t*'s. But in these same thirty days, you'll be on a quest to find the truth."

Well, she was sort of heading in that direction, anyway. The fantasy stuff just wasn't working for her anymore. Lately, she'd been thinking about being kissed. For real. Not as part of some reenactment.

"And after thirty days, you'll no longer be a virgin," her mother added in a discussing-the-weather tone. Vita took something from her pocket—a foil-wrapped condom— and handed it to her. "Use this, though. It's a rubber, and it'll stop you from getting knocked up. You put it on the man's secret place when he's decided not to keep it secret from you any longer."

Mila stared at her. "I know what a condom is."

"Well, good." Vita patted her hand. And kept on patting. It went on for so long that Mila had to stop her or else she was going to have a red mark.

"Is something wrong?" Mila came out and asked.

Vita nodded, got to her feet, but not before patting

her hand again. "I need to take a little trip back to see my family."

She might as well have announced she was going to Pluto. Vita never traveled. Heck, her mother never left Wrangler's Creek. "To Romania?"

Another nod. "I want to see them while they're still around to be seen. Just don't hate me when the shit happens. I had my reasons for doing what I did."

Color her confused. What did Romanians, upside down, devirgining and bad juju have to do with her hating her mother?

"All will be revealed in time," Vita added, and she started to walk to her bicycle, which was next to Mila's fence.

She was still confused. "Want me to give you a ride home?" Her mother owned a car but rarely used it. Instead, Vita preferred to pedal the two miles from her place and into town.

Vita shook her head and kept moving. Mila would have gone after her if her phone hadn't rung, and she saw her best friend's name on the screen. Sophie Granger McKinnon.

"I'm at the hospital," Sophie said the moment that Mila answered.

That was not something she wanted to hear from anyone but especially one who was seven and a half months pregnant with twins. "Are you in labor?"

"No. I'm fine. It's not me. It's my mom. She had some chest pains so I brought her in." It sounded as if Sophie was crying. "Mila, they think she might have had a heart attack."

Oh, mercy. "Just stay calm. I'll be there in a few minutes. Who's with you now?"

"Clay."

Good. Clay was police chief Clay McKinnon, Sophie's husband and a rock under pressure. He would help Sophie rein in her worst fears. Still, Mila needed to be there, too. She'd known Sophie's mother, Belle, her entire life, and while Belle wasn't exactly Miss Sunshine, she didn't put curses on people.

"Garrett and Nicky are on the way, too," Sophie added. Her brother and his fiancée. "Garrett was off buying some cattle, but he should be here soon. Anyway, I've tried to call Roman, but he's not answering. I hate to ask you to do this, but could you try calling him again for me? If he still doesn't answer, would you drive to his house in San Antonio and tell him what's going on?"

"Of course," Mila said without hesitation.

"I know Roman and Mom are at odds, but he'll want to know. Convince him to come home."

"I will."

Mila wasn't sure she could do that. Roman wasn't an easy-to-convince sort of person. Plus, she always got a little tongue-tied around him. But surely once he heard about his mother, Mila wouldn't need to do much convincing. He would hurry to be by her side.

She scrolled through her "favorites" contacts, found Roman's number and pressed it. Since he hadn't answered his sister's call, Mila expected this to go to voice mail, but she was surprised when he immediately answered.

"Mila," he said.

One word. Her name. There was nothing unusual about it, other than Roman had been the one to say it. And, like any other time she heard him speak, her stomach did a flip-flop. She so wished there was some way to make herself immune to him.

Mila gathered her breath, ready to tell him about his mom, but Roman continued first. "It's Tate," he said.

Her stomach did another flip-flop but for a different reason this time. That's because she heard the concern in his voice. "What's wrong?"

"He ran away again, and I've been looking all over for him. By any chance, did he go to your place?"

It wasn't an out-there kind of question. Tate had run away before, nearly two years ago, and he'd gotten someone to drive him to her house. That's because Tate's mother, and therefore, Tate, were Mila's cousins.

Once Valerie and she had been close, too, since Vita had raised Valerie as her own. But it didn't matter that Mila had once thought of her as a sister because she hadn't seen Valerie in years. That didn't matter to Tate, either. He just seemed to want a connection with anyone who was blood kin with his mother.

Something Mila understood, because she missed having that with her father.

Plus, Tate knew that Mila kept a spare key in the verbena plant so he'd be able to get into her house. She checked, and it wasn't there now.

"I'm going inside to see if he's here," she assured Roman.

Mila got the door unlocked as fast as she could, and her gaze fired all around. Her house wasn't that large— two bedrooms, a living room, kitchen and bath. So, it didn't take her long to check out the place.

And spot him.

Tate was on the sofa, asleep on top of her Buttercup dress.

"He's here," she told Roman.

Roman said something she didn't catch. Profanity mixed with a prayer, maybe. "Put him on the phone. I want to talk to him." That didn't sound like a prayer, though. More like the profanity tone.

Mila was about to tell him to take it easy on the boy, but she froze. "Oh, God."

That's because she spotted something else. Something in Tate's hand.

A bottle of pills.

Tate didn't have a firm grip on it. In fact, he didn't have a firm grip on anything. His hand was limp, the bottle resting on its side in his palm, and he was as white as a sheet of paper.

"Call an ambulance," she managed to say to Roman.

Mila dropped the phone and ran to Tate.

CHAPTER THREE

THAT WHOLE LIFE flashing before a dying person's eyes applied to fathers, too. Roman now had firsthand proof of that.

In that moment when Mila had shouted for him to call an ambulance, Roman saw it all. His childhood on the ranch. His screw-ups. His arrest for underage drinking. Another arrest for reckless driving only a year after that. The arguments with his parents those things had caused.

He was probably being punished for all the crap he'd done, but Roman wished to hell that the powers that be had taken that punishment out on him instead of Tate.

In that life-flash, Roman had seen Valerie telling him that she was pregnant. They'd both been just eighteen and in their senior year of high school. He'd felt the sickening feeling of dread that this was yet something else he had screwed up. The feeling hadn't lasted though, not after Tate had been born. The moment Roman held his boy in his arms, he knew he'd never love anything or anybody the way he did his son.

And now he might lose him.

Tate was breathing, that much he knew, and Mila had said something about Tate holding a bottle of medicine. Roman didn't know what he'd taken or how much, but he knew what this meant.

His son had attempted suicide.

Hell.

Roman was damn perceptive when it came to his job, but he hadn't seen that his own son was on the brink of doing something like this. It made the fight at school and being expelled fade way, way to the background.

"How far out are you now?" Mila asked from the other end of the phone line.

Roman wasn't sure he could speak because his chest and throat were so tight. "About five miles. Anything from the doctor yet?"

Though he knew the answer to that. If there'd been something, *anything*, Mila would have told him. After he'd called the ambulance about thirty minutes ago, he had called her right back. She hadn't gotten off the phone with him since then and had been updating him every step of the way.

The ambulance's arrival.

The drive to the hospital, which thankfully was only a few minutes from her house.

And Tate and her going into the emergency room.

The medics had immediately whisked Tate away, but they hadn't allowed Mila in there with him. Instead, she was outside the examining room.

"Nothing yet from the doctor, but I'm certain that Tate will be fine," Mila said. It was hard to tell if she was BS-ing, but Roman decided to take her at her word. He just couldn't wrap his mind around anything else right now. "Focus on your driving," she added. "Make sure you get here in one piece because we don't need another Granger in the hospital."

That was for sure. One was more than enough.

He wanted to know if Mila had learned what meds

Tate had taken. Or where he'd gotten them. But again, if she knew something she would have told him.

Unless it was bad, that is.

People kept all kinds of old meds in their bathrooms. Maybe Tate had even gotten into the Percocet that was left over from when Roman wrenched his knee. Or, hell, he could have gotten it from some kid at school or stolen something from the nurse who'd been cleaning his busted lip. Tate could have taken something that could kill him.

Roman heard his too-fast breath, felt himself losing focus, so he forced himself to keep talking to Mila. "Were you able to get in touch with Sophie and Garrett?"

Mila didn't jump to answer that. Something that caused Roman's chest to tighten even more. "Yes, Sophie's here," she finally said. Then Mila hesitated again. "You want me to put her on the phone?"

It was tempting because he loved his sister, and it might have soothed him to hear her voice, but Sophie was mega-pregnant, and there was nothing in his own voice that would soothe her. He damn sure didn't want her going into early labor because she was upset.

"No. I'm taking my exit now," Roman told her. "I'm almost there. Meet me at the ER doors so I know where to go. Oh, and try to get Sophie to sit down or something."

He hit the end call button and started the last couple of miles. They crawled by. Too bad, though, that his thoughts weren't crawling. Apparently, the life-flash was the only thing that was going to fall into the fast category today because his truck suddenly felt as if it were in snail gear. It didn't help that Mila was right.

He had to focus on his driving because it wouldn't help anyone if he got in an accident.

It was the second time today that he screeched into a parking lot, and he hit the ground running as soon as he brought his truck to a stop. It took another lifetime for him to run to the ER, and just as he had known she would be, Mila was there.

"This way," she said, and he pulled her into a quick hug as they ran. "The doctor is still in there with him."

Roman got another hug from Sophie, who wasn't sitting but rather pacing outside an examining room while she had her hands on her back. Roman didn't knock. He just threw open the examining room door and went in.

Only to see Tate barfing into a bedpan.

His son was alive, conscious and sitting up. Roman wasn't sure how many prayers of thanks he said in those next few seconds, but he had to have set a world record.

Tate wasn't alone. In addition to the doctor, a nurse was there. Wanda Kay Busby, and she immediately smiled and winked at him. Roman hoped she had something in her eye to make her do that, because the last thing he wanted right now was a flirting nurse.

Or a cop.

There was one of those, too. His brother-in-law, Chief Clay McKinnon, was in the corner of the room, his back against the wall. Maybe Clay was there as family, but it was also possible he'd been called in because this was a suicide attempt.

Roman went to Tate and put his arms around him. He couldn't tell if Tate was glad to see him because he was still heaving.

"Does your son have any known allergies?" the doctor asked. His name was Alan Sanchez, and Roman had known him most of his life. In fact, Dr. Sanchez had stitched him up a few times.

Roman shook his head and tried to think. "Sometimes dairy upsets his stomach." Which probably wasn't relevant here, but Roman's thoughts were all over the place. He sorted through the tornado in his head and came up with some questions for Tate.

"Are you okay? What did you take? And why the heck did you do this?"

Tate couldn't answer because he was still barfing.

Dr. Sanchez pulled a medicine bottle from his pocket and showed it to Roman. Not prescription stuff, but rather over-the-counter meds. Cramp Relief Nighttime, Roman read from the label. Beneath it was something that got Roman's attention: "Nighttime relief of menstrual discomfort, PMS, bloating and headaches."

"Tate took period medicine?" Roman asked, certain that he'd missed something.

"Well, it's also a general painkiller," the doctor explained, "and it has a sleep aid in it. A medicine similar to Benadryl. That's why Mila wasn't able to wake him when she found him in her house."

"Period medicine?" Roman repeated. That told him just how bad off Tate was for him to down something like that. "Why did you do this?" he said to Tate.

Tate lifted his shoulder, which wasn't an answer. At least not the answer Roman wanted to hear.

"He'll be drowsy for a while," the doctor went on. "We pumped his stomach, but that was just a precaution. We think he only took three. While that exceeds the recommended dosage, it's not enough to be life threatening."

All right. That was an answer Roman wanted to hear.

Tate was going to be okay. The relief flooded through him, but it was quickly followed by another emotion.

Anger.

This was intentional. If he'd simply had a headache, he could have almost certainly found something else to take care of it, and he wouldn't have needed three pills.

"Any idea how Tate got that cut on his mouth?" Dr. Sanchez asked.

That didn't help with the anger that was quickly eating up the relief. "School fight." Roman wouldn't mention the other stuff about Tate being expelled and running away. No, that was something he would discuss with his son as soon as he quit puking.

"Why don't we step outside and go over some paperwork?" the doctor added. "It's going to be a while before Tate feels like talking."

Yeah, and he might never feel like talking to his father. Well, that was about to change, because Roman was tired of sweeping all that teenage angst under the rug. It had brought them here, to this, and it was going to end.

Clay stayed put with Tate and the nurse, and Roman let the doctor take him by the arm and lead him into the hall. The moment the door opened, Mila was right there. No Sophie, though.

"How is he?" Mila immediately asked. "God, Roman, I'm so sorry. I swear, I didn't know he would do anything like this or I wouldn't have left that spare key in the verbena."

Roman waved off her apology. "Thanks for finding him and getting him here. Where's Sophie?"

Mila tipped her head to the other end of the hall.

"Cafeteria. She's getting a snack. But she'll be back in a few minutes."

Good. Then he'd make her sit. Maybe even talk her into going home with her husband. That would clear out the cop along with getting Sophie into a more comfortable place where she could get some rest.

Roman turned to the doctor. "Did those pills damage Tate in any way?"

"Probably not. At most he'll have an upset stomach and be sleepy." He looked down at a tablet where it appeared he'd made some notes on a medical form. "But I do need to keep him at least overnight. Tate will also need a psychiatric evaluation."

Those two words felt like a punch to the gut. Obviously, the doctor thought this was more than teenager angst to request something like that.

"You'll want to give Tate some time, too," the doctor went on. "He seemed scared of what your reaction would be. Terrified, actually. When he first woke up, he asked me not to tell you. In fact, he said he didn't want to see you."

Roman felt Mila's hand on his arm, probably because he was breathing like an asthmatic. His son was terrified of him. Great. Something else to add to his résumé of shitty screw-ups. He'd been right to worry about that when Valerie had told him she was pregnant.

"He's a teenager," Mila whispered to him. That was likely meant to comfort him and explain all of this away, but nothing could do that right now.

The doctor wisely gave him a moment by looking over his notes again. "It'll take me a while to set up the psychiatric eval. A while to get him into a room, too.

In the meantime, if you want to check on your mom, the nurse will stay here with Tate."

Because Mila still had her hand on his arm, Roman felt her fingers tense. "I didn't tell him," Mila jumped to say. "I thought he already had enough on his mind for the drive here."

Roman huffed. She was right, he had had enough on his mind, but he wasn't someone who needed sheltering. "What's wrong with my mother?"

Even now, just saying the word *mother* caused him to have a bad reaction. That's because there'd been bad blood between them for so long that Roman's go-to expression upon hearing her name was to scowl.

"Sophie brought her in a little while ago," the doctor explained. "Belle was having chest pains, shortness of breath—"

"A heart attack?" Roman interrupted.

The doctor shook his head. "It's called stress cardiomyopathy or broken heart syndrome."

Roman just stared at him, wondering if this was some kind of sick joke. Apparently not. On the day his son had swallowed PMS meds, his sixty-year-old mom had had a broken heart reaction.

"It happens to some women her age," the doctor explained. "We're not sure why, but I'll be keeping her for a day or two, as well. She's in room 112, and you can look in on her now if you like."

That was an offer that most sons could answer with a resounding yes, but he hesitated. "She doesn't always have a good reaction when it comes to me. I don't want to upset her."

Again, like his son.

Roman was seeing a pattern here.

The doctor made a sound of agreement because he almost certainly knew all about Belle's and his parting of the ways. A feud that'd come to a head when Roman and Valerie had refused to get married just because she was pregnant. His mother had considered that an embarrassment and a "slimeball" thing to do.

Her exact words.

It hadn't helped, either, when Valerie had run out and left Roman to raise Tate alone. Ditto for not helping—the fact his mother and he were both mule-headed. But, by God, Roman had gotten plenty tired of having her judge him.

The doctor made some more notes. The way this was going, he might be scheduling a psych eval for Roman, too.

"Hold off on seeing Belle, then," Dr. Sanchez said a moment later. "She might ask about Tate, and it's not a good idea to tell her about him just yet. Let's wait a few more hours until I'm certain she's stabilized."

Good idea. A few more hours might give Roman a chance to find level ground. The tornado was starting to spin in his head again.

The doctor looked at him. "I'll need you to fill out some insurance paperwork." He pointed to the reception desk at the front of the waiting room. "Just see the woman who's seated there and she'll get you started."

Dr. Sanchez walked away, leaving Roman alone with Mila. He was too exhausted to figure out the right thing to say to her, but it was obvious she was worried.

"Bad day?" she asked. She didn't crack a smile. In fact, Roman wasn't sure he'd ever seen Mila smile. But this seemed to be some attempt at humor.

He didn't smile, either, but yeah, it'd been a bad day.

His son's life was a mess, and Roman wasn't even sure how to fix it. Now, his mother was having heart problems. A problem with a weird name, at that. And even though it was minor in the grand scheme of things, his side was hurting—bad.

"Maybe this means you've gotten all the awful stuff out of the way," Mila added. "That's what my mom always says, anyway." She made a face. "Except she says you have to flush the toilet to get rid of the poop and have clean water. My mom says a lot of weird things," she added in a mumble.

She looked at him, her expression changing, and Mila reached out for him. Not as some kind of comforting gesture, either, but with both arms. And she lurched toward him. At first, Roman didn't know why she'd done that.

Until somebody turned off the lights in his head.

And he dropped to the floor like a sack of rocks.

CHAPTER FOUR

"I DON'T WANT whipped cream in my boxer shorts," Roman mumbled. He wasn't sure why, but it was hard to speak.

"All right," someone agreed. "Seems like a reasonable request to me."

It took Roman several moments to process the comment. It wasn't easy because, in addition to it being hard to speak, it was also hard to think. His head was whirling like an F5 tornado. But, despite the whirl, he thought he might recognize the voice. Not Tiffany Ann, standing in his living room.

But rather his mother.

Hell. Even in a dream he didn't want to talk to his mother about whipped cream sex, so Roman forced himself to wake up. Maybe there was glue or something on his eyes because he had to struggle to get them open.

Bad idea.

The light stabbed in his eyeballs and therefore his head. In addition to the whirling thoughts and dreams, he was also in pain.

"Would you like whipped cream somewhere else?" she asked. "Maybe like in some hot chocolate or on a piece of pie?"

Definitely his mother.

Roman got his eyes open again, expecting the remnants of the dream to vanish. It didn't. His mother was right there, standing next to his bed. Except it wasn't even his bed. Not his room, either.

"Where am I?" he asked.

"The hospital. We both are."

That's when he noticed his mom was indeed wearing a hospital gown. And he remembered. She'd been admitted for the heart problem with the funny name. His son was here, as well, and that caused Roman to jackknife to a sitting position so he could check on Tate.

Another bad idea.

Because the pain wasn't just in his head. It was also in his side where the bronco had kicked him. His mom caught on to his shoulders and eased him back down on the mattress. Roman was already going in that direction, anyway, because he didn't have a choice. He had to get control of the pain before he could walk.

"Your appendix ruptured a couple of hours ago," Belle explained. "You had surgery."

Yes, he remembered falling. Remembered the concern he'd seen on Mila's face. But he didn't have a single memory of the surgery. Later, he would want to know more about that, but for now there was something a lot more pressing.

"Where's Tate?" he asked. "I want to see him."

"He's with the doctor right now, but he'll be done in a few minutes." Belle motioned toward the two other beds that were to Roman's left. "Doc Sanchez fixed up this room for all of us. Isn't it nice? It used to be two rooms, but it had one of those squishy dividers that he pulled back. This way we can be together but still have two bathrooms."

Maybe it was the fog in his head or the pain, but Roman didn't get it. "All of us? Here? Together?"

Belle nodded, smiled. "He thought it would be a good idea for you, me and Tate to be close to each other."

It wasn't a good idea at all. "He knows that you and I don't get along," Roman reminded her.

Belle shrugged. "Maybe he thought it'd be good therapy or something."

Well, it was *or something*, all right. It was stupid.

As soon as he could, Roman would request another room. Better yet, he'd get out of here the moment he could stand up. No way did he want to be trapped with the woman he'd left town to escape.

"You want me to see if the nurse will bring you some whipped cream now?" Belle asked. "That's all you've been mumbling about since they brought you in from recovery."

Hell's bells. He hoped he hadn't said too much. Of course, unlike Tate, his mom probably didn't know what a Brazilian strip wax was.

"But I have to tell you," she added. Any time she started a sentence with those six words, Roman knew that nagging would shortly follow. "I think it's a bad idea to eat all that sugar right after surgery. Of course, you always were a rebel like that even when it wasn't good for you. I don't think you can argue with me about that."

Oh, he could, but Roman chose not to.

"No whipped cream," he assured her. He glanced down at her arm and realized she had an IV pole next to her. An IV needle in her arm, too. Roman had one, as well, but he wasn't standing. "Shouldn't you be in bed?"

"Probably, but when you started talking, I thought we should have a little chat first before Tate gets here."

Roman groaned. "I don't want to hear anything from you about Valerie and me not getting married—"

"Agreed."

It was a good thing Roman was lying down because he would have collapsed from shock. In the past thirteen years, his mother had never passed up an opportunity to harp on him. Maybe she was drugged up or something.

Heck, maybe *he* was drugged up.

"Tate needs peace and quiet right now," she went on. "I'm supposed to have that, too. And I'm betting the doc won't like it if you're all agitated and wanting to eat whipped cream. Might cause you to pop a stitch. Anyway, I thought we could each come up with a safe topic to discuss like the weather or whipped cream. We could even have our own safe words."

"Safe words?" Maybe his mom would have known about a Brazilian, after all. Mercy, he hoped not. He had enough unresolved issues with her without putting that in his head.

"Yes, you know like bumfuzzle or Dippity-do," Belle explained. "Words that we wouldn't normally say. We could say one of them if the conversation is taking a direction that might hit one of our hot buttons. Then we would immediately stop talking about whatever it is we were talking about. I mean a complete verbal shutdown on the subject." She paused. "You don't use Dippity-do in conversation, do you? Because if you do, we could go with another word."

Roman was certain that even with the pain and fog, he managed a blank stare. "I don't use Dippity-do. I don't know what the hell it is."

"Hair gel," she said as if the answer were obvious. "And bumfuzzle is when you're confused. My granddaddy used to say it. But I have to tell you, Roman, you've got more hot buttons than I do. Any little thing will tick you off. You've always been that way, and I think it's gotten worse—"

"Dippity-do," Roman snarled through clenched teeth. He didn't expect it to work. But it did.

Belle hushed—a complete verbal shutdown on the subject—but she did add an indignant wobble of her head as if disapproving of the shushing.

"Well, this was your idea." He stared at her, daring her to disagree with that, or with anything else he might add to it.

"Bumfuzzle," she mumbled.

Good. They'd reached a truce. A weird one with words he didn't especially want to say aloud, but the truce was in the nick of time.

Because Tate came into the room.

His boy looked better than he had when Roman had seen him earlier. Tate wasn't throwing up at least. But he was in a wheelchair, and Sophie was pushing him. That caused Roman to try to jolt from the bed again to help her, but Sophie waved him off.

"Don't even think about getting out of that bed," Sophie scolded Roman. "You scared the living daylights out of all of us when you collapsed. How's your head? You smacked it pretty hard when you hit the floor."

Roman touched his fingers to his forehead. Yep, that was the source of the pain, and he remembered hitting it. Also remembered Mila trying to break his fall.

Sophie maneuvered the wheelchair close to the middle bed, and Tate got out of the chair and onto it.

"Are you okay with this sleeping arrangement?" she asked, glancing at all three of them.

Roman would have slept in a pit of rattlesnakes if he could be near his son. Since there was a sudden lump in his throat, he settled for nodding. Tate nodded, as well. Maybe because he figured Roman wouldn't chew him out in front of Belle. He wouldn't. But not because Belle was there. He needed to have a long, serious talk with Tate, but he had to keep his temper out of it.

Even if he was hurt and furious that Tate had done what he had.

"Are you okay?" Roman asked him.

Tate shrugged and grunted. It was more of a response than Roman normally got so he'd take it.

"The doctor said he'd be in soon to talk to you," Sophie explained. "And a nurse will be by to take Tate to meet the therapist."

Tate grunted again, a sound that could have meant anything. Roman hoped it was a sound of approval because Tate certainly needed to see someone.

"Garrett and Nicky will be here in a couple of minutes," Sophie went on. She dropped down into the wheelchair and rubbed her belly. "Clay's on his way, too. They won't stay long, though, because visiting hours end at nine."

Roman tried to check the time, but he wasn't wearing his watch. He didn't have his phone, either. But since it was dark outside, it had to be past eight.

"Is Clay gonna arrest me?" Tate asked.

Sophie glanced at Roman and Belle again, maybe to see if either of them had put that idea in Tate's head. Roman certainly hadn't. Belle shook her head, as well, and got back in her bed.

"No, of course not," Roman assured him, and Clay had better not try, either. He wasn't sure if attempted suicide was illegal or not, but it didn't matter. "Any idea how long we'll all be here?" he added to Sophie.

"If she doesn't have another episode and agrees to bed rest at home, Mom will be released tomorrow. Tate will stay until you're discharged. That'll be two or three days, depending on how you behave," Sophie quickly added when Roman opened his mouth to complain that he didn't want to spend that much time in a hospital. "If you try to rush this, you could mess up your stitches."

That bit off whatever complaint he was about to make. Plus, there was a silver lining to this that he was just now seeing. Once Belle was discharged, Tate and he would be in here alone. Where they could maybe talk.

There was a soft knock on the door, and since it was already open, Roman saw Mila. Her expression was as tentative as the look in her eyes. As it usually was whenever she was around him. She was already nibbling on her bottom lip.

"Come in," Sophie insisted. She went to Mila and pulled her into her arms for a hug. They'd been best friends for as long as Roman could remember, and it was clear their friendship was still strong.

Roman wished he could feel the same way about Mila. After all, she'd been damn good to Tate, and today she'd probably saved his life. He owed her for that, but sometimes when he looked at her, she reminded him of Valerie and the heart-kicking he'd taken from her.

When Mila and Sophie finished the hug, Mila lifted a bag. "My mom sent gifts. Sorry," she immediately added. "They're wrapped so I don't know what they are."

She took out a pink box for Belle, a blue one for Tate

and a bright red one that she handed to Roman. He was a little surprised that Vita would remember to include him in the gift giving. Or, for that matter, that she even knew he was in the hospital. Of course, everyone in town probably already knew. If they'd had a local TV channel, it would have been on the news.

Belle opened her box right away and took out what appeared to be a small jar of ointment. "It says on the label it's for healing." She unscrewed the lid, smelled it, and some of the color blanched from her face. She quickly resealed it. "Well, it's the thought that counts. Please tell your mother thank you."

After the face his grandmother had made, Tate was a little hesitant opening his. He touched it the way a person might if they were trying to avoid poison ivy. But there was nothing smelly inside. He took out a yo-yo. Tate glanced at him, Belle, Sophie and then Mila as if they might have an explanation for the gift choice.

None of them did.

Roman wasn't sure Tate even knew what it was, but his son forced a smile. "Please tell Mrs. Banchini thanks and that I like it."

Mila smiled, not forced, and all attention then turned to Roman. He nearly feigned being too weak to deal with opening presents, but one of them would just open it for him. He was going to have to man-up and deal with whatever Vita had given him. Considering, though, that the woman put curses on people, he approached his with the same caution that Tate had.

There was a gold foil wrapper inside.

At first, Roman thought it was candy, but no, it was a condom.

He quickly shut the lid, cleared his throat. "It's, uh,

personal," he said because everyone was clearly waiting for the big reveal. "Tell Vita thanks," he added, and hoped it sounded sincere.

He wasn't.

Did the woman expect him to be having sex while he was in the hospital? Good gravy. He really had to do something to tone down his badass reputation.

"Is it an egg with poop on it?" Mila asked. "Because my mom likes to send stuff like that. She gave me chicken poop earlier when—" She stopped and suddenly got very interested in looking in the empty bag that had once held the gifts.

Roman didn't think there was anything else interesting in there, but he did wonder why Mila hadn't finished. And why Vita had given her chicken shit. He had no intention of asking her either of those things—he could probably find out from Sophie, anyway—and besides, they were interrupted.

A nurse stepped into the doorway. Not the Busby sister, but it was someone Roman knew well. Alicia Dearman. He'd lost his virginity to her way back when, and judging from the smile she gave him, she was remembering that in great detail. Roman remembered, too, and it wasn't something he wanted to repeat.

He could almost feel his testosterone levels drop with that thought.

Still, Alicia was a barracuda in bed. And yes, teeth were involved, and even if he hadn't just had surgery, he wasn't looking for sex. He wanted to focus on his son.

Even though Vita obviously thought the sex would win out.

"How are y'all doing?" Alicia asked. She spared

Belle, Mila, Sophie and Tate only a glance and kept her attention on Roman.

Roman adjusted his badass expression and added a bunched-up forehead so it would look as if he was in pain. He was, so it wasn't that hard to do.

"Poor baby," Alicia said. "I'll see about getting you some meds. For now, though, I need to borrow this little guy. Dr. Woodliff wants to see him."

That was a name Roman didn't recognize, but he figured it was the therapist. "Can I go with him?" Roman asked.

"No, that's okay," Tate quickly said, and Alicia made a sound of agreement.

Roman tried not to let that sting. Especially since it would have been hard for him to get out of bed right now. Still, he wanted to know what the therapist was going to say to Tate. And vice versa.

Especially the vice versa.

Tate might tell the doc that the reason he took those pills was because he hated his dad. Hell, Tate could think Roman hated *him*. He didn't. But for some reason, Tate just wasn't feeling the love. Maybe because he was feeling Valerie's rejection even more.

"I'll just walk with them," Sophie said when the nurse wheeled Tate out into the hallway. "That way, I can maybe find out how long Tate's session will take."

Roman thanked her. Sophie wouldn't listen at the door or anything, but she might be able to get a sense of how Tate felt about all of this. His son was far more likely to open up to his aunt, or even to the janitor, than he was to Roman.

"I should be going, too," Mila said. She headed for

the door, but Belle practically scurried off the bed to stop her.

His mother looked in the hall and shut the door. She also pulled Mila closer. "I had one of those life-changing moments when I thought I was dying," Belle said to her.

His mom probably thought she was whispering softly enough for Roman not to hear her. She wasn't.

"I've heard that can happen." Mila glanced at him as though he knew what this was all about. Maybe Belle was going to give her some safe words, too. If so, he hoped they were better than bumfuzzle or Dippity-do.

"It got me thinking," Belle went on. "I stopped living my life when I lost my husband. It was as if I buried myself right along with him, and I want that to change. I'm only sixty, not a hundred and sixty."

Mila gave him another uncomfortable glance, but his only response was a "you're on your own here" shrug.

"Anyway, I know you love those online fantasy sites," Belle went on. Now, that got his attention, and Roman found himself trying to quiet his pulse just so it wouldn't drum in his ear and he could hear better.

Fantasy sites? Maybe this had something to do with books. After all, Mila did own a bookstore.

"I'm off those for a while," Mila whispered. Her voice was considerably softer than Belle's, but he still heard it.

"Yes, the Buttercup fiasco. I heard you talking to Sophie about it on the phone. But that was just one negative experience out of a dozen or more, right? And honestly, as pretty as you are, no wonder Wesley wanted to get in your pants."

That really got his attention. Was this Wesley guy

real? From the sound of it, yes. And also from the sound of it, he'd done something to Mila to upset her.

"I want the name of the site," Belle went on. "I want to have a *10* movie experience. You know, Bo Derrick running down the beach with her hair braided."

Mila shook her head. "I'm not familiar with that—"

"'Cause you're too young, but I remember it." His mother made what appeared to be a dreamy sigh. "And I always wanted to do it. I want to do that beach scene where the seaweed washes over the kissing couple, too."

What the hell?

Roman must have made some kind of sound, probably a grunt of uncomfortable confusion, because both women looked at him.

"Did you hear us?" Belle asked, her tone one of pure shock. He wasn't sure why it was hard to believe he'd heard her since he was only about ten feet away.

"I heard some of it. What's this about, anyway?"

Mila couldn't have looked more uncomfortable if he'd put wet Pop Rocks in her panties. "Nothing. Just a way to keep myself entertained." She brushed a quick kiss on Belle's cheek. Waved an equally quick good-bye to Roman. "We'll talk tomorrow," she added to his mom, and hurried out.

Roman waited for Belle to explain. And waited. And he waited some more. When it was obvious she wasn't going to spill all, he opened his mouth to ask her about it. But opening it was as far as he got.

"Bumfuzzle," she said. His mother made a locking motion with a key over her lips and got back in bed.

Heck. Roman hadn't expected the safe word to work in her favor. But he didn't press it. One way or another, he'd just get the truth from Sophie.

CHAPTER FIVE

"WHAT DO YOU mean Roman was asking about my sex life?" Mila asked Sophie, who was on the other end of the phone line.

This wasn't exactly a conversation Mila wanted to have while walking across the hospital parking lot, but it wasn't something she wanted to put off, either. Anything about Roman, especially Roman mentioning her, had a way of capturing her complete attention.

"He heard you talking to Mom about the fantasy stuff," Sophie explained, "and when I went to see him earlier, he worked it into the conversation."

"How the devil did he work that in?"

"He asked if you were still a virgin."

Mila wasn't sure why that caused her to blush. Everybody in town probably talked about that, but it caused a little tingle inside her to know that it was something on Roman's mind. It likely wasn't a deep interest for him, though. More like a curiosity.

"I told him yes, you were still a virgin," Sophie went on, "and that he was the reason for it."

Mila gasped and nearly dropped her phone. "You didn't."

"No. Just kidding. But it's the truth."

In part, and in a very roundabout way, it was the truth. Mila put her hand to her heart to try to steady it. She needed to regain her composure and get rid of the flushed cheeks before she went into Belle's hospital room.

Where Roman would be.

Mila had wanted to wait to have this conversation with Sophie's mom until after the woman got home, but Belle had called earlier and asked her to come over on her lunch break.

"Admit it," Sophie went on, "no man has ever lived up to Roman in your eyes. Though I don't have a clue why you feel that way. He's pigheaded and sullen."

Yes, but he was also alarmingly handsome. The kind of handsome that made a woman stop breathing. Stop thinking. And start feeling warm in all the secret places of her body. The Grangers were all good-looking, but in her opinion Roman was at the top of that good-looking man-heap.

And now he was here. And hurting.

Not just from his surgery but because of what'd happened with Tate.

"How was Tate when you saw him earlier?" Mila asked.

"Changing the subject. You always do that when I talk about Roman. But in this case I'll give you a pass because I know you're worried about Tate. So am I. The doctor said the pills didn't do any harm, but that he'll need to keep seeing the therapist."

Mila had expected that. "Did Tate say how the first therapy session went?" She stopped outside the hospital doors since she didn't want to continue this conversation while she went through the waiting room.

"He grunted when I asked. Have you noticed that Roman's and his grunts are identical? It's weird."

Yes, she had noticed. For some reason, even the little things about Roman jumped into her head and stayed there.

"One more thing, and I'll let you go," Sophie said. "If you help Mom set up one of the fantasy dates, give Clay the guy's name so he can run a background check on him. The way we do for you."

Clay did indeed do that for her. He'd started it shortly after one of her "dates" had gotten drunk and broken into the bookstore. There'd been no real damage, but it was better to be safe than sorry.

Mila assured her that she would, ended the call and made her way into the hospital. The waiting room was packed, making her wonder if these people all needed medical attention or if they were there to find out what was going on with the Grangers. Sometimes, it was tough being the richest family in town. People admired them, wanted to be them, but there were some who would probably like to see Sophie and her family brought down a peg or two.

And they had been.

Only two years ago Sophie and Garrett had nearly lost the family business when one of their accountants got involved in money laundering. It'd been a huge scandal. In part, because at first the main suspect was their CFO, Billy Lee Seaver. Since Billy Lee was also godfather to Sophie and her brothers, it had made the gossip even juicier.

Shortly after that, Garrett's then-wife had gotten caught having sex with another man. That had fueled the worst of the busybodies for a while, but now that Garrett had divorced her and was engaged to someone else, it appeared that Roman and Tate would be the next up in the gossip barrel.

Mila would do what she could to nip it in the bud.

In part, she could do that just by being seen in public with her mother. Vita had a way of diverting attention simply by showing up. A way of making Mila uneasy, too.

Bad juju, her mother had said. *An ill wind blowing.*

Well, it had blown, all right. That's why Mila was visiting three people she cared about in the hospital. She doubted Vita had known what was going to happen, but people did have gut feelings about this sort of thing. But if so, what gut feeling had prompted her to give Mila the condom?

And to say that Mila was going to have her life turned upside down and lose her virginity in thirty days?

Yes, definite unease, considering that Roman was back in town and that he was probably the only man in the universe she'd take to her bed.

Mila made her way to the hall of the hospital ward, and she immediately spotted Belle. Not in her room, but sitting in a wheelchair just outside the door. She wasn't wearing a gown, but rather a dress.

"I'm waiting for the doctor to say I can go home," Belle said right away to her. She moved the wheelchair toward Mila, halving the distance between them.

Mila glanced at her watch. "Why didn't you just wait in bed?"

"Because Tate's been out of the room most of the morning at appointments, and I've already had to use my safe word with Roman three times. My son certainly knows how to start a fight."

Yes, and so did Belle. Mila kept that to herself, though.

And she wondered about safe words. That wasn't something she'd expected Belle to say, but Sophie's mother was a little like Vita. You couldn't be certain what would come out of her mouth.

Like now.

"Why would a man want whipped cream sprayed in his boxer shorts?" Belle asked.

Mila was certain she got a deer-in-the-headlights look. "I'm not sure," she settled for saying. "Why?"

"Because that's what Roman was going on about yesterday when he was waking up from surgery." She took Mila's hand, pulled her closer. "You think women have been doing that to him?"

Mila suspected that women had done a lot of things to Roman. Probably whipped cream along with other edibles. She might be a virgin, but she wasn't clueless.

"That nurse, Alicia, has been flirting with him," Belle went on. "I told her to take care of my bedpan. I didn't have a bedpan, mind you, but I thought it would remind her that she's not there to play under the sheets with my son. Will you talk to her about it?"

Mila would rather eat a cactus. But she nodded. If Roman gave her any hint that it was a problem, she would say something to Alicia. What, exactly, Mila didn't know, but Roman was here to recover. That might not happen if Alicia managed to give him an erection.

"Now, to the fantasy," Belle went on. "Did you bring me the webpage address?"

Mila nodded and took the paper with the info from her purse. She didn't hand it to Belle right away, though. She moved the woman closer to some chairs and sat so she could make eye contact with her.

"Are you certain you want to do this?" Mila pressed.

"Of course. Didn't you hear what I said about wanting to live my life? Lordy, I can hardly wait to get started. I've missed so much."

Mila knew the feeling. But she also knew something else. "The fantasies can be fun, but they shouldn't be a substitute for a real relationship. If you want to start dating, I'm sure there are several men in town who would love to go out with you."

One man, anyway. Billy Lee Seaver. Mila didn't think it was her imagination that the man had stars in his eyes when it came to Belle. Probably the only reason he hadn't asked her out already was because she'd been his best friend's wife.

Belle just stared at her. "You let the fantasy dating be a substitute for your life," the woman pointed out.

"Yes. But I'm not doing that anymore. I've put the fantasy dating on hold." Maybe permanently. It only made her feel even emptier when she went through the motions.

"Does that mean you're going to date for real? I hope so." Belle didn't give her a chance to answer. "That's why I copied this for you. One of the nurses let me use her computer. Not the one swishing her tushy around Roman. But one of the other ones." She took a piece of paper from her pocket and handed it to Mila. "It's three dating sites."

Mila recognized them since they were the very sites she'd recommended to Sophie a couple of years ago. Sophie had gone on one date, and it hadn't worked out so well. Besides, Mila really wasn't up to going out with a bunch of men with the hopes of finding a prince among frogs.

"I don't know about this." Mila couldn't have sounded

more uncertain if she'd tried. But what she really felt was *unconvinced*, and nothing was going to get her to change her mind.

"Well, how about someone local, then?" Belle asked. She smiled, a sneaky little smile. "There are plenty of men in town who'd love to go out with you." Belle didn't add *gotcha*, but she could have.

"I'm thinking more about a hiatus from dating," Mila said.

"Or we could double." Belle suddenly got very excited as if that were a wonderful idea.

It wasn't.

Mila would rather eat two cacti than double date with her best friend's mom.

"And there's Roman," Belle added a moment later.

Mila silently cursed, wondering if the woman was actually going to start playing matchmaker. But Belle wasn't looking at her. Instead, her attention was on the room she shared with Tate and Roman.

And Roman was there.

In the doorway.

Mila got another of those tingles again. An especially warm one that went all the way to places that should be no-tingle zones. Because Roman didn't see her that way. He only saw her as Valerie's and Tate's cousin.

"Oh, there's Twila Fay Betterton," Belle said. "Yoo-hoo, Twila Fay!" she called out, and waved at the woman. "She's probably here because her hemorrhoids are giving her fits again," she added in a whisper to Mila. "Why don't you go check on Roman while I talk to her?"

Again, without waiting for Mila to respond, Belle took off, wheeling her way toward Twila Fay, who did indeed look as if she were suffering from some kind of anal pain. Or maybe that was her usual expression.

And speaking of expressions, Mila tried to fix hers before she started toward Roman. She went with what she hoped was a friendly but casual smile. It faded quickly, though, when Roman staggered a bit and caught on to the doorframe to steady himself. Mila shoved the dating site list in her purse, hurried to him, and just like that, he was in her arms.

"Dizzy spell," he snarled.

"Then you shouldn't be standing. Come on. Let me get you in bed."

Bad choice of words. Very bad. Because she went stiff, and there's no way Roman could have missed that since they were touching in several places. Not the tingly place, thank goodness.

He chuckled, all low and husky. It sent out a Texas-size amount of pheromones. Mila quickly tried to rein in any effect that might have on her.

Too late.

The effect was there.

Roman put a stop to that, though, by brushing a kiss on the top of her head. It was the kind of thing a man might do to his sister. Or a friend. It was a kiss of death for any woman wanting romance. Which she wasn't, Mila assured herself.

She led him to the bed and had him sit. Again, not a bright idea because she ended up between his legs, too close to him and with their gazes practically colliding.

"Thank you again for what you did for Tate," he said.

Another nail in her kiss-of-death coffin. He felt obligated to her. And he shouldn't. "Tate wasn't in any real danger," she reminded him. Thank God. "Someone would have found him soon enough, or he would have woken up on his own."

Mila was about to add that when she took those particular meds the drowsiness only lasted a couple of hours, but she really didn't want to discuss anything to do about the discomforts of her menstrual cycle with Roman.

"So, did you give Mom those dating sites?" he asked.

She stepped back from him. Nodded. And, in turn, Belle had given her a list. "If she goes through with any dates—" she put *dates* in air quotes "—then Clay will vet the guys."

"Like he does for you?"

Mila didn't make eye contact with him. Didn't confirm what he'd just said, either, but she suspected this had come up in his conversation with Sophie.

"It works," she answered, trying to sound light and carefree. "I'm in one piece."

Physically, anyway. Whenever she was around Roman, she felt a little damaged. As if all the pieces were there but not in the right places.

Maybe that's why there was tingling in her panties.

"You're too good a person to not have someone in your life," he added a moment later.

"Pot calling the kettle black." She hoped that would cause him to chuckle again just so she could hear that pheromone-y sound.

But no. Roman shook his head. "I'm not a good person."

Mila nearly jumped to argue with that. There were better than *good* things about him. He'd raised his son on his own. He'd built a business. And he hadn't been in trouble with the law in years.

All right, that last part wasn't so much good as it was that Roman had learned to follow the straight and narrow. Or maybe he'd just learned not to get caught.

"I don't want anyone in my life," he continued. "I only have room for Tate right now."

Of course, she'd known that, but it was a little soul-crushing to hear him say it aloud. And this time, the words really sank in. Not just his, but Belle's, too. And Sophie's.

Because Mila did indeed want someone in her life.

She always had. She'd just wanted the wrong person, and it was obvious that wasn't going to change. In fact, it could get worse. After what'd happened, Roman probably was going to spend even more time and energy just being a dad.

Mila glanced down at her purse. It was still open, and she could see the note with the dating sites that Belle had given her. She'd planned to toss it first chance she got, but that wouldn't happen now.

Maybe it was time to move past the fantasy level and find someone who could fill all these empty places in her life.

Maybe it was time for clothing removal, after all.

CHAPTER SIX

ROMAN HADN'T BEEN sure there was anything worse than his mother's annoying verbal jabs. But there was. And it was his son's silence.

Now that Belle had been sent home the day before, Tate and he had the room to themselves. Something that Roman had wanted. That's because he'd envisioned it giving them a chance to have some long, meaningful conversations.

It hadn't.

Tate was playing with the yo-yo Vita had sent him while he watched some show about soy farmers. Not that there was a good channel selection on the hospital TV, but it was a hit to the ego that his son preferred organic soy farming to him. Before that, Tate had preferred a documentary on dwindling fly-fishing spots. Before that, he'd played a game on his phone until the battery had died. When no one had been able to find him a charger, the marathon of *compelling* TV had started.

Roman wasn't sure how much longer this would go on. They were waiting on Dr. Sanchez to give them a yay or nay verdict. Nay would mean they'd have to stay in the hospital one more day.

A yay would mean they could go home.

Tate was fine physically and probably could have already left, but Roman was thankful the doctor had kept the boy with him. This way, they could leave for home together instead of Tate having to stay with the housekeeper, Garrett or Sophie.

"As soon as we get home, I'll start looking for a new school for you," Roman threw out there. Like everything else he'd said to his son, he rethought that. Maybe Tate wasn't mentally ready for school yet, but he couldn't imagine that it would be a good idea for him to just sit around in between therapy appointments.

And there *would* be therapy.

Dr. Woodliff had already made it clear that he wanted to see Tate indefinitely.

"I can drive you back here for your sessions," Roman added, rethinking that, too. It was possible that just the thought of therapy was depressing for Tate.

It sure as heck was depressing for him.

So was the fact that he was getting behind at work. Of course, that depression was to a much lesser degree than what he was feeling for Tate. Roman had delegated some of the work to his assistant, and his business partner, Lucky McCord, had taken on some, as well. But sooner or later, Roman needed to tackle at least some of the paperwork. The trips he'd have to hand off, too, since he didn't want to be away from Tate until things were back to normal.

That was another depressing thought.

Normal hadn't been exactly stellar what with Tate's surly moods. Roman hoped the new normal was an improvement, but he would settle for a life where his son didn't feel the need to take pills to dull his pain.

"Will my mom be at my appointments with the doctor?" Tate asked.

It wasn't an out-of-the-blue question. Dr. Woodliff had said that Valerie should come for some of the therapy sessions. Roman had nixed that at first, but then the doctor had reminded him that Valerie was at the root of this.

Root.

Yeah, she was. But that didn't mean she would help matters if she came. She could only stir up Tate and make things worse. She'd stir up Roman, too. Not in a good way, either. There was no trace of the love he'd once felt for her, but there sure as heck was a lot of resentment.

Still, Roman had tried to call Valerie, using the last phone number he had for her. It was no longer in service so he'd asked Clay to try to track her down. Roman had even had his housekeeper take Clay the envelope that had arrived for Tate the day of the suicide attempt. There hadn't been a return address on it, nor any hint of Valerie's whereabouts inside. It had been just another recycled card, this one for his birthday. But there had been a postmark, and it was possible Clay could track her down using it. That was one of the few advantages to having a cop in the family. That, and the fact that his sister was crazy in love with the guy.

There was a knock at the door, and Roman sat up, figuring it was Dr. Sanchez. But it was Garrett. His big brother glanced at him, at Tate, the yo-yo and then at the TV.

"Well, hell. No wonder you're down in the dumps," Garrett said, clearly not afraid to address the eight-hundred-pound gorilla in the room. "Here, this might help." He dropped a phone charger on the bed and handed Tate a brown paper bag. "Burger and fries from the diner. I asked them to add some extra grease for you."

Tate reached for both right away. "Thanks, Uncle Garrett." He sounded so happy that Roman was surprised he didn't add some "gee-whizzes" to that. Tate plugged in his phone and started in on the burger.

"Is that an extra grease burger for me?" Roman tipped his head to the second bag his brother was holding.

Garrett shook his head. "The doc said you're still on a restricted diet so I got you some crackers and vanilla pudding." He flashed his golden boy smile, the one that made him the darling of Wrangler's Creek. "It's not whipped cream, but it'll have to do."

Roman scowled at him. A long, mean scowl. Obviously, Belle had been blabbering. Thankfully, Tate didn't ask about the whipped cream reference, probably because he couldn't hear over his own chewing. He was wolfing down the burger as if it were the cure for everything that ailed him.

"So, when are they springing you from this place?" Garrett gave Tate's bare foot a tug.

Tate shrugged. "Dad was just talking about that. Soon, I guess." He stopped in midbite and perked up again. "Do I have to go back to San Antonio? Can I stay with you, Aunt Nicky and Kaylee at the ranch?"

Kaylee was Nicky's four-year-old daughter. Hardly a companion for a teenager. In fact, there was no one at the ranch anywhere near Tate's age.

Garrett looked at Roman. "That's up to your dad, but you know you're welcome anytime. Your dad owns the ranch, you know?"

"Yeah, I know, but he hates it there because of Grandma fussing at him. But I don't hate it there."

Roman nearly pointed out that Tate hadn't spent a

single night at the ranch, but he had visited a couple of times. However, this probably had more to do with Tate not wanting to return to his friends, because he would have to give some kind of explanation about why he'd been gone. Of course, most of those friends already knew he'd been expelled from school so they might think he'd already moved on.

Garrett turned to Roman, and while he didn't smile exactly, Roman thought his brother might be fighting back doing so. That's because Garrett wanted Roman back at the ranch. He was the person in the family who was always trying to get them all under the same roof.

But his mother was under that roof, too.

"I'd love for both of you to stay," Garrett said to Tate. "But it's up to your dad. He probably has something pressing back in San Antonio."

Yes, Roman did. His sanity was what was pressing. It was bad enough being here in town, and despite the safe words his mother had come up with, Roman doubted she'd stick to using them. No, once the shock of her heart problem had worn off, she'd be back to her own harping self. And he'd be back to snapping at the harping. Not exactly a peaceful environment for his son.

Then Tate said something that changed everything.

"Please, Dad."

That was it.

Two little words that had plenty of emotion behind them.

Roman's kneejerk reaction was still to say no. Their life and home weren't here. His job wasn't, either. Plus, there was that whole other part about the ranch being a crap-pit for him. Too many memories. Too much bad blood.

"Please," Tate repeated. "Can we go there together?"

And that question erased any argument Roman could have given him. However, Roman could put some conditions on it.

"Okay, we can stay at the ranch." Roman was surprised a thunderbolt didn't hit him because he'd sworn he wouldn't go back there. "But only for a couple of days. Just until you're feeling better." Until he was feeling better, as well, since Roman wasn't sure how fast he'd be back at full speed.

Judging from Tate's frown, he didn't like Roman's condition. "Uh, I was thinking I could finish out the school year here. It'd only be for six weeks," he quickly added. "I could go to school here and keep on seeing Dr. Woodliff without having to drive back and forth."

Obviously, Tate had given this a lot of thought. Too bad he hadn't let Roman in on it so he could have figured out if this was a good solution or a disaster in the making. Garrett was of no help. His brother just shrugged.

"You might not be able to get into school here," Roman reminded him. "They might not take transfers this late in the semester."

"Dr. Woodliff said they would. He said his wife is a teacher there and that he could help me with it if that's what we decided to do."

So, Tate hadn't only thought about this, he had also talked to his therapist about it.

"You wouldn't have to go to the ranch with me," Tate went on. "I know you're busy and all with the rodeo stuff. But I'd be okay there without you. I mean, it's not like I need a sitter or anything."

No. But Tate did need a father.

And Roman needed his son.

Garrett lifted his eyebrow but didn't smile. That's because he knew what Roman was about to say. Best not to gloat especially when the gloatee might punch him first chance he got.

"Okay," Roman said. "We'll stay at the ranch."

Tate smiled. Actually, it was more of a grin. "Thanks, Dad."

He would have said it a thousand times just to get that kind of response from his boy. But saying it and living it were two different things entirely.

Roman hoped like the devil that he didn't regret this.

ROMAN REGRETTED THIS.

The moment he stepped into the house at the ranch, he felt as if he'd gotten sucked into a circle of hell that Dante had forgotten to mention.

Home.

Home was a good place to be if it wasn't filled with shit memories. And this place was doused in them. Added to that, there was a hoard of people there to greet Tate and him. Alice, the housekeeper. Lawson, his cousin. Sophie, Nicky, Kaylee, Clay, his mother and an old family friend, Billy Lee Seaver. They didn't exactly shout "surprise" when Tate and Roman walked in with Garrett, but it was obvious that this was some kind of celebration.

No Mila, though. Roman had thought she might be here for this. But she was probably still at work.

The hugs started, and even though they tried to keep them gentle because of his surgery, Roman winced a few times. Winced, too, when his mother told him he needed a haircut. He probably did, but he made a mental note not to get one while he was there. Yes, it was childish, but his mother brought that out in him.

"You have your old rooms, of course," Sophie said.

She took the gift bag from Vita and some flowers that Roman was holding. Actually, there were six bouquets in all, most sent by his business associates. Tate and Garrett had those, and Alice hurried to take them so that Sophie could show them to their rooms.

Roman didn't need her help finding his, but he didn't know exactly where his mom had set up a room for Tate. He only knew that she had done it because she'd mentioned it any time he was around her. Of course, she always mentioned it as a complaint that Roman had never let the boy stay there.

The house was sprawling by anyone's standards, and they went down the hall where there were several bedrooms. His was exactly as he'd left it thirteen years ago, right down to the rodeo trophies he'd won, and the motorcycle magazines. It was like walking into a time capsule preserved in that circle of hell.

"Your room's right next door to your dad," Sophie told Tate.

It was a good room. Big and with windows that overlooked the barns and pastures. Roman knew that because it was the same view he had.

"Your housekeeper brought some clothes and such," Sophie went on. She tipped her head to a suitcase on the floor in Roman's room.

Garrett came in and put the flowers on the desk. His mother was hovering right behind his brother. At least the others hadn't followed for this part of the homecoming. Not that Roman didn't want to see them. He did. He just didn't want to see them right now.

"You want to go for a ride?" Garrett asked Tate. "We got in some new horses this morning, and we can see how they do."

"Yeah." Tate was obviously eager to do that.

"I would ask you, but you're not in any shape to get in a saddle," Garrett added to Roman.

"He's supposed to be on bed rest," his mother reminded him.

"So are you," Roman reminded her right back.

Hell. He had to stop this snapping. Roman didn't want to drag Tate's mood down to his own shitty level.

"You want to take a nap?" Sophie asked him when Garrett and Tate headed out. His mother finally left, too.

"Sure." That was a lie. Roman just wanted a moment so he could steel himself up for the rest of this visit. Six weeks. It suddenly felt like an eternity.

Sophie smiled, kissed his cheek. "My advice? If you need a place to escape, come to the guest cottage. That's where my office is and there's plenty of room. There's enough office space for you, too. Temporary office space," she added.

"Thanks. For both the offer and the temporary part."

"I know this isn't easy for you, but it'll be nice to have you around."

"So Garrett won't have to courier all the paperwork from the ranch that I need to sign," he commented.

"That, and we love you. You didn't forget that, did you?"

No. It was the one thing that had given him any sort of anchor. Especially after Valerie had left. Roman took hold of her arm, eased her closer. Well, as close as he could, considering her huge belly, and he brushed a kiss on the top of Sophie's head.

"I love you, too, Prissy Pants," he said.

Because it was an old childhood nickname that she hated, it got the exact reaction he expected. Sophie punched his arm. And she was good at it, too. It stung like hell. He'd obviously taught her the right way to punch.

"You know I can always smother you in your sleep, Quick Zipper," she fired back.

Ah, good one. Roman hated it as much as she did Prissy Pants. He hadn't always hated it, though. Once he'd thought it was cool that the other teenagers had considered him, well, a guy-slut who got a lot of action. But after he'd knocked up Valerie, the label just made him feel like a guy-slut who should have been more careful.

Sophie's gaze went to the window where Roman saw Garrett and Tate heading for the barn. "Can Tate ride?" she asked.

"Yeah. He's had lessons."

Lessons. That made him wince, too. He was an eighth-generation Texan from a long line of ranchers. It seemed a little like nails on a chalkboard to realize that his son hadn't grown up riding. Maybe he could change that. Since Tate was going to have to move schools, anyway, maybe Roman should buy a place in the country where they could have horses.

Sophie put the gift bag on the desk, and even though he didn't actually see her look inside, she must have gotten a peek of the condom. "Did Vita expect you to need that while you were here?"

"Who knows with Vita."

She made a sound of agreement. "Because Vita gave

Mila a condom, too, along with some mumbo jumbo about there being some big changes in her life."

Judging from Sophie's tone, she thought this was all connected. It was, but the only connection was in Vita's warped mind.

"Mila and I aren't hooking up," he assured his sister. "I don't hook up with virgins."

"Good."

Well, he hadn't expected that. Roman had always gotten the feeling that Sophie was trying to matchmake Mila and him.

"Despite what Mila thinks right now," Sophie continued, "she's not the casual sex type. And she shouldn't have sex with some guy from a dating site just because she no longer wants to be a virgin."

Since Roman could see himself in the dresser mirror, he knew he made a face. "Is that what she's doing?"

Sophie made a face, too. One of disapproval. "She's considering it. Mom gave her these dating sites, and Mila said she was going to use one of them."

Roman had to do a mental double take. "Why would Mom give Mila anything about a dating site? It was Mom who was asking Mila about them."

"No. That was Mila's fantasy dating sites." She stopped. "How'd you know about that?"

"Mom has zero whispering skills, and it wasn't as if I could get up and walk somewhere else. They were talking about it right after my surgery."

Sophie nodded as if all of this was crystal clear. It wasn't. He motioned for her to continue with her explanation.

"Before I started seeing Clay, Mom looked up some regular dating sites for me. Those are the ones she gave to Mila, though I can tell you from personal experience that it was a sucky ordeal. Anyway, Mila gave Mom the sites for fantasy dating, but I'm hoping Mom will decide against doing those."

So did he. On both counts. A woman shouldn't have to risk a "sucky ordeal" for her first time, and he didn't want to think about his mother having fantasies of any kind.

"I plan to talk to both of them about it. Now, you go ahead and get some rest." Sophie gave him another kiss and walked away.

Well, rest had been the game plan, but Roman wasn't sure that would happen now. If he tried to nap, he was certain the only thing that would be going through his head was the conversation he'd just had with his sister.

Crap.

Why did he even care a rat's butt about this? His mom and Mila were grown women. And plenty of people used dating sites, even strange ones like those that catered to the fantasy experiences. One of his business associates had found a site that catered to men who liked threesomes. Then foursomes.

Since it was obvious he wasn't going to get any rest, Roman used the French doors in his room to go into the backyard. As a teenager, he'd used them to sneak in and out of the house, and he was sort of doing that now. He wanted a moment to himself. And he got it. No one, including any of the hands, was around. Not a surprise, really. On a nice spring day like this, there was plenty of ranch work to do, and Garrett and Tate would have gone out through the other side of the barn once they'd saddled up.

The stitches in his side were still letting him know

he wasn't completely healed, so Roman kept his steps light as he walked across the yard and to the corral where he spotted two palominos. Probably some of the new horses that Garrett had mentioned he'd just bought.

His brother had certainly made this place successful. Roman had the proof of that in the financial reports that Sophie sent him each month. Not just for the ranch, but for Granger Western, as well.

The bottom line was they had plenty of money.

But then, they always had. They hadn't done anything to get that seed money started. They could thank their ancestors for that, but his siblings had certainly built on that, and built big. Roman had done the same with his rodeo promotion business, but he never forgot that it wouldn't have been possible without those silver spoons they'd all been born with. Most of the time, though, people forgot about all the hard work that it took to keep those spoons polished.

He made his way to the corral fence to get a better look at the horses. He not only got that, Roman also got a jolt from the memories. There were memories everywhere on the ranch, but there was a bad one here.

This was where he'd had one of those pivotal moments in his life. Well, actually, the pivoting had started earlier that day. He'd been about the same age as Tate and had ridden his bicycle over to his great-grandfather's old house. Not far, just a half mile or so, and it was a trip he'd made plenty of times before. That day, however, he'd seen his father's truck, pulled off onto one of the trails that led to the house. Roman had stopped because he thought his dad had broken down, and he'd looked around, expecting to see his father fixing a flat tire or something.

But Roman hadn't seen that.

Instead, he'd gotten an eyeful of his father making out with the new waitress from the Maverick Café. Roman couldn't remember her name, but he sure as hell could remember seeing his dad kissing her and running his hand into her unbuttoned squirrel-brown uniform top. Even though Roman knew little about sex in those days, he was well aware of what was going on and recognized the heat-glazed eyes and the groping.

When his dad had spotted him, he'd stopped, bolted from his truck and gone after him, but Roman had ridden his bike into the woods and hidden.

Roman had also cried.

He hadn't exactly put his dad on a pedestal because, in addition to being his father, his dad was also an asshole. Always wheeling and dealing. Always playing mind games. But the bottom line was he was still his dad. And Belle had still been his mom. In those days, Roman had had her on a pedestal. That had been before the harping, before the constant flood of criticism. When he still had respect for her.

But it all changed that day.

His dad had finally found him a few hours later, right here, next to the corral fence. He'd been neither apologetic nor remorseful. Just the opposite, in fact. He'd simply said to Roman if he told anyone what he'd seen in that truck, that he would ground him and sell his favorite horse, Lobo. After that, his father had walked away as if he'd just delivered some kind of decree that Roman would obey.

He didn't.

That "decree" had made Roman feel dirty, as if he'd

been the one to do something wrong. It hadn't been fair, and in those days, Roman still believed in fairness.

It'd taken a week for him to build up the courage, but Roman had finally gone to Belle to tell her. He had waited until she was alone in her rose garden, and even though he'd fumbled with what he was saying, Roman had spelled it out for her.

Her husband was cheating on her with a woman—a girl, really—who probably wasn't old enough to vote. And not only that, he'd threatened Roman into keeping his secret. A secret that was twisting and tearing his insides apart as only bad secrets could.

His mother hadn't even looked at him the whole time he was talking. She'd kept clipping those roses, kept placing the flowers in a perfect, flat row on the basket looped over her arm. No tears, no denials, no falling apart as he had feared she would. She simply said the words that still echoed in his head.

"Go inside and wash up, Roman. Your hands are filthy."

Even now, her reaction stunned him, and he'd tried to repeat what he'd told her, in case she hadn't understood. But she had. When her watery blue eyes had finally met his, Roman had seen it all. She not only knew about her husband's cheating, but she also wasn't going to do anything about it.

He'd gone to his room and cried again.

The last tears he had ever shed.

Roman had tried to make sense of it. Hard to do that with his thirteen-year-old's mind. And he hadn't wanted to tell Garrett, his big brother, because he had known that Garrett would confront their dad. Garrett was the good guy even back then. He would have confronted their father, who would have given him a punishment equal to or possibly worse than the threats he'd issued to Roman, and it wouldn't have made any difference.

Belle would have condoned the cheating with her silence.

Maybe his mother hadn't wanted to give up being a Granger. Maybe all of this—the house, ranch and money—meant more to her than her self-respect. Maybe she'd just been too weak to walk out of the marriage.

Whatever it was, Roman had lost respect for her that day, too. And for his father. Because his dad had indeed grounded him and sold Lobo.

Roman hadn't expected Belle to go to his father and tell him what he'd said. But obviously she had, and she didn't lift a finger to stop her husband from carrying through on his unfair threats. Then she'd tried to fix things by leaving him a picture of Lobo on his bed.

As if that would help.

It hadn't. Not that day, anyway. But he'd kept the picture and looked at it from time to time. Still did. Because it was a reminder that things you loved could be snatched away. It was also a reminder, though, that there'd been something important enough in his life to love.

After that, Roman said fuck-you to fairness and to his mom and dad. He'd said fuck-you to a lot of things. And he had done that right here, standing at this very corral fence.

His father had continued the unfair shit for the next ten years before cancer claimed him. He'd made Roman the owner of the ranch when Garrett was the one who wanted it. Maybe that had been his father's way of trying to pull Roman back into the family, but it hadn't worked.

Ironic, though, that Tate had been the one to get Roman back here.

His father was probably laughing his butt off in the grave.

He was so deep in thought that he didn't hear the footsteps until it was too late to duck for cover. But at least it wasn't his mother. It was his cousin Lawson.

"Pretty, aren't they?" he asked, tipping his head toward the horses. He walked to the fence, stood next to Roman.

They were the same age and looked more like brothers than cousins. On occasion, they'd raised hell together by drinking and making time with some of the more willing girls in Wrangler's Creek.

"Garrett loves this place," Lawson went on.

That caused Roman to look at his cousin. Because it sounded as if there was a "but" coming.

Roman cursed. "Please tell me Garrett's not thinking about leaving here once Nicky and he get married."

"No way. Nicky and her kid love it here, too, and you couldn't get Garrett to move away if you stuck dynamite up his ass. There might be trouble coming, though."

Hell. "What kind of trouble?"

He motioned to the back part of the ranch. "You know that land by the creek?"

With just that question, Roman got an inkling of what this was about. Because that land had been in dispute for more than six decades. It was an old family history lesson, but Roman's great-grandfather, Zachariah Taylor Granger, or Z.T. as people called him, had a brother, Jerimiah, who was Lawson's great-grandfather. Both Z.T. and his brother had built not only the town of Wrangler's Creek but the ranch, as well. However, after a falling out, they'd split the land.

Except for about a hundred acres that, at the time, had been leased out to another rancher.

The lease had long since expired, and that meant the ownership of the land was in question, and it was a prized chunk of acreage to own because the creek coiled through it. Garrett needed the creek water to keep the ranch growing.

"Your brothers don't even ranch their land," Roman said, though he was certain Lawson needed no such reminder.

"That might change. Lucian is thinking about bringing in large herds."

"Lucifer," Roman grumbled.

Lawson didn't object to the nickname for his oldest brother, especially since he was the one who'd given it to him. Roman's family wasn't the only ones on the outs with Jeremiah's kin. Lawson had parted ways with his three brothers, as well. That was mostly due to Lucian. Roman was a badass novice compared to Lucian and the man's cut-throat business tactics. Lucian and his brothers already had a huge ranching operation in another part of the county, but if they were looking to expand, they'd definitely be looking here.

"Did Lucian tell you this?" Roman asked.

Lawson shook his head. "Dylan."

Another of Lawson's brothers. Roman was a novice womanizer compared to Dylan, but at least he wouldn't stab you in the back. Dylan fell into the lover rather than the fighter category.

"I've already told Garrett all of this," Lawson went on, "but he's not spreading the news just yet. Especially since it might not happen. Dylan's trying to talk Lucian out of doing this."

Okay, maybe Dylan had some fighter in him, after all.

"Tell Dylan thanks," Roman said. It wasn't thanks because of him but because of Garrett. This place did mean everything to his brother.

"I will. I'm seeing Dylan later this week. He's coming into town to meet Mila for a drink." And with that, Lawson walked away.

"Mila?" Roman cursed in pain when he moved too fast to catch up with Lawson.

When Roman did step in front of him, Lawson looked at him as if he didn't understand what had to be a look of concern on Roman's face. "A friend set them up on a blind date," Lawson explained. "Of course, it's not really blind because they know each other. Not well, though… Say, what the hell's wrong with you? Are you about to keel over again from the pain?"

Roman took a moment to decide how to answer that. He took another moment to try to figure out why it bothered him that Mila was going on a date with his cousin. And it *did* bother him. There was no mistake about that. It bothered him because Dylan was a love-'em-and-leave-'em type.

Just like Roman.

And considering what Sophie had told him about Vita giving her a condom and Mila using a dating site, maybe she had decided to lose her virginity to Dylan.

Dylan would take it, too, because he wouldn't care if he broke her heart in the process.

"Are you okay?" Lawson asked.

No. He wasn't. Roman had to stop Mila from making a huge mistake.

CHAPTER SEVEN

"I DON'T WANT to risk getting seaweed and sand in my hoo-hoo," Belle said.

Mila just nodded. Something she'd been doing a lot since Belle had shown up at the bookstore at nine a.m. and had brought her list of fantasy dates with her. The list now included discarded ones, the possibilities and her favorites. Despite the fact that Mila had told her she needed to order some books and do paperwork before she opened the store at ten, Belle had sat down as if this were a social call.

"That's why I've decided against *From Here to Eternity*," Belle added. "Plus, I'd have to drive a long way to get to a beach."

Good point, but she had convinced Mila at the no seaweed or sand in the hoo-hoo. At least she was convinced if *hoo-hoo* was Belle's word for her lady part. If not, then Mila had no idea what the woman meant.

"That brings us to the pottery scene in *Ghost* and the scene from *Twilight*. The one where they're in the woods, and he tells her to 'say it.' I like that scene a lot." Belle sighed like a schoolgirl. "I like the one from *Ghost*, too, but I don't want to fall in bed with my undies showing."

Mila wasn't sighing. The first one would mean very close contact, and if Belle got someone like Wesley, then it could turn ugly. There was also a problem with the *Twilight* scene because it was indeed in the woods where Belle would be alone with this guy.

"Uh, you just got out of the hospital a couple of days ago—" Mila started.

"Four days," Belle corrected. "That's plenty of time, considering I wanted to jump-start my life. This is the slowest jump-start in history, since it'll take me at least a week to set this up. And that's after I decide which one."

Since it was obvious she wasn't going to be able to use Belle's health to get her to rethink this, Mila took the list and looked it over again. And mentally ticked them off one by one. Great day, but the woman had lofty fantasies that ranged all the way from Tolkien scenes to *Pretty Woman*.

"How about Scarlett O'Hara?" Mila suggested. "You could do the scene where she visits Rhett in jail." That way, "Rhett" wouldn't be able to get his hands on her.

Belle stared at her, huffed. "All right, what's wrong? You did this fantasy stuff for a couple of years. If it was okay for you, why isn't it okay for me? And don't say it's because I haven't had a date in over forty years because you haven't had a real date in ages, either."

The woman had a point, but Mila thought maybe she picked up on bad vibes a little better than Belle. Maybe not, though, since she had had that encounter with Wesley.

"Honestly," Belle went on, "I see just as much risk in you going out with Dylan later today as in me doing *Twilight*. And my name's already very close to the character so that might be a good sign."

Mila froze. "How'd you know about Dylan?"

Belle froze, too. "Uh, Lawson mentioned it."

Great day. That meant it was all over town. "It's not a date. It's just coffee." Mila was thinking of it as more of a prequel to a possible date.

Belle just stared at her. "Dylan isn't the 'just coffee' type. He could charm the panties off a nun. Or you."

Maybe, but it would be a nice change of pace from the other guys in town who were trying to do the same.

"How'd Dylan set up this date with you, anyway?" Belle asked.

"He's friends with Julie Dayton. She's the librarian at the school." Basically, Julie had played matchmaker, and Mila didn't know whether to thank her yet or not.

Mila braced herself for Belle to tell her all the reasons she shouldn't go out with Dylan. After all, it wasn't her coffee meeting that folks were chattering on about. They were also talking about the possible lawsuit that Dylan's brothers might file against the Grangers.

"I have an idea," Belle said, lowering her voice to a whisper despite the fact they were the only two people in the entire store. "Go out with Dylan. Let him think you're falling for his charming ways. It won't be hard because all those boys are lookers. Anyway, while he's charming you, you could pump him for information about the lawsuit. You might even be able to convince him to tell his brother to back off."

Mila lowered her voice to a whisper, too. "No." And she didn't have to think about it, either. "This is just for coffee at the café in about an hour. No pumping. No spying. In fact, I don't plan to stay for more than thirty minutes."

Her plan also included ordering iced tea so she wouldn't even have to wait for it to cool. To say she was having second and third thoughts about this was an understatement. Still, she would go since it seemed cowardly to back out now especially since she'd arranged for her part-time help, Janeen Carlin, to cover the store.

Belle didn't say anything for several long moments. "Do you want a short date because of Roman?"

"What?" A conversation with Belle was rarely easy to follow, and this one was no different. "Why would you think of Roman?"

"Because he's right outside the window. I guess it's the opposite of out of sight, out of mind. Instead, he's in sight, in mind."

Mila turned toward the window so fast she heard her neck pop. And Roman was indeed there. He was peering through the window at them. He lifted his hand in an awkward wave.

"I hope nothing went wrong with Tate," Belle commented. "He was supposed to start school today."

Mila had already moved toward the door, but that caused her to go even faster. "Is Tate okay?" she immediately asked the moment she unlocked it and threw it open.

Roman pulled back his shoulders, surprised by her question. Or maybe he was just surprised that her voice was so intense.

"He's fine. I got all the paperwork done for him to go to school here, and I just dropped him off…" His words trailed off when he spotted his mother. "Did I interrupt anything?"

"No." Belle snatched her fantasy paper from Mila, folded it and put it in her purse.

Obviously, this wasn't something the woman wanted to discuss with her children. Probably because they all disapproved. Sophie and Garrett had already called Mila with their concerns. So had Billy Lee. Apparently, though, Belle had no hesitation about discussing it at length with Mila.

"I need to be going," Belle said. She kissed Mila's cheek and spared her son a glance on the way out. "And you need a haircut," she added to Roman.

"Dippity-do," he grumbled to her.

Mila didn't have a clue what that was about, and she didn't have time to ask Belle because the woman hurried out.

"Are you here about your mom's fantasy dates?" Mila asked at the same time that Roman asked, "Was my mother here about your date with Dylan?"

Neither answered.

They just stood there, obviously surprised and also waiting for the other to say something. There was no need for her to ask him how he knew about Dylan. Gossip. No need for him to explain how he knew about his mother because he'd overheard their conversation when they were at the hospital.

And speaking of hospitals, she looked at his side. He wasn't hunched over in pain as he'd been the last time she'd seen him. "Are you supposed to be driving, walking and such?"

His mouth tightened a little, probably because he thought she asked in an effort to avoid answering his question. She had. But Mila honestly wanted to know how he was doing.

"The doctor didn't say I couldn't do those things," he answered. Then added, "I'm fine. Practically good as new."

She doubted that, but it was nice to see him up and

about, especially since he had given her a scare when he'd collapsed.

"So, why are you here?" she pressed when he didn't continue.

He glanced around. "Books. I thought I'd get some for Tate. You know what he likes, and I thought you could help me pick out a few. I don't want him to get bored while he's at the ranch."

She doubted that would happen. From what she was hearing, Tate was riding a lot and even helping Garrett with some of the ranching chores. Now that he was back in school and had his therapy sessions three times a week, he probably wouldn't have a lot of spare time. Still, it wouldn't hurt for him to have some books on hand.

Mila headed to the Young Adult section, specifically to the postapocalyptic books that Tate preferred. Roman followed her, and that's when she noticed he was hobbling a bit. Definitely favoring his right side.

"I also wanted to thank you again," he said.

Mila should have just let that pass, but she couldn't. She whirled around to face him but hadn't realized that he was so close. She practically knocked right into him.

"Please don't tell me thank you. Or hug me." She hadn't meant to blurt that last part out, but maybe her visit with Belle had put her close to her tipping point.

"Hug you?" he questioned. Roman huffed. "Does that have anything to do with you seeing Dylan?"

Mila could see no correlation, but obviously Roman could. "No. Why would you ask that?"

He shrugged. "Because I know you're going out with him today, and maybe you think he won't like it if you and I are…friends."

So, perhaps that was the correlation, but it required a huge stretch to get from a coffee date to dictating her friendships. Of course, Roman might believe Dylan would feel that way because of this potential lawsuit. Because Dylan and his family wouldn't be just suing the Grangers.

They would be suing Roman since he owned the ranch.

Mila forced herself to turn back to the books and took several from the shelf. *"Friends,"* she repeated. She didn't make it sound like a question. She just tossed it out there to see how Roman would react.

He hesitated. A long time. "Yeah. We've been friends since we were kids."

That hurt. He could have at least said *good* friends. Or *dear* friends. Something to distinguish her from the cashier at the grocery store.

Mila handed him the books with a little more force than she'd intended and started back to the front. Again, he followed her.

"Are you mad at me?" he asked.

"Yes! No," she quickly amended, and then went with a "Maybe."

She was toying with the idea of playing with fire here. If she said she didn't want to be just his friend, it could put him on the spot. He could reject her.

Heck, he probably would.

She wasn't anywhere near his usual type, and it didn't matter that she wanted him to feel more for her. Mila couldn't force him. And that's why she needed to keep that coffee date with Dylan.

God, she had to move forward instead of being stuck in gear over Roman.

"It's okay," she assured him. It was a lie, of course. Mila stopped, turned and gave his arm a friendly pat.

Or at least that's what she'd intended. He reached out, lightning fast, with his left hand and caught her wrist. He was so close again. So close that she caught the scent of his aftershave. It smelled expensive. And dangerous.

"Are you going out with Dylan to prove some kind of point to me?" he asked.

Again, with the precursor to playing with fire, she answered, "No. I'm going out with him to prove a point to *me*."

That wasn't a lie. And she could tell from Roman's expression that he knew that, too.

"I need to take off the swimming floaties of life and venture into the deep end of the pool," Mila continued, and wished that she'd come up with a better analogy.

"And you can do that with Dylan?"

She hated to say that any man would do, but at this point, any man would. "It's a baby step. Coffee and conversation. I'll work my way up to dating and a relationship."

His grip melted off her wrist, and he looked down at it as if trying to figure out why he'd been holding her in the first place. "Why do you have to work your way up?"

Of course that didn't make sense to a Granger. "I didn't exactly come from a normal family, and in high school, boys were afraid of me because of my mother."

"I wasn't."

"You were the exception rather than the rule." And he'd only had eyes for Valerie back then. "So, I dated a couple of misfits who only reminded me how much of a misfit I truly was."

He shook his head. "But you went to college. You roomed with Sophie. You would have met guys who didn't know about Vita."

"Yes, but I didn't meet anyone who was more interesting than the characters in the books I was reading." And certainly not more interesting than Roman. "The weeks turned into months. Then years. Eighteen-year-old guys don't mind a shy, awkward date, but that doesn't fly when you're thirty-one."

Roman studied her, processing that. It was all true. Well, everything after the part about her being okay.

"Don't let Dylan hurt you." But it was as if he'd said too much because Roman lifted the books. "Can you go ahead and ring these up? I need to get started on those other errands."

"No charge. They're a gift."

After she'd scolded him for thanking her, Mila thought maybe he'd scold her right back for giving his son books. But he only nodded and went toward the door. He stopped again.

Causing her heart to stop, too.

For a couple of moments, she thought he might say something about them. Not that there was a *them*, but in those moments, the fantasy started. Roman, shirtless, turning to her, dragging her into his arms and kissing her.

But that didn't happen.

He walked out, leaving her to stand there and curse herself. She was still cursing when Hilda Meekins, the mail carrier, came by. Mila dredged up a smile for her so that Hilda wouldn't think anything was wrong. Mila especially didn't want her thinking something was wrong since she'd seen Roman leave. In fact, Hilda still had her attention on Roman and nearly walked into the door.

"Yum," Hilda said. She handed Mila a stack of letters she took from her mailbag. "I think I had an orgasm just walking past him."

Mila knew how the woman felt. Well, she could imagine it, anyway.

She looked through the letters while Hilda went to the window so she could no doubt continue to gawk at Roman. The first six were bills or info about new books, but the last one got her attention.

It was from her mother.

A first. But it was also a first for Vita to take a vacation to go see her family. The postmark, though, was from Wrangler's Creek, which meant her mom must have mailed it right before she left. Strange, though, that she hadn't just given it to Mila when she'd driven her to the airport.

Then again, strange and Vita went hand in hand.

She should probably take it to her office to open, carefully, in case it contained some kind of charm that was disgusting or smelly.

"Oh, that can't be good," Hilda mumbled, and for a moment Mila thought the woman was talking about the letter. She wasn't. "There's Dylan Granger. You think they'll get in a fight right here on Main Street?"

That sent Mila hurrying to the window. Not because she wanted to see a fight, but because Roman might be involved. But it wasn't Roman talking to Dylan.

It was Garrett.

And yes, judging from their body language, there might indeed be a fight. Mila dropped the letters on the counter and hurried out to them. She was still several yards away when she could hear what they were saying.

"Any reason Lucian didn't come straight to me with this chicken-shit notion of a lawsuit?" Garrett asked.

Even though Dylan had a much friendlier look on his face, that tightened his mouth a little. Maybe because he didn't like having his brother insulted. "You'd have to ask Lucian about that."

"I would, but he's not returning my calls." Yes, Garrett was definitely pissed off. A rarity for him. That was usually Roman's territory. Thank goodness he wasn't there or Mila would have stood no chance of diffusing this.

"You made it," she said to Dylan, and she hoped it sounded as if this were a planned meeting.

Dylan smiled. It was dazzling and perfect, but then he'd had a lot of practice over the years flashing it at every woman who caught his eye.

Garrett wasn't smiling, though, and judging from the glance he shot her, he knew all about this date.

"I hate to interrupt," she went on, speaking to Dylan, "but could we go for coffee now? Something's come up in the shop, and I need to get back a little sooner than I'd originally planned."

Dylan looked at Garrett, probably considering if he should stand his ground and continue an argument that should be between Roman and Lucian, not him and Garrett. Mila fixed that. She hooked her arm through Dylan's and got him moving.

"Tell Sophie and Nicky I said hello," she said to Garrett.

She didn't wait around for his reaction. Mila just led Dylan across the street to the bookstore. "If you don't mind, we can have coffee in here," she said. That way, she wouldn't have to lock up. Or walk into the diner after people had just witnessed what'd happened.

Of course, most wouldn't know what had been said, but the gossips would embellish it. They'd embellish this, too. After all, she was taking a known womanizer into her store where they'd be alone. At least, they would be until Janeen showed up. Which hopefully wouldn't be long. Too bad Hilda hadn't stuck around.

"You know you didn't fool Garrett about switching the time of our coffee date," Dylan remarked. "He knows you were running interference. Which he didn't need by the way."

Probably not.

"And for the record, there really wasn't anything to break up," Dylan added. "Garrett's a reasonable man, not the sort to swing his fists."

Yes, normally he was reasonable, but the ranch was like his own child, and tensions were high right now what with Tate's, Roman's and Belle's recent medical problems.

She let go of his arm and motioned for him to follow her into her office. Such that it was. It was actually a converted storage closet, but at least she had a pot of fresh coffee and a desk. A desk that would be between Dylan and her.

Mila got busy pouring two cups of coffee, but she'd barely gotten started when Dylan took her hand. He doled out another of those smiles that she was certain had coaxed plenty of women into his bed.

"I'm not much of a coffee drinker," he said. "And you're not much of a dater. So, why don't we just sit down and chat? You can tell me why you agreed to go out with me. Oh, and if it's to poison me to stop a possible lawsuit, then let me down easy. I have a fragile ego."

She seriously doubted there was anything fragile about this cowboy. And he was a cowboy, all right. A charming one. He had the Granger looks. Granger money, too. But it was packaged in that lanky body with the great-fitting jeans. Mila might not have been the dating type, but she wasn't blind.

With a trace of that smile still on his mouth, Dylan took the chair across from her. She sat in the one behind the desk.

"No poison attempt," she assured him. "In fact, when I agreed to see you, I didn't know anything about the potential lawsuit."

He looked at her with those sizzling eyes that managed to be both hot and cool at the same time. "So, this is about Roman."

She nearly got choked on her own breath. Good grief. Did everyone know she had a thing for Roman? Apparently so. She considered denying it. Considered trying to convince Dylan that he was wrong.

But maybe he wasn't.

By her own admission this "date" was like a prequel, but now that she was face-to-face with Dylan, she knew there was no spark. And if she couldn't have sparks with a guy like Dylan, then there was no sense lying to herself. This was indeed about Roman. Not to make him jealous or anything, but because she was simply trying to get over him. If that was even possible.

Dylan shrugged. "I'm okay with that. Truth is, along with wanting to see you again, this is sort of a reconnaissance mission. I don't want this lawsuit. Garrett and Sophie probably don't, either. That leaves Roman."

He stopped, clearly waiting for her to pick up where he'd left off.

"If you think I have some kind of insight into Roman's mind, you're mistaken. But if you have any control over this, please talk Lucian out of whatever he's planning. Or at least get him to delay it. The timing couldn't be worse."

Dylan sipped his coffee, looked at her from over the top of his cup. He winked at her. "I knew there was a reason I always liked you. You're loyal. With a scary-as-shit mother, but loyal." He paused. "I did hear about Roman's boy. Is he okay?"

She nodded. He was out of the woods for now, but there were no guarantees. Tate had a lot of issues to work out. So much anger.

Like his father.

Mila knew the reasons they both were like that. Tate because of Valerie, and Roman because of his parents.

Roman had no idea that all those years ago she'd overheard him tell his mother about his father's cheating, but she had been inside Sophie's room with the window open. Sophie had been wearing headphones and listening to music, but Mila had heard enough of the conversation to understand that this had crushed Roman.

Crushed boys became angry ones.

And carried that anger with them when they became men.

"So, you want to make this a real date or what?" Dylan asked. "Before you say no, I promise you that it'll just be a date. No recon, and you won't have to nip arguments in the bud between me and a cousin." He smiled. "Other nipping, however, is optional."

Mila smiled, too. This was what it was like to have

someone flirt with her. She liked it. But she shook her head. "If I say yes, then everyone will think I'm just trying to make Roman jealous. You might even think that. It wouldn't be true because Roman would actually have to care for me that way to feel jealousy. Still, if I can get a rain check, maybe we can go out after he's left town. That way, the gossip won't include him. It'll be just about us."

Not that she wanted an *us*, but Mila wasn't going to close any more doors. Especially since she'd just opened them.

Dylan nodded, took her hand and kissed it. "Absolutely. And you can make sure your mom doesn't put a spell on me." He tipped his head to the shop. "I noticed the letter from her on the counter. That wasn't about me, was it?"

He winked again. Obviously, he was joking, but it did get her thinking. Maybe it *was* about Dylan. After all, her mom had said all that stuff about an ill wind. Vita might be trying to give her some kind of juju guidance.

Suddenly, Mila couldn't wait to read it so she was very glad when Dylan stood to leave. Of course, that wasn't exactly a good step in her door-opening process. She could encourage him to stay so they could chat, break some ice, and maybe she would get the urge to do some "nipping" with him. But for now, she let him walk away, and Mila followed him to the door.

Dylan turned as if he might kiss her goodbye, but he settled for skimming his index finger down her cheek. "That was the shortest, and best, date I've had in a while."

Mila figured the "best" part was an out-and-out lie, but she didn't call him on it. She let him go, and since it was still fifteen minutes until opening, she locked the door and tore into the letter from her mom.

It was handwritten, only two short paragraphs so it didn't take Mila long to read it. It took a little longer, though, for her to get what her mother was saying in those handful of sentences.

Oh, God.

This couldn't be right so Mila read it again. And again. By the fourth time, the tears came, and Mila sank to the floor with the letter clutched in her hand.

CHAPTER EIGHT

ROMAN WAS STALLING, and he wasn't even going to pretend that he wasn't. In part, he wanted to be in town near the school in case something went wrong and Tate called. The ranch was only a short drive away, but there was something comforting about being able to see the school building as he went from one errand to another.

First, to the bookstore, then the diner for some coffee to go, then the grocery store to pick up some of Tate's favorite snacks. All of that had left his incision aching a bit. That's why he'd decided to sit in his truck and watch for the other reason he was stalling.

Mila.

More specifically, Mila and Dylan.

Main Street really was the catbird seat, and Roman had caught the tail end of what appeared to be a conversation with Mila, Garrett and Dylan. Garrett had headed to his truck after that, and Mila had taken Dylan into the bookstore.

Taken.

As in she'd grabbed hold of Dylan's arm and led him there.

Apparently, this was a change of venue for their date. Too bad his catbird seat didn't allow him to see in the bookstore windows or have eavesdropping equipment. Plain and simple, he didn't trust Dylan, and if Sophie was right and Mila truly was ready to jump into bed with someone—anyone—then Dylan would almost certainly be glad to accommodate her.

Why that riled Roman, he didn't know, but he continued to watch. However, since he didn't want anyone to think he was just watching, he called his office and put out some fires there. Rodeos went on all year, but the spring was an especially busy time. Roman could delegate some of the work, could do some from his laptop or phone, but there was no substitute for getting in a vendor's face when there'd been a screw-up.

That was one of the advantages to being a badass. Vendors listened when he got in their faces.

The bookstore door opened, and he saw Dylan come out. Roman hadn't timed it, but it seemed a tad short for a date. Even one where they were only supposed to have coffee. Maybe that meant Mila had called it off. Or Dylan could have done something to upset her.

In case it was the latter, Roman decided to walk past the store so he could look in on her. He wouldn't go in again. Considering he'd only been in her store one other time, it would look suspicious if he made two visits in one day.

He got out of his truck, but before he even made it to the sidewalk, he saw Dr. Woodliff coming toward him. Since the doc was on his to-do list, Roman welcomed the chance meeting.

"I saw you sitting out there, watching the bookstore," the doctor greeted him. "Thought I'd come out and say hello."

So, not a chance meeting, after all. Roman frowned and would have to rethink his whole catbird seat theory. It was clearly too visible of a spot for spying.

"How's your incision?" he asked Roman.

"Healing. How's my son?" Roman hadn't intended to be so blunt with that question, but Tate wasn't giving him any hints about how the sessions had gone.

"Healing," the doctor repeated.

Dr. Woodliff's gaze drifted toward the school, and he got an *aha* look in his eyes. Roman didn't figure the guy was a gossip, but now he might at least rethink Roman's bookstore gawking. "I don't think Tate will have any problems. The teachers are all good. Most of the kids, too."

Most. But not all. If Tate ran into one of those not-good kids, then he could get bullied. Hell. The bullying could get pretty ugly if word spread about his suicide attempt. Roman reconsidered checking on Mila. Maybe he should go park outside the school instead. Perhaps even take a stroll through the building. Of course, if Tate saw him, he'd be mortified.

"Any luck reaching Tate's mom for some family therapy sessions?" the doctor asked.

Roman had to shake his head. "But I have two private investigators working on it. Chief McKinnon, too. They'll find her."

Finding Valerie wasn't the problem, though. It was whether or not she would come. And if she did, what she would say or do once she was here.

The doctor gave him a pat on the arm, said he would see him at their next appointment and walked off. Leaving Roman with a decision to make. Risking Tate's wrath by looking in on him or risking Mila's wrath by looking in on her.

Roman decided to do both.

Badasses didn't mind a little wrath every now and then.

He started with Mila because she was closer and because she'd be opening the store soon. In fact, she was late doing that. It was already a quarter past ten, and she still had the closed sign in the window. That caused him to walk a little faster. Roman looked in the window, didn't see her, so he tried the door.

Locked.

From the glass panels on the door, he had a perfect line of sight to her office. Not there, either. Maybe she was in the storage room. But then he looked down and spotted her.

On the floor, crying.

In that moment he wanted to track down Dylan and beat the crap out of him, and while he still might do that, Roman knocked on the door.

"Let me in," he insisted.

Mila shook her head, turning her face from him, but it was too late. He'd already seen those tears and wanted to know what the hell Dylan had done to put them there.

He kept knocking, and Mila must have realized he wasn't going away because she finally reached up and unlocked it. She also turned away again, but Roman just closed the door and stepped in front of her.

"What happened?" he snapped.

She didn't jump to answer that. "Do you remember my father?"

In the grand scheme of things, Roman hadn't expected that to be the topic of conversation. Probably because he was still in an ass-whipping mood and had a specific ass in mind to whip—Dylan's.

"I do remember him, some. I was about seven or so when he died. He used to buy me a Coke whenever he'd see me at the grocery store." No one else had done that, probably because of the Grangers' money. Everyone else figured that Roman could afford his own Cokes. And he could have, but it was a nice gesture. "And he'd tell corny jokes."

"Yes," Mila agreed, her voice a whisper. "What do you call a sleepwalking nun?"

Roman remembered that one because it was one her father liked to repeat. "A Roaming Catholic." He nearly smiled at the memory, but because of her tears, this was not a smiling kind of situation.

"I loved him," Mila went on, "and when he didn't come home that night, I thought I'd died, too. Nothing was the same after that. Nothing."

Crap. This was probably the anniversary of his death or maybe his birthday. Though it wasn't easy to do, Roman sat down on the floor next to her and pulled her into his arms.

"I'm sorry. If you want, I can go with you to the cemetery," he offered. "Or I can sit with you. Just let me know what to do."

She lifted her left hand then, and he saw the paper she was holding. Actually, she'd crushed it in her grip.

"It's from my mother," she said, handing it to him.

Roman still wasn't piecing this together, but he soon did when he started reading the letter.

Dear Mila,
This is going to be a hard letter to read, so sit down. Take a drink if you have one nearby. When you're done reading, just remember that I'm still your mother. I always will be, no matter how much you hate me for keeping this from you. I'm sorry for that.

Well, that sure as hell wasn't a good start, especially since Vita didn't seem to be the type to dole out apologies.

Frankie wasn't your daddy. Yes, I know that's hard to hear, but it's the truth. I got pregnant with you and went to stay with my cousin in Houston so I could have family with me when you were born. That's when I met Frankie. You were just a baby, and he loved you right from the start. We got married, and I came back to Wrangler's Creek with both of you.

"I'm not who I thought I was," Mila said. "I'm not Mila Banchini."

"Yeah, you are. This doesn't mean anything." He hit the paper with the back of his hand. But it did mean something.

Mila's life had just turned on a dime.

Something that Roman knew a little about.

"Read the rest," she insisted.

Roman wasn't sure he wanted to know what those last couple of sentences said, but he did it, anyway.

Your daddy, the one who put you in me, is from here in Wrangler's Creek. Please don't ask me who he is because it would mess up his life if he was to know about you. That's why I never told you, Mila. He has a good life here and wouldn't want folks to know about his goings-on with me. Forgive me if you can.

Love, Mother

Well, there it was. A bombshell on paper. Roman didn't know exactly how he would feel if Belle sprang something like this on him. Considering his father had been an asshole, it might be a relief. But Mila had loved her father, and he'd been a good man.

"He's here in town," Mila went on. "And my mother won't be back from this trip until the end of the summer. She doesn't have a cell phone and didn't give me a number for any of the relatives she's visiting. I have to go all that time without knowing, and maybe I won't know even then. She doesn't plan on telling me."

Not from the sound of it, but if he had Vita in front of him, he might be able to convince her to spill it. Then again, she might just give him chicken shit or put a curse on him.

"Why would Vita be telling me all of this now?" Mila blinked back tears. "And why do it in a letter? Why not just tell me in person?"

Roman could only guess at that. "Maybe she was scared. Maybe she didn't want to see you upset when you learned the truth."

Though it was cowardly of her to do it this way.

"And as for the timing," he went on, "she could have read tea leaves or looked into a crystal ball that told her she should do this now." That would have sounded like BS if it'd been anyone but Vita.

"Who do you think he is?" Mila asked.

Roman tried to go through the possibilities. The man would be in his fifties at least, maybe a lot older. And it would be someone who'd been here at least thirty-two years. Someone who still had a "life" here, which probably meant another family. He could think of at least a half dozen men who fit that, including the two ministers and Dr. Sanchez. Roman couldn't see any of those men having an affair with Vita.

Actually, that applied to all men. Vita just didn't seem the type of woman a man would risk knocking up. Though Roman was thankful someone had. Or else Mila wouldn't be sitting next to him.

"I'll put together a list of possibilities," Mila said. "Later, though."

Yeah, definitely later. Once she got past some of the hurt and feelings of betrayal over her mother lying to her.

There was a knock at the door, the sound echoing through the room. Neither Mila nor he answered. Didn't move a muscle. They just sat there with her in his arms.

Ellie Stoddermeyer, the dispatcher who worked at the police station, pressed her pinched face against the glass, looking inside. Thank God she didn't look down because she was one of the biggest gossips in town and would have told everyone about Roman and Mila being on the floor together.

After mumbling something about "some people being late," Ellie walked away.

"I can put a sign on the door," he offered since obviously the Closed one hadn't stopped Ellie from knocking. Of course, it hadn't stopped him, either. "Maybe a sign that says something about you being closed for inventory. And what about Janeen? Will she be coming in?"

"I texted her and told her to take the day off," Mila explained. "And don't put out a sign. If someone sees you doing that, they'll think something's going on between us."

Something was. He was comforting an old friend,

but Mila was right. She wasn't going to want any new gossip, especially since it would almost certainly take her a while to wrap her mind around this.

"Do you have any booze in this place?" he asked. Because that was a good suggestion on Vita's part.

"It's still morning," she said. Then shrugged. "I have some in my desk drawer."

She got to her feet, lowering the blinds on the front windows and door. Of course, if anyone had seen Roman go in there, they would think Mila and he were about to have a round of sex only minutes after seeing Dylan, but Roman would just have to try to diffuse the gossip somehow. No way was he leaving Mila alone right now.

He got up, as well, not easily, and when Mila heard him grunting and struggling she came back to help him. That meant her looping her arm around him and pulling him close. It meant body-to-body contact, which was a dangerous thing right now with all the energy zinging in the room.

He followed her to her office but didn't sit. He was afraid if he got in the chair, he might not be able to get out of it.

She sat, though, behind her desk and took out a bottle of Irish cream liqueur and a glass. "I can't drink stuff that tastes like battery acid so this is all I have." She used the glass for his drink, poured hers into a cup that still had coffee in it.

Roman didn't normally drink anything other than whiskey or beer, but he'd make an exception in this case. Plus, it was a little like having a breakfast pastry.

"When I first saw you crying, I thought Dylan was responsible," he admitted.

She nodded, gulped down what was in the cup and poured another one. This time, it was just the booze, not watered down by coffee. "I figured you had. But no, Dylan was fine. Polite, even."

Roman frowned. For such mild words, he didn't like that they tightened his stomach. But that could be the drink. "He didn't try to work his *magic* on you?" He made sure magic had the same tone as *toenail fungus*.

"No. I'm still a virgin." She made that sound a little like toenail fungus, too. "Yes, I know it's archaic in this day and age. And yes, I do know I can have sex without it being a commitment."

Roman mentally tested out a few ways to respond to that, and he decided silence was the way to go.

"Sometimes, I want that," she continued. *"Sex,"* Mila corrected. "Not the commitment. Sometimes, I just don't want to be me." She paused. Laughed. But it wasn't a funny ha-ha laugh. It was hollow and sad. "Turns out I'm not the person I thought I was, since I'm not Frankie Banchini's daughter. So I guess I got what I wanted."

He eased down on the desk, moved the bottle slightly out of her reach. If she was getting drunk, her eye-hand coordination might go first, and she might not be able to pour another drink. Roman knew from experience that a drink or two could help a rotten situation, but six or seven drinks just made you shit-faced and more susceptible to doing something stupid.

Since they were talking about sex and were alone in her office, it wasn't a good idea to toy with doing anything stupid.

"You're still you," he repeated, but Roman doubted she heard him. Or if she did, it didn't sink in. The pain and shock were too close to the surface now, but maybe she'd remember this later.

And believe it.

"Think of all the good things," he went on. "You have your own business. Your own house. And, other than keeping a spare key in a potted plant, you make smart choices."

Like not falling for Dylan.

But he didn't mention that.

Instead, Roman tried again to help her put things in perspective. "Until you got that letter, you were happy. You'll be happy again. You'll see."

She gave another of those laughs, and it sounded a little drunk. Or maybe that was a sugar high. "Right, happy." More of that fungal tone. "Those fantasy dates you've been wondering about?" she went on. "I go on them because someone's not trying to get in my pants. They haven't made me happy in a while now."

"Someone getting in your pants is the only way you'll lose your virginity."

He frowned again. Had he just said that? Yep, apparently he had. He was moving into the stupid zone. It didn't help when Mila stood because with him sitting on her desk and looming over her—yes, he was looming now—it put them practically eye-to-eye.

Mouth-to-mouth, as well.

Then hand-to-hand when she slid hers over his.

She smelled like dessert, felt like silk and looked like Christmas. Not a good combination.

"I don't want it to be a conquest." No trace of that drunk laughter now. She wasn't dodging his gaze, either. She was looking right at him. "Like—'yay, I did it. I went where no man has gone before.' Why are guys like that, anyway?"

"Not all are. Personally, I avoid virgins. Sorry," he added.

He definitely didn't say present company included. Because here he was. Not moving. And thinking about something he shouldn't be thinking about.

Like the condom he carried in his wallet.

Or the hard-on he was getting.

If there was a highway to hell, then he was on it right now. Along with coming close to messing up things big-time with Mila. Like that letter she'd just gotten, a kiss would change everything.

Sex would change everything times a thousand.

"You know those cans people use for pranks?" he asked. "The ones with the fake snake inside that jump out when you open the lid?"

Clearly, she hadn't been expecting him to say that. Roman saw the surprise in her eyes. He couldn't miss it because she was still only a couple of inches away. He also didn't miss the glance she made at his crotch. Maybe Mila thought he was talking about his hard-on jumping out at her.

"Well, it's very difficult to put that snake back in once it's out of the can," Roman assured her.

When he'd first thought of the metaphor in his head, it'd made a lot more sense than it did when he said it aloud. And it hadn't been sexual in his head, either. Of course, pretty much anything he said or did right now would have some sexual overtones to it.

"What if I don't want to put it back?" she asked.

This was one of those defining moments in a man's life. The badass in him wanted to answer that by showing her. But the other part of him that wasn't badass knew this was a bad idea.

One that would feel very, very good, though.

Somehow, even with that understanding of all those *very*s, Roman had to decline.

He stood, risked brushing a kiss on her cheek and started toward the door. "I'll call Sophie and have her come stay with you."

"No, don't. She's in Austin this morning on business, and I don't want her to have to drive back. Plus, I really do want to be alone right now. In fact, I'd prefer you not mention this to Sophie or anyone else. Not until I get a handle on it. Okay?"

Roman turned, studied her to make sure she wasn't about to fall apart. Mila certainly looked stronger than she had a couple of seconds ago.

Hotter, too.

He groaned because he needed to get out of there fast.

She didn't follow him. Good thing because it was hard to walk with an erection and with his side still literally in stitches.

"Will you ever change your mind about this?" she asked when he made it to the front door.

Absolutely. In fact, he might change it before he could even get outside. But that wasn't what Mila needed to hear right now, whether she thought it was or not.

"I'll get back to you on that," he settled for saying, and Roman left before he let his hard-on do the talking for him.

CHAPTER NINE

TATE WISHED HE could put on a magic cloak or ring or something and make himself invisible. That way, he could go from class to class and not have anyone see that he was there. Because everyone was seeing him.

That was the problem with going to a small school. Everybody knew everybody. And they all knew he was new. They probably had heard about him, too. Probably knew he'd taken those stupid girl pills. Something he hadn't thought about when he'd first talked his dad into staying in Wrangler's Creek.

This had been a shitty idea.

And it'd been his.

He considered calling his dad but then looked up at the clock on the wall of his English class. Only ten-thirty. He'd been here two and a half hours and was ready to quit. His dad wouldn't like that. Heck, he didn't like it much, either, but when he got home, he could tell his dad that he wanted to do homeschooling. Anything to stop everyone from seeing him.

The teacher hushed talking about sentence structure and stood to write something on the chalkboard. He was old, tall and skinny, and if his hair would have been long, he would have looked like Gandalf from *Lord of the Rings*. That was one of Tate's favorite books, but it wasn't what Teacher-Gandalf wrote on the board for their reading assignment.

Al Capone Does My Shirts.

Tate doubted there'd be any wizards in a book with that title.

Shit. He hated this school. Hated his life.

The bell rang, and everyone started out of the room, heading to the next class. Tate took out his schedule again even though he had it memorized, and this was his free period. He needed to make his way back to homeroom so he could sit there while everyone looked at him and whispered about those girl pills.

He waited so he'd be the last one out, and he went into the hall. It was packed, of course, and looked like the cows Uncle Garrett sometimes herded into a corral when they needed medicine and junk. Most of the kids here had the same blank looks as those cows. They probably didn't have the kind of stuff going on in their lives like he did.

They probably had mothers who gave a shit.

"You're Tate Granger," someone said from behind him.

Tate glanced over his shoulder and saw two girls. They'd both been in his English class but had sat at the front. One was blonde and about his height. The other was taller and had red hair with purple streaks in it. He figured the blonde had been the one to say that because she was smiling. The other one was giving him a "get out of my face" look.

He nodded.

"Well, I'm Chrissy Beaumont." Yep, it was the blonde, all right. "My dad owns the grocery store. The pharmacy, too. He knows your dad real well."

Since that might not be a good thing, Tate just shrugged. He'd heard that his dad used to get in trouble a lot when he was his age.

"I've been riding at your family's ranch a couple of times," Chrissy went on. "The Grangers own a big house and lots of horses," she added to her friend. She paused, maybe just so she could take a breath, and then fluttered her fingers toward the other girl. "Oh, this is my half sister, Arrie. Well, it's really Arwen like that fairy or whatever in that movie."

"Lord of the Rings," Tate said.

"Yes, that one. Anyway, Arrie is hanging out with me today."

Arrie didn't look very happy about that. She didn't look happy about anything, but he did like the name and thought her nose ring was pretty. So were the three rings in each of her earlobes. One of the earrings was a tiny cowbell.

"My mom said I wasn't to let Arrie out of my sight," Chrissy added. "She's grounded for skipping theater arts. Weird, right? I mean, if you're gonna skip, skip math or something." She didn't even try to whisper that or anything.

Arrie just huffed.

"I gotta get to class." Tate turned to leave, but Chrissy stepped in front of him. "I'm having a little pool party at my house on Friday. Would you like to come?"

Tate had seen the way that some women looked at his dad. Actually, a lot of women looked at his dad that way. But it was the first time Tate had seen that look aimed at him. Chrissy was thinking that because his family had money and a big house that he'd make a good boyfriend.

He wouldn't.

Especially since being a boyfriend would mean going to her party. Here at school, at least, people probably wouldn't bring up that he'd tried to off himself, but it could come up at a party. And even if it didn't people would still look at him like some kind of freak.

Tate shook his head. "I can't go to your party, sorry. I've got to do something else that night."

It wasn't a lie. He had books he planned to read and would maybe go riding with his uncle.

"Oh, well," Chrissy said. Her voice wasn't as happy as it had been a few seconds ago. "Maybe some other time. Come on, Arrie."

Chrissy walked away. Arrie stayed put. "Did you really try to kill yourself?" she asked.

It was the first time anyone had come out and asked that. Even Dr. Woodliff had tiptoed around it by asking Tate if there was anything he wanted to talk about. His dad hadn't brought it up at all. His dad and the rest of his family were treating him as if he were bad-off sick.

And that scared him.

Because he just might be.

"Arrie?" Chrissy called out, waggling her fingers at her half sister. "Come on. You're gonna make me late again."

Arrie ignored her, but it was pretty clear that she was waiting for Tate to answer her question. He'd taken those pills because the bottle said it would make him sleepy. He'd just wanted to sleep so he could turn off the bad feelings in his head.

"No. I didn't really try to off myself," he answered. "It was just something stupid that I did. It was an accident."

She looked at him. A long time. Long enough for Chrissy to yell for her two more times. "If you ever think about doing anything else stupid, just call me." Arrie took his hand, scribbled her phone number on his palm, and that's when Tate saw it.

The white scar on her wrist.

Not something like you'd get from a scrape. It was straight across, and he could even see the little scars from the stitch marks.

She followed his gaze, and even though her look didn't get any friendlier, it did soften a bit. "Yeah," Arrie said. "For me, it wasn't an accident."

MILA STOOD IN Sophie's office in the Granger guesthouse and waited for her friend to finish reading the letter from Vita. Mila had gone over every word so many times that she knew it by heart. Knew, too, the reaction Sophie would have.

"Holy crap on a cracker," Sophie said. Since she wasn't much for profanity, that was pretty harsh for her. Sophie looked at the back of the letter as if to find some explanation there, but it was blank. They had all they were going to get in the explanation department for now. At least until Vita got back from her trip.

"It came a week ago," Mila added. Actually, nine days. She could probably come up with the exact hours if need be.

"And you're just now showing it to me?" Sophie asked.

Mila had known she'd say that, as well. "I wanted some time to come to terms with it."

Sophie stared at her. Then winced. But the wincing wasn't because of Mila. It was because one of the babies had kicked her. It was hard enough that Mila saw Sophie's belly move from beneath her maternity top.

"You should have called me the minute you got this," Sophie went on. "I would have come right away."

"That's why I didn't call. I know you're trying to wrap up some things at work before you take time off for the babies, and I didn't want to bother you."

"Turkey squat," Sophie snarled, giving Mila yet another example of Sophie's G-rated notion of cursing. "We're best friends, and you shouldn't have had to go through this alone."

"I wasn't alone. Roman read the letter, too. He came by the shop shortly after I got it. And he's been texting me every day to make sure I'm okay."

Sophie made a quick sound of surprise. "That was sweet of him. Not so sweet, though, since he didn't tell me about it."

"I asked him not to." However, Mila was surprised he'd carried through on her wishes.

"Wait," Sophie said. "Was Roman there that day because of your coffee date with Dylan?"

Mila nodded. "First, he came by to get some books for Tate. I think he wanted to talk to me then about Dylan, but your mom was there."

"Fantasy date stuff." Sophie sighed. "We'll get into that later, but for now, tell me about Roman's visits that day."

"Well, he came by a second time, only a few minutes after Dylan left the shop." She had told Sophie about the coffee date. Such that it was. Mila had also told her that she wouldn't be going out with Dylan again. "I had just finished reading the letter and was crying when Roman came in."

Sophie mumbled some profanity again. "You cried? Of course you did. And I wasn't there. I should have been there." Sophie's pregnancy emotions were about to get the best of her. She looked to be on the verge of tears.

Mila hugged her. "Roman was a good substitute so don't worry about it. He stayed with me for a little while and even had a drink with me." She paused. "I gave him an erection."

Sophie's head whipped up, fast. "W-what?" Clearly, she was surprised, and Mila didn't think it was left-over shock from the letter that caused Sophie's mouth to drop open like that.

"I didn't do it on purpose," Mila explained. "We were just drinking and talking, and we were standing very close to each other. I'm not sure what happened, but the air changed between us or something. I got all tingly, looked at him, and I could see that he was getting tingly, too."

"Roman, tingly?" There was skepticism in Sophie's voice.

Good point. He probably didn't tingle. He just got hard. Mila had seen the outline of it behind the zipper of his jeans.

"Do you think it means anything?" Mila asked. "Other than the obvious. I mean, men get erections all the time so it might not have had anything to do with me."

Sophie rolled her eyes. "Of course it had something to do with you. Roman isn't fifteen. He doesn't get an erection because he's standing next to a woman. He got it because you were a woman he wanted to sleep with." She smiled. "Isn't this what you've been wanting for years?"

Yes. Mila had always wanted Roman to get uncomfortably aroused in her presence. She just hadn't realized it was going to cause her to feel like this.

Confused.

Maybe it's because all of this was coming on the tail of that letter. Also on the tail of Tate's suicide attempt. Or maybe she just hadn't thought this through.

"Roman won't like taking my virginity," Mila pointed out.

Another eye roll from Sophie. "Oh, he'll like it, all right. Maybe he'll have doubts afterward, though."

There was no maybe about it. He *would* have doubts. Because Roman expected her to expect something from him.

"You should have just gone for it," Sophie said. "Not just once but three times, and then you could have tested that stupid rule of his."

Mila had to shake her head. "What rule?"

She dismissed it with a wave of her hand. "Some dumb thing he has about only having sex with a woman a maximum of three times. I heard him talking to Garrett about it, and I could tell it didn't make any more sense to Garrett than it did to me."

Well, it wasn't making sense to Mila. "Why three? Why the rule?" she added.

"Because more than three is the C-word. And no, I don't mean that C-word," Sophie said, motioning toward her lady parts. "I mean *commitment*. Roman's scared spitless about it so he figures if he doesn't spend much time boinking a woman, then he also won't feel any obligation to commit."

Mila could see that side of an argument, but three times with Roman might be enough to fulfill every fantasy she'd ever had. And some she hadn't even thought up.

"All of this explains why Roman's been so antsy lately. Antsier than usual," Sophie corrected. "He wants to have sex with you." She stopped, looked up at Mila. "You think your mom knew that and that's why she gave him the condom when he was still in the hospital?"

Mila had to go with another question. "What condom?"

"It was in the gift bag that you brought him from Vita."

Oh, mercy. If she'd known that, Mila wouldn't have given it to him. "I thought it was chicken poop or something." And then she remembered what else her mother had done. "She gave me a condom, too. It was the same day Roman, Tate and your mom ended up in the hospital. Vita told me I was going to lose my virginity within thirty days."

Sophie must have had the same idea she did because she moved some papers off her calendar desk map and looked at the dates. All of that had happened thirteen days ago. In some ways it seemed a lifetime. In other ways, it wasn't much time.

"Only two and a half weeks left," Sophie said. "And that's if you use the entire thirty days. Vita could have just been giving you a general reference. It could happen before then."

Mila was about to agree with her, but she stopped and came to her senses. "My mother's predictions and visions don't always come true." She certainly hadn't kept track of the success to failure rate, but Mila was positive there'd been failures.

Except she couldn't think of a single one at the moment.

And her mother had said all that stuff about an ill wind. That had come true. Again, though, she stopped.

"We're talking about Vita here," she reminded Sophie. "She could have given the condoms to Roman and me as a way of nudging us to become lovers. Not because she truly wants that but because she thought it might make me forget that she'd never told me the truth about my real father."

Sophie didn't, and couldn't, argue with that. "But Vita did give you clues as to who your father is."

"Yes, and I've already started a list. I went to the library and found a copy of the town's old phone book from the year I was conceived. Thankfully, nearly everybody had landlines. I was able to rule out some because they were too young or too old. Like Ned, the pharmacist, because I figured, since he won't touch anyone unless he's wearing latex gloves, then he probably wouldn't have had unprotected sex with Vita."

Sophie's face bunched up, and Mila knew why. "Hey, that's not a fun image in my head, either," Mila assured her. "In fact, none of these are fun images. I prefer to think of my mom as asexual."

Which she probably was these days. Mila had certainly never seen her in the company of a man since she'd become a widow.

"I also ruled out anyone who's dead," Mila went on, "because Vita said in the letter that he was still alive."

That part had actually been a relief once Mila gave it some thought. Because Roman's father had slept around. Not once in a million years had Mila thought that Roman and she might be related, but it was good to have it confirmed that they weren't.

"So, how many candidates do you have on your list?" Sophie asked.

"Nineteen."

Sophie frowned right along with her. "You've got to start whittling that down. Let me see it. Maybe I can help."

"I didn't bring it," she lied. It was on her phone. "Besides, you've got enough to do. You're only four weeks from your due date, and the doctor said the twins would come early. I know you've still got plenty of things to do to get ready for that."

Again, Sophie couldn't argue.

Mila patted Sophie's belly. "Just think, soon we'll get to hold these little guys, and you won't have to carry them around with you all the time."

"Soon I'll be able to see my feet again. And bend over. And go more than twenty minutes without having to pee. Soon, Clay and I can have sex. I miss sex, and the doctor said to hold off because I've dilated some."

Mila's shoulders snapped back. "What does that mean?"

"It's normal. It just means my body is getting ready to have these guys. Then I'll know if Clay and I will have two sons, two daughters or one of each." Unlike many couples, Clay and she hadn't wanted to know the gender of their babies before they were born. "And after four weeks, sex. I really miss sex," she added.

Mila missed it, too. More so now than she ever had. That perhaps had something to do with her seeing Roman at that exact moment. He was coming out of the barn and heading to a corral where some horses had just been delivered.

He had obviously recovered from his surgery. Considering how he was dressed, he had also decided to help around the ranch. He always wore jeans, cowboy hat, boots and his rodeo buckle but usually still managed to look as if he ran a business. Not today, though. His shirt was unbuttoned, the sides shifting when he walked to give her a peep show of that toned chest and pecs.

Seriously, the man had a six-pack.

He even managed to look good sweaty, and she couldn't take her eyes off him when he grabbed the hose and ran some water over his head. It snaked down that perfect body, sliding right into the waist of his jeans.

Exactly where Mila wanted her hand to be.

"If women could get an erection, you'd have one right now," Sophie said. The sound of her voice jarred Mila back to reality. But she came back with little "side effects." She was breathing too fast and was warm and damp in the wrong place.

Mila hadn't even been sure when Sophie had moved to the window to see what she was gawking at. That probably had something to do with her heartbeat drumming in her ears. She was a mess.

And very aroused.

"You should go out and…talk to him," Sophie suggested. "And you can do that after you tell me about my mom and this fantasy dating stuff. Do I need to worry about her?"

"No." Of course, Mila would have said that even if there had been something to worry about and then she would have gone to Garrett or Clay to fix the situation.

But Mila thought she had it under control. "Belle set up the first date. It's the 'frankly, I don't give a damn' scene from *Gone with the Wind*. Clay vetted the guy, and he's a retired software developer, widowed, no red flags to indicate he's a pervert."

In some people's minds, though, he was a pervert simply because he did fantasy dating.

"They'll be doing it at the bookstore after hours," Mila went on. "Belle has the props and her costume. But as a precaution, Clay's going to put in a security camera that he can access from the police station."

Sophie shook her head. "You two set all of this up and didn't let me know?"

"You've had other things on your mind." Mila gave her stomach another pat and got a kick on her palm from one of the babies. Even though she'd felt them move before, it always still seemed like a little miracle.

"Okay," Sophie agreed. "But I wish you could talk Mom into ditching this whole fantasy idea."

"Trust me, it's not doable right now." But Mila did think of something else that Clay and she hadn't *vetted*. "What about your mother's heart condition? Will something like this aggravate it?"

"No. I already asked the doctor. Of course, he wouldn't discuss specifics with me about Mom's medical records. Privacy laws. But he said there's no reason she can't resume a normal life. Personally, I don't think this is normal, not for her, anyway, but he refused to try to rein her in on this."

Well, at least this wasn't going to kill Belle, but Mila still needed to keep an eye on the woman, anyway.

"Mom should just go on a real date," Sophie added, "and she wouldn't have to look far for someone to take her out. Billy Lee has always had a thing for her, and he's on his way over here right now to bring me some papers to sign."

Billy Lee Seaver. He wasn't just the CFO of Granger Western, but he was also on Mila's possible dad list. She wouldn't mention that to Sophie, though, because he was her godfather. Besides, he didn't look like the sort who'd go for Vita. Belle and he seemed like a better fit.

"Now you can go out there and get Roman," Sophie said. "He should be healed up enough for a romp in the hay if you're so inclined."

Mila smiled. But the truth was—she was inclined. Now, she just had to get Roman on the same inclination with her.

She kissed Sophie's cheek, put the letter in her pocket and headed toward the back door. She didn't want to go out the front because she spotted two of the hands out there. No need for her to advertise that she was moving in Roman's direction. She could just go out the back and make her way to him. Of course, someone would probably still see her, and Sophie would likely peek from the window, but the fewer people she encountered, the better.

Mila had barely made it to the back porch before her phone rang, and Mila saw the "unknown" caller on the screen. Since she figured it was a telemarketer, she let it go to voice mail, and a few seconds later, her phone dinged to indicate she had a message. She listened to it while she started walking again. She made it to the bottom step of the porch.

And then she had to stop when she heard the caller's voice.

"Mila," she greeted her. "Call me when you can, coz."

Valerie.

Mila hit the callback button immediately, but it took several rings for Valerie to answer. "I've been trying to get in touch with you—"

"Yeah," Valerie said. "Just about everybody I know has been calling to say Roman and you've been bugging them to find me. Well, here I am. What's so urgent that you just had to talk to me?"

Mila wished she had rehearsed this, but even if she had, she probably couldn't have made this sound better. "Tate maybe tried to kill himself. He was in the hospital, but he's all right," she quickly added when she figured Valerie would interrupt her. She didn't. "Are you there? Did you hear me?"

"Of course I heard you. You said he was all right. How'd he try to kill himself?"

"Pills." Mila hoped Valerie didn't ask what kind because it would maybe make this seem like a foolish attempt. But in Mila's mind, any attempt was serious and a cry for help.

"What kind of pills?"

Mila bit back a groan. "Does it matter? The point is he took them."

"Sure it matters. A friend of mine took an entire bottle of Oxy, then some benzos, and he chased it down with some rum. He really wanted his ticket punched. But if Tate just took a couple of benzos on their own, then maybe he was just trying to get some sleep."

Mila wasn't even sure what a benzo was, and while Tate did indeed go to sleep on the pills, that wasn't why he had taken them.

"So, what did he take?" Valerie pressed.

"I'm not sure," Mila lied. "And you're missing the

point. Tate needs help. He's seeing a therapist, and Roman and he decided it would be best to stay here at the ranch in Wrangler's Creek for that."

"Roman's at the ranch?" Valerie laughed. "I thought I felt a chill on the bottom of my feet. That's because hell must have frozen over." Another laugh. "I'll bet Belle's bugging the shit out of him."

Mila would have liked to think that Valerie was in shock over hearing about her son, but unfortunately, this was typical behavior. Valerie was the ultimate party girl, out to have fun, and if it wasn't fun, she didn't want to deal with it. Which was why she'd left Tate when he was just a baby.

"Roman would do anything to help Tate," Mila continued, not even addressing Valerie's comment about Belle. "But Tate needs you here, too, so you can go through a family counseling session with them."

"Counseling? You mean with some head doctor with a bunch of degrees? That's not the way to heal the mind. Art and meditation are the way to fix that. You need to get Tate to a yoga class."

Mila had to relax her jaw so she could speak. "Then maybe you can suggest that to the therapist when you come for the session. Please come," she added. For Tate's sake, she would resort to begging.

"Please?" Valerie repeated. "You must think this is serious."

"I do," Mila assured her.

Valerie laughed again. "Oh, I see what's happening here. Helping Tate is a way for you to get cozy with Roman. Don't lie. It's something you've always wanted. You, the little bookworm mouse. Roman, the renegade cowboy with a great dick. You must be in seventh heaven, having Roman practically right on your doorstep."

Mila had no idea how to answer that. If she agreed and tried to placate Valerie, she might refuse to come. Heck, the woman might refuse, anyway, so Mila just went for broke.

"Come to Wrangler's Creek ASAP to help your son," Mila warned her, "or I will find you and drag you back here myself."

Another laugh. "You think you can kick my ass, little coz?"

"I know I can."

Valerie didn't laugh that time, but she did end the call, making Mila wonder just how long it was going to take her to find that coldhearted witch's ass and kick it all the way back here to the ranch.

CHAPTER TEN

ROMAN HELD THE hose over his head again and let the cold water cool him off. Or at least that was the plan. But even the water wasn't helping much.

It was Texas hot, way too humid, and his body was aching. When he'd agreed to help Garrett move the horses from the corral to the back pasture, he'd forgotten how much work it could be. He wasn't out of shape, but ranching required a different set of muscles than the ones needed for the gym or for testing out a new bronco for the rodeo. Still, it was satisfying.

Something he wouldn't mention to Garrett.

His brother might use that *satisfying* feeling to try to lure Roman back here for good. It wouldn't work. Roman couldn't live in the same house with his mother. But that wouldn't stop Garrett from trying.

Roman glanced up from his hose-dousing and spotted Mila in the window of Sophie's office. It'd been over a week since he'd walked out of her bookstore and left her with that letter and her tears. If it'd only been those two things, he would have stayed, but he'd seen that look in her eyes. Had known what she wanted from him.

And what she wanted was something he couldn't give her.

Even if his body disagreed.

He'd always been well aware that Mila was attracted

to him. He wasn't stupid. But Roman had also known she'd held back. Maybe because she was Valerie's cousin. Maybe because he scared her. She wasn't the sort to want to play with fire. But that look in her eyes had told him that she might want to sample a little fire, after all. That's why he'd left. That's why he hadn't gone back to the bookstore. However, he had listened to make sure there wasn't any gossip about her falling apart or anything.

There wasn't.

In fact, the only gossip was that several people had spotted him limping out of her bookstore and that maybe she'd kicked him in the balls when he'd tried to rid her of her virginity.

Mila glanced in his direction, looked away and then she disappeared. Not out the front door, which meant she was probably going out back. Roman turned off the hose and headed there, too. Not for more of those lustful looks or hard-ons, but because he wanted to find out how she was doing.

When he made it to the side of the guesthouse, he still couldn't see Mila, but he certainly could hear her. She was talking on the phone to someone, and her tone let him know that the conversation wasn't going well.

"Come to Wrangler's Creek ASAP to help your son, or I will find you and drag you back here myself," she snarled to the person on the other end of the line.

Valerie.

He hurried to the back porch just as Mila was hurrying in his direction, and they darn near collided. Roman had to catch her by the shoulders to stop them from doing a full body slam.

Just like the day at the bookstore, there were tears

in her eyes again, but this time he didn't have to guess the source of them. She also didn't have to guess that he'd heard what she said because he saw the realization in her expression.

"I'm so sorry," she said, and despite the fact he was trying to hold her at bay, he ended up just plain holding her instead. "I shouldn't have threatened her. I kept it together until she started talking about your dick."

Roman felt his muscles tense. "That must have been some conversation."

She huffed, wiped away her tears and stepped out of his arms. "It was Valerie being Valerie." And that said it all.

His ex had a way of riling people even from hundreds of miles away. Apparently, that's exactly what she'd done, since Mila's warning had been about Valerie coming here to help Tate. He wasn't sure how his dick fit into that, because Valerie hadn't been near that part of him since she'd been pregnant with Tate.

"Valerie accused me of using Tate to get close to you," Mila went on. "I'm not. I've always loved Tate."

"I know." No argument from him on that, but he did have some questions. "Is she coming and why didn't she call Tate or me?"

"She probably thought I'd be the easiest of the three to roll over. She'd actually have to be a mother if she talked to Tate, and you would have threatened her with more than butt-kicking."

Yeah, he would have. "Valerie knows exactly where my hot buttons are and how hard to push them. And no, that wasn't a dick reference."

Mila didn't smile, but the corner of her mouth lifted a little. "She pushed my buttons, too." The sadness returned to her eyes, making them even darker than they already were.

Exotic eyes. Dark brown but with flecks of gold in them. Though Roman wasn't sure why he was noticing that at a time like this.

"If Valerie comes, she comes," he said to try to chase away some of that sadness. "Nothing you said to her would make her stay away if she truly wants to be here." That worked the other way, too. Roman did want to talk to her, but that was only so he could say he tried. Valerie would do what she wanted, and to hell with anyone else.

Including their son.

"Did she say anything about calling me?" Roman asked.

"No. But she pretty much blew off what Tate did. She suggested yoga or meditation."

Definitely a good thing he hadn't talked to her. He wouldn't have made things better. "You probably think I'm stupid to have gotten involved with her," he said.

Mila immediately shook her head. "No. I remember her in those days. She was fun. Alive. Outgoing. Everything that I was too afraid to be."

He couldn't argue with any of that, either, but he'd never understood the last part. "Why were you afraid?"

Another head shake, followed by a shrug. "I just didn't fit in. I thought perhaps because of my mother and because I didn't have a dad, but now I wonder if I sensed that I wasn't who my mom was telling me I was."

"Maybe." He paused. "You think it'll help if you find out who your father is?"

"Maybe," she repeated. "I have a list." She pulled out her phone from the back pocket of her jeans and showed him the file she'd placed in her notes.

Roman did more than just glance at it. He took her phone and scrolled through the names.

"Yes, Billy Lee is on there," she volunteered. "And the minister. Along with Waylon Beaumont."

The man who owned the grocery store and pharmacy. He was on his second family since he and his first wife had divorced, and he'd remarried a woman a lot younger than he was. If memory served, they had daughters about Tate's age. That probably wasn't someone Mila wanted to go up to and ask if he was her biological father. But there was someone on the list she could tackle first.

"Billy Lee will be here soon," he told her. "Why don't you talk to him about this?"

She was shaking her head before he even finished. "No. Didn't you remember that part about my mother's letter saying it would mess up my birth father's life if he knew?"

"I remember. But that doesn't apply to Billy Lee. He's not married, never has been. He's not dating anyone, either, so there's no relationship to mess up if he finds out he has a daughter."

"His reputation," Mila quickly supplied. "Granger Western does business with a lot of people, and some of them might not appreciate that the CFO fathered a child out of wedlock." She winced. "Sorry."

Mila was probably referring to the fact that he'd done the whole fathering out of wedlock thing, and he had, but the difference was Roman had nothing to do with Granger Western except occasionally signing some paperwork. He certainly wasn't a "face" of the company the way Sophie and Billy Lee were.

"Is that what you were talking to Sophie about—Billy Lee?" he asked.

"No. In fact, I didn't mention it to her yet. I showed Sophie the letter, though. We also talked about your mother…and some other things."

Since she didn't volunteer what those things were, Roman didn't ask. Though he was curious. Lately he was a lot more curious about anything that involved Mila.

Damn.

It was this attraction again. It was sliding right through and undoing the slight cooling off he'd gotten from the hose. Best to say something instead of just standing there simmering.

"I can talk to Billy Lee for you," he suggested. "I won't come out and ask unless that's what you want me to do."

"I don't."

That's what he'd figured. "I can just ask in a round-about way." After all, Billy Lee always asked Roman about his love life, in a roundabout way, too, so the subject was bound to come up. Roman would just turn the tables on him.

Mila motioned toward her car that was in the side driveway, and it looked as if she was ready to leave. She didn't move, though. She stayed put and looked at him. Well, she looked at his clothes, anyway.

"Ranch work?" she asked. "It looks good on you."

He shrugged. "It's temporary. Hell, that describes a lot of things in my life right now. Tate seems to be set-tling into school all right, but in another few weeks, the term will end, and we'll go back to San Antonio. I have to go sooner than that actually."

Her forehead bunched up. "You're leaving?"

"Again, just temporarily. I've got a meeting I can't put off. I'm driving into San Antonio tomorrow and hope that Tate will be okay without me for a night or two."

"I can check on him," Mila volunteered. "Not sure he'll need it, though, since Garrett will be around."

Yeah, his brother had really stepped up with Tate, and Roman wasn't going to forget that. It was one of the reasons he was doing ranch work today.

"Do you really have a rule about only having sex with a woman three times?" she asked.

Roman certainly hadn't seen that question coming, and he scowled. "Who told you that?"

"Sophie."

Great. So, that's what Mila and she had been talking about. His dick was certainly the topic of conversation today.

"Well, do you?" she pressed.

Since this wasn't an easy thing to explain, Roman considered lying, but it didn't seem right to lie to a woman who was jacking up his testosterone. "Yes."

Clearly, she wanted more than that because Mila just stared at him.

"It's a rule that makes things simple," he went on a few seconds later. "That way, a woman doesn't think sex will lead to anything more. And even if you tell someone that it's just sex, the longer you're with that person, it might start to feel like, well, more."

"Familiarity breeds commitment?" Her tongue wasn't actually in her cheek, but it should have been. She glanced away, smiled. "It's a good rule. It's sort of like a genie giving you three wishes. I like it."

Mila was certainly keeping him on his toes. "Most women hate it. Or they think it's a rule I'll break. I don't."

"Good." She took in a quick breath. "Then this should make things easier for both of us. I want to have sex with you, Roman. Once is fine, but three times works, too."

Mila brushed a kiss on his lips. Considering his mouth had dropped open, it nearly turned French.

"Think about it and let me know what you decide," Mila added, and she walked away.

She left him there, in shock. Wondering.

Wanting the hell out of her.

Shit.

He was going to say yes.

MILA TRIED TO look confident as she strolled toward her car. If it was working, it was pure facade because she wasn't confident about anything right now.

Well, nothing except that she really did want to have sex with Roman.

Three times was a bonus. She'd thought simply to ask him to be her first. With no strings attached, of course. But now, he could be her first, second and third. Most people didn't count actual times, just lovers, but she liked the idea of Roman topping her lovers' list.

If she ever got a list, that is.

But this was a start to getting one. Mila refused to dwell on the fact she might get a broken heart out of this because that was overdue, too. She was fed up with being Mila Banchini, and while she didn't want to go full-Valerie, she at least wanted a taste of what others had.

She didn't look back at Roman. In part, because she

wanted to pretend that he was drooling over her and not standing there with a dumbfounded look on his face. Besides, she had no doubt thrown him for a loop, and he might need days or longer to come up with a decision. Best to leave and give him some time and space.

When Mila was still a few feet away from her car, she heard the giggling and at first thought it was Sophie. But it was Belle. She was in the sunroom just on the other side of the back porch of the main house. She wasn't alone, either.

Billy Lee was with her.

They didn't see Mila at first so she was able to notice the way they were standing. Close, for one thing. And Billy Lee was smiling at whatever had caused Belle to laugh.

"There you are," Belle said when she spotted her. "I saw your car and figured you'd gone out to chat with Sophie. Come on in so we can talk, too."

This would no doubt be about the fantasy dating, something Mila didn't want to discuss, but she did want to get a better look at Billy Lee. She had gotten looks before, of course. Over the years, he'd dropped by dozens of times while she'd been visiting Sophie, and she had also seen him in the hospital a lot when Sophie's dad was dying.

Billy Lee aimed a smile at her as she made her way up the steps, and Mila tried to study his face without drawing attention to what she was doing. She didn't see anything that she hadn't noticed about him before. She certainly didn't see herself in him, but then most people said she looked like Vita when her mother was younger.

"I was just telling Billy Lee about how good it was to see Roman doing some real work for a change," Belle remarked. "I hope it sticks and he doesn't go back to that rodeo stuff."

It hadn't stuck and he was going back, but Mila kept that to herself. Easy to do since the house phone rang and Belle scurried off to answer it.

"I'm glad we've got a few minutes," Billy Lee said, glancing back at Belle, who was now in the kitchen on the phone.

Her stomach sank a little. Oh, mercy. Had he heard about her daddy list?

"I wanted to thank you," Billy Lee went on. "I don't know what you said to Dylan, but it worked. Dylan was able to talk Lucian out of the lawsuit. Or rather, he was able to talk him into putting it on hold. That's good enough for now."

This was the first Mila was hearing of it, and it seemed as if Billy Lee was waiting for her to tell him how she'd managed it. She didn't have a clue. "I just asked Dylan to consider it," she settled for saying.

"Sometimes, a mention is all it takes." He glanced back at Belle again.

Mila was probably reading way too much into this, but it seemed as if he was…cozier than usual. Maybe because of the relief he felt over the lawsuit. Maybe because he felt a genetic bond. Either way, he moved closer and lowered his head.

"Is Belle really going on a date?" he asked. "One where she dresses up and pretends to be someone else?"

Oh, so that's why he was acting cozy. He was concerned, maybe even jealous. "Yes, it's a fantasy date."

Another glance at Belle. The woman was still on the phone. "I want to set up one for Belle and me. A surprise one. Do you think you could help me with that?"

"Sure." Since Billy Lee could be her father, it was a little strange talking to him about dating, but Mila heartily approved. Billy Lee was someone Clay wouldn't have to vet, and judging from the way Belle had giggled around him, she liked the man.

"Which fantasy do you think she'd like?" Billy Lee asked.

"Well, she likes the scene in *Twilight* where Bella tells Edward that she knows he's a vampire."

Mila had never seen a blanker stare in her entire life.

"It was a very popular movie and book," Mila added. "But she also likes the pottery scene in *Ghost*. And the scene in *Pretty Woman* where she gets the necklace."

Yet another blank stare.

"Tell you what," Mila continued, "the *Pretty Woman* scene will be easier to set up, and I can maybe borrow a dress for Belle from the theater department at the high school. All you would need to wear is a tux and bring a necklace to give her. Just text me the date when you'd like to do this, and I can set up everything in my bookstore."

"Drat," Belle said, putting her hand over the receiver of the phone. "Mila, this call will take a few more minutes. Garden Club stuff. Can you wait for me in the family room? My costume is in there, and I want to show it to you. Billy Lee, you can see it, too, if you like."

"No, thanks. I need to go have a word with Roman. Thank you," he added in a whisper to Mila as he walked out toward Roman, who was near the barn now.

Billy Lee probably wanted to tell him about the lawsuit, and while Mila didn't especially want to be in on that discussion, she didn't want to talk antebellum dresses, either. Still, she'd see it, make a few minutes of polite conversation and then get back to the bookstore so she could help Janeen close up.

While Belle was still in the kitchen, Mila made her way to the family room and immediately spotted the dress. Hard to miss. It was huge, taking up nearly the whole sofa, and it wasn't an especially nice shade of green. Obviously, Belle was going for the jail-visiting scene where Scarlett had worn a curtain.

Mila checked the time after a few minutes crawled by, and she was about to leave a note for Belle to let her know that she'd had to go. However, the sound of a vehicle stopped her, and she glanced out the front window and saw the school bus driving off. That meant she'd get to see Tate before she had to leave.

She heard voices. Except Tate wasn't alone when he was coming up the porch steps to the house.

There was a girl with him.

A girl with purple and red hair.

"This way," he whispered to her. "Keep quiet so they won't hear us."

And he led the girl in the direction of his bedroom.

CHAPTER ELEVEN

SEX. WITH MILA.

Even though it was obvious that Billy Lee was headed his way to talk to him, Roman wasn't sure he'd be able to manage anything as complex as human speech. All of his brain had gone straight to his dick.

Not a good place for his brain to be since he needed it right now.

And what he needed was to be rethinking this stupid idea of having sex with Mila. If he wanted something that risky in this life, he should just climb up in the barn loft, jump into a pile of hay and play dodge the pitchfork.

"Looks like old times," Billy Lee greeted him. "You were always with the horses. Garrett was always off with the cows. Though I suspect in your brother's case, it was more of a way for him to be by himself."

Roman suspected the same thing. While he was suspecting, he added that Billy Lee was here on some kind of fishing expedition. Maybe to find out if Roman had plans to make ranch work permanent.

"I'm not staying," Roman said right off, shaking Billy Lee's hand when he offered it.

The man smiled. "I figured as much, but I thought I'd ask for your mother's sake." He hitched his thumb toward the house. "I just told Mila thanks for running interference for you with Lucian."

Lucian via Dylan. Roman still wasn't happy about that, but yeah, their lawyer had called him earlier that morning to say the lawsuit was off. He should have mentioned it to Mila, but his brain had started to go south from the moment she rounded the corner of the guesthouse and he'd seen those tears in her eyes.

Then the heat.

Yep, that was the way to make him forget something. But Roman hadn't forgotten what Mila and he had talked about.

"Did you ever spend any time with Vita when you were younger?" Roman asked. Not very subtle, but Billy Lee wasn't much for subtleties. He was a numbers man. Great with spreadsheets and cost margins. People and conversation, not so much. That probably explained why he was still single.

Roman expected the man to be surprised, though, by the question, Billy Lee clearly wasn't. Roman had seen bull calves look more comfortable after having their balls clipped than Billy Lee was looking right now.

"Did Vita say something to you?" Billy Lee countered.

In a general sense, answering a question with a question wasn't a good sign. So, Roman just laid it out there for him. "Did you knock up Vita? This would have been about nine months or so prior to Mila being born."

Now, there was some surprise, and Billy Lee actually staggered back a step, along with putting his hand over his heart. "Shit."

That wasn't a good answer, either. Well, it wasn't good if Billy Lee had plans to deny Roman's knocking-up theory.

Billy Lee shook his head. "Vita never told me she was pregnant." He shot a glance back at the house. "Is Mila my daughter?"

"You tell me. Do the math and figure it out."

Of course, that was asking a lot even from a math person because it had been over three decades ago.

"Shit," Billy Lee mumbled after thinking about it a few moments. "It's possible, I guess."

Roman wasn't even going to address the part about Vita not looking like someone Billy Lee would take to his bed. He was just going to assume that Vita hadn't always looked like an eighty-year-old woman.

Or that alcohol had been involved.

"I thought Frankie was her father," Billy said, still shaking his head.

"No. Vita recently confessed to Mila that she gave birth to her and met Frankie shortly thereafter. Vita said Mila's father was from right here in Wrangler's Creek, and you lived here back then."

Billy Lee nodded. "And the timing could work. Hard to believe it, but Vita was once an attractive woman. Not nearly so strange as she is now, either. She had plenty of men interested in her. Also, I was drinking a lot in those days."

Bingo. Alcohol had played a part.

But there was something that Billy Lee had said that Roman latched on to.

"Plenty of men were interested in Vita?" Roman repeated.

"Yes." He didn't hesitate, either. "She had this whole hippie love-child thing going on then. Long hair, fresh face, and she used to make her own wine."

Again, alcohol. But was Billy Lee saying Vita had

slept around? If so, then this might be the start of a very long search. Still, it was a start.

"So, here's what you're going to do." Roman put his arm around Billy Lee's shoulders because the man didn't look too steady on his feet. "You'll need to take a paternity test. Mila, too. You can get a test for yourself, swab the inside of your cheek and then, once Mila has done hers, a lab can compare the DNA."

Roman waited to see if Billy Lee would balk at any part of that.

"You sure know a lot about this," Billy Lee remarked.

"I did some reading right after Mila learned she had a father here in Wrangler's Creek. Mila needs to know the truth," Roman added just in case Billy Lee was still thinking about balking.

But the addition wasn't necessary. "Of course. I'll do it as soon as possible." He groaned, scrubbed his hand over his face. "Could you tell your mother that something came up and that I had to go?"

Billy Lee didn't wait for Roman to respond. He practically ran to his car, which was parked next to Mila's. He wasn't sure why she was still there, but he was apparently about to find out.

Roman opened the back door of the house, and he immediately heard the loud voice. Not Mila's. But his mother's.

"I'm sorry, but I can't tolerate that sort of thing in my house," Belle was saying.

Roman was instantly pissed. Belle had better not be talking to Mila that way. And she wasn't. When he followed the sound of her voice to the hall, he saw Tate and a girl he didn't recognize. Mila was there, too, but she was in between Tate and his mother.

"What's going on here?" Roman asked.

Tate and Mila groaned. The kind of groans people made when they thought something was about to get worse. Roman figured it was when his mother flung an accusing finger at Tate.

"He brought that girl to his bedroom," Belle said. "I told him he couldn't do that."

"He can't, but you're not the one to tell him that. I am."

Tate and Mila groaned again. The girl looked as if she wanted the floor to swallow her up. Roman wished he could have a do-over and assure her that she wasn't about to be burned at the stake, but his mother had already lit the proverbial fires.

And she started fanning the flames.

"Tate's just like you," Belle went on. "Sneaking around. Bringing girls into his bedroom."

"They weren't doing anything," Mila spoke up. She had one arm around Tate. The other around the girl. "This is Arwen Beaumont, a friend of Tate's. She's in his grade at school."

Beaumont. Her dad, or rather her stepdad, owned the grocery store.

"We weren't doing anything wrong," Tate grumbled, but Roman could already see his son detaching himself from this. He felt he hadn't been treated fairly.

Something Roman knew all too well when it came to his mother. He didn't think he was projecting about that, either.

"They were on the floor," his mother went on. "Mila was just standing outside the door doing nothing about it. She even tried to stop me when I opened the door."

"I didn't do anything about it because nothing inappropriate was going on," Mila argued. "I was just listening at the door to make sure it stayed that way."

Later, Roman would thank her and then ask her why she hadn't texted or called him when Tate had taken a girl into his room.

"I was teaching Tate meditation," Arwen said. "You know, to help when everything starts boiling around inside him. Like now."

There wasn't as much anger in her voice as Roman was feeling. In fact, she just seemed embarrassed about being caught in the middle of a family squabble.

So did Mila.

Mila turned to Roman. "Is there anything you need me to do before I go?"

He shook his head. Best if she wasn't there for the rest of this. She gave Tate a reassuring look, a kiss on the cheek and walked away.

"I should be going, too," Arwen insisted. She was right behind Mila.

Roman didn't know how the girl had gotten there, but if she'd walked or ridden a bike, Mila would make sure she got home all right. He could add that to his list of things he needed to thank her for. But there was one person here he wasn't going to thank. Make that two.

Tate for getting himself into this.

And his mother for making it worse—something she was a pro at doing.

"I still think they were about to have *s-e-x*," Belle said the moment Mila and Arwen were gone. She huffed. "It's not right for a boy to have a girl in his room. Especially when he didn't get my permission."

"He didn't need your permission. He needed mine."

And he didn't have it. Wouldn't get it, either, because Roman knew it wasn't a good idea for two thirteen-year-olds to be behind closed doors. Meditation could lead to sex. Hell, anything, including breathing, could lead to sex at that age.

Because Roman felt some of his own temper reaching that bubbling point, he turned to Tate first. "Go ahead and pack your things while your grandmother and I talk."

"Pack?" Belle yapped.

"Pack?" Tate echoed. "I don't want to leave."

"And I don't want him to go." That came from Belle.

Roman wasn't sure which one to scowl at first. He aimed one at both of them. "Your grandmother just crossed the forbidden zone of parenting," he said to Tate. "She had no right to yell at you. No right to discipline you."

He turned to her when she opened her mouth. "This isn't your house. It's mine, remember?"

Tears sprang to her eyes, and even though Roman didn't want to react to them he did. He cursed himself and cursed this fucking situation.

"I don't want to leave," Tate repeated. This time, there was a lot more anger than there had been just a few minutes earlier. "I don't want to switch schools again. I'm tired of you and everybody else running my life!"

He went in his room and slammed the door.

Belle hurried to hers up the hall and did the same thing. That's when Roman saw Garrett standing there. He wasn't sure how much his brother had heard. Probably more than he wanted to hear.

Garrett went to him, and Roman steeled himself up for a lecture. Instead, he gave Roman a pat on the back.

"Why don't you go to the Longhorn and have a beer?" Garrett suggested. "Better yet, drink more than one and have Hermie Walters drive you home when you're ready."

Hermie was the town's only taxi driver and often parked outside the Longhorn just because he knew he'd earn some bucks from someone who'd gone in there to drown his sorrows.

"I'll stay here and make sure everyone is okay," Garrett added.

Roman blew out a long breath and was about to say no, that this was his responsibility.

But Garrett continued before Roman could speak. "You remember the times when you'd be so mad at Mom that you wanted to smother her, and yet she'd still come in your room and insist on hashing things out? She could have waited until you both cooled down, but she didn't. And by hashing out, I mean she would want you to see things her way."

Roman would like to have said he didn't have any recollection of that. But he did. Belle had done that too many times to count.

"Remember how things played out?" Garrett went on. "You just got madder. She got madder. And it ended up being a shouting match where you both said things you regretted and you got grounded."

Again, it had happened.

"Now, what's the wise choice to make here?" Garrett asked him.

"Smart-ass," Roman grumbled. But he started walking. Apparently, he was going to the Longhorn Bar.

"I can walk home," Arwen insisted.

"No. The Busby boys like to toss tacks and such on the road as a prank, and you could step on one."

Too bad Mila couldn't think of a better argument to give Tate's friend, but she really didn't want the girl to walk. She wanted to drive her so they could talk along the way. Of course, it wouldn't be a long talk, but Mila just wanted to make sure she'd be okay.

Mila stood there with the passenger's side door open while Arwen volleyed glances between her car and the road. It wasn't far, less than two miles to her house, but maybe the threat of the tacks had worked because Arwen finally got in.

"I know you've been warned not to take rides from strangers," Mila added once Arwen had put on her seat belt, "but I'm not really a stranger."

"I know. You're the lady who owns the bookstore. The one with the weird mom. People say you're an old maid, and that your mother will put a curse on people who piss her off."

Yep, that was her life in a nutshell. Now, she wanted to hear about Arwen's life so she could figure out if this girl was out to help Tate or mess with his head.

"How did you get into meditation?" Mila asked as she drove away from the ranch. She stayed well below the speed limit so it would give them more time to talk, and she'd take the back way. Again, to give them more time.

Arwen looked at her, huffed. "I don't like it when adults do that. You know the answer, but you want me to tell you things. Why not just come out and ask what you really want to know?"

Mila nodded. "Fair enough. For the record, though,

I actually don't know how you got into mediation, but I'm hoping you truly believe it'll be helpful. Tate is my cousin, and I love him. He's been through a lot, too much, and I don't want him hurt."

"I don't want him hurt anymore, either." Arwen didn't snap that or say it in an angry voice. It was a whisper. "I know what he went through because I went through it myself. Can't believe you haven't heard gossip about it." Still no anger, but Mila heard the hurt.

"I treat gossip like white noise. And I've had a lot of practice tuning it out."

She waited to see if Arwen would talk more about what'd happened, but the girl just sat in silence for the next few minutes. "The meditation will help," she finally said. "If Tate's grandmother doesn't want me to teach it to him, then there are plenty of books and videos on the internet."

Mila frowned, not at Arwen but herself. The only reason she'd dismissed meditation was because Valerie had suggested it. But Mila thought Valerie's suggestion was minimizing Tate's situation. She didn't think Arwen was doing that.

"I know you don't think much of me," Arwen went on. "I mean, Tate is rich, and his dad owns a big business."

"Your dad owns a business, too," Mila pointed out.

"Stepdad," she corrected, and she repeated it under her breath. "Since you've tuned out the gossip, you might not know that my mom was a cocktail waitress in San Antonio where she met my stepdad. She already had me then, but I was just a baby, like only a year old. I don't know my real dad. My stepdad divorced his wife

to marry my mom, and nine months later, my half sister was born."

The situation wasn't identical to Mila's, but there were some similarities. Frankie had met Vita when Mila was a baby, and a couple of years later, Valerie had come to live with them after her folks had pretty much abandoned her. That hadn't been an ideal situation for anyone, and Mila got the feeling that Arwen's life had been much worse than ideal.

But there was another facet to this.

Arwen's stepfather, Waylon Beaumont, was one of the candidates on Mila's list. Too bad she didn't have the man in front of her so she could look at his features the way she had Billy Lee. But what Mila really wanted to do was dismiss him as a possibility. Nothing she was hearing about the guy was making her wish he was her father.

Mila took the turn to Arwen's house and drove a couple of miles until she reached the place. She pulled into the circular driveway in front of Arwen's home. It was just on the edge of town, and the third largest house—right behind the Grangers' and the one that Roman's great-grandfather had built. On the outside, it looked like a great place to grow up, but Mila had the feeling it hadn't been for Arwen.

There was a girl sitting on the porch. Mila recognized her as Waylon's daughter, the one he'd had with Arwen's mother. She stood, folding her arms over her chest as if she'd been waiting—impatiently—for Arwen.

"Will you be in trouble for going to Tate's house?" Mila asked her.

"No. That's my half sister, and she won't tell anyone. She won't want to explain why she let me out of her sight." Arwen opened the car door, but she didn't get out. "I tried to kill myself, too."

Oh, God. Arwen's confession made Mila feel as though someone had punched her. Mila had never considered suicide, and she figured there must have been a lot of pain and misery for it to come to that.

"My mom and stepdad tried to keep it quiet, and they don't want me to talk about it." She glanced down at her wrists, at the watch there. It was silver with a wide band. "That's why I'm supposed to wear this, to keep it covered. I forgot it the other day. Tate saw it, and that's how we started talking."

So, Tate knew. That would indeed give him some familiar ground with Arwen. "If he invited you to the house, he must want to learn how you're managing things. You are managing them, aren't you?" Mila asked.

"Yeah. Don't worry. I'm not gonna do anything stupid like that again."

Mila nearly asked—what about Tate? But even if Arwen thought she knew the answer to that, she probably wouldn't want to break a confidence. At least, Mila hoped Arwen and Tate were talking to each other enough that they'd build a relationship like that. Tate had his therapist and his family, but Arwen had personal experiences that might help him.

"Thanks for the ride," Arwen said. The girl got out and started walking toward the house.

Mila considered going to her. Hugging her, even. But she hardly knew Arwen, and she might not want that. Plus, Arwen probably wouldn't want to explain a hug to her half sister. Judging from what Arwen had said, the girl was supposed to be watching her or something.

Mila waited until Arwen was on the porch. The sister said something to her, something Mila couldn't hear. Arwen didn't seem to hear it, either, because she went inside with the girl following close behind her. Mila wasn't sure if she could help Arwen in any way, or even if the girl wanted her help, but maybe she could invite Tate and her to the bookstore under the guise of a new release or some special discounts.

She considered texting Janeen and asking her to close up so Mila could go straight home, but sometimes being around the books steadied her. That was because of the man she thought was her father and his love of reading.

Which meant that stress reliever was built on a lie.

Still, she drove there, anyway, parked and then sat for a few minutes to compose herself before she went in. No Janeen, but there was someone else in the shop.

Roman.

He was sitting on the sofa in the reading area, a bottle of beer in his hand. "Garrett told me to get drunk." He lifted up the rest of a six-pack, and she saw a second one in a plastic bag on the floor next to the sofa. "Wanna get drunk with me, and then we can talk about that sex offer you made?"

CHAPTER TWELVE

MILA DIDN'T EXACTLY jump at his offer, and that's when Roman noticed that she looked a little shaky. He was shaky, too, but he was hoping the beer could help with that. Mila, as well.

"We're going to have sex?" she asked. Not in a heated "I want you right now" kind of way. There was something in her voice that hadn't been there at the ranch.

Doubt.

That was good. Roman had wanted to think and rethink this until she either pulled the off switch or jumped him. Whichever way she went, he just wanted her to be sure.

Mila glanced around the store. "Where's Janeen?"

"She just left a few seconds before you walked in. I've only been here a couple of minutes myself. I told her I'd wait here for you and that she could go. She's got a hot date."

Mila nodded. "Thanks." She locked the door, turned the closed sign around and made her way to him. She didn't sit next to him but rather across from him, and she helped herself to one of the beers. "How's Tate?"

Roman had been mulling that over in his head, and despite Garrett's insistence about him drinking, the beer wasn't helping. "He wants to stay at the ranch even after what happened."

He thought maybe the breath Mila took was one of relief. "I guess that means you worked things out with your mother." She paused. "Or did you evict her?"

"I considered eviction," he admitted. "Dismissed it. Then got pissed about considering it and dismissing it. My relationship with my mother is complicated."

She smiled a little. "I think we can both say that. I'm glad you didn't kick Belle out. You would have regretted it, especially since you plan on leaving in a few weeks." Mila looked at him. "That is still the plan, isn't it?"

He nodded. At the end of the school year, he wouldn't ask Tate to pack—Roman would insist on it.

Mila took a tiny sip of her beer, made a face. Obviously, she wasn't going to be able to get drunk on that. Not that he especially wanted her drunk. He didn't want to be in that state, either, since he had to leave on a business trip first thing in the morning.

"I drove Arwen home," Mila continued. "She has a complicated relationship with her family, too."

So, maybe that's what had caused Mila to look shaky. Then he remembered her list. Yeah. Waylon didn't look to be the sort who'd be thrilled about the town finding out he'd made a baby with Vita. From the sound of it, Waylon also wasn't being a good stepfather to Arwen.

"Is Arwen trying to help Tate or is she a screw-up?" he asked. "And no, I'm not judging her if it's the latter since I had that label when I was her age."

Hell, in his mother's eyes, he still had it.

"I think Arwen's trying to help," Mila answered. "She's gone through something similar, and it appears she's found a way to cope."

Roman hadn't come here expecting that. He'd thought, at best, that Arwen was just looking for sex.

But maybe that's because Roman had had sex on the mind lately.

Like now.

While he was looking at Mila.

He started to bring up her sex offer, but there was something else he needed to get out of the way first. "I talked to Billy Lee, and he did sleep with Vita."

Judging from the strangled sound of surprise Mila made, he should have eased into that a little better.

"Billy Lee doesn't know for sure if you're his daughter or not," Roman went on, "but he agreed to take a paternity test. He said he'd get the kit right away." Mila was breathing too fast now. So fast that Roman put his beer aside and went to her. He stooped down, looked her in the eyes. "I'm sorry. I thought you wanted to know."

"I do," she quickly assured him. "I just hadn't expected him to say it could be him. God, it could be him. I mean, what are the odds that Vita would have slept with two men around the same time?"

This time, Roman took a moment to try to figure out how to say this. He didn't want any other shaky looks from Mila and no more of those startled gasps. But even after giving it some thought, Roman didn't know how to make this sound better.

"Billy Lee said a lot of men thought Vita was attractive when she was in her twenties," he settled for saying.

"She was. I've seen pictures of her, and she was beautiful. She just didn't age well—" Mila stopped. "The odds might be pretty high that my mom slept with more than one man. Is that what Billy Lee meant?"

Shit. He'd stepped in it, and now he might get Mila riled at Billy Lee. Definitely not something he wanted since the man could turn out to be her father.

"I'm not sure what he meant," Roman lied. It was one of those little white lies to fix the shit he'd stepped in. He hoped it did, anyway. "But just put that all aside for now and focus on Billy Lee. He'll take the paternity test, but you'll need to take one, too, so your DNA can be compared to his." He took the kit from the bag next to the beer and handed it to her. "I bought this for you at the pharmacy."

She took it, glanced at the label. "You've been busy."

"It was just one aisle over from the beer. Of course, the clerk will tell folks that I bought it, but no one's going to consider it juicy gossip or much of a surprise if I buy a paternity test." He motioned toward it. "There's a second kit in the bag for Billy Lee, but I can take it to him if he hasn't bought one already. You won't have to see him unless you want to."

"I don't want to see him yet." Mila took the kit and opened it. "Was he…upset?"

"No. Not really." And if he had been, Roman would have chewed his ass out and given him a safe-sex lecture that would have fallen into the "day late, dollar short" category. It was a lecture Roman had gotten plenty of times from his folks after he'd gotten Valerie pregnant. "He was surprised more than anything."

Mila made a sound of agreement. She knew a little about feeling surprised over this, as well. Of course, until today Mila hadn't even known that Billy Lee could be her father whereas Billy Lee had known it was at least a possibility.

She used the swab on the inside of her cheek, slipped it back in the little plastic case and handed it to him.

Roman put it away in the shopping bag. He'd get it

to Billy Lee before he went in for his business meetings in San Antonio.

"One more thing," Roman continued. Best to clear the air before he clouded it with more sex talk. "Billy Lee told me that Lucian put the lawsuit on hold. He seemed to think you had something to do with that."

She lifted her shoulder. "I asked Dylan to talk to him. Didn't figure he would, but yes, Billy Lee mentioned things had worked out that way."

For now they had. That didn't mean Lucian wouldn't change his mind down the road. "I don't want you to feel you have to run interference for me with my cousins."

"I don't feel that way." She huffed and had another sip of beer. Made another face. And her attention slid from his face to his crotch.

Wait.

Not his crotch.

His side.

"Have you healed?" she asked.

He eyed her with some suspicion. "That sounds like a sex question."

"It is."

Roman certainly hadn't expected her to jump right into this, but then again she'd been the one who'd first brought it up at the ranch.

"I'm healed," he admitted. That was more or less true. "But I'm still not sure it's a good idea."

"Oh, it's not." She laughed. Not a full-out laugh. It was low and a little sultry. If warm brandy could laugh, that's how it would sound.

Roman tried to push aside the effects of that sultriness and make his point. "Most people don't jump into something if they know it's a mistake."

"Sure they do. Well, many people do, anyway. I've spent most of my life trying to avoid mistakes, trying not to be like those other women who took you to their beds. I've missed out. They didn't."

Roman frowned because she made it sound as if he were some kind of guy who had sex with any woman he met. He didn't. But he hadn't exactly qualified for monk status, either.

He geared up to try one more time to talk her out of this or at least have her rethink it, but Mila reached out and put her hand around the back of his neck. Maybe she hadn't remembered that she was still holding a cold bottle of beer. Emphasis on cold. He made a sound of surprise, or rather he tried to do that, but it got muffled because she put her mouth on his and kissed him.

For days now, he'd been dreaming about kissing Mila. Not one of those friendly pecks, either. A real, full-blown kiss.

And he got it, all right.

Mila might not have experience when it came to sex, but she sure had the kissing down pat. Even with the cold bottle on his neck, Roman felt the heat go from his mouth straight to his groin.

That was the sign of a good kiss.

She wasn't tentative and she tasted like sin. Not necessarily a good combination for a man who was still trying to figure out how to talk her out of this. Now, thanks to that kiss, he had to talk himself out of it, as well.

With her eyes half-closed and a dreamy look on her face, Mila eased back, gulped in a breath. Finally, he thought. She was going to rethink this.

Or not.

Apparently, that break was just for air because she

moved to the edge of the chair. Her grip tightened around the back of his neck, she dragged him closer and she ran her tongue over his bottom lip. When she came back for seconds, she proved that she understood the subtleties of French kissing.

Even with all that, Roman managed to hold back and keep his senses. Hard to do when she continued the dragging. The motion pulled him forward so that he landed on his knees right between her legs.

And she just kept on kissing him.

Kissing, tugging and adjusting their positions as if she was ready to have sex with him right then, right there.

"I knew you would be good at this," she whispered against his mouth.

He wasn't doing it. She was. And she was good at it. Of course, that got him thinking that maybe that was so because he suddenly wanted her more than his next breath. That's why Roman was the one to up the ante. He took hold of her, hauling her against him.

Not the brightest idea he'd ever had.

She tumbled out of the chair, and without breaking the kiss, she kept tumbling, and the impact of her body against his sent them both to the floor. Bottles clanged. Beer spilled, and he hit his head against the leg of a coffee table.

And then there was his side.

Mila's knee landed there, and while it wasn't exactly a screaming-out kind of pain, it did hurt and made him rethink if he was physically ready for this. If Mila had been any other woman, he would have said yes. That she could just be on top. But she probably hadn't planned on having to do all the work on the day she lost her virginity.

That last word flashed in his head.

A reminder of what was at stake here. There was that whole thing about heartbreak and commitment. Things that he was certain he didn't want, and he would have told her that, too, if she hadn't kissed him again.

She rolled partially off him, still pinning him to the floor with her upper body while the kissing raged on. Mila adjusted, moving her knee until it was between his legs. Right against his dick. Probably not the best place for it, but it wasn't the worst, either. At least it wasn't on his incision.

"Breathe," she whispered. At first he thought she was talking to him, but he was breathing. She was the one who was struggling with her air intake.

Roman did something about that. He kicked the beer bottles aside and eased her off him and onto her back. He didn't kiss her mouth. He left that part of her alone for now so she could fix that oxygen issue, and he went after her neck. She clearly liked that because she made a sound of pleasure and stopped grappling for position.

Good.

Less grappling meant less possibility of him getting kicked.

That didn't stop her hands, though. They were all over his chest, and she was trying to unbutton his shirt. He figured once she got that done, she'd attempt to unzip him next.

That couldn't happen.

His dick really hated this idea, but Roman knew this couldn't lead to full-blown sex. However, it could lead to something. Something that would hopefully be a lot more pleasurable for Mila than it would be for him.

First things first, he checked their position, and he did that without breaking the kiss. In fact, he made some progress with that by going lower. He shoved up her shirt and kissed the top of her left breast while he checked the window from the corner of his eye. Anyone walking by would really have to be looking to see them, but he didn't want to take any chances.

Roman started rolling with her.

He rolled over the beer bottles, one of them digging into his back, the other his butt. Or maybe that was Mila's hand. She'd apparently gone lower, as well, and was trying to slide her hand into the back of his jeans.

Roman let her keep doing that since it was better than a hand-slide to the front of his jeans, and he rolled a few more times, this time through the spilled beer and across the small carpeted area until they were on the other side of the sofa. Now, they had some privacy. Of course, her office would give them even more of that, but judging from the urgency of Mila's sounds and gropings, he didn't have that kind of time.

"I have a condom," she said.

So did he, but he wasn't going to need it. He hoped. He just needed to hang on to his willpower and remember that the stakes were sky-high here. After he'd taken the edge off Mila's need, she might remember that, too, and be thankful they had left their condoms in their wrappers.

Roman levered himself up, pushed down her bra and did some kissing to please himself. Of course, all of this was pleasing to him, but her breasts were especially nice. For one thing, they were real, which meant they were soft. Small. Perfect. Roman kissed them for a while, taking her nipples into his mouth until she started pinching him.

Not to get him to stop, he realized.

She was pinching his arm and leg because she was trying to pull him on top of her. A place he wanted to be, badly. Like small natural breasts, he liked missionary position, too. But there'd be no missionary-ing in his position today.

He unzipped her jeans. She cooperated with that, even lifting her hips to help. Probably because she thought this was going to lead to sex. And it would. Just maybe not the kind of sex she'd envisioned. It sure as hell wasn't the sex he'd envisioned, either, but it was going to have to do.

While he rid her of her panties—which were white lace and barely there—Roman kept kissing her, kept making his way down. To her lower stomach. Then to her thigh. She clearly hadn't given up on him being inside her because she was tugging at him. Roman fixed that.

He pushed her legs apart and gave her a kiss she wasn't likely to forget any time soon. He sure as hell wouldn't. The taste of her gave him the erection from hell. He was so going to pay for this.

But it was so going to be worth it.

She continued to struggle until her struggle-to-moans-of-pleasure ratio was where he wanted it to be. That's when he nipped her with his teeth.

That moan was very loud.

And she stopped struggling. However, she did grab on to his hair, hard, and she anchored him there right between her legs. Not that he had plans to go anywhere, but Roman appreciated the enthusiastic help.

Her moans stopped. She tensed, and she plowed her fingers all the way to his scalp. That might have had something to do with Roman using his own fingers to go along with his mouth. It must have been the right combination.

Because Mila had herself a big, moaning climax.

THERE WERE LITTLE gold sparkles behind her eyes. Sparkles in her mouth, too. In fact, Mila thought she might be sparkling all over.

Her body was slack. Every muscle felt puddled on the floor along with the spilled beer, and there was only one thought going through her head.

Amazing.

Simply amazing.

It wasn't her first orgasm, of course. That had come during a rare make-out session with Tommy Tucker back in tenth grade. She'd dated him long enough for them to have some pretty serious kissing bouts, and one time they'd bumped and grinded against each other enough to finish them both off.

This one with Roman was much, much better.

That probably had everything to do with the fact that Roman had been on the giving end of it. He hadn't done any receiving, though.

Roman made his way back up her body, kissing her along the way, but instead of unzipping his jeans and getting started with his own "receiving," he pulled her into his arms to cuddle. One where she was naked from the waist down and her butt was on the beer-soaked rug. Since it seemed as if the cuddling was just getting started, Mila decided to say something to keep moving this along in a sexual direction.

"I know how to put a condom on a man using only my mouth. Sophie and I saw it in a magazine, and we practiced on bananas."

As expected, that got Roman's attention. He lifted his head, looked at her, and because his secret man place was against her leg, she felt him harden even more than he already was.

"That was an offer by the way," she added.

He nodded, eased a couple of inches away from her. "Yeah, I got that. And while it's a damn good offer, it's one I'm going to have to turn down. Sorry."

Well, there went her gold sparkles. Mila sat up, stared at him, and she was certain she was frowning. "When we were talking at the ranch, I offered you sex, not half-sex. I figured if you came here, you must have thought that was a good idea."

Another nod. "It was. I wanted to be with you. *Want* to be with you," he amended. "But I don't want to fuck up your life."

Too late. Well, her life had changed, anyway. Mila didn't see that as particularly bad in a screw-up kind of way. She'd been waiting to get naked with Roman for years, and she'd finally accomplished it. She should have amended that fantasy, though, to include his nakedness, as well. And real sex that involved a condom and him inside her.

"Is this about that three-times rule?" she asked.

He kissed her, picked up her panties and jeans and proceeded to dress her. "It's about you. I want to give you some time to think this through. I don't want you hurt."

It was about that rule. He wasn't going to budge on

that, and Mila wasn't even sure he wanted to budge. Roman did this sort of thing all the time. Clearly, he had plenty of experience with it, and maybe he just intended to keep on doing it.

With a string of women who would come after her.

If she'd had any sparkles left, that would have dissolved them. A dose of reality came in their place, and it definitely didn't shine. It made her feel, well, naked and exposed.

Roman was right. She did need to think this through, and it took all of two seconds for Mila to push away that exposed feeling and realize something.

"I'd rather have temporary with you than permanent with someone I would just be settling for," she said.

There. She thought that might relax his tense forehead, that it might stop him from shimmying on her jeans.

It didn't.

He kept shimmying. "You deserve better than temporary. You deserve better than me."

There was nothing better than Roman. He wouldn't see that, of course. In many ways, he was still that hurt little boy who felt betrayed by his parents.

"I should go," he said when he finished dressing her. "I need to check on Tate."

That wasn't total lip service coming from him, either. After what'd happened with Belle, Roman did indeed need to make sure all was well. Garrett would keep an eye on Tate, but like the offer she'd just made to Roman, that was temporary. The boy needed his dad.

Roman stood, pulled her to her feet and kissed her again. It might have stayed short and sweet, some post-partial-sex gesture. But Mila slipped her arm around his waist and kissed him the right way. The way that he would know there could be more if he wanted it.

He moved into the kiss, then moved away from her. He groaned and cursed. "What the hell am I going to do with you?" he grumbled.

Mila had a couple of suggestions. One involved her putting that condom on him with her mouth. But obviously it wasn't a question he wanted answered because he headed for the door.

Roman walked out, leaving her to wonder something.

Did that count as one of their three times? Because if it did, she only had two more to go.

CHAPTER THIRTEEN

There were a dozen things on Roman's mind. Unfortunately, they weren't the right things.

He needed to be going through the invoices and schedules for his rodeo business. That was one of the main reasons he'd come to his office in San Antonio. That, and so he could go to a bunch of meetings with people who either wanted to do business with him or wanted to go through existing contracts and make changes. Normally, these were things he could practically do in his sleep.

Apparently, not today, though.

Or the day before.

Yeah, he'd had this mind haze for a while now, and he could pinpoint the exact moment it started. When he'd gone down on Mila and given her that orgasm. For something that had only taken twenty minutes or so, it was certainly having some lasting effects.

He was worried that he'd already done too much damage, that he'd hurt her. Roman didn't know that for sure because she hadn't called him in the two days he'd been gone. She had texted but that'd only been in response to his text to ask her if she was all right. Mila had sent back a one-word reply: Peachy.

What the hell did that mean?

Was she upset and that was her sarcastic way of blowing him off? Or did Mila truly use a word like that?

"Who's Mila?" his assistant, Joe O'Malley, asked.

Roman frowned, shook his head, and then he realized he'd scribbled her name on notes he was supposed to be making so that Joe could draw up a contract. Hell. What'd happened between them wasn't just bad news for Mila. It apparently was for him, too.

"Don't tell me," Joe went on. "You've met your three-sex limit with this woman and now she's wanting more." He chuckled. "Women need to find a cure for you."

Roman's frown turned to a scowl. Joe wasn't just his assistant, he was a friend, and sometimes Joe had witnessed him having a bad breakup. Bad as in when Roman had moved on, and his sexual partner hadn't. It didn't happen very often, but when it did, it was memorable. Painful, too. It didn't matter that he hadn't wanted a relationship with those women. He'd still hurt them.

Exactly what he had been trying to avoid with Mila.

"Well?" Joe pressed.

"I've met my limit with her," he settled for saying. He couldn't go back for a real first round with Mila because it would be a mistake. He was certain of it. And that's why he didn't understand when he took out his phone and sent her another message.

You're sure you're okay? he texted.

Since she should be at the bookstore today, he didn't expect her to answer right away. But she did.

Mila texted him a smiley face.

WTF? Was she trying to drive him crazy?

Joe chuckled again and gathered up the papers they'd been working on. "If that was Mila, I think you should consider changing your rule from three to four. Obviously, this woman's gotten in your head."

Yeah, and she wanted to get in his pants, too.

Well, maybe she did. It could be that once had been more than enough for her and that she was over her teenage crush. If so, that was a good thing.

But why did it make him feel like shit?

His phone dinged again with another text. Not Mila this time, but from Billy Lee.

Overnighted the paternity test day before yesterday as soon as you gave it to me, Billy Lee said. I paid for expedited processing and might have the results as early as tomorrow.

That was a good thing, too. Mila and Billy Lee would soon know, and if he was her father, they could figure out how they wanted to handle it. Roman suspected that Billy Lee secretly hoped Mila was his daughter, but there might be a problem.

Belle.

His mother could be judgmental as all get-out, and she might get mad at Billy Lee for having sex with Vita. If so, it could put a rift between not just Billy Lee and her but also between Belle and Mila.

Roman fired off a response to Billy Lee, thanking him for keeping him posted, and he added, Tell me the results before you give them to Mila.

That way, Roman could maybe set the stage for what was to come next—the beginning of a father-daughter relationship, or if Billy Lee wasn't a match, moving on to the next step in the search for her father.

If Mila still wanted him to help with that.

He decided not to ask her. Not after getting "peachy"

and smiley face responses to his texts. He'd just wait until he got back to Wrangler's Creek tomorrow.

Roman glanced at the paperwork and then at the three pictures he kept on his desk. One was of Tate when he was actually smiling. A shot Roman had taken of him at a rodeo. The second picture was of Garrett, Sophie and him when they'd been teenagers. They were smiling, too, and acting goofy, which was exactly why he had the photo on his desk. Sometimes, he needed to remember that there had been happy times at the ranch. He tempered that happiness with the third photo.

The one of his horse, Lobo, that he'd found on his bed.

It was the picture his mom had left to make up for what his father had done. It definitely didn't make up for it, but Roman smiled now, thinking about Lobo and the rides they'd had.

There was a knock at his door, and Joe stuck his head inside. "You've got a visitor. He's got a name like a country music singer, but he looks like a barber. It's Waylon Beaumont."

Roman certainly hadn't been expecting a visit from Arwen's stepfather, but he motioned for Joe to send him in. About a minute later, the man appeared in his doorway. He'd known Waylon his whole life, but Roman couldn't say he actually *knew* the man. In fact, he wasn't even sure they'd ever spoken to each other. Apparently, though, they were about to speak now.

And Joe was right—the guy did look like a barber.

His hair had some kind of junk in it, and it was practically plastered to his head.

"This won't take long," Waylon said. He came closer to Roman's desk, but he didn't sit. "I brought my wife into town on a shopping trip, and I'll need to be getting back to the mall soon. When I found out that your office was close by and that you were here today, I thought it'd be a good time for a visit."

Roman wasn't certain how Waylon had found out he'd be there, but it was possible he'd heard it from Arwen if Tate and Arwen were sharing that kind of info.

"What can I do for you?" Roman asked.

"You can keep your son away from my stepdaughter."

All right. No mincing of words. Roman would have appreciated it more if this hadn't been about Tate.

"Arwen's messed up," Waylon went on, "and she doesn't need your boy messing her up any more than she already is."

Roman didn't stand, mainly because it would put him in too good of a position to punch this clown. "And how do you figure Tate's making things worse for her?"

It was something Roman genuinely wanted to know. He wanted to know the reverse, as well—if Arwen was a bad influence on Tate.

"She sneaked over to your house," Waylon explained. "She's not supposed to go off anywhere without her half sister, Chrissy. Chrissy's a year younger than Arwen, but she's a hell of a lot smarter. And she doesn't screw up the way Arwen keeps doing."

Roman took a deep breath. "You think Tate coaxed Arwen into coming to the house?"

"I do. It wouldn't have taken much coaxing, either. Arwen's not very bright."

Roman hardly knew the girl, but he felt the need to defend her. "She seemed plenty bright when I talked to her."

Waylon's shoulders went back. "When?"

"The day she was at the ranch. She was teaching Tate how to meditate to help him with his stress."

"Meditation," Waylon grumbled. He added some profanity. "That's just a way of tuning us all out."

Yeah. And after listening to Waylon, Roman could see why she wanted to do that. The guy was a dick.

"You shouldn't want Arwen around your boy, either," Waylon went on. "She's only thirteen, and she's already started sleeping around."

Roman tried not to react to that, but he didn't want Tate having sex yet. Sex complicated the hell out of things, and Tate already had enough complications in his life.

"You know for a fact that Arwen is 'sleeping around'?" Roman asked.

"I haven't caught her in the act if that's what you mean, but just look at her. Her hair and all those piercings. She did that to herself with a needle."

She was indeed a little holey, but Roman didn't think it was extreme. Ditto for the hair color.

"So, if a girl has piercings and purple hair, she's a slut?" Roman didn't bother to take out the sarcasm.

"Who cares if she is or not—people will think that about her."

"I didn't."

The look that passed between them said it all. Waylon thought Roman was a slut, too. In some ways, he was. Since it sometimes took one to know one, Roman was pretty sure Arwen didn't fall anywhere near the slut category.

Obviously, Roman's "I didn't" response displeased Waylon because the man's eyes narrowed. "She tried to kill herself. Slit her wrist. Now, I know your boy tried to kill himself, too, but common sense should tell you that these two shouldn't be seeing each other."

Roman heard every word, but he got mentally stuck on the first part of that.

She tried to kill herself.

Hell.

Now, he had to consider at least part of what Waylon was saying. If both Arwen and Tate were depressed and had each considered suicide separately, then maybe they'd consider it again—together.

"I'll talk to Tate," Roman finally said. "But I won't order him to stay away from Arwen." For one thing, it might not even be necessary, and for another, it might be like waving a red flag in front of a bull. Tate might continue to see the girl solely because Roman disapproved.

"Do that. I don't want Arwen on the Granger ranch again."

Roman probably should have just let the dick walk out, but two could play the dick game. "Did you ever fuck Vita Banchini?"

That stopped Waylon in his tracks, and he turned back around to face Roman. "What did you say?"

So, Roman repeated it word for word.

Maybe Waylon objected to the crude word. Or maybe just the question itself. Either way, he wasn't pleased, and every tightly stretched muscle on his face proved that.

"What did Vita tell you?" Waylon snapped.

Now, Roman was doing some cursing. Not aimed at Waylon. But at himself for asking. If he hadn't wanted to know the answer, he shouldn't have brought it up, and Waylon's response was an answer.

The man hadn't denied it, and that said it all.

Great. Just great. He didn't want this jackass to share any DNA with Mila. And maybe he didn't. If Vita had slept with two guys, maybe she'd gone for his favorite number—three.

"What did Vita tell you?" Waylon repeated, his voice louder this go-around.

"Nothing." That was the truth. "I just heard some things, that's all." That was the truth, too.

Sort of.

Roman had heard from Mila that Waylon was on her list as a potential father even though Waylon had been married at the time Vita had gotten pregnant.

Waylon aimed his index finger at Roman. "I don't know what you heard, but I want to talk to whoever said it."

It was petty, but Roman aimed his middle finger at Waylon and shot him the bird. The man cursed him and walked out.

Well, he'd successfully kept his badass title, but that wouldn't help Mila if she needed to get a DNA sample from Waylon. It wouldn't help Tate, either, but at least Roman could do something about that. Even though Tate would still be in school, he could leave him a message for his son to phone him back. But there was no need for a message because Tate answered on the first ring.

"Did she call you, too?" Tate asked before Roman could say anything.

Roman certainly hadn't been prepared for that question, and his first thought was that the *she* was Mila. "Did who call me?"

"Mom."

Roman hadn't been prepared for that answer, either. "When?"

"Just now while I was on my lunch break." He had no trouble hearing the excitement in Tate's voice. "She's coming, Dad. Mom's coming to the ranch."

Roman got up, and he grabbed his truck keys. "I'm on my way."

MILA HAD ALREADY used an entire can of air freshener, and she might have to use more. The bookstore still smelled like beer and sex. She hoped that last one was only her imagination, but she wasn't wrong about the beer. Maybe the smell would clear before Billy Lee and Belle showed up for their fantasy date in about two hours.

This wasn't an especially hard fantasy to set up, which was partly why Mila had suggested it to Billy Lee. It also would give him a chance to flirt with Belle and maybe bring her a gift. Plus, the dress she'd managed to get for Belle was beautiful. Not a perfect match to the one Julia Roberts had worn in the movie *Pretty Woman*, but it was lipstick red and with enough of a shine to the fabric that it looked like silk.

Mila put a gold throw on the sofa and some glitzy pillows that she'd bought on sale years ago but had never used. She went back into her office to get some candles they could use for ambiance instead of the harsh overhead lights and the scripts she'd printed out, but before she could get back to the scene, the door opened.

She mentally cursed that she'd forgotten to lock it and was about to tell whoever it was that she had closed early.

But it was Arwen.

The girl glanced at the "decorated" reading area, then at the candles Mila had been reaching for on her desk. "Sorry, looks like you're expecting someone or something."

"It's not for me." But Mila decided that was all the explaining she should do. "Are you finished with school for the day?"

Arwen nodded. "I don't have a sixth period so I'm allowed to leave. I'm not skipping or anything. I wanted to see if you had *The Walking Dead* volume ten, but if you're closed—"

"No. I have it." Mila motioned for Arwen to follow her to the graphic novel shelf because the girl looked ready to run. She also looked as if she could use a friend. Mila couldn't qualify for that because she was so much older than Arwen, but she could be there if the girl wanted to talk.

"You look different," Arwen told her. "Like you're happy or something."

Or something was closer to the truth. Mila doubted she was glowing from an orgasm she'd had three nights ago, but it was possible. She was also trying to figure out what to do about Roman. But that was a long debate she would have with herself later.

"Are you happy?" Mila asked her, and then winced. "Sorry. Not very subtle. It's just you seem sad or something."

"Mellow," Arwen corrected. "Trust me, that's better than some other things I could be." She took the graphic novel from Mila when she pulled it from the shelf. "I won't hurt Tate, you know. I know that's what his dad and you are worried about, but I'm not going to talk him into doing anything stupid."

"That's good," Mila assured her.

"Already done the stupid stuff," Arwen added in a mumble. "It didn't work out so great, and I won't be doing it again."

It hadn't worked out so great for Tate, either, but Mila thought he was getting better. She'd been going out to the ranch in the evenings to check on him, and it seemed as if his surliness was easing up a bit.

Mila considered not charging Arwen for the book, but the girl took some money from her purse and went to the cash register. "Thanks for giving me a ride home that day," Arwen told her. "And thanks for being nice to me."

She wanted to hug Arwen, but that might be too much coming from someone she hardly knew. That's why it surprised Mila when the girl hugged her. It didn't last long, though, because the door opened again, and Sophie came in. Not exactly walking. More like waddling. Arwen broke away from Mila, took her book and the change, and she headed out.

"Wasn't that the girl Tate's been seeing?" Sophie asked.

Mila nodded. "I like her."

"Good. My nephew has enough going on in his life without adding a troubled girlfriend." She paused, glanced around at the fantasy date area. Then sniffed the air. "It smells like beer." She turned toward Mila probably as fast as she was capable of turning. "You've been with Roman."

Jeezum Pete. Was she wearing some kind of sign around her neck that others could see and she couldn't? First Arwen had said she looked happy and now this.

"What does the smell of beer have to do with Roman?" Mila asked her.

"Well, you wouldn't be drinking beer in here. You'd be sipping wine or Baileys. And I doubt you'd be with any other man. That leaves the obvious. Roman and you had sex in here."

"No, we didn't." Mila didn't like telling half-truths to her best friend, but she didn't want to get into the details of oral sex and spilled beer.

Sophie stared at her as if ready to challenge that, but she must have gotten a cramp or something because she caught on to her back and hobbled her way to the sofa.

"Are you all right?" Mila asked, helping her to sit down.

"Fine. I just finished my OB appointment, and he said all is well in here, that it shouldn't be much longer." She patted her huge belly. Frowned. Then looked to be on the verge of tears. "I think I saw a penis."

Okay. "Uh, where did you see that?" Because judging from Sophie's reaction, it hadn't been on Clay. Maybe someone had flashed her.

"On one of the babies when I was having an ultrasound." Now, the tears came, and Mila hurried to get her a tissue.

Mila was willing to give all the comfort and tissues that Sophie needed, but she wasn't understanding this. "Are you disappointed it's a boy?"

"No. I'm just really disappointed I saw it, that's all. And I'm hormonal. I cry at everything. The other day I cried because my pancake looked like a bunny."

Mila had witnessed some of that, and she figured it was something like PMS on steroids. All she could do was keep hugging Sophie while she cried it out.

"I wanted to keep the genders a surprise," Sophie went on. "I usually close my eyes, but this time I sneezed and then I looked at the screen. I'm pretty sure it was a penis complete with little balls and everything. Well, one ball, anyway. It was like a blob beneath this little missile-looking thing."

Mila wished she could come up with an alternative suggestion, but she was drawing a blank. There weren't many things on a baby's body that could resemble a missile and a blob.

"Where was Clay during this?" Mila asked.

"He was there, but he didn't sneeze or look at the screen so I pretended that I hadn't seen it. I don't think he believed me."

Probably not. After all, Clay was a cop, but he likely hadn't wanted to make Sophie feel worse.

"You only saw one penis, right?" Mila clarified, and waited for Sophie to nod. "That means you don't know the gender of the other baby. That'll still be a surprise."

Sophie perked right up. That was the hormone reaction again because she was literally smiling through the tears. "You're right. I don't know, and if I need another ultrasound before I deliver, I'll put on a blindfold."

"Great idea." At this point Mila would have concurred with anything to make Sophie feel better.

"So, did you have sex with Roman?" Sophie asked.

Mila groaned. Obviously, Sophie wasn't going to drop the subject, but Mila was saved from answering because the door opened again. This time, however, it was someone expected even if he was a little early.

Billy Lee.

He was carrying a garment bag over his arm. Probably his tux, but he got a very uncomfortable look on his face when he saw Sophie. "Uh, I thought the fantasy date would be just Belle and me."

"It will be." Sophie tried to make a dismissive wave of her hand at the same time she tried to get up. Mila caught her around the waist to keep her from dropping back down. "Don't worry, I'm going." She went to the door but then stopped right next to Billy Lee. "Just make this work for Mom, please. She really needs to get her own life."

Billy Lee made a sound of agreement. "I'll try." He glanced down at her belly. "Are you okay to drive?"

"Oh, I don't fit behind the wheel anymore. I'm walking over to the police station and Clay and I can go home together." She kissed Billy Lee on the cheek. "Have fun."

"Is she okay?" Billy Lee asked after Sophie had left. "She looked as if she'd been crying."

"She saw a penis on one of the babies in an ultrasound. She didn't want to know the sex," Mila added.

He nodded, glanced at the marginally decorated reading area and nodded again. His nerves were showing, and Mila didn't know if that was because of the date or because he now knew that he could possibly be her father. When he didn't say anything, she just motioned toward the bathroom.

"You can change in there," she explained. "If Belle gets here before you finish, I'll have her change in my office. Oh, and I've got champagne and music. The soundtrack is already loaded, and all you have to do is press the button on the old intercom on my desk."

She tried to remember if there was anything she'd forgotten. And there was something. "Did you bring a necklace?"

He took out a box from his jacket and opened it. It was emeralds and gold. It definitely didn't look like a fantasy prop.

"It's real," Billy Lee volunteered. "I thought it might make the fantasy better if it wasn't fake."

Well, it wouldn't hurt. Unless Belle thought it was too much, that is.

"Roman wanted me to call him with the paternity test results," Billy Lee said out of the blue. "He wanted me to tell him first, before you."

She automatically frowned. Then shrugged. She doubted that Roman was doing that to hide anything from her. No. It was more likely that he just wanted to be there to help her process whatever she was feeling.

And maybe have sex with her.

But that last thought was just something she'd tacked on. Probably because she'd been thinking way too much about Roman and sex. Maybe he had, as well, because he had texted her twice.

"We could know as early as tomorrow," Billy Lee went on. Then he paused. "I didn't have a clue that you could be my daughter. I just figured if Vita had gotten pregnant, she would have let me know."

You'd think that. But they were dealing with Vita here. "Maybe you'd started dating someone else by the time she found out."

He made a sound to indicate that was possible but not likely. "It could be because things didn't go so well between us." He stopped again, groaned. "This is hard for me to talk about, but your mom and I just didn't hit it off in bed. And that's all I'm going to say about that."

Good. Mila was sorry she'd heard that much. Still, bad sex shouldn't have prevented Vita from telling him he was going to be a father. Which meant he might not be.

She took out her phone, pulled up the list of possibilities and showed it to Billy Lee. "If we're not a match, who would be your guess as to who would be?"

He took her phone, looking through it, but instead of her reading the list, she watched his expression. It changed when he reached one of the names. Billy Lee made a sound, a barely audible sigh.

"Who?" she pressed.

"Waylon Beaumont."

Of all the names on the list, that was the one Mila dreaded. Maybe because he seemed like a hard man. "You really think he'd sleep with my mother?"

He lifted his shoulder. "Roman and I talked about this the other day. It was a different time. All of us were young, and we made mistakes. And no, I'm not saying you were a mistake. I'd be proud to call you my daughter."

Mila hadn't expected that to hit her so hard, but just as Sophie had done earlier, tears sprang to her eyes. "And I'd be proud to call you my father," she managed to say.

He pulled her into his arms, kissed the top of her head. This was exactly what she'd missed, and she hadn't even realized it until now.

"Tell you what," Billy Lee said, easing back and looking her in the eyes. "If you want, I can cancel the paternity test, and we can just assume that I'm the one who got Vita pregnant."

It was a generous offer, and in the end it might cause her far less grief than learning the truth, but she had to shake her head. "Thank you, though."

Billy Lee still had her phone when it rang, and she saw Tate's name pop up on the screen. Mila automatically checked the time. School had probably just let out so it might mean that he had missed the bus and needed a ride.

She took the call, and the moment she heard Tate's voice, Mila knew it wasn't just a missed bus.

"Can you come to the school right now?" he asked, the anger running through every word. "There's been some trouble."

CHAPTER FOURTEEN

ROMAN PULLED INTO the parking lot of the Wrangler's Creek school. It had been less than a month since Tate had run away and taken those pills, and the memory was still way too fresh. He prayed it was nothing that serious.

Or worse.

Of course, Roman had imagined the "or worse" when he'd gotten the call from the principal asking him to get there right away. After Tate had told him that Valerie was coming, Roman had already been on the road heading to the ranch so this wasn't much of a detour.

Had Valerie shown up at the school and caused a scene?

That was one of the possibilities that came to mind. He hadn't had many dealings with Valerie since she'd left, but when she was younger, she was a person who could definitely stir up some trouble. If that's what she had done, Roman might have to rein in his temper again for the second time today. That conversation with Waylon was still fresh, as well.

He got out of his truck and made his way into the school. Most of the students had obviously already left, but there were still a few in the large hall that fed off the entrance.

Roman made his way down that hall and to the

principal's office. He knew where it was because he'd
had to go there often enough when he'd been in school
way back when. The place hadn't changed a bit in all
that time. It smelled like a boys' locker room that'd been
doused with floor wax and Pine-Sol.

"Roman," a woman greeted him right off. It took him
a moment to recognize her. Mindy Morgan, one of his
old high school flames. She smiled, and then she must
have remembered that he wasn't there for a social visit
because she fluttered her fingers in the direction of the
closed door of the principal's office.

"Tate's in there," she said.

"With Valerie?"

Mindy blinked, obviously surprised by his question.
"No. With Mila Banchini. Is Valerie back in town?"

He didn't know yet, but Roman would find out as
soon as he made sure his son was all right. Because if
this wasn't about Valerie, then maybe Tate had tried
to do something to harm himself. What Roman didn't
understand, though, was why Mila was there.

The moment Roman walked into the office, the relief flooded through him. Tate was okay. But the relief
didn't last long because he saw the anger on his face.
He also saw the concern on Mila's.

"I didn't do it," Tate snarled. Since he'd been at the
ranch, his son had dialed down his attitude, but he certainly wasn't dialing it down now.

"Tate called and asked me to come," Mila volunteered. She stood. "But now that you're here, I can go."

"No," Tate snapped. He repeated it, but in a much
softer voice. "Please stay."

Mila looked at Roman, and he could tell she was
silently asking if it was okay for her to be there, but

Roman didn't know. That's because he didn't know what the hell was going on.

The principal was Doug Morgan, the father of the woman who'd been at the reception desk, and Roman knew him, as well. In fact, he'd had some run-ins with the man not only when he was dating Mindy but also when he'd gotten in trouble. In fact, Roman had sat in that very chair where Tate was now. The only difference was that Doug had had more hair when Roman had been in the hot seat.

Maybe Doug remembered this wasn't an especially warm and fuzzy place for Roman because he didn't greet him, didn't ask him to sit. He merely showed Roman a photo on his phone.

"I didn't do it," Tate repeated.

It didn't take Roman long to see what Tate was claiming he hadn't done. The photo was of a row of lockers that had been spray painted. The black paint really stood out on the industrial-gray metal lockers, and despite the scrawl, he could also make out the words.

Fuck You, followed by several exclamation marks.

Obviously, the person who'd done that was pissed off. Much like his son was at the moment. But he'd never known Tate to use that kind of profanity. It didn't mean he didn't, though.

Roman took the phone and turned it for Tate to see. "Do you know anything about this?" He didn't ask if Tate had done it since he'd already denied it twice. Best to go at this from a different angle.

And it was a good angle to take.

Because Tate immediately glanced away.

Roman wasn't an expert in body language, but he

was a parent, and he knew when Tate was dodging something.

"I didn't do it," Tate repeated, which was just another way of dodging Roman's question.

So, if Tate hadn't done it, who had?

The answer quickly came to mind. Arwen. Tate could be protecting the girl. Of course, maybe the only reason her name came to mind was because of that conversation Roman had had with Waylon. Still, it was easy to believe that Arwen was troubled and could therefore act out.

Roman handed the principal back his phone. "What makes you think Tate did this?"

Doug huffed, and Roman could practically hear what was going on in his head. He thought Roman was dismissing the possibility of Tate's involvement. He wasn't. His son might indeed be involved if he was trying to cover up something for Arwen.

"I found a can of black spray paint in his locker," Doug answered.

Damn. That was certainly a big-assed clue. But it wasn't necessarily a clue left by Tate. "Did you put the can in your locker?" Roman came out and asked Tate.

"No," Tate said without hesitation. "I don't know how it got there."

All right. That was a dead end so Roman turned back to the principal. "How'd you know the can was in his locker? Did someone actually see him put it in there?"

Doug's mouth went into a flat line. Perhaps because he was remembering all the other times Roman had challenged him when he'd gotten in trouble. That was too bad. Because Roman didn't want his past coming back to haunt his son.

"No, I didn't see him do it," Doug answered, "but it was there when I opened the locker."

"So, who tipped you off?" Mila asked.

Good question, and apparently Doug didn't have an especially good answer because he did that flat mouth thing again. "I don't know. It was anonymous, but that doesn't mean Tate didn't do this."

"That's exactly what it means," Roman argued. "The person who gave you that tip could have set Tate up."

"And why would anyone have done that?" Doug fired back just as fast. "To the best of my knowledge, Tate hasn't made enemies here. In fact, everyone has gone out of their way to be nice to him."

Because he's a Granger.

Doug didn't actually include that, but Roman could almost hear him saying it. Yeah, some people were nice to the Grangers and their money. Others didn't feel the same way, though.

There was another possibility, too. That the person who'd done this hadn't intended to get back at Tate but rather Arwen. Roman nearly brought up the girl's name, but he figured that wasn't going to lessen the steam that he could practically see coming out of Tate's ears. Best to try to resolve this fast before both Tate and he said something that would only make this worse.

"How do we fix this?" Roman asked. And he hoped like hell that Doug wasn't going to start talking about suspending or expelling Tate.

Doug glanced down at Tate's school records, which he had opened in front of him. Records that no doubt included the problems Tate had had in San Antonio.

"It's his first offense *here*," Doug said. "So, I can go easy on him. A week of detention and he'll have to pay for the lockers to be repainted. *He'll* have to pay," the man emphasized. "Tate won't learn his lesson if you give him the money."

Tate got to his feet, his hands clenched at his sides, his face tight and flushed. "I didn't do this, and I shouldn't have to pay for it or go to detention."

Roman's knee-jerk reaction was to get just as mad, tell Tate that he would indeed pay and get him out of there. But he stopped and rethought this.

"You really didn't do this?" he asked Tate.

"No! I didn't." Again, no hesitation.

This was a gamble since Tate had lied to him before, but Roman thought it was a gamble worth taking. "Here's what I want you to do," Roman said. He put his hands on the principal's desk, leaned in and put his bad-ass expression to good use. "Ask around and find out who gave you that tip. Then call the hardware and grocery stores and find out if any student recently bought a can of that brand of black paint."

"The pharmacy, too," Mila provided. "They sell spray paint, as well."

Good point. "And the pharmacy," Roman added. "If none of that gives you a name, then call me, and you and I can talk. Maybe I'll even hire a PI to get to the bottom of this. In the meantime, there'll be no detention for Tate, and I'll pay for the locker to be repainted."

Roman took out five twenties, all that he had in his wallet, and put it on Doug's desk.

Doug huffed. "I told you it wouldn't be a good lesson for Tate if you paid for it."

"True. It wouldn't be a good lesson if Tate had done it, but he just said he didn't. And I believe him. The person who did this can pay me back when you find him, or her, but I'm sure you'd rather get that painted before the kids show up for class tomorrow."

The man glanced at the money, then slid his gaze to Mila, Tate and Roman. It gave Roman a good jolt of déjà vu because he'd had to wait other times to learn his own fate. The difference was his father had never once stuck up for him. In fact, his father had always suggested something even harsher than the principal had.

"All right," Doug finally said. "I'll do some checking and get back to you. But no PI. I won't allow someone questioning these kids."

Roman didn't care about him blowing off the PI suggestion or even that this might be a temporary fix. It still felt like a victory. It must have to Mila, too, because she made a soft squeal and hugged Tate. Tate didn't exactly hug her back, but some of the venom had faded from his eyes. He picked up his backpack and headed out with Mila following right behind him.

"Call me the minute you have anything," Roman added to Doug.

"You do the same. Because I think Tate knows more about this than he's saying."

So did Roman, but he didn't confirm that. Old habits. He just thanked the man and hurried to catch up with Mila and Tate. They'd covered a lot of distance in those couple of seconds because they were already out of the building by the time Roman spotted them. They were headed to Mila's car, which was parked on the other side of the school. Roman hadn't even noticed it when he'd first driven up, but then he'd been in the semipanic mode.

He still was.

They'd dodged a bullet, but if the principal didn't

follow through on this, Tate might end up with detention. Roman figured that could send Tate to a whole new boiling point that wouldn't be good for anyone. This called for something drastic. Something he'd sworn he would never share with anyone.

"When I was your age, I saw my dad with another woman," Roman threw out there.

Tate turned around to face him. No venom, just plenty of surprise. Maybe because he had no idea where this was going.

But Mila wasn't surprised.

In fact, she glanced away, which meant she knew about this. How, he didn't know, but Roman would find out later.

"Long story short," Roman went on, "I did what I thought was right and told someone, and I got in trouble for it. It wasn't fair, it sucked, and I'm still pissed off about it. That doesn't mean I get a free pass to do something stupid. Understand?"

He wasn't certain Tate would. Nor was he certain Tate wouldn't point out that Roman had indeed done plenty of stupid things. That's why it was a relief when Tate nodded.

"What kind of trouble did you get into for doing the right thing?" Tate asked.

"I got grounded and had something taken away that I loved. A horse."

Tate stayed quiet a moment. "Did Grandma ground you? Is that why you're so mad at her?"

Roman considered lying, but since he was in this deep, he just went for broke. "My dad grounded me, but she knew about it and didn't do anything to stop it."

"Maybe because she was scared to tell the truth," Tate said.

Now, it was Roman's turn to have a couple of moments to consider that. His mother certainly hadn't been afraid that her husband would hit her or anything. But there were other kinds of fear.

Like losing someone she loved—her husband.

Funny, that it'd taken his thirteen-year-old son to point that out to him.

Funny, too, that Mila picked right up on how she could apply this to the current situation. "Are you protecting someone you care about?" she asked Tate.

It wasn't a good time for more quietness, but that's what Tate did. Hell.

"Did Arwen paint those lockers?" Roman pressed.

"No," Tate snapped. Then he paused again. "But I think her sister, Chrissy, could have done it. She's mad because I won't come over to her house and because I'm hanging out with Arwen."

Roman was ready to march right back into the building and tell the principal that, but Tate caught on to his arm. "If Chrissy gets in trouble over this, their dad might take it out on Arwen. He's not very nice to her, and this could make it worse."

Yeah. Roman had heard some of that in his chat with Waylon earlier. However, that didn't mean he was going to let Chrissy skate. If the girl was anything like her father, then she was not only capable of this, she also needed to be held accountable. This shit could have set Tate back in the worst kind of way.

"Arwen came by the bookstore earlier," Mila said. "I got the feeling she wanted to talk to me about something. She left, though, without saying much."

Roman wondered if Arwen's visit had anything to do with Waylon stopping by his office in San Antonio. That was something he needed to find out, as well. But for now, he just wanted to get Tate home. Plus, he had to make sure Valerie wasn't already at the ranch.

"My truck's over there," Roman said, tipping his head to it.

Tate nodded, hugged Mila and started in that direction. Roman wanted to hug her, too. Actually, he wanted to kiss her, but he wasn't sure how things were with them so he settled for thanking her before he turned to leave.

Roman didn't get far, though, because Mila's and his phones rang at the same time. He doubted that was a good sign.

"Clay," Roman said, showing her the screen.

"Your mom," she said, showing him hers.

They answered them together, but it wasn't a long conversation from Clay.

"Sophie's water broke," Clay said. "Get to the hospital now."

ROMAN CERTAINLY HADN'T forgotten about his sister being close to the time to give birth to her twins, but with everything going on, he had pushed it to the back of his mind. Well, it wasn't there now.

This was a huge day for Clay and Sophie—for the entire family—but it was also a worrying one, too. Valerie had had some complications with Tate and had needed an emergency C-section. Things had been touch and go there for a while, but Roman remembered the terror of not knowing if they were going to make it. Of course, that terror had vanished when he'd held his son for the first time, and it'd been replaced with a new fear.

Worry that he would screw it up.

Soon, Sophie and Clay would get to go through all those emotions, too.

Tate, Mila and he hurried into the hospital, and Roman looked around for his family. He spotted one member, Belle, and she wasn't hard to miss. That's because she was wearing a bright red ball gown that took up a significant amount of space. Billy Lee was next to her in a tux.

"Fantasy date," Mila whispered to Roman.

That. He hadn't forgotten about that, either. *"Gone with the Wind?"*

"Pretty Woman. It was your mom's idea," she added when Roman glanced at her.

He'd glanced at Mila with what had to be a strange look considering the character in that movie was a hooker. But then, his mom often made weird choices.

"Where's Garrett?" Roman asked while Tate and Mila were hugging his mom.

"He's with Clay and Sophie," Billy Lee answered. "He won't be back there much longer, though, because they're getting ready to take Sophie to delivery."

Already. Things were moving a lot faster than they had with Tate.

"Nicky's on her way," Billy Lee added. "She just had to get somebody to watch her little girl first."

"I'm sick with worry over Sophie," Belle volunteered the moment Billy Lee finished his explanation. "In fact, I need to go back to the bathroom again." And she scurried off as fast as she could scurry considering she was dragging fifteen yards of fabric.

"Belle's been throwing up," Billy Lee admitted.

"She threw up a lot when Tate was born, too," Mila said.

Roman wasn't surprised that she remembered that since she'd stayed at the hospital the entire time. In fact, Mila had been the second person to hold Tate. Valerie had been too woozy to even see him until he was several hours old.

"Did you just get out of school?" Billy Lee asked Tate, and Tate nodded. "Then let's go to the snack bar so I can get us both a bite to eat. You want us to bring you back something?" he asked Mila and Roman.

Both shook their heads. And Tate and Billy Lee started walking, leaving Mila and him there alone. Roman debated if he should bring up what'd happened between them. Debated asking her about her *peachy* text and that smiley face, but in the grand scheme of things, that seemed trivial so he decided to go with something more important.

His visit with Waylon.

However, Mila spoke before he could say anything. "When you were a kid, I heard you tell your mother about your father cheating. I didn't mean to eavesdrop, but I was in Sophie's room, and the window was open."

That explained why she hadn't looked surprised when he'd told Tate.

"Sophie didn't hear," Mila quickly added. "And I didn't say anything to you because I didn't know what to say. That's why I left that picture of Lobo on your bed."

Now, Roman was certain he looked surprised. "I thought my mom had done that."

She shook her head. "I had taken the picture a couple of months before, but I had it printed out at the pharmacy. I'm sorry I sneaked into your bedroom to leave it, but I thought sneaking was better than giving it to you in person. I swear, that's the only time I went in your bedroom."

Roman couldn't help it. He smiled. Only Mila would apologize for doing such a thoughtful thing. Before he even realized he was going to do it, he pulled her to him and kissed her. It wasn't one of those long lingering kisses that would lead to thoughts of sex, but it was enough to remind her that kissing was an option for them.

Maybe sex was, too.

She looked up at him, their eyes connecting, and it seemed as if they had an entire conversation without saying a word. She wanted to know what was going on between them. He wanted to know that, too. But he also wanted to tell her that he was glad he had these moments with her. Since this nonverbal stuff was going pretty well, he decided to tell her with another kiss. He pulled her closer for this one. He also lingered a little longer.

It lasted until Roman heard someone clear their throat.

Belle.

And she wasn't alone. Nicky and Alice, the housekeeper, were next to her.

If Roman had planned on keeping this—whatever *this* was—solely between Mila and him, he'd blown it. But he figured the gossip had already made it back to his mom and everyone else in town.

Or maybe not.

"Are you having *s-e-x* with Mila?" Belle whispered. She didn't sound as if she would approve of that, either. Probably because she thought Mila deserved something better. Or maybe just deserved someone who wasn't a badass screw-up.

Thankfully, Roman didn't have to answer because from the corner of his eye, he saw Billy Lee and Tate hurrying back toward them. Garrett was only a few steps behind them, and Roman's heart went to his knees.

"Is Sophie all right?" Mila asked, and he was glad she had because Roman's throat had clamped shut.

"She's fine. She had the babies. Fast," Garrett added. He looked as shaky as Roman felt. "They're all crying."

Well, hell. That didn't sound good, and then Roman remembered that babies cried, and Sophie had been shedding tears at the drop of a hat these days. The other day he'd caught her crying because she'd seen a puddle of water that was shaped like a puppy.

"Sophie's okay," Belle whispered. "My baby's okay." With Billy Lee's help, she sat down. Good thing, too, because his mom didn't look steady on her feet.

"The doctor shooed me out." Garrett went to Nicky and kissed her much as Roman had kissed Mila a few moments earlier.

"So, what did she have?" Mila again. "I know one's a boy because Sophie accidentally saw something on the ultrasound—"

"The other's a girl," Garrett answered. He no longer looked shaky. He was grinning from ear to ear.

"No C-section?" Roman managed to say. "No problems?"

Garrett shook his head. "They're all good. Except for Clay, but the doctor said a lot of men throw up in the delivery room."

Poor Clay. That wouldn't help his tough guy image as the town's top cop. Still, he had to be on cloud nine.

"It might be a little while before we can see them," Garrett went on, "so if you all want a bite to eat or something, I'll wait here."

Roman wasn't going anywhere. Apparently, neither were the rest of them because they all found their way to seats. He ended up between Mila and Tate.

"It's all coming together," his mother muttered. "Just like Vita said it would."

Everyone turned and looked at her. "Vita?" Roman questioned.

Belle nodded. "She said Sophie would have a boy and a girl, someone to carry on Granger Western." She made eye contact with Roman. "And she said you would have an encounter with someone shortly after that happened. An encounter with someone you shouldn't be with."

His mother certainly knew how to silence a room and stomp on some of the joy Roman was feeling. It didn't help that Vita might be right. After all, Roman had indeed been considering having full-blown sex with Mila, and he probably should rethink being with her.

"Vita said after Roman's encounter with the wrong woman that he'd finally find someone who wasn't so wrong for him," Belle added.

Wasn't so wrong? Not exactly an enthusiastic endorsement.

"My mother also told me that a poop-streaked chicken egg could ward off an ill wind," Mila pointed out to Belle. Obviously, she wasn't any happier about this than Roman was, and it wasn't necessary for Mila to add other examples, but she must have felt the need to do that. "She buys her charms and curses from the craft store with discount coupons. She spits on her smudging weeds, and she lied to me about who my father was."

Judging from the way Mila went stiff, she probably hadn't intended to blurt out that last one. Garrett glanced at Nicky. Billy Lee glanced at Tate. And Belle glanced at all of them.

"The point is," Mila went on, "that my mother is the last person in town who should be doling out advice, especially about encounters with women that Roman shouldn't be with."

It was well said and would have been much more effective if the hospital doors hadn't opened, and at that exact second, someone walked in.

The wrong woman.

"Mom!" Tate called out. He ran to Valerie and pulled her into his arms.

CHAPTER FIFTEEN

MILA WAS TOO stunned to speak. Considering what she'd just been babbling on about, that wasn't a bad thing. God, had she really just spilled the beans about her father?

Apparently so.

And she'd done it on the very day she should be talking about nothing but Sophie and the birth of her precious babies.

"Told you," Belle mumbled to her.

It didn't take long for Mila to make the connection between Valerie and the *wrong woman* prediction from Vita. A connection Mila dismissed as she did most of what Vita said. Normally, Belle and others dismissed it, too, so Mila wasn't sure why Roman's mother had latched on to this particular prediction as if it were a nugget of gold.

No reason except that it had seemingly come true.

"My mom came," Tate said, smiling. No, not just smiling. Beaming. "She came."

Mila wasn't sure she'd ever seen him this happy, but he was the only one in the waiting room who apparently felt that way. One by one, they each stood and pinned their attention to her cousin.

It'd been years since Mila had seen Valerie, and yet the woman hadn't aged a day. In fact, she looked younger. Her hair was blond now with copper and purple highlights, and she had it gathered in a bohemian-supermodel kind of ponytail. Even her tie-dyed shirt and jeans managed to look catwalk-ready.

"Of course I came," Valerie said as if there'd never been any doubt she would. There had been plenty. "I wouldn't miss seeing my boy, but when I got to the ranch, one of the hands told me you were here, that Sophie was having her baby. So, do you have a boy cousin or a girl cousin?"

"Both," Tate proudly announced. He continued to keep his arms around Valerie as she came closer to them.

"Belle," Valerie greeted her. She said her name as if she were the mother-in-law Valerie was so glad she didn't have. She didn't mention a word about Belle wearing a ball gown. "Billy Lee. Mila." She barely spared her a glance and practically ran her name together with Billy Lee's. "Garrett. And this must be your fiancée, Nicky. The ranch hand mentioned her, too. Congrats on your engagement."

Garrett and Nicky were still mumbling a thanks when Valerie shifted her attention to Roman. "Still good-looking as ever. Did you know your daddy swept me off my feet when I wasn't much older than you?" she asked Tate.

Tate shook his head. Probably because he knew very little about his mother. That's because there was little that Roman and Mila could have told him about her that wasn't bad.

Mila hoped her cousin had changed for the better. And if she hadn't changed, maybe Valerie wouldn't do any harm while she was here. Which brought Mila to her next question.

Just how long would Valerie be staying?

Considering the way Tate had latched on to her, he didn't ever want her to leave, but Valerie might have a different notion about that.

Or not.

That was a hungry smile she aimed at Roman. When she shifted her attention to Mila, though, it was neither a smile nor a hunger. Mila didn't think she was wrong that Valerie was questioning why she was there—at a Granger family event. Valerie would give Billy Lee a pass in that department since he was Sophie's godfather.

Mila wondered if Valerie would even care that Billy Lee might be more than that to Mila. He might be her father.

Valerie shifted her finger back and forth between Mila and Roman. "So, are you two…together, or what?"

"That's what I asked them," Belle volunteered. "Except I spelled it out." She tipped her head to Tate. "Didn't want to say it in front of him."

"Tate knows how to spell," Roman said to Belle without even looking at her. "How long are you in Wrangler's Creek?" Roman asked Valerie. He didn't appear to be on the verge of answering Valerie's question, but Mila knew the answer.

It was the *or what*.

What Roman and she had was not quite a relationship and with no promise that it ever would be. Still, Mila could feel her heart hanging on. Which made her stupid, of course, but then she'd always been a little bit stupid when it came to Roman.

Valerie smiled, gave Tate a squeeze with her arm

around his shoulders. "I'll stay as long as my boy needs me. And don't worry. You won't have to put me up at the ranch. Lick and I are staying at the inn just up the street. Room four."

"Lick?" all but Tate said in unison. It sounded like the nickname of a rocker.

"He's a friend." Valerie aimed her answer at Tate even though he was the only one who hadn't said anything. "You'll love him, honey. Very cool guy. He's the lead singer in a heavy metal band."

Bingo. Mila hoped she wasn't right about the other bad feelings she was getting from this.

"I didn't bring him with me because I didn't want to spring a bunch of introductions on him at once," Valerie went on. "Sometimes, he gets anxious around new people. I know that sounds crazy, considering he performs in front of a crowd, but he says that's different, that he doesn't have to talk to them. And no, he won't meditate, though I tell him it'll help."

Tate glanced away. Belle cleared her throat. Both were obviously remembering Arwen's visit to Tate's room, but Valerie didn't seem to notice that she'd just brought up a touchy subject.

"Why don't you come with me to the inn now, and you can meet him?" Valerie asked Tate.

Tate immediately looked at Roman. "Can I?"

Roman certainly didn't jump to say yes, and Mila knew why. Lick might be an idiot. Or a male version of Valerie.

"Don't you want to see the babies?" Roman asked him.

"Sure. But Uncle Garrett said it might not be for a while."

He had indeed said that, but Mila knew Roman

wished that Garrett hadn't. "All right, you can go meet *Lick*. But I'm going with you."

"Uh, probably not a good idea." Valerie chuckled as if that was actually funny. "Lick is a little jealous, and once he sees you, those misplaced feelings will go up a notch."

Great. A jealous musician boyfriend named Lick who disliked people. Nothing could go wrong with a combination like that.

"I can go with Tate and Valerie to the inn," Mila offered. "After he's met Lick, Tate and I will come back here."

"Or better yet." Billy Lee made a show of checking the time. He moved between Mila and Roman, slipping his arms around both of them. "I could use a bit of fresh air. Why don't I walk over there with them because I know Sophie will want to see her best friend and brothers first chance she gets. Let me do this for you," Billy Lee whispered to them.

Even though Roman trusted Billy Lee, he was probably wondering if he should allow the man to place himself in the middle of this. Still, Mila could see the exact moment that Roman gave in.

"Don't be long," Roman said to Tate.

Tate nodded, and there was a lot of enthusiasm in it. Billy Lee gave Roman what he no doubt hoped was a reassuring pat on the back. "I won't let him out of my sight," Billy Lee promised.

Roman followed the three to the door, and he stood there watching them for several moments. The inn wasn't that far, and from his position he would have been able to keep his eyes on them until they actually went inside.

"You can come and see the twins now," Clay called out to them. "They just moved them from the delivery room and into the nursery."

Mila spotted Clay in the hall, and he was motioning toward him. He certainly didn't look like a man who'd thrown up less than a half hour ago. He looked happy to the point of being giddy.

Unlike Roman.

Roman had to practically tear himself away from his Tate-watching before joining the group as they followed Clay. He was still wearing a green paper robe over his clothes that rustled when he kept motioning for them to follow him.

The hospital was old, built back in the fifties, and while some of it had been updated, the nursery still had a large glass window with the babies in clear bassinets. The room was large enough for a dozen or more infants, but right now there were only two.

"Uh, they're wrinkly," Garrett commented just as Nicky said, "Oh, they're beautiful. Perfect, in fact."

Mila was with both of them on this. They were wrinkly. Perfect, too.

"Meet Kyle and Katelyn McKinnon," Clay proudly announced. "I can't wait for my sister and her boys to see them. They're on vacation right now but will be back tomorrow."

His sister, April, and her twin boys had been the only family Clay had had until he married Sophie. Now, they had a set of twins of their own. Sophie and Clay were finally getting the lives they both wanted.

"When will we be able to see Sophie?" Belle asked. She had her face pressed right against the glass. "And when can I hold them? The one on the left looks like it needs burping."

"That's Kyle," Clay provided. "You probably won't be able to hold them until later tonight. They only want Sophie and me to do that for now. But you might be able to see Sophie soon. The doctor wants her to try to feed the babies first, and he said it wasn't a good idea for family to be in there until Sophie's gotten comfortable with nursing."

"Hogwash," Belle complained. "Sophie won't mind me being with her for that."

Oh, yes, she would, and this was where Mila could help. "It probably isn't a good idea to hold the babies while you're wearing that dress. You could trip on it or something. Why don't you let me take you home to change, and then I can bring you back?"

After Sophie and Clay had had some alone time with their son and daughter.

Belle looked down at her dress, frowned. "I suppose you're right. Billy Lee will want to change, too. That way people won't wonder why we're dressed like this."

No, they wouldn't. Probably everyone in town already knew about the fantasy date, but Mila didn't bring that up.

"Why don't you let Nicky and me take Mom to the ranch?" Garrett said. "Then we can all come back in an hour or so." He put his arm around his mother to get her moving.

"The babies are so beautiful," Nicky added as they left.

Clay left, too, when a nurse motioned for him to come into the nursery. He practically ran, and Roman and Mila waited and watched while the nurse had Clay sit in a rocking chair and she put one of the babies in his arms. It seemed a perfect moment. Private, too.

Roman must have felt the same way. "I'll walk up the street and wait outside the inn."

"I can go with you," Mila offered.

"No." He answered a little fast for it not to hurt some. "I need to talk to Valerie. *Alone.*"

ROMAN WAS STANDING so still and was so lost in thought that he nearly let Mrs. Abernathy's Yorkie pee on his leg. Maybe the dog thought he was a statue or something, and it didn't help that Mrs. Abernathy—who was a hundred if she was a day—had stopped, too, to look at what Roman was staring at.

The door to the Red Rooster Inn. Or Rooster's as everyone called it.

"No, no, Toodles," Mrs. Abernathy scolded the dog. "No tinkling on people." It had already hiked up its hind leg and dribbled pee as she pulled him away from Roman. "The sign doesn't change, you know," she added to Roman.

It took him a moment to realize she was talking about the old pub-style sign that was dangling on chains outside the inn. It was of a red rooster, of course, and it was gazing, if roosters could indeed gaze, at a pair of hens in the distance.

"Once somebody painted the chicken eyes with glow-in-the-dark paint," the woman went on. "It sort of changed then when you'd look at it from different angles. Made 'em look like aliens or zombies. But Alford had it repainted."

Alford Crenshaw was the owner who lived in the back part of the inn, and the glow-in-the-dark paint story was plenty familiar because Roman had been the one who'd given the poultry glowing eyes. Like some other bad decisions that he'd made in his life, beer and encouragement from a friend had contributed to the prank. And the friend had been none other than Valerie.

When Toodles tried to pee on Roman's boot again, Mrs. Abernathy gave another scolding and said something about it being time for her to start the walk home. She'd made it sound like a long journey, but her house was about twenty feet away.

Roman kept an eye on her to make sure she got there safely, but it was hard to pull his attention away from what was going on inside Rooster's. More than anything he wanted to be in there. He doubted that Valerie and a guy who called himself Lick were careful about what they said to Tate, but maybe Billy Lee could head off trouble if he saw it coming. Then Roman could do what he always did after a Valerie-storm had moved through.

He'd pick up the pieces.

Repair things as best he could. Much as Alford Crenshaw had done to the rooster sign. But even now, after all these years, Roman could see bits of the glow-in-the-dark paint in the corner of the rooster's eye. Valerie was like that. Always leaving shit behind.

He glanced up the street again and saw Mila coming out of the hospital and heading toward the parking lot. That probably meant she'd already gotten to have a visit with Sophie and was now going home. She didn't look in his direction, and he'd like to think it was because she was in dreamy thought over seeing Sophie so happy, but Valerie's arrival had no doubt shaken her.

And Roman hadn't helped.

He'd dismissed her when she asked to come with

him to the inn, but he'd had his reasons. For one thing, he had needed some time to think. Time to rein in his emotions so he didn't say something stupid to Valerie, and he'd needed to figure out how to tell his ex that he was going to smother her in her sleep if she hurt Tate again. His son had been through enough and, coming on the heels of what could have been another suspension over the locker, Tate might be near the breaking point.

The minutes crawled by, and just when Roman thought he was going to need to text Billy Lee for an update, the front door of the inn finally opened. Tate came out first, shoulders slumped, his hands in his pockets.

Crap.

Something had gone wrong.

It hadn't gone wrong, though, in Valerie's mind, because when she came out, her arm was hooked through Billy Lee's and she was laughing. "I told you Lick was fun," she said. "But you know us creative types. We get cranky when we aren't creating."

Roman had no idea if Lick was truly creative, but he'd seen some of the stuff that Valerie called her art, and it looked like something done in a pre-K class. Still, she could consider herself an artist until the cows came home, but she couldn't hurt Tate.

"Are you okay?" Roman asked Tate.

Tate shrugged, so Roman looked to Billy Lee for answers. "Lash wanted to work on his music."

"Lick," Valerie corrected with a giggle. She nudged Billy Lee in the ribs as if he were joking, but Lash might have been what the idiot had done to Tate, as in lash out.

"He said we had to go," Tate added.

Valerie dismissed it with a wave of her hand. "He

was just a little testy. And he didn't mean it when he called you a brat. That's a term of endearment for him."

Maybe, but it was a term that had Roman seeing an even brighter shade of red than was on the rooster sign. Billy Lee picked up on it right away.

"I thought Tate and I could walk down to the hospital and see Sophie and the babies now," Billy Lee suggested. "Then maybe I can drive Belle and him back to the ranch?"

Tate shrugged at that, but since he didn't refuse any part of that offer, Roman gave a nod to Billy Lee. "Thanks." He took hold of Tate's arm when he started to walk off. "We'll talk when I get home."

Tate yawned. "Can it wait until tomorrow? I really do want to see the babies, and I've got a bunch of homework to do."

It might be true, but it could be that something had just happened that Tate didn't want to discuss. Fine. Then Roman would have a little chat about it with Valerie. At least she had the decency to drop the fake giggles and smiles once Tate and Billy Lee were out of earshot.

"You're supposed to be here to help Tate," Roman snarled. "Did the meeting with your boyfriend do that?"

"Don't you lecture me." She came down the steps. "I took time out of my busy life because you asked me to come. I came."

Roman waited a moment to try to talk himself out of yelling. It worked, but he had to speak through clenched teeth. "Did that meeting with your boyfriend help or hurt Tate?"

Judging from her suddenly tight jaw, it was the latter. So, Roman had his answer. He pushed past her and went inside.

"Roman, don't you dare say anything to him," Valerie insisted. She was trying to keep a grip on his arm and hold him back.

It didn't stop him. Roman went straight to room four, didn't knock, and he threw open the door. The TV was blaring with some loud music, and there was a buff guy with stringy blond hair on the bed, a bottle of beer in his hand. He was wearing only a pair of boxers with pussies on them. Not of the cat variety, either.

"What the fuck do you want?" he grumbled to Roman. "First the brat and the old fart and now you?" He looked at Valerie. "Didn't I tell you I was tired and didn't want any more interruptions? It was bad enough I had to come to this cow-shit town with you, and now I have to put up with this asshole?"

Roman hadn't been certain what he was going to do, but that clarified things for him. He went to Mr. Wonderful, dragged him off the bed and slammed him against the wall. Hard.

Lick might have muscles, but it was obvious from the puny punch he tried to throw at Roman that he'd gotten those muscles in a gym and hadn't had an older brother who'd beaten the crap out of him.

Roman dodged the first punch, then a second one all the while Valerie was shouting for him to stop. He didn't stop. When Lick tried to kick him in the balls, Roman slugged him in the gut. It had the intended effect. It knocked the breath out of him, and Lick quit fighting and cursing.

"If you call my son a brat again," Roman warned

him, "I'll rip off your dick and shove it up your ass. Understand?"

Lick garbled out a few sounds and nodded.

"Lick didn't mean it," Valerie insisted. She was crying now and trying to pull him out of Roman's grip.

Roman let go of Lick and turned to her. "And you will not let this dipshit anywhere near Tate again. You'll go to a therapy session with Tate and do everything you can to help him. Understand?"

"You don't have the right to talk to me that way!"

"Understand?" Roman yelled right in her face.

From the corner of his eye, he saw Lick come at him again. Roman was thankful for it. He had a lot of dangerous energy churning inside him, and he hadn't known how he was going to burn it off.

Now, he knew.

When Lick raised his fist to hit him, Roman gave him an upper cut to the jaw that knocked him on his pussy-clad butt, and because he was pretty sure there wasn't another point he needed to make, Roman walked out. Valerie didn't follow him. She hurried to her piece-of-shit lover and started kissing, hugging and apologizing for what had just happened.

Roman figured he should be worried if Lick was going to take out his anger on Valerie, but his concern meter for her was at zero right now. Besides, if Alford heard a ruckus going on, he would call the cops. In fact, he probably already had, and Roman hoped like the devil that no one bugged Clay about this.

He started walking toward the hospital when he left the inn, and he figured by the time he got there, he would have calmed down some. He hadn't. So, he kept on walking. He definitely didn't want Sophie to see him like this. Nor Tate. In fact, there was only person he could risk seeing him right now.

Roman walked straight to Mila's house.

It wasn't far. Nothing in Wrangler's Creek was, and when he saw her car in the driveway, he knew she was there. He went straight up the steps. Knocked. Then knocked again when she didn't answer right away. A few seconds later, the door opened.

"Roman," Mila said on a rise of breath.

He didn't give her a chance to say anything else. Roman dragged her against him and kissed her.

CHAPTER SIXTEEN

MILA HAD BEEN about to ask Roman what was wrong. And something was indeed wrong. She could see it on his face.

She felt it in his kiss.

At least for a couple of seconds, anyway. It was hard to feel anything but pleasure when Roman was kissing her.

He backed her inside, kicking the door shut with his foot, and he turned, pinning her against the wall. The kiss continued, raging on as if there were some fierce battle going on inside him.

"Are you okay?" she finally managed to say when he broke for air.

"Lick had pussies on his shorts, and I punched him."

Mila didn't have time to react to that, though she was surprised. Not that Lick was a guy who deserved punching but because she didn't know what the other thing meant. She hoped Lick hadn't smelled of sex while Tate was there. If so, Roman had obviously handled it.

And now she was getting the aftermath of that.

Mila decided just to ride this incredible wave and then she'd sort it all out later. Not that Roman gave her much of a choice about that. He kept kissing her, kept pressing his body against hers, until Mila thought she might be melting. She didn't care if she did. She just wanted Roman to fix this fire that he had started inside her.

He did. Without breaking the kiss, he scooped her up and headed to her bedroom. Or rather the guest bedroom since it was first off the hall. He carried her inside, dropped her on the bed and in the same motion he yanked off his shirt.

That distracted her for a moment. His body could always do that to her. And it was obvious things were going to move pretty fast. She didn't mind, but Mila took a moment to touch those toned muscles on his stomach while he was unzipping her jeans. As he'd done in the bookstore, he peeled them off her, rid her of her top and went after his own zipper.

She helped with that and saw the scar from his surgery. It'd healed from the looks of it, but she wanted to make sure he didn't hurt himself with this anger sex.

Anger sex, she mentally repeated. Then smiled.

Mila had always suspected that sex with Roman would be intense, and this was off to a good intensive start. That start got better when he pulled off his boots, jeans and boxers.

Oh, my.

Someone had sucked all the oxygen out of the room. There wasn't a drop left in her lungs, and she couldn't speak. Turned out, though, that speaking really wasn't necessary.

Roman took a condom from his jeans pocket, but he didn't put it on. Instead, he put his knee on the bed, the mattress dipping down with his weight and sending him forward. On top of her. He kissed her again, dragging off her bra and panties.

Touching her.

While he kept up those wildfire kisses, he played with a new fire source. Her breasts. Many, many kisses there. He circled her nipple with his tongue and took her into his mouth. Then he located yet another fire source.

Between her legs.

She'd known he could do magic things with his mouth there, but his fingers were equally clever. Maybe too much so. Because for a moment Mila thought he was going to finish her off right there. She didn't want that and maybe managed to make a protesting sound.

Roman listened because he tore open the condom, put it on and pinned one of her hands to the bed.

"Slap me if I hurt you," he said.

The offer surprised her, much as his greeting had done at the door, and with that sound of surprise shaping her mouth, Mila lost her virginity to the only man she'd ever wanted to have it.

There was no pain. At least, she didn't think there was. It was hard to tell because she went flying to a place where there was only pleasure. The delicious pressure of him inside her, filling her. And then he was moving.

She liked the moving part best.

There was a rhythm to it. A frenzy, too. And the need. The need was growing with each of those moves. He didn't stop with the kissing and touching, either. Roman managed to connect with her mouth, and he reached between them to touch her in the very spot that would cause her to climax. Of course, she doubted that she would need his fingers when she had something much bigger and better suited for climax-giving.

This was so much better than oral sex or the orgasm in high school with her clothes on. Roman thrust inside, and each time sent those gold sparkles exploding all around her.

He wasn't especially gentle.

She would thank him for that later. Because he wasn't treating her like a virgin who'd been waiting her whole life for him. He was treating her like his lover. She decided to treat him like a lover, too, and not just lie there and moan while he gave her all this pleasure.

She kissed him, lifted her hips. In theory it was a good idea, but at that moment he pushed into her again, catching that "right place" just right.

"There you go," Roman said, his voice all low and dripping with sex.

And there she went.

Though she wasn't sure how he knew it was about to happen. But it did. The sparkles multiplied times a billion and then shattered. Mila felt herself shatter, too.

Roman gathered her in his arms, buried his face in her neck, and one thrust later, he shattered right along with her.

Two times.

Those were the words going through his head. Roman couldn't pretend that the first time didn't count, either. They hadn't actually had sex, but he'd gotten Mila naked. Naked plus climax counted. Now, though, he'd crossed the sexual Rubicon because he'd taken her virginity. Perhaps hurt her, as well, so Roman lifted his head to look at her and make sure she was all right.

Oh, no.

That was more than an "I'm just all right" look on her face. Her lids were lowered halfway. Her facial muscles were slack. And she was smiling. That definitely wasn't the expression of someone who knew there could be only one more time—at most—for them to have sex.

Mila located his mouth, kissed him and then fully opened her eyes. "Oh, no," she said, making him wonder if she was just repeating what he'd said in his head. But unless she had ESP, she didn't know that had been his reaction.

Unless, of course, she was reading his expression as he'd done to her.

"Are you regretting this already?" Roman asked, and because he thought they could use some levity, he added, "Because usually the regrets don't come until the postorgasmic fog is gone."

"No. I'm not regretting it. But you are. Does this count as one time or two?"

It would have been much easier to answer if she hadn't kissed him or if her body hadn't had a really nice little aftershock contraction. He liked to call those the gifts that kept on giving because it gave his dick a squeeze to remind him of just how good this had been.

And it had been darn good.

"Two times," he answered, causing her to frown.

"Did I hurt you?" he asked at the same moment she asked, "Did I hurt you?"

He had to smile. "No. The incision is fine." He probably wouldn't have noticed if it'd popped. An orgasm was a cure for a lot of things. "And you? Did it hurt?"

She flexed her hand. "Nope. It was a tight fit, but I think that's what made it so good." Her eyes widened, and she blushed.

Clearly, she wasn't used to talking about her private parts with a man. One who'd just introduced that part to sex. But yeah, a tight fit had made it pretty damn memorable.

"I'm glad it was you," she said, pressing her hand to his cheek. "I wanted it to be you."

He'd figured that, but the jury was still out on whether or not this was a really, really good thing that would open her up to new experiences or if this was just going to cause her to build a shell around her to guard her heart.

Since she got that dreamy look in her eyes again, Roman decided it was time to put a little distance between them so they could both have some thinking time.

"Bathroom?" he said so he could take care of that first.

She pointed to the hall.

He kissed her because she looked so damn tasty lying there. Her hair tumbled all around her face, and she had a "fuck me again" smile. It was tempting to use up his third shot, but that was something he could think on, as well.

Roman gathered up his clothes, located the bathroom. Not hard to do because the house was small. He decided to take a quick shower just in case he ran into Tate when he got back to the ranch. He doubted his son would pick up on it, but it was best not to walk in there with Mila's scent all over him. He took a last whiff of that scent before he stepped under the showerhead.

Mila would need to know about what had happened at the inn. If for no other reason than so she could make sure Tate didn't have another encounter with Lick. In fact, everyone in his family should know. Once Mila heard what had gone on, she'd probably figure out that's why he'd come to her. She might feel used. Might be pissed off.

If that happened, he would deserve anything she dished out.

He'd hoped that the silence would help him come to the right answer. And it did. There was really only one answer here and that was for him to leave Mila alone. This wasn't going to turn into a relationship. He didn't do those. Especially the kind of relationship she would almost certainly want.

She wasn't exactly a white picket fence kind of person, but it was close. She wanted *normal*, and she wanted it here in Wrangler's Creek. Roman couldn't give her either of those things.

So, there.

It was settled.

He should just go in the bedroom, tell her he was sorry and then hit himself in the head with the biggest skillet he could find. Maybe punch himself a couple of times, too, because he'd really screwed this one up. Then he could focus on what he should be focusing on— Tate and this shit-storm situation with Valerie and the turd she'd brought to town with her.

Roman took a little more time in the bathroom to give Mila a chance to catch her breath, and when he was finished dressing, he went back into the bedroom, expecting to find her there. She wasn't. And her clothes weren't lying on the floor, either.

He went to the room across the hall—her bedroom, he realized when he saw the stack of paperbacks on the nightstand next to what appeared to be an old cup of tea and some candy bar wrappers. There were plenty of pillows all stacked up, which meant she probably used this as her reading spot.

"Mila?" he called out in case she was naked in the closet.

No answer.

In a house this size she should have been able to hear him no matter where she was. That sent a jolt of alarm through him, and he went into the living room. No sign of her there or in the kitchen. Roman called out to her again and got the same response.

Nothing.

Since she hadn't vaporized, he glanced around, trying to figure out where she could be. Maybe she'd taken out the trash or something. He was heading to the side door off the kitchen to check when he saw the note on the counter.

"'I decided to go back to the hospital and say goodnight to Sophie,'" he read aloud. "'Don't worry. I won't say a word to her about what happened. Just lock up on your way out. Oh, and thanks bunches.'"

Roman read it again. And again. He frowned.

Thanks bunches?

Well, he hadn't thought that would be Mila's reaction after losing her virginity to him. He had figured she'd be picking up the pieces of her heart or else picking out china patterns. Apparently, though, she was in a different state of mind than he'd ever imagined she would be, and the PS at the bottom of the note proved that.

"Never thought I'd get to have a one-night stand with Roman Granger. Ha!"

To deepen his frown even more, Mila had added a smiley face and that one word he was starting to hate. "Peachy!"

MILA DROVE AWAY from her house, not speeding exactly but she wasn't dawdling, either. She hadn't lied to Roman when she'd said she wanted to go back to the hospital, but even if Sophie hadn't been there, Mila would have just figured out somewhere else to go.

She'd seen that look in Roman's eyes. The panic. The regret. He was probably thinking that having sex with her could only lead to some kind of commitment.

It didn't.

She had fallen hard for him years ago, and sadly that "commitment" of her heart would have stayed that way even if they hadn't had sex. But the last thing she had wanted was for sex to make him feel trapped. Apparently, Roman wasn't ever going to be the friends-with-benefits type.

Mila felt the tears burning her eyes and blinked them back. Cursed them, too. She had fantasized about having sex with Roman, and it had lived up to the fantasy. That wasn't a reason to cry. It was a reason to celebrate. Maybe now she could truly get past the massive obstacle in her heart that was there because she just hadn't been able to stop caring for him. She would always care. But it was time to maybe look at other possibilities.

Even if that made her heart ache even more.

She drove up the street toward the hospital, a trip she could have easily walked, but she wanted to drive around a little while before she went in to see Sophie. Maybe Sophie would be so caught up in her precious babies that she wouldn't sense that something about Mila was different.

It was dark now, and there was that old saying of the town rolling up the sidewalks at night. The sidewalks were still there, of course, but no one was out and about. At least, there wasn't until Mila made it to the inn.

Valerie was outside, pacing and smoking a cigarette.

Mila considered just driving right past her, but she suspected the reason Roman had ended up at her place was because of something that had gone on here. Since she might not hear it from Roman, she pulled over to listen to what Valerie had to say.

"Fuck Roman," Valerie snarled the moment Mila got out of her car.

Because Mila had done just that, she just stayed quiet and waited. She didn't have to wait long for Valerie to continue.

"You can tell Roman I said that, too. Fuck him. Do you know what he did?" But she didn't give Mila a chance to venture a guess. Her guess, though, would have been that Roman had punched Lick because of something he said to Tate. "He punched Lick. Twice."

Yep, Mila had been right. "Was Tate there when it happened?"

Valerie stopped in midpace and gave her a "what the hell are you talking about" look. "No. This all went on after Tate left. Roman was being a dick, and now Lick's packing to leave."

Great news. Well, maybe. "You're not going with him, are you? Because the doctor wanted you to be there for a therapy session."

Valerie grunted and kept puffing on that cigarette. "Tate's fine. He didn't even get upset when Lick called him a brat. And Lick didn't mean it. He's just tired, that's all."

Everything inside Mila went still. "He called Tate that?"

"So what? I'm sure Tate's been called worse. He's a teenager, for Christ's sake."

"He's never been called worse by his mother's boyfriend." Mila tried to tamp down her anger, but it was too late. She wanted to go inside and punch Lick herself. "Why would you bring Lick here with you, anyway? This visit isn't about him. It's about your son."

Valerie huffed. "You think you have the right to give me advice just because you're fucking Roman? Well, you don't. No one has the right to give me advice when it comes to me and my son."

There was probably nothing Mila could say to her that would help. Plenty she could do to hurt, though, and Mila was wishing she could slap some sense into her cousin. That would only make things worse for Roman and Tate.

"Tate idolizes you," Mila settled for saying. "Whenever you send him a card or call him, he tells everyone. Just those small gestures from you make him happy. Think how much good a therapy session with him would do. It would let him know that you love him."

"Of course I love him. He's my kid," Valerie snapped. For a moment it seemed Valerie was about to jump into another tirade about Mila minding her own business. She didn't. She cursed, but Mila thought that might be aimed at herself.

"I'm not good at this," Valerie said under her breath. "That's why I talked Lick into coming with me. Because I will never be good at this, and I thought it'd help to have him here."

Mila wasn't sure what *this* encompassed, but maybe Valerie meant motherhood. She also wasn't sure why

Valerie would have thought a guy like Lick would have been of any help whatsoever.

"Tate doesn't need you to be perfect," Mila explained. "He just needs you to be there."

"That's just it. If I'm *there*, I'll screw it up. I always do." When Valerie looked at her, Mila saw the tears.

Valerie had done so many hurtful things that it was hard to be affected by those tears and feel sorry for her, but Mila did. She could never dismiss all the things Valerie had done to Tate, but it was obvious she was at least aware of the damage she'd been doing. Until tonight, Mila hadn't even been sure Tate was on Valerie's radar.

"I left the hospital because I could see you were all judging me," Valerie went on. "The only thing I could think of was to pretend that I wanted Tate to meet Lick."

Mila just sighed. "Obviously, that didn't work. And as for judging you, I wasn't. I was actually thinking how beautiful you are, how beautiful you've always been. It's no wonder that Roman was attracted to you."

She hadn't meant to say that last part aloud. She'd learned the hard way not to bring up Roman because it usually caused Valerie to go into the insult/attack mode.

But Valerie only dismissed it with another grunt. "When Roman picked me in high school, I couldn't believe it. Here we lived, in a trailer. With Vita. And he still picked me. That's when I knew something was really wrong with me. Because I didn't love him. And I kept thinking if I can't love someone like Roman Granger, then there must be something seriously broken inside me."

This was the first Mila was hearing of any of this. When Valerie had been with Roman, the only thing she'd ever talked about was the sex. Mila had assumed there'd been some love involved but apparently not.

Not on Valerie's part, anyway.

But Mila was almost positive that Roman had been in love with her cousin. Ironic that he'd fallen in love with the very person who wouldn't love him back.

Valerie's tears started up again, and this time she couldn't blink them away. They spilled down her cheeks. Mila hoped she didn't regret this, but she put her arms around Valerie and hugged her. She expected Valerie to push her away and start the barb-flinging, but she stayed there a few seconds, then eased away.

"How can I fix this?" Valerie asked.

"You can go to that therapy session with Tate." Mila didn't have to think long to come up with that answer. "You do what the therapist tells you to do. You rebuild your relationship with Tate and make it the way it should be." Now, here was the hard part, and Mila had to tamp down years of jealousy to say it. "Even if that means moving closer to Tate so you can see him more often."

Valerie didn't jump to nix that. What she didn't do was verbally agree. She also didn't even show any signs of agreement with her expression. Still, it was a start.

The start came to a quick halt, however, when the door to the inn flew open, and a man with greasy blond hair came out. He had a suitcase in each hand and a woman's purse on his shoulder.

This had to be Lick.

Mila amended her thought about punching him. She'd rather kick him in the nuts instead.

Lick thrust the purse and one of the suitcases at Valerie. "Are you coming with me?" he asked. He took some keys from his pocket, pointed them toward a rental car parked in front of the inn, and he hit the button to unlock the doors.

Valerie shook her head, caught on to his arm. "Please, don't do this. I have to stay for my son's counseling session. Just one more day, and then we can go."

"I'm not staying in this hick-hole another minute much less a day. You can either come with me or you can go to the session with your ex."

More head shaking from Valerie. "Roman won't be at the counseling. It'll be just Tate, me and the therapist."

"I don't care." Judging from his face, he was telling the truth. He didn't. Not about Tate, or Valerie for that matter.

Lick waited what had to be three seconds at most before he threw off Valerie's grip with far more force than was necessary, and he started for the car.

"Please, don't go," she begged. But Valerie was talking to the air because Lick got behind the wheel and started the engine.

Valerie looked at Mila as if asking her what to do. Again, Mila didn't have to think about this for long. "You need to stay and be here for Tate."

"Get in or I'm leaving!" Lick shouted, and it was loud enough for them to hear it even though he didn't lower the window.

Valerie fired glances back and forth between Lick and her, and Mila gave it one last shot.

"Stay for Tate's sake," Mila told her.

For a moment she thought she was getting through to her cousin. But it only lasted for a moment.

"Tell Tate I'll call him," Valerie said, and she ran to the car. The moment she was inside, Lick gunned the engine and sped away.

CHAPTER SEVENTEEN

ROMAN CURSED, AND because it didn't help his mood, he cursed again. He was in Sophie's office in the guesthouse on the ranch. There was a stack of paperwork for Granger Western on one side of the desk. A stack of paperwork for his own business on the other side. Now, Buck Williams, one of the hands, had dropped off some ranching business contracts that needed his signature.

He didn't want to do any of this and considered putting a closed sign on the door of the guesthouse the way Mila did at her bookstore.

And speaking of Mila, he cursed her, too.

It'd been three days since they'd had sex and she'd left him that stupid-assed "peachy" note. No calls, no texts. Nada. And it wasn't as if she didn't have something to talk to him about.

Not sex, either, but Valerie.

Since Mila had been the one to call Tate and tell him that his mother was leaving with Lick, Limp, Lash or whatever the hell his name was, then Mila must have some clue as to what had happened.

Of course, Roman had a clue, too. Valerie, being Valerie, had just skipped out again, leaving him to pick up the fucking pieces. Still, Mila might have some insight that she could have passed along to him, but the one time Roman had walked by her shop to see her, she'd been doing story time with a bunch of little kids from a preschool group. She'd simply waved at him and smiled.

Smiled!

As if there was something to smile about.

He reminded himself that a smile was better than her crying over him or feeling sorry about what they'd done. But apparently she wasn't having any regrets. She was sailing on with her life as if nothing had happened. Pretty damn strange for a woman who'd hung on to her virginity for over three decades.

"I'm busy," Roman snarled when there was a knock at the door. Tate wasn't home from school yet, Mila would be working at the bookstore and Sophie was at home with her babies. That meant there was no one else he wanted to see.

Including the woman who opened the door and popped her head in.

His mother.

"I just need a minute," Belle said. She frowned. "Why are you so cranky?"

"You know why. And I'm not cranky. I'm busy." He scribbled his signature on a bull sperm purchase and on an order for some deworming meds.

"Sounds like crankiness to me," Belle mumbled. Despite his having stated not once but twice that he was busy, Belle came in, anyway, didn't close the door, and she sank into the chair next to the desk. "Does your mood have anything to do with Mila?"

She didn't give him a chance to give a "why the heck would you ask that?" stare.

"Because of Mila and those dating sites," she added. This time his stare was more along the lines of *WTF?*

"Mila's looking at the dating sites again," Belle continued as if he'd actually asked that. "Not the fantasy ones, either. The real sites. She asked me for some old links I had gathered for Sophie before she fell for Clay. Anyway, I emailed them to her, but I left a couple of them off. I mean, she doesn't need a webpage for well-endowed men."

Roman just went with another *WTF?* stare. He wouldn't even address the well-endowed part, but he did have a question. "When did this happen?"

"A couple of days ago."

He'd had sex with her a couple of days ago. What, had she decided that once was enough with him and it was time to try someone else?

Of course, that's what he'd wanted her to do. Just not this bloody soon.

"I think she looked at Sophie's happy life," Belle explained, "Garrett and Nicky's, too—and Mila must have decided to go for the gold and get her own happy ending." She paused only long enough to draw breath. "Maybe you're cranky about Valerie, too."

"Valerie certainly didn't help matters," he growled, and he wasn't sure he wanted to drop the subject about Mila. His mother obviously didn't intend to go along with that, though.

"Valerie helped by leaving. Do you really think it would have done Tate any good for her to stay around?"

It was one of the wisest questions he'd ever heard his mother ask. Too bad he was in a shitty mood that *wise* couldn't help. "No, but Tate doesn't get that, and it means he takes it out on me and everyone around him."

"Well, he has been cranky," Belle agreed. "But that should ease up soon once he figures out that she's never going to be the mom he wants her to be." She paused. "You figured it out when you were about his age."

Roman's hand froze in midsignature, and he looked up at her. Were they actually going to talk about this? "You know why and how I figured it out," he reminded her.

She nodded. "And it made you very angry. You're still angry."

Hell, yeah, he was. Like Mila and her virginity, Roman had also hung on to that anger for over three decades.

"Have you ever done something that changed your and someone else's life?" she asked. She didn't look at him when she spoke. Belle twisted her wedding rings around her finger, the diamonds catching the light and giving off little flashes.

Roman knew she wasn't talking about Mila, but that was the first thing that came to mind. He had done something to change everything. And he wasn't sure he'd changed it for the better. His mother certainly hadn't twenty years ago, either.

"I loved your father," she continued. "I thought I would never love someone as much as I did him. That's why I kept hanging on. Those other women didn't mean anything to him, and he wasn't going to leave me for them."

"He had sex with other women," Roman pointed out. "He disrespected you, your marriage vows and those other women."

Again, she nodded. "And because of that, you don't respect vows, either." She gave him a nervous smile. "I watch those celebrity shrinks on TV. Plus, there's something like this going on in one of the other TV shows."

Probably not the most reliable sources to get therapeutic help, but at least Belle finally seemed to be connecting the dots.

"I'm sorry about how I handled that," she went on. "God, am I sorry. I was wrong, and I didn't know how to fix being wrong."

Roman opened his mouth to tell her that it was too late for an apology, but it hit him.

It wasn't too late.

Maybe because he wasn't filtering all of this through a thirteen-year-old mind, he couldn't see any benefit to hanging on to this any longer. His parents had screwed up, he had screwed up, but it was time to let it go. Well, let it go as much as he could. It was hard to wash away a festering hurt with just a chat and an apology.

He reached over and brushed his fingers over her arm to get her attention. And because he just wanted to touch her. "Truce?" he offered.

Judging from the smile, you would have thought he'd offered her the world. Hell, maybe it was something like that because if Tate offered him a truce, Roman would be in seventh heaven. That didn't mean he thought everything was suddenly going to be perfect between his mother and him. Belle would always be Belle. But Roman would take just not being at war with her. He had enough battles in his life without continuing to fight this one with his mother.

"Truce," she repeated. She used her pinkie to catch a tear that was about to fall. Roman was hoping that was a tear of the happy variety.

She stood, gave his hand a squeeze. "I'll let you get back to your work, but I wanted to ask your opinion first. Billy Lee wants to have *s-e-x* with me, and I'm considering it."

Oh, man. He hadn't seen that coming. Roman had thought this was going to be about gardening or baby-sitting the twins. He did not want to talk sex with his mom. Still, with Sophie tied up, maybe he was her only option.

"Do you want to have sex with him?" he asked. "Because I'm thinking if you have to spell it instead of saying it, then—"

"I really want to," she interrupted. "But I don't want to mess up our friendship. He's always been there for our family. Heck, he's like family, and if this turns out to be a mistake, it could ruin things, you know?"

Yeah, he did know. Firsthand. Because he'd done it with Mila.

"Then just take things slow," he said. Not stellar advice since his mother had been a widow for years and Billy Lee had been waiting in the shadows for her all this time. Billy Lee was a walking metaphor for taking things slow.

"Yes, thank you," she said. She headed for the door, but then she hurried back to his desk and hugged him.

His mom was still hugging him when Mila stepped in. "Uh, am I interrupting anything?"

"No, we're done," Belle assured her. "I'm going to have *s-e-x* with Billy Lee." His mother moved away from him and hugged Mila. "And if you really want that site for well-endowed men, I'll send it to you."

Mila had a similar *WTF?* look on her face that Roman was certain he'd had earlier. "That's wonderful about Billy Lee, but I'll pass on the site. You already sent me quite a lot of them. Thank you, by the way."

"My pleasure. I just want you all to be as happy as I am right now." Humming—yes, humming—his mother left, and Mila walked in.

His heart did a fluttering thing, maybe because he wasn't sure how he was supposed to feel about this visit. Especially since she was moving on with those dating sites.

She motioned in Belle's direction. "Are you okay with her and Billy Lee?"

"Yeah." But even if he hadn't been, he hoped that his mother would go for it, anyway. She didn't need her grown kids dictating who her sex partners should be.

"I'm sorry about Valerie leaving the way she did," she added. "For the record, I did try to talk her out of it."

He'd already figured that out.

"And to set another record straight," she went on, "your mother thinks that well-endowed site is about men with a lot of money."

He'd also figured that out. The one thing he hadn't figured out was the woman standing in front of him.

"How's Tate?" she asked.

Roman made a so-so motion with his hand. "I'm thinking when school ends, I should take him on a vacation. Maybe we can go on one of those cruises geared to kids his age."

She made a sound as if that were a fine idea. "He also wants to do the junior bronco riding in the town festival this summer. Maybe you can work with him on that since you won it a couple of times?"

Seven times. Every year from when he was thirteen until he quit competing right after Tate was born. But this was the first Roman was hearing about his son's interest in it.

"How'd you find out Tate wanted to ride broncos?" Roman asked.

"He emailed me and asked if I had any books about it. I had two so I dropped them off at school yesterday during his lunch period. He asked me to stay and eat with him so I did. The cafeteria food is still just as awful as it always was. I had the mystery meat with a side of limp fries," she added, smiling.

The smile didn't last long.

He hated that she was standing there so stiff. Formal, almost. Yes, he had messed up their friendship for twenty minutes of sex.

Great sex.

But still…

"You left me a note with a smiley face on it," he said, and left it at that. Something to get the ball rolling on a conversation he'd been wanting to have with her.

And not wanting, too.

This could be a Pandora's box kind of thing, but crap in a basket, he wanted to know if their time together had truly been as insignificant as a one-night stand.

Mila nodded. "I didn't want you to think I'd just run off because I was upset. I wasn't. Like I told you afterward, I'm glad it was you."

She had indeed said that and then had gotten that life-planning look in her eyes. At least, Roman had thought that was what had been going on, but maybe he'd been wrong.

"No regrets," she added with a quick smile. "I hope it's the same for you."

"No regrets," he repeated. None about the actual sex, anyway. Roman wasn't sure what he actually regretted about this, but something didn't feel right. "What made you decide to start using the dating sites?"

She looked away before he could see what was in her eyes. Too bad. And he tried not to read anything into that. Maybe she was just uncomfortable talking about other men with him. He was certainly uncomfortable, but he wanted to know.

"You," she answered.

All right. Roman hadn't counted on her being quite that blunt.

"Look, I know you don't do relationships," she added. "You told me that right from the start. So, if I mope around, that's only going to make you feel bad. It'll make me feel bad, too, and I don't like wallowing in misery."

"Misery?" he repeated. "Are you really miserable?"

"I would be if I were just sitting around, and that's why I'll use the dating sites. I don't expect to find love at first sight, but it'll be nice if I could find someone for dinner dates, movies...that sort of thing."

Sex would no doubt be part of that *sort of thing*. Which was good. Normal. And he didn't want Mila to live like a nun. She'd already lived like that for too long, and it was obvious she enjoyed sex. Now, she would just be enjoying it with men who didn't have three-fuck rules and a bias against relationships.

Roman would have maybe rethought that rule if it'd been the right thing for Mila. But it wasn't. She really needed someone who had their shit together.

"Do you want me to be mad at you?" she asked.

The question threw Roman for a moment. The obvious answer was no, but she maybe should be mad at him. "I showed up at your door, practically barged my way in—"

"I'm not mad," she interrupted. "And I'm not going to be mad at you for that night. I knew exactly what I was doing and wouldn't have changed anything."

He would have changed that stupid note, but he kept that to himself because it was starting to feel petty that he was hanging on to it.

She walked closer, her eyes never breaking contact with his, and she smiled another of those small smiles. Before she leaned in and brushed her mouth over his.

Man, it felt as if a mule had kicked him.

The kiss slammed through him, and Roman might have caught on to her and pulled her to his lap if she hadn't backed away.

"There," she said. "That proves I'm not angry."

No, it only proved that this attraction between them had turned scalding hot. At least, it was scalding on his part.

"I did have a reason for coming here," Mila continued a moment later.

She took a deep breath. The kind of breath a person would take if they were about to say something they didn't want to say. He hoped like hell this wasn't some kind of goodbye and that she never wanted to see him again.

Mila took out her phone and handed it to him. "One of the kids from school sent me that about an hour ago," she explained.

Roman looked at the phone. Maybe this wouldn't be a photo of Tate doing something bad.

It wasn't.

It was a video. Not an especially clear one, but he

could see the row of lockers in the school. The very ones that Tate had been accused of vandalizing. He could also see someone spraying paint on them. Not Tate, though. Roman didn't know who it was until the sprayer started to run off.

"Chrissy," Mila provided.

Roman stopped the video, enlarged the frame where he could best see the girl's face. And yes, it was Chrissy, all right.

Shit.

"She probably won't be out of school yet," Mila explained, "but I heard from another student that she usually goes to the grocery store so her dad can drive her home."

He got up from the desk, hoping that Mila wouldn't try to stop him when he went to have a chat with this little witch. She didn't.

In fact, Mila took out her keys. "Come on. I'll drive."

"WHO SENT YOU that video?" Roman asked as they drove toward town.

Mila figured Roman was feeling plenty of anger, just like that night with Lick. Unlike that night, he wouldn't be able to punch Chrissy or curse at her, but he sure as heck could let the girl know that she was not going to get away with this.

"It's from the youngest of the Busby boys, Arnie," Mila answered. She had such a white-knuckled grip on the steering wheel that her hands were starting to ache. "He didn't want me to tell Chrissy, though, because he said she can be mean."

The girl must have been especially "mean" to cause

a Busby to say that because Arnie and his brothers were Wrangler's Creek's resident troublemakers.

"I figured we could show it to Waylon first," Mila continued, "and once he calms down, we can deal with this rationally."

She could hope, anyway.

Mercy, this was hard. And not just because she had to have a confrontation with the girl who might be her half sister, but it was hard because she was having to be with Roman and pretend that she wasn't unraveling inside.

It was as if he'd caught on to a single thread and just kept pulling.

No way would she tell him that, though, because despite what he'd said about not having regrets, she figured he had plenty. They were still friendly, but things would never be the same between them. And it had come at a time when she truly needed a friend. She couldn't go to Sophie because she had her hands full with the twins. Even her last-ditch sounding board, Vita, wasn't around.

"Hell," Roman grumbled, and he reached over from the passenger's seat and loosened her fingers on her left hand from the steering wheel. She'd been gripping way too tight. "I didn't think about Waylon being on your list. You don't have to do this. I can handle it myself."

Maybe. But since she could feel the anger coming off Roman, she didn't want him punching Waylon if things turned ugly.

"This isn't about me," she assured him. "It's about Tate. I'll deal with the list stuff later."

Mila hoped that sounded believable so that Roman wouldn't worry about her. She couldn't just tuck those feelings away in a neat little box. They would always be there right at the surface until she learned the truth. She was only hoping that the truth would lead her to Billy Lee and not Chrissy's father.

When Mila pulled into the parking lot of the grocery store, she immediately spotted someone she hadn't expected to see.

Tate.

"What's he doing here?" Roman mumbled as he got out.

"Arnie sent me a text, too," Tate explained. "He got worried that Mila might not try to fix this. I knew he was wrong, though. Mila wouldn't have just blown off something like this. She'd try to help."

Mila wasn't certain she could fix this, but she intended to do her best. She only wished that Arnie had held off on telling Tate because she would have preferred this initial confrontation to take place without him. Still, this situation had affected Tate more than anyone else so he deserved to be there. Roman must have felt the same way because he didn't stop Tate when he followed them inside.

There was no sign of Chrissy, but they got the attention of the cashier and the handful of customers. Mila tried to smile, just to defuse some of the gossip, but there'd be speculation no matter what she did.

Roman went to the back of the store, to the narrow hall in between dairy and meats, and he knocked on the door to Waylon's office. He didn't wait for the man to invite them in, though. Roman opened the door and went inside.

Mila thought that maybe Chrissy would already be there, but she wasn't. Waylon was alone, reading a magazine, and he scowled as he dropped it on his desk.

"I thought we said all there was to say when I visited you in San Antonio," Waylon grumbled.

This was the first she was hearing of a visit, but Mila guessed it was about Tate leaving Arwen and maybe Chrissy alone. Unless Waylon had gone to talk to Roman about possibly being her father. But no. If Waylon had done that, Roman would have mentioned it.

"Is there a problem?" someone asked from behind them.

It was Waylon's wife, Bernadette. Even though her age put her past the trophy wife stage, she was still an attractive woman with her auburn hair and green eyes.

"Is there a problem?" Waylon repeated to Roman. He didn't even acknowledge Tate or Mila.

Mila handed Roman her phone, and he in turn passed it to Waylon. "Hit Play," Roman instructed, "and you'll see your daughter spray painting some lockers at school. After she did that, someone—probably her—gave the principal a fake tip that Tate had done it."

"Arwen," Waylon spat out. Bernadette hurried to his side to look at the video.

"Chrissy," Roman corrected.

"No way in hell—" But Waylon stopped when he got to the point on the recording where he could see Chrissy's face. The muscles in his jaw started stirring. "This has been Photoshopped." Now, he looked at Tate. "Are you trying to get Chrissy in trouble?"

Tate shook his head. "I didn't Photoshop anything. Chrissy did this."

Waylon's grunt sounded as if he wasn't buying that, and he hit the delete key on the video. Smiling, he handed the phone back to Mila.

"Waylon!" Bernadette said on a gasp.

"It's a hoax," Waylon assured her. "And now there's no proof of it."

"No proof except Tate has a copy," Mila informed him. "Oh, and I put it on a storage cloud. One that's protected with a password. I thought that would be the easiest way to send copies to the principal and the school board."

She added that last part only because she wasn't sure if the principal and Waylon were friends. Mila didn't want this swept under the rug.

Waylon's eyes narrowed. "Why are you doing this?" Waylon asked Tate. "Is it because you want to get back at Chrissy after she rejected you?"

"Wait a sec," Roman said, holding up his hand. His phone rang, but he didn't even glance at the screen. He let the call go to voice mail. "When you came to my office in San Antonio, it was to warn me to keep Tate away from Arwen. You said she was *messed up*. You didn't mention Tate showing a bit of interest in Chrissy."

"And I don't have any interest in her," Tate quickly added. "She's not very nice. Or smart. The only thing she wants to talk about is makeup and music. She brags that she hasn't ever read a book."

Mila braced herself for Waylon to try to jump down Tate's throat. But Bernadette spoke before her husband could say anything.

"You told him that Arwen was messed up?" she asked Waylon.

"Yeah. Because she is, and you know it. Chrissy's the good girl, and that kid of yours somehow managed to put Chrissy up to this."

"I thought you believed it was Photoshopped?" Roman snapped.

If looks could kill… "If it's not, then Arwen's behind this. I'll tell Doug that, too, when and if you show him this piece of shit video."

Doug as in Doug Morgan, the high school principal. Mila had been right about them being friends. Or at least that's what Waylon wanted them to think, perhaps as a way of getting them to back down.

"Waylon," Bernadette said again, but this time there were tears in her eyes. It gave Mila hope that there was at least one person in Arwen's family who cared about her. "How could you do this?"

"How could I do it?" Waylon flung his hand in Mila's direction. "Ask her why she's really doing this, why she's going after Chrissy."

Bernadette looked at her as if expecting an answer. But Mila didn't have one. Until it hit her.

Was this about her paternity list?

"What are you talking about?" Bernadette asked her husband.

"I'm talking about her making waves," Waylon snapped. "Trying to find her daddy."

It *was* about the list, and Mila was so shocked that she couldn't speak. Roman took hold of her arm, moving her slightly behind him. Maybe trying to protect her, but Mila didn't want protection. She wanted the truth, and since Waylon had brought it up, she wasn't going to hold back.

"Are you my biological father?" she came out and asked. But the moment the words left her mouth, she regretted them. She shouldn't have dug all of this up in front of Tate.

Judging from Bernadette's gasp, she hadn't heard the

gossip that her husband obviously had. Though Mila had no idea anyone was gossiping about it until now.

"Are you?" Bernadette asked him.

Waylon leaned back in his chair, shrugged. However, it was an angry shrug. "Could be. But if you're waiting for me to do a DNA test or welcome you with open arms, that's not gonna happen. *Ever.* I won't do a test because it doesn't matter. Even if you are a product of that night, you're not my daughter any more than Arwen is."

Mila hadn't expected Waylon to pull any punches. And he hadn't. She also hadn't expected him to admit possible paternity or say that it didn't matter. Mila wasn't the only one stunned in the room, though. Bernadette had serious tears in her eyes now, and shaking her head, she ran out.

Mila figured Waylon was waiting for her to do the same, but she actually had a functioning brain and spine. "I'm sorry," Mila said first to Tate, then she repeated it to Roman while she downloaded the video from storage. "And I'm sorry that you're a worthless human being," she added to Waylon.

He got to his feet, but she ignored him for the time being so she could send it out to every one of her contacts. Then she loaded it on YouTube.

Tate smiled. "Guess you won't have to bother sending it to the principal now. He'll see it soon enough."

"See what?" Waylon howled. "What did you do?"

Probably something she would regret later, but Mila didn't regret it now. It felt damn good. "Google 'Waylon Beaumont's daughter doing her dad proud,'" she told him, and then walked out.

Waylon cursed her so Mila hurried. No way did she

want Tate to hear that. But she soon realized Roman wasn't following them.

Heck.

She didn't want Roman punching this idiot, and that's exactly what it looked as if he might do. She needed to do something drastic again, and this time she hoped it wasn't something she would regret.

"Roman, I'm in love with you," she said to him. "Now, please, let's go."

Roman stopped moving toward Waylon, and even Waylon froze. The only saving grace in this was that Tate was out of earshot. At least, she hoped he was. Thankfully, it stunned Roman enough that it gave Mila time to take hold of his arm and get him moving.

"I really hope you didn't want to keep that video a secret," she said, her voice shaking. Actually, she was shaking, too.

"To hell with the video. What did you just say?" Roman demanded.

"I said I was in love with you. Now, put it on the back burner, and let's make sure Tate's okay." She didn't wait for him to agree. Mila hurried toward the front door where Tate was walking out.

"I'm so sorry," Tate said. He wasn't crying, but it appeared that could happen at any second. Since she doubted he would want anyone to witness that, Mila took him to her car and had him get in the backseat. Roman was right behind them.

Roman looked at her the moment he got in. "Did you say that so I wouldn't punch Waylon?"

She ignored his question and tipped her head to Tate. That got Roman turning around to have a harder look at his son.

"It's all right," he said to Tate. "None of this was your fault."

"But it was. Mila was here because of me, and Mr. Butthead was mean to her."

Roman probably considered telling Tate that it wasn't a good thing to call someone a name like that, but since Waylon was clearly a butthead, he let it pass.

"Is he really your dad?" Tate asked her.

"Possibly." Of course, that meant she'd just confessed her mother's sexual escapades, but it was better for him to hear it from her than from someone else. "But as he said, it doesn't matter. I had a father. A good one. And I don't need another one."

Roman glanced at her as if trying to decide if that was true. Part of it was. She didn't need another father like Waylon, anyway, but she was still holding out hope for Billy Lee.

"We should go to the school and show the video to Principal Morgan," Mila suggested. Though Waylon was almost certainly on the phone with the man to put his own spin on the situation. Hard to spin the truth, though, when it was right in someone's face.

"I can do it," Roman said. "You should probably go home and have a drink or something." He took her hand and lifted it to show her how much she was trembling.

She nodded because he was right. Besides, Roman was Tate's father, and he should be the one handling this.

Roman got out, went to the driver's side and motioned for her to move to the passenger's seat. She did because she really didn't want to drive while her nerves were unsteady.

"I'll drop you off at your house," he said. "Then Tate

and I can go to the school. When we're done, I'll have someone from the ranch pick us up and bring you back your car." He paused. "Maybe later we can talk."

He meant talk about the *I'm in love with you*. It wasn't something Mila especially wanted to discuss, but maybe by the time Roman had finished with the principal, she would figure out what to say to him.

It would possibly involve a lie or two.

Roman had barely made it out of the parking lot when there were dinging sounds on both Roman's and her phones. They'd both gotten a text message only a few moments apart. Probably some kind of threat from Waylon.

Mila looked at the screen almost afraid of what she might see. But it wasn't from Waylon.

It was from Belle.

"Tired to cell roaming but no answer so am testing," she read aloud.

"Tried to call Roman but no answer so I'm texting," Roman interpreted. "Mom's not good at texts." He pulled over and took out his own phone. "She sent me the same message."

He stopped, froze, and Mila knew why. It was because he read the rest of what Belle had messaged.

I decided to have sax with Billy Lee so were on the way to Vegas now to get merry. See you tomorrow.

CHAPTER EIGHTEEN

Normally, a hard ride into the pastures helped Roman clear his head. But not this time. Of course, that was asking a lot out of a ride because there was way too much in his head to clear.

He didn't even want to think of his mother just yet. Maybe she truly had meant *merry* and not *marry*, but even if she hadn't, that wasn't his rodeo. Billy Lee was a decent guy, and even if Belle was rushing into this, it wouldn't be a big mistake.

Unlike the one Roman had made with Mila.

He'd known right from the start it hadn't been a good idea for him to have sex with her, and now she might have fallen in love with him. Or not. Truth was, he wasn't sure what was going on in Mila's head and that was one of the reasons he'd saddled up and gone all the way to the back pasture. He would have stayed out there longer, too, if it hadn't been getting dark.

Roman led the horse into the barn, automatically glancing at the windows of Tate's bedroom. The lights were on, and Tate might be doing the homework he said he had. It was just as likely, though, that he was moping—much the way Roman was doing. Unlike him, though, Tate had managed to get that whole locker/vandalism thing straight.

But not without some pushing from Roman.

At first, Principal Morgan had pretty much spouted

what Waylon had said—that the video could be Photo-shopped, but then Arnie Busby had manned up, called the principal and told him that he'd recorded it.

Morgan hadn't wanted to believe it, Roman could tell, but in the end the principal's friendship with Waylon hadn't overshadowed the fact that Chrissy had committed a malicious act for the sole purpose of getting Tate in trouble. Principal Morgan had suspended Chrissy for three days, told her to pay for damages and write an apology to Tate. She might write it, all right, but Roman figured that the only thing she'd truly be sorry about was that she got caught.

Perhaps this would be the end of it, and Chrissy would steer clear of Tate. And even if she didn't, there were only another two weeks of school. After that, Tate might never have to see the girl again.

Might.

Tate was already asking if he could stay the summer. That was another thing that had prompted Roman's ride. He wasn't sure what the hell he was going to do about that. And speaking of things he was uncertain about— one of them walked into the barn.

Mila.

"I got your text reminder about wanting to talk to me," she greeted him.

He had indeed sent her a text. Not one that could be vaguely interpreted like his mother's. Roman had made this one pretty clear.

We need to talk, he'd texted.

And here she was.

She wasn't wearing her usual jeans but rather a white summer dress and sandals. His stomach did that flip-flop thing that it'd been doing around her lately, but this time there was more flop than flip. That's because Roman didn't think she'd gotten dressed up to come to the barn to chat to him.

"You have a date?" he asked.

She shrugged. "I'm meeting someone just for a drink at the Longhorn. He's a bull rider from San Antonio."

Roman automatically scowled and not because he was jealous. It was because most bull riders were half crazy. The others were all the way crazy. "Anyone I know?" As a rodeo promoter, he knew plenty of them.

"Caleb Armstrong."

Yeah, he knew him, all right, and Caleb was a decent guy. That was good. So, why didn't it feel *good*?

"Those dating sites work fast," he commented.

She shook her head. "Sophie set this one up for me. Caleb and Clay are friends, and since Caleb was in town to see the twins, Sophie thought I should meet him."

Sophie? Apparently, his sister didn't have her hands as full with the twins as he'd thought if she was playing matchmaker. And why the hell was Sophie doing that, anyway?

For that matter, why was Mila letting her?

He finished brushing down the horse and led her into a stall while Mila walked into the barn. Clearly, she had something on her mind and wanted to talk before her "date." Well, Roman had something on his mind, too.

"You said you were in love with me," he threw out there. "But since you're doing this—" he motioned toward her clothes "—then that must have been a ploy to keep me from punching Waylon."

She nodded. "In part."

Roman huffed and put his hands on his hips when she didn't add more to that. "In part?" he repeated.

"Because being a little bit in love is like being a little bit pregnant."

"Yes," she admitted. Mila huffed, too. "Look, neither one of us want me to be feeling what I feel for you, and I'm not stupid. I know when to cut my losses and move on. This drink with Caleb is about moving on. That way, you won't feel guilty for what happened between us."

Hell. That actually made sense. Well, it made sense for Mila. She was a nice person who wanted to do the right thing by him. Even if it might not be the right thing for her.

"You're going out with Caleb to make me feel better," he grumbled.

Since he suddenly needed a drink, he went into the tack room and came out with two beers he took from the fridge. Garrett didn't normally keep anything but water in there, but Roman had added the beer since he liked to have one after he finished a ride. He twisted off the tops, handed Mila one and then had a long drink from his bottle.

She looked at the beer, then at him, and for a moment Roman thought she was going to refuse, but she finally had a sip. Then made a face.

"Sorry," he said, leaning against the barn wall. "I don't have any of the Irish cream stuff."

"It's okay. I don't want to drink too much, anyway."

No. Because she might be planning on doing that with her date.

Roman cursed himself for wanting to ask her to cancel that date. Then he cursed himself for wanting her. It would definitely be sending the wrong message if he kissed her again.

"How's Tate?" she asked.

"Better." At least he thought that was true. "He asked if we could stay here for the summer."

"Is that possible? I mean, with your job?"

"It's doable." After all, Sophie ran Granger Western from the ranch, and that business was in Austin. San Antonio wasn't as far from the ranch as Austin was. "But I'm not sure this is the best place for him. I doubt Chrissy is going to turn angelic, and that means future run-ins with her."

She made a sound of agreement, had another sip of beer and walked closer. Not over to him exactly, but just a few feet where she sank down onto some stacked hay bales.

"Of course, there are Chrissys everywhere," she said.

It was true. That still wasn't a reason to stay. Three more months here would feel a little like putting down roots. Something Roman wasn't sure he could do even if things were better with his mom.

"There are Waylons everywhere, too," he pointed out. "Anything on Billy Lee's DNA test yet?"

"He hasn't called, but I'm sure it's back by now. That probably means he doesn't want to tell me that it's not a match."

Yeah, it probably did mean that, and when Mila took the next sip of beer, he got a good look at her eyes in the dim light. This was eating away at her.

"Part of me wishes my mom had never told me," she added. "And she did warn me that it would mess up my birth father's life if he found out about me. What she didn't say was that it would mess up mine, too."

Hell. It was a dangerous thing to do, but he went to her, sank down and put his arm around her. "This might be one of those things that you just have to accept and move on. If Waylon's your father, he's an asshole. Nothing you can do about that."

"Your father was an asshole, and you left," she pointed out.

True. He couldn't deny that. "But I was getting double-whammied from both my mother and him." Except he had to rethink that. "At least my father didn't harp on me to marry Valerie the way my mother did."

"I'll bet Belle doesn't feel that way after the stunt Valerie pulled by leaving." Now, Mila made a sound as if she were rethinking that. "She does know people can have sex without being married, doesn't she?"

"She knows it, but she doesn't believe in it." Which probably meant she was a married woman by now. Roman didn't mind that part, but he didn't want the image in his head of Billy Lee and Belle having sex so he pushed it aside.

Pushed it aside and looked at Mila.

At the same moment, she looked at him.

And their eyes locked.

There it was again. That slippery slope of attraction. It was coupled with the worry over her dad situation. Coupled, too, with more worry about Tate. Maybe even him. Not a good combination because it made Roman want to do something to ease that look in her eyes.

Mila pressed the backs of her fingers and part of the beer bottle against his mouth, and that's when Roman realized he was moving in on her. In fact, he'd been just a very short distance from kissing her.

"If you kiss me," she said, "I don't want it to be because you're feeling sorry for me right now."

Since that was a part of it—a small part—he pulled back.

"If you kiss me," Mila went on, "I want it to be for one reason. Because it's what you really want to do."

Oh, he really wanted to do it, all right, but that was because of the slippery slope stuff. And because his dick was suddenly in on this. He didn't just want to kiss her. He suddenly wanted a lot more.

"Another thing," she said. "Do you honestly intend to stop with just a kiss?"

No, he didn't, and even though he didn't say that aloud, Mila nodded in agreement.

"There's one more time on my three-rule," he reminded her. "But then, you have that drink date with Caleb. It hardly seems right to have sex with me and then meet him."

"Good point." She stood, handed him her beer, and Roman thought that was it, that she was about to walk off.

But instead she took her phone from her pocket and fired off a text.

"The date's canceled." She put her phone back in her dress pocket, and in the same motion Mila leaned down and kissed him.

"It's our last time together like this," she added. "So, let's make it count."

MILA REFUSED TO regret this even though she had come to see Roman to tell him that she had to do a better job of guarding her heart. But heart-guarding would apparently have to wait a little while longer.

Maybe sex would, too.

She'd gotten so caught up in seeing Roman—specifically, his unbuttoned shirt, damp hair and those scorching eyes—that Mila had forgotten they were in a barn where one of the hands, Alice or a family member could come walking in. There were barn doors, of course, but no way to lock them from the inside.

"Sorry," she said. "I didn't think about the logistics of this."

Apparently, Roman had, though. He put the beers on the ground, pulled her out of the open doorway and against the barn wall. And he kissed her. It was one of those kisses that matched the look in his eyes.

Scorching.

And it generated enough heat to light up a small country. It certainly lit her up and rid her of plenty of doubts that this wasn't doable.

Yes, it was doable. Mila just didn't know how. After a few more kisses, she didn't care how as long as it happened.

Roman had a special way of keeping the uncertainties out of her head. He pressed his body against hers, aligning his erection with the notch of her thighs, and he kept kissing her. Wonderful, delicious pressure that she was sorry she had lived so long without. But what really sealed the no-doubts was when he shoved up her dress and slid his hand over the front of her panties.

Yep, no more doubts.

Mila had even forgotten about them being in a place where someone could walk in and see them, but again Roman fixed that. Without breaking the kiss, he hooked his arm around her waist, lifting her, and he carried her into the tack room, which was only a few steps away. He got her inside, used his elbow to shut the door, and then he pinned her against the back of it.

"No lock," he said.

It took a moment for it to register that if they were against the door, then no one could just come walking in. It took that moment to register because his hand went under her dress again, and this time he didn't touch the front of her panties. Those clever fingers went into them.

Then into her.

He touched her. Kissed her. And he touched some more.

Mila got so caught up in all the kissing and touching, but she soon figured out that this was about to come to a quick end for her. That might be Roman's intentions.

Sex without actually having sex.

He'd already done that to her once, and it had become like a first strike in his three-strike rule. She didn't want half sex to count as a whole so she caught on to his hand, pushed it aside and turned him so that he was pinned against the back of the door.

The room was darker than the barn, the only illumination coming from the clock on a small microwave that was sitting on an equally small fridge, so it took Mila's eyes a couple of seconds to adjust. That meant a short delay in her seeing Roman's reaction to what she'd done. The corner of his mouth lifted into a smile.

She fixed that by kissing him. Not that she minded him smiling, but he had a hot smile, and she was already primed and ready to go. Best not to add anything to the mix if she wanted even a short amount of foreplay.

Which she did.

If this was going to be her last time with Roman, she wanted to savor it a little. Mila wanted to be able to look back on these memories and think about how perfect it had been.

But it wasn't perfect.

The door was rough wood, and when she went to put her hands on his butt, Mila was certain she got a splinter. It seemed a small price to pay, though, and she especially felt that way when his kisses returned to her mouth. She didn't give up on her butt-grabbing quest, but it did slow her down a little.

Yes, this was what she wanted from him. That slow, dreamy feeling of pleasure sliding through her body. The kisses that could dissolve industrial-grade steel. His left hand, moving over her breasts while his right hand pushed her dress the rest of the way up. Roman didn't stop with the dress pushing, either. He slid down her panties and used his foot to push them the rest of the way off.

"Sorry about this," he said, unzipping his jeans. "You deserve better."

There wasn't anything better than her getting Roman, but she nearly asked him about how they were going to make this happen. The answer to that, though, suddenly became very clear. He lifted her until her thighs and knees were anchored against his hips. They shifted positions again so that her back was against the door.

He put his hand between them again, and since she wasn't wearing her panties now, she had no trouble feeling his fingers.

"I don't want a hand job," she managed to say.

"Good. Because you're not getting one. You're getting me."

That's when she figured out what he was doing down there. He was putting on a condom that he'd taken from his wallet. The wallet was now on the floor, along with the condom wrapper.

Mila was so thankful that her eyes had finally adjusted to the darkness because she was able to see Roman's face when he pushed into her. Of course, she only

got a glimpse of him because that push blurred her vision and thinned her breath enough that she felt ready
to pass out. She didn't care if she did.

As long as she had an orgasm first.

Roman worked hard to make sure that orgasm happened, too. He held her in place, making all the right
moves in exactly the right spot. He certainly knew what
he was doing. Maybe that's why after only a few of
those maddening strokes, Mila was ready to let everything shatter into gold sparkles again.

Still, she tried to hang on, tried to make this last, and
she did that by cataloging as much as she could. That
warrior look on his hot cowboy face. His hard muscles
that made her own body feel soft. The taste of him when
he kissed her. All of that rolled into one perfect ball of
memories that she would have to make last a lifetime.

Because this was number three.

And Mila struck out with an orgasm that shuddered
through her from head to toe. All in all, not a bad way
to finish. So, she helped him finish, too. She pushed her
hips against him, taking him deep inside all that shud-
dering. She kissed him, and with her mouth against his,
Roman said the only thing she wanted to hear.

Mila.

She held on to the sound of her name for a few seconds until Roman added one more word. A word that
didn't sound as needy or romantic as when he'd said
her name.

Fuck.

ROMAN COULDN'T BELIEVE he'd used his last shot with
Mila on a door-fuck. Really? He wanted to hit his head
against the wall.

"This should have been wine and roses," he mumbled. He maneuvered her to a standing position, which made it much easier for him to see her expression.

Her left eyebrow was raised. "I'd rather have a climax than wine or roses," she informed him.

He kissed her because he was thankful that she wasn't pissed, and he made a quick pit stop in the small adjoining bathroom. Actually, it was just a toilet and a tiny sink, but it was enough for him so he wouldn't have to return to the tack room with his dick hanging out.

However, Mila's butt was hanging out when he returned.

She had located her panties and had hiked up her dress to put them on, but she was hobbling around, trying to keep her balance. He went to her and helped even though it went against every grain of his manhood to help her cover up that great ass. The front of her body wasn't so bad, either.

"You deserved wine, roses *and* a climax," he told her, and because he needed it, Roman kissed her.

It put a knot in his stomach to realize that might be the last real kiss they ever shared. He couldn't risk another because kissing with Mila led to sex. No way around that so he stepped back.

She stared at him, not smiling exactly but not looking as if she'd been disappointed by this. He was. And worse, Roman was starting to think that maybe that first time they were together hadn't counted.

But it did.

There were reasons he'd come up with that rule, and the reasons were still there. Even if he wanted a relationship, he didn't have time for one because it would take his attention away from Tate. Right now, Tate needed a lot of attention.

"Am I going to have to say something shocking or inappropriate to get that cranky look off your face?" she asked.

"I always look cranky." He paused. "What would you consider inappropriate?" Because if it was sexual…no, best not to go there. He waved it off.

"I have an idea." Now, she smiled. "Want to go on a fantasy date with me? No sex allowed. I've always wanted to do a spanking scene but not a hard one like in *Fifty Shades of Grey*." This time she was the one who waved it off. "Any kind of spanking like that usually leads to sex."

Yes, he'd been there, done that, and while he wasn't a fan of spanking, the idea certainly seemed appealing. Maybe because he'd just seen Mila's bare butt. But she was right. That would lead to sex.

"How about the sign scene in *Love Actually*?" she asked. "It's just a little kiss at the end."

He'd seen the movie and knew what she was talking about. "Kissing is still kissing." And he doubted they'd keep it *little*.

She nodded. "We should probably go with something G-rated. I'll give it some more thought. You, too, and we could plan it for the day after Tate finishes school. That way, if you decide to head back to San Antonio, it wouldn't interfere with your plans."

Roman was about to tell her that he didn't think a date, even a sex-less one, was a good idea, but Mila was clearly ready to leave. She threw open the door, but she only made it a few steps into the barn before she froze.

Hell.

Was Tate out there? Or had Mila's drink date come to the ranch looking for her? But it wasn't either of them. Or Garrett or one of the hands. Roman hurried out to see someone he hadn't expected to see.

Vita.

Mila's mom was standing just outside the barn door, and she shifted her gaze to each of them. "If you're done having sex," Vita said. "It's time for us to talk."

CHAPTER NINETEEN

EVEN THOUGH MILA was pretty sure her clothes were all fixed and in the right place, she checked to make sure. But her mom probably hadn't guessed about the sex because of Mila's clothes being askew. No, Vita had likely figured that out because there weren't many reasons she would have been in the tack room with Roman.

Plus, Roman did look a little askew. His shirt was still unbuttoned, and he seemed ready to dig a hole and crawl in it. Mila doubted he'd wanted anyone, especially her mother, to know about their temporary relationship. One that might not have ended just yet if Mila could talk him into one last fantasy date. But for now, it was obvious she was going to have to have a different kind of conversation.

"When did you get back?" she asked her mother.

"About an hour ago. I came here looking for you. Sensed you'd be here," she added. "And I knew you'd want to talk about the letter I sent you. About your father, as well."

Oh, yes. Mila definitely wanted to discuss that but not here. Apparently, her mother and she were of a like mind on this.

"I thought we could sit in the sunroom," Vita suggested. "You, too," she added to Roman. "Because there are some things you need to hear, as well. Things you're not gonna like much, but I had my reasons for doing what I did."

Roman and she both groaned. It was never a good thing when her mother said something like that. Actually, Vita rarely said anything that made people feel good. Mila figured this time would be no different, especially since there was the hot topic of her biological father.

"First of all, I'm sorry things are over," Vita said, making her way up the steps. "I had hopes you two would get together, but sometimes hopes are like a thimble of spit—yucky and useless."

Mila frowned. She didn't like having her time with Roman compared to spit. It'd been wonderful. Life-changing. But Vita was right. It hadn't worked out. Roman had gotten that shell-shocked look in his eyes only seconds after the orgasm had worn off. If Mila was a betting woman, she would wager he was getting ready to run. The only reason he hadn't already was because of Tate.

And speaking of Tate, Mila checked the area surrounding the sunroom to make sure neither he nor Alice were around to hear any of this. She definitely didn't want him to know that his father and she had become temporary lovers.

Mila had been so concerned about looking for Tate that she hadn't noticed Roman's expression. That's because he'd been behind her when they'd walked up the steps, but now that they were inside, she could see he was scowling. Not an unusual expression for him, but he wasn't scowling at her mother. He seemed to be aiming his expression at everything in general.

"How'd you know anything had even started between Mila and me?" Roman asked.

Vita made an isn't-it-obvious sound and sank down into one of the white wicker rocking chairs. She motioned for them to sit, as well, and that's when Mila noticed both her mom's suitcase and a cup of half-finished tea. Apparently, she'd been here at least a little while before she'd gone out to the barn. Mila hoped Roman and she hadn't made sex noises and that's what had clued Vita into what was going on.

"Sometimes, sex can clear the head," her mother went on. "It doesn't appear that happened with you two but never mind. You'll be able to figure this all out whether your mind is clear or not."

Mila definitely wanted to switch subjects. "Is this about my birth father?"

"It is."

"Why didn't you tell me sooner?" Mila demanded when her mother didn't add more. "Why wait thirty-one years?"

"The tea leaves." Maybe it was Mila's narrowed eyes that prompted Vita to add more than that. "And I figured you should know the truth before you settled down and started your own family."

Those reasons might make sense to Vita, but they didn't to Mila. "You should have told me. Not in a letter, either. You should have told me face-to-face."

"It wouldn't have helped. You would have still been mad, still would have had to work out all of this on your own, and I knew it would complicate things if you found out the truth. And it did, right?"

Mila threw her hands in the air and took the love

seat across from Vita. "It might complicate things if I knew for sure. I don't. Billy Lee took a paternity test—"

"It's not him," Vita interrupted.

The emotions hit Mila a lot harder than she thought they would—especially since she'd already suspected he wasn't the one.

Roman sat on the love seat beside her. "Are you okay?" he asked, slipping his hand over hers.

She nodded, looked at her mother, waiting for more. Much, much more. Mila wanted an explanation as to why Vita hadn't told her this in that letter, and then she wanted to know the identity of the man whose DNA she had.

Vita took a moment before she continued. "It's too bad, though, that it's not Billy Lee because now that he's eloped with Belle, it might tie things together nicely."

"How did you know they'd eloped?" Judging from Roman's tone, he wasn't very happy with her mother right now. Neither was Mila. "ESP?"

Vita gave him a flat look. "Alice. She told me when she was fixing me some tea. She said Belle sounded happy. That's good. There needs to be at least one person around here who's happy."

"I might be happy if you hadn't sprung that bombshell on me with a letter," Mila told her. "What you did wasn't right."

"No," Vita quietly agreed. She dragged in a long breath. "I did have sex with Billy Lee, but it was just sex."

Mila so didn't want to hear about her mother's love life, even if it might be pertinent to the discussion. "Skip the parts about Billy Lee and tell me about who did get you pregnant."

"You know." Vita looked her straight in the eye. "And I did try to warn you about him. Waylon will never admit it, though I did go to him and I told him I was carrying you. He said he didn't even remember us being together, that he was too drunk."

For the first time in her entire life, Mila thought she might have seen the beginnings of tears in her mother's eyes, but Vita quickly looked away.

"I know this is hard, but he'll never be your father," Vita added.

That wasn't hard at all. Waylon wouldn't be. He was a jerk and didn't deserve a moment of her time. Too bad that she couldn't stop thinking about him.

And that led Mila back to sex.

This probably wasn't a can of worms she wanted to open, but she had to know. Roman beat her to it, though.

"What possessed you to be with an asshole like that?" Roman asked her mother.

"Sex," Vita readily answered. She sighed, and there were no more threatening tears. She even gave a wistful smile. "I used to enjoy it in those days, and I was young and single."

Mila had hoped there might be something deeper. Something like love. After all, Waylon had been married twice so there had to be something lovable about him.

"I was only with him two times," Vita went on. "He had this stupid two-time rule in those days. Twice with a woman and then nada." She used her hand to make a cutting motion across her neck.

Because Roman still had hold of Mila's hand, she felt him go a little stiff. "You have nothing in common with that man," she assured him. Maybe it's because she was punchy from the recent orgasm and her mother's arrival, but Mila had to laugh and then she turned to Roman. "My stepsister, Arwen, and your son have a thing for each other."

She wasn't sure why she found that amusing because clearly Roman didn't. Maybe because he saw the pain behind her attempt at humor. He leaned in and despite the fact her mother was sitting there, he brushed a kiss on Mila's mouth.

"Oh, no," Vita said, getting their attention.

Both Mila and Roman looked at her. "Oh, no?" Mila repeated.

"I really thought it'd be over between Roman and you by now." Vita stood. "That's what was in the tea leaves, anyway. That you'd be together three times and that it'd be over."

Mila wasn't sure how to respond so she went with the simple answer. "Roman and I aren't *together.*"

"Whew." Like her mother's teary eyes, Mila had never seen that much relief on Vita's face. It was definitely a night for firsts.

"Why are you whewing?" Roman snapped. He obviously knew this wasn't going to work in their favor.

"That's what I wanted to talk to you about," Vita said as if the answer was obvious. It wasn't. Roman and Mila just gave her blank stares.

"Valerie," Vita finally answered. "I've talked her into coming back to Wrangler's Creek. She's inside right now. Valerie's here to try to make a go of it with Roman and Tate."

ROMAN SURE DIDN'T thank Vita. In fact, he wanted to tell her to mind her own business while punctuating it with a whole bunch of cussing. But he didn't have time for that. If Valerie was really inside with Tate, then he had to get to them before she caused any more damage.

That damage was especially possible if she'd brought that idiot boyfriend with her.

"You shouldn't have done this," he warned Vita before he went inside. Mila was saying something similar to her mother, and she was also adding the curse words. Vita had overstepped her boundaries in a huge, shit-kicking way.

Roman ran through the house, looking for Valerie, Lick and Tate, and he soon found two of them. Valerie was sitting on the foot of Tate's bed. Tate had his back against the headboard, and even though she was talking to him, his attention was on a book that was in his lap.

No Lick, thank God, but that didn't mean he wasn't there somewhere in his pussy shorts and with his bad attitude.

"Roman," Valerie said. She stood, rubbing her hands along the sides of her jeans.

Since he didn't want to curse in front of Tate, Roman gave her a glare that he hoped conveyed his feelings. That's when he saw the bruise around her left eye. It had makeup caked over it, but it was still visible. Like Tate, she suddenly got very interested in not making eye contact with him.

"Lick and I are over," she added.

Roman was relieved about that because it meant the clown wasn't here. But that didn't mean he wouldn't show up. Valerie was a turd magnet, and Lick was a first-class turd.

"Tate, are you okay?" Roman asked him.

Tate nodded but didn't spare him a glance. That told

him his son probably wasn't okay at all, that he was conflicted about his mom's visit. Roman wasn't conflicted, though. Plain and simple, he didn't want Valerie there.

"We need to talk," Roman told her. He motioned for her to follow him. Valerie did, but only after she gave Tate a hug.

"Why the hell are you here?" Roman demanded the moment they were out of Tate's room and at the end of the hall. He kept his voice as low as he could manage, but there was no way he would take out the anger.

"Vita." Valerie sighed, pushed her hair from her face. "She found me, somehow." She stopped, looked up at him. "You think she really does have ESP?"

"No. I think she has decent Google-search skills. Your boyfriend started posting trash reviews of my business. Trash talk about me, too, on social media. And no, I didn't find it. One of my business associates did. Lick allowed his location on the posts. It's not hard to find someone in a New Mexico town that only has three hundred people."

"Oh, Roman. I'm so sorry." She sounded genuine. And surprised that her nutjob boyfriend had done something like that. "Did it hurt your business?"

He nearly said yes just to make her feel bad, but the feeling bad part had already been accomplished. Well, unless this was all an act. But acting wasn't Valerie's style. Especially acting so that somebody would have sympathy for her. She usually preferred to shock people with her god-awful behavior.

"My business is fine." Booming, in fact, thanks to some of Garrett's connections, but he wasn't going to get into that, either. Not when there was something much more important to discuss. But Valerie spoke first.

"I learned my lesson with Lick," she said. She touched her fingers to the bruise. "He did this to me."

"Yeah, I didn't figure you were going for the raccoon look with one eye." Roman instantly regretted that. Old habits when it came to Valerie. They'd fought and slung barbs for so long that he wasn't even sure how to do something as simple as have a normal conversation with her.

When he continued, Roman tried to tamp down that anger in his voice. "I don't want you here messing with Tate's head again. Every time you pull one of your stunts, he's the one who gets hurt."

"I know. Vita made me see that. She's crazy, but sometimes she makes sense."

The anger returned. "And sometimes she sticks her nose where it doesn't belong. She shouldn't have gone to you and talked you into coming here. And there's no way she should have talked you into trying to get back together with me."

Valerie's eyes widened, causing that bruise to look even bigger. "I'm not here for that. I'm here for Tate." She shook her head and cursed. "You think Vita's matchmaking?"

Maybe.

But there was a more obvious reason that occurred to Roman. This could be Vita's way of making sure he didn't end up with Mila. Vita could be just trying to protect her daughter from getting involved with a guy like him. He wasn't a turd like Lick, but he wasn't exactly husband material, either.

"Honestly, I only came here for Tate," Valerie went on. "I want to go to that therapy session with him and try to fix things. Not with you. I think we both know we're not good together."

He did know that, and he was glad Valerie did, too, but that didn't mean everything was hunky-dory here. "I don't want you doing something to make this worse for Tate," he spelled out for her.

Roman expected her to get defensive. She didn't. Valerie nodded. "I'll try very hard to help him."

It was the right thing to say, but none of this felt right. Not only because he was worried about how this would affect Tate but also because of what Vita had said to Mila and him in the sunroom.

Valerie's here to try to make a go of it with Roman and Tate.

Mila might think that was what should happen. Vita might even be able to convince her that it was the time to back off so that Tate, Valerie and he could have a shot at being a family. Vita was wrong. There was no shot at it. But Mila might not know that.

"Mila?" Valerie said.

Roman shook his head. "What about her?"

"Uh, you just said her name."

Hell, now the thoughts were leaking out of his mind and finding their way to his mouth. "She's in the sun-room," he explained. Which, of course, didn't explain much. "I need to see her for just a minute."

He didn't wait for Valerie's approval. Didn't need or want it. But he wouldn't stay with Mila for long since he didn't want Valerie spending too much time with Tate unless he was there.

Roman hurried back to the sunroom, and when he saw the empty love seat, his stomach twisted a little. Vita, however, was still there.

"She went home," Vita said, looking over her shoulder at him. She stood, faced him. "Now, you've got to decide if you've hurt my daughter enough or if you're man enough to let her go."

How did that make you feel?

Dr. Woodliff had said that so many times that it just came to Tate's mind whether the doctor said the actual words or not. Usually Tate hated the question because it made him think of things he didn't like thinking about. But today, the doctor was asking that just as much of his mom as he was Tate.

And his mom was answering, too.

Just as his dad had done in the sessions the doctor had had with Tate and him. His dad hadn't liked the question much, Tate could tell, and it seemed to make his mom jittery or something. That probably wouldn't get better if they did what the doctor wanted and had a session with all three of them. Tate figured there'd be some yelling during that therapy.

"It made me feel like shit," she said. "Like crap," she corrected, maybe because the doctor had already told her it wasn't a good idea to cuss in front of her son. "I knew it was wrong to leave town when Tate was a baby, but my head wasn't in a good place then."

She probably didn't know it, but it wasn't hard for Tate to see that. Because the couple of times he'd seen her, she'd been kind of messed up. Not like the potheads but more like it was her usual way of thinking and acting. Tate figured it was much easier to fix a pothead because all they had to do was quit smoking. But it was harder for his mom because it was going to take more than just not lighting up.

Sometimes, he was afraid she might never find a way to fix it.

Even with the doctor's help.

"I felt crappy for a long time," Valerie went on, "but I always loved my son. Always." She patted Tate's hand and smiled.

He liked having her smile at him, even though the smile never quite made it to her eyes. She was like one of those nurses who was looking at a really sick person in a hospital bed and wanted him to feel good even when he couldn't. Tate figured he must be pretty bad for her to look at him that way.

"I want to be a good mother," she continued, "but I don't think like most moms. I mean, I get bored. Not that Tate's boring," she quickly added. "He's not. It's just it gets boring here. It's hard for me to be in one place because my mind is always racing. I feel if I don't move or go somewhere that I'll explode."

"And how do you feel about that?" the doctor repeated, but this time he said it to Tate.

Tate thought he could understand that. There had been times when he'd felt like exploding, too, but it hadn't come from staying in one place too long. It had been when he thought about how much his mom must hate him. He didn't say that, though, because it really wouldn't make her eyes smile. He couldn't say it to his dad, either, because it would piss him off.

So, Tate just shrugged.

The doctor's mouth tightened a little because he wanted Tate to answer with words, but sometimes a shrug said it all. It made him feel shitty, and there was nothing he could do about it.

"I don't want Tate punished because I'm a crappy

mom," she went on. She looked at him. "And I don't want you taking any more pills."

This time a shrug wasn't going to be enough. "I won't." It was true. Even those times when he was feeling lower than the grass beneath cow shit, he wouldn't try to off himself.

Arwen had helped him see that.

She'd told him that doing stuff like that only hurt the people you didn't want hurt. Like his dad, Mila, his grandma, aunt and uncle. And him, of course. It didn't hurt his mother. Not really. It just made her feel bad that she couldn't be the mom he wanted her to be. The only thing it changed was that people were looking at him with those nonsmiling eyes.

"Tate is working through his feelings," the doctor told his mom. "Of course, part of those feelings is his anger at you."

Tate nearly shook his head and corrected Dr. Woodliff. It wasn't anger. Anger was what his dad felt. It made him grouchy, and that's when he cursed a lot.

"Anger can be expressed in many ways," the doctor explained. Maybe because he was a head doctor—as Grandma Belle had called him—he could see that Tate hadn't agreed with the anger stuff.

"He took those pills because he was angry at me?" his mom asked. Shit. Now, she was looking all sad, as if she might cry.

"Were you angry?" the doctor came out and asked him.

This was one of those times when Dr. Woodliff wasn't going to let him get away with a shrug. "Yeah," Tate said.

It was the truth, too. The anger had kept growing and growing inside him until it hadn't felt like anger anymore. It'd felt like the shot the dentist gave him one time when he needed a filling. All numb and funny. Not funny-funny, either, but wrong.

His mom did start to cry, causing Tate to feel all numb and wrong again. He looked at the doctor, hoping he could fix it.

"We've covered a lot of ground today," Dr. Woodliff said. "Our time is up, but I'd like for both of you to come back tomorrow—with your dad. How does that sound?"

"Great," his mother said without hesitation.

Tate shrugged.

When the doctor stood, Tate and his mom did, too, and she smiled again as if they'd just covered all that ground that Dr. Woodliff had said they did. Tate thought the only ground they needed to cover was something they hadn't even touched on. It might take weeks for them to get to the single question that Tate wanted to ask. He figured he didn't have that kind of time with his mom.

They went out the side door of the hospital. A door probably put there so that people wouldn't see crazy people, or people like him, coming out of a head-doctor's office. He immediately spotted his dad, sitting in his truck. He didn't get out. Probably because he didn't want to talk to Valerie. Even though she was staying at the inn and not the ranch, the air got thick whenever they were around each other.

Tate didn't think that was a good thing.

"I'm so glad I got to do this with you," his mom gushed. He didn't think it was a good thing, either, that she was starting to look all around. She reminded him of a steer that was trying to get away from one of the hands with a lasso. "I've got a painting I want to work on, and I know you need to get back to school, but maybe we can have dinner together at the inn."

He nodded, figuring there was about a fifty-fifty chance that she would change her mind and want to keep working on the painting.

"Do you hate me?" he came right out and asked.

She gasped, put her hand over her heart. "No. Of course not." She looked at him. Really looked at him. And she repeated it as she shook her head. "I just hated the person I became after I had you."

The doctor had talked to him about people changing, and maybe she had. But from what he'd heard people say, she had always been that way. The other thing the doctor had said was something about stupidity being when you kept doing the same thing and expected it to be different. Or something like that. Tate wasn't saying his mom was stupid, but maybe she couldn't see what everyone else could.

"You heard what I told Dr. Woodliff," she added. "When I'm here, I feel like I'm about to explode, and I knew you were going to be all right even if you had a crappy mother. Because you know how much your dad loves taking care of you."

She made that sound as if there was no doubt about it. Tate had doubts, though. "Sometimes, he likes it," Tate semiagreed.

His mom took hold of his arm and turned him to face her. "No, he loves it. He loved you from the first moment he held you. I could see it. He changed right before my eyes. More than anything, he wanted to be a good father to you. That's why I knew it was okay for me to leave."

"It wasn't okay."

But right off he regretted saying that. Because maybe it *was* all right. If she'd stayed, she might have exploded. She might have taken some pills or shit. And even if she hadn't, she might have spent the last thirteen years shrugging and feeling numb and wrong.

He didn't want that for himself, and he didn't want it for her, either.

"It's okay for you to go," he told her.

She looked at him, blinked, and he saw she was blinking back tears. She opened her mouth but nothing came out. Sometimes, that happened with his grandma Belle when he surprised her too much like with a bad word that had slipped out.

"I'm not a little kid," he added. "I know you can't be here, and I'm all right with that." It was mostly true, anyway.

She kept staring at him, the way people did when they thought you were lying. Maybe she saw what she wanted to see or at least saw that it wasn't an out-and-out lie.

"You should go back to New Mexico." He kissed her cheek. "Maybe you can come back on my birthday or something."

"Of course. Absolutely." Now, the smile made it to her eyes, and that meant Tate had finally figured out how to make someone happy.

He could let her go and not whine about it.

Except maybe it was okay to whine about it a little.

She hugged him, kissed his cheek, and still smiling, she said, "I love you, baby."

He wasn't a baby, but he didn't want to correct her and risk her smile going away. That's why he waved at her as she headed in the direction of the inn.

His dad opened his truck door and stepped out. Maybe because he thought there was something here he needed to fix. There wasn't. Tate made his way to the truck and got inside.

"Is everything okay?" his dad immediately asked.

He wasn't ready to tell him just yet that it would be a long time before Valerie came back. That she'd still forget his birthdays. And send those stupid cards with the names scratched out. He wasn't ready to tell his dad that nothing had changed.

Nothing except him.

He wasn't the one who was broken. His mom was. And she wasn't someone that he or his dad could fix.

"Are you okay?" his dad pressed.

Tate just settled for a shrug.

But yeah, he was okay.

CHAPTER TWENTY

IF ONE MORE person asked her if she was okay, Mila was going to scream. It had been going on for nearly two weeks now, and she was tired of it. Nearly every customer who'd come into the store had asked in some way or another. Her mother, too. And even Roman had texted her a couple of times to ask.

She'd sent Roman a Sure with a smiley face.

Mila had told her customers, "Of course. Why wouldn't I be?" And then she'd looked at them as if daring them to bring up the fact that Valerie had left town again and now Roman was preparing to do the same. He wouldn't be going to Valerie, but then he wouldn't be staying in Wrangler's Creek, either.

Roman hadn't brought up their fantasy date in those texts, and she was sort of glad that he hadn't. While she would have enjoyed one last night with him—even a nonsexual one—it was obvious he needed to focus on Tate. There was no telling what the boy was going through now that his mother had abandoned him again.

Mila had refrained from texting Tate to ask if he was okay. She knew just how irritating that could be. But she had sent him an email to let him know she'd gotten in the graphic novels he had wanted her to order. That way, she opened the door to communication if he wanted it.

He apparently hadn't.

Tate had messaged back to say he was busy with finals and that he would be in soon. Soon hadn't happened, though, since it'd been two weeks.

The bookstore door opened, and Mila immediately saw Sophie struggling to get it. That's because she was trying to squeeze a double stroller through the narrow opening. Mila hurried to her and lifted the front so they could shift and wiggle the stroller inside. Despite all the shifting and wiggling, the twins stayed sound asleep.

"Did you know that boy babies pee in your face?" Sophie asked.

Well, at least Sophie hadn't asked if Mila was okay. Mila shook her head.

"They do," Sophie assured her. "You have to keep your mouth closed when you diaper them. When you burp them, too, because they'll throw up in your mouth. But girl babies also do that."

Sophie wasn't making motherhood sound particularly fun, or sanitary, but Mila knew her friend was the happiest she'd ever been. The most exhausted, too, because Sophie immediately sprawled out on the reading sofa. Didn't sit, but sprawled as if ready for a nap.

"I took the babies by the police station to see Clay," Sophie explained. "I figured since I was out, that I'd stop by and say hello. Did you know it takes nearly an hour to get everything ready just to get the twins in the car? And then I had to stop along the road and nurse one of them."

Mila had guessed the nursing part because from beneath Sophie's shirt, she could tell that the cup to her nursing bra was undone, and her nipple was pressing against the fabric. Mila motioned for her to fix it, and Sophie mumbled some profanity.

"No wonder the Busby boys whistled at me when I walked by them. Apparently, they were noticing a different kind of twins than the ones in the stroller."

"How are you, anyway?" Sophie asked, fixing her bra.

Mila frowned. Apparently, she hadn't dodged that bullet, after all. So, she decided to tell Sophie everything she probably didn't want to know. "Business is good. My mom and I have made peace with each other. I haven't made peace with Waylon, though. And I've found a few interesting matches on a couple of the dating sites. I'm considering going out with one of them."

Sophie sat up, stared at her. "Roman," she spelled out. "Are you okay with what he's doing?"

"You mean leaving? Yes, I heard Tate and he were moving back to San Antonio in a day or two."

"Bet you didn't hear it from him because he's not talking about it. In fact, he's back to his cranky self. Tate's better, though. Roman said he would get him bronco riding lessons from some guy who works for him in the rodeo business."

Mila wanted to blow out a breath of relief. That was good about Tate. Not so good about Roman. "Why is Roman cranky?"

Sophie flopped back down on the sofa. "He won't say, of course, but I think it's this whole fantasy date thing he's planning. He knows this will probably be the last time he'll get to play lover boy with you. Without any actual loving, that is."

Mila heard every word Sophie said, but it was as if her mind was on some kind of time delay because it took several seconds to sink in. "Fantasy date?"

"Yes, you know the one you asked him to do with

you. FYI, he sucks at planning, and you can thank me for nixing the first few ideas he came up with. *The Godfather*," Sophie quickly supplied. "And *Braveheart*. But I think the only reason he wanted that one was so he could paint his face blue."

Mila was still hearing every word, still having trouble absorbing it. "Roman's planning a fantasy date?"

Sophie sat up again. Stared at her. "You didn't ask him to do that?"

"I guess I did, but I just figured it was off since he hadn't mentioned it."

Sophie made a slight gasp, one that caused both babies to wake up and start fussing. "Crud. Maybe it was supposed to be a surprise. Please act surprised if he goes through with it."

Mila wouldn't have to act. She would be surprised. "Uh, is the date he's planning...romantic? Because neither of those movies you mentioned scream romance."

"Maybe to a guy they are." At least, that's what Mila thought she said. It was hard to hear with the babies crying now.

Sophie went to the stroller, scooped up one of them, and smiling, she showered some kisses on the baby's face. Mila would have done the same to the second one if the door hadn't opened, and Belle hadn't waltzed in.

Literally.

The woman twirled around as though she were dancing when she came in, and in the same motion, she swooped in and picked up the other baby.

"Oh, my little darlings," Belle said. "I've missed you." She gave kisses to the baby she was holding and then kissed the other one.

"You saw them just an hour ago," Sophie pointed out.

"An hour's too long without some grandbaby sugar. Sorry I haven't been by sooner," Belle added to Mila. "But being a newlywed keeps me busy. These little snoogums do, too."

"Mom has been babysitting some each day so I can nap," Sophie explained.

"Billy Lee helps," Belle added, motioning to the door where her husband was walking in. Judging from his big grin, it was obvious that marriage agreed with him. With Belle, as well.

Billy Lee hugged Sophie and the babies before going to her. He took her by the shoulders. "I got the DNA results back a while ago," he whispered. And shook his head. "I'm sorry. I really wanted it to be me."

"So did I." She kissed his cheek. "But it's okay."

He raised an eyebrow. "Okay with Waylon being your father? Vita told me. She came by to see us yesterday to make sure there weren't any ill feelings between Belle and her. She gave us an egg."

"With some crap on it?" Mila asked.

He nodded. "She said it was a good thing, but I have my doubts."

"She meant for it to be good. She gave me one, too."

"And Clay," Sophie added.

Mila hadn't been sure Sophie had heard Billy Lee's and her conversation, but obviously she had.

"I need to be going," Sophie said, putting the baby back in the stroller. Belle did the same to the other one after she gave him a dozen more kisses.

Sophie also gave Mila a kiss on the cheek. "Are you sure you're all right?"

For once, Mila didn't mind the question. She nodded. "I am." Not just with Billy Lee not being her father but with everything.

Well, she was mostly okay. But *mostly okay* was the story of her life.

"We'll talk soon," Sophie assured her, and she got busy hauling out the stroller. Billy Lee and Belle helped, and Mila stood at the window, watching them until they were out of sight.

She waited until she was certain they wouldn't be back, and she locked the door and turned the sign to Closed. Mila definitely didn't want anyone walking in on this conversation that she hoped she was about to have with Roman.

Mila pressed his number and heard it ring. But the ring sounded much closer than it should have. She soon figured out why.

Roman was at the door, and he was trying to get in. In fact, he was almost frantically motioning for her to open up. Mila did and came face-to-face with another surprise.

Roman in a suit.

She'd never seen him in anything but jeans so she had a few moments of stunned silence before he practically pushed his way inside.

"I didn't want anyone to see me like this," he said, "or they would have known something was up." While he was locking the door and pulling down the blinds, he thrust a plastic bag at her. "Your costume."

So, this was about the fantasy date, and since his face wasn't blue, and he wasn't wearing a kilt—too bad about that—he hadn't gone with *Braveheart*. But she still couldn't rule out *The Godfather*. Brando had worn plenty of suits in that movie.

She hoped there wasn't a horse's head in the bag.

"Uh, I wasn't really expecting the fantasy date," she told him.

He finished with the blinds, turned and looked at her. "It was your idea. And you said you wanted it to happen when Tate finished school. Well, he was exempt from a couple of his finals because he has good grades so he's done."

Talk about bittersweet. The good grades part pleased her, but Mila wasn't counting on having to face this day until tomorrow.

"What I meant was I wasn't expecting you to plan the date," she explained.

He lifted his shoulder. "I thought it was something I could do for you."

Roman didn't add that it would be a nice way to say goodbye, but Mila was pretty sure that's what he meant.

Yet another bittersweet moment.

She wanted to be with Roman, and having him plan this was not just a surprise, but it also made it even more special. The trick would be for her to enjoy it without thinking this would be the last time they'd be together like this. Oh, he would come back to Wrangler's Creek, all right, but he'd already reached his three-count limit. That meant he'd stay friends with her.

Definitely bittersweet.

She smiled and looked in the bag to see what adventure he had planned. It wasn't a horse's head but rather a gray halter dress. The kind of dress you'd wear to a party.

"I had to order it," he said. He took out his phone and turned on some music.

Both the music and the dress were suddenly very

familiar. But what was confusing to her was the wad of yellow foamy-looking material at the bottom. Mila pulled it out and nearly screamed.

Because it was a fake snake.

She was certain her mouth was gaping when she turned back to him.

"I didn't think you'd want me to spank you with an actual belt, and that was the only soft thing I could find." Roman smiled. "Are you ready for a spanking, *Anastasia*?"

ROMAN FELT LIKE an idiot. A horny one.

Definitely not a good pairing for someone trying to hang on to his badass image.

Plus, he was wearing a monkey suit that felt as foreign to him as if he'd put on a tutu. It was too bad Mila's fantasy hadn't included some rodeo stuff, but she had mentioned the *Fifty Shades of Grey* scene when she'd first brought up this fantasy date idea.

"You actually did this for me?" Mila asked.

Her breathing was already a little too fast so maybe this was indeed some kind of turn-on for her. It was a turn-on for him, as well, but not because of the fantasy. His body just seemed to start firing on all cylinders whenever he was around Mila.

"I wanted to do something so you'd remember me," he said.

She laughed, a short burst of air. "Trust me, I'll remember you."

He'd expected her to go into her office and change, but she didn't. She shucked off her top right there and slipped out of her jeans. That sent his horniness up a significant notch.

She wasn't wearing frilly underwear. It was plain white and cotton from the looks of it, but Mila still managed to make it look amazing. She slipped on the dress, and he got another dose of *amazing*. Mila didn't give him time to savor the eye candy, though, because she took hold of his arm and led him to the reading sofa.

"Use your hand," she said.

Because his mind was in the gutter, it took him a moment to realize she was talking about the actual spanking. He didn't mind that. In fact, his hand was rather pleased about it. His dick was even more pleased when she lay belly-down across his lap. She hiked up the dress.

And pulled down her panties.

Of course, he'd expected some seminudity. He just hadn't expected it to make him rock hard. Mila noticed, too, because she looked up at him and smiled. Not the kind of smile someone might have at the start of a roller coaster ride. This was more the look Mrs. Robinson had given in *The Graduate*.

He looked at that smile, then at her bare ass, and it occurred to him that this might be harder than he'd thought it would be. And no, he wasn't talking about his dick now.

"I've never spanked anyone," he confessed.

The smile stayed on her mouth. "Then it'll be a first for both of us. If you like it, I can spank you."

No, he'd pass on that. In the state his body was in, it wouldn't take much for this to go from a spanking to a fucking. Something that couldn't happen. Mila wanted a fantasy, no-sex date, and that's what she was going to get. Mostly, anyway.

"I forgot the dialogue," he told her.

"Improvise," she said, her voice all soft and silky.

Actually, that soft and silky also described her butt. Roman ran his hand over her left butt cheek before he gave it a tap. Since it didn't even make a sound, he tapped a little harder. And got a very nice reaction from Mila.

She made a slight gasp of pleasure.

So, he did it again, harder. But not too hard. After the first spank, he could see the general appeal of this. Not for his own sake, but because Mila definitely seemed to be getting some enjoyment from it. So he made things a little more interesting. Roman moved her legs apart, lifted her hips and landed the next one at the very bottom of her butt cheeks.

A much louder sound of pleasure from Mila.

So, he did it again.

This was more like a glorified hand job, and while it wasn't supposed to get sexual, Roman didn't think Mila would mind if they did this for a while longer. Just short of an orgasm, of course, because that would be sex. After that, he could leave and find a tub of ice to jump into because he was going to need some way to cool down.

But Mila didn't let it reach the orgasm stage.

She got up onto her knees and unzipped him.

"Uh, this isn't part of the fantasy," he managed to say.

"I'm improvising. We can't have sex because of your rule, but the first time we were together, it was just half sex since only I climaxed. So, that means I can do this, and it'll be the other half."

This was a blow job.

Roman was about to tell Mila that he didn't think it

was a good idea, but after she took him in her mouth, he forgot all about what he intended to say. Hell, he forgot how to talk.

She wasn't very good at *this*, but it didn't matter. He was already so primed and ready that her breath alone probably could have gotten him off. Roman just sat back and let her take care of finishing that half portion of his man-rule.

All in all, there was a lot to be said for this fantasy date stuff.

"Well?" Mila asked him.

Roman was still coming back down to planet earth, and his head was still in the clouds, so he wasn't sure what Mila was asking. He hoped it involved doing to her what she'd just done to him.

But apparently not.

She got off the sofa, pulling up her panties and shoving the dress back down. Since Roman didn't want to sit there with his dick hanging out, he zipped up and waited to see if she would give him a little more info so he could answer that vague question. Maybe it wouldn't involve her getting sad.

"I learned how to do that from an internet article I read," she finally said. She tipped her head to his crotch. "In this case, I thought the act was better than the article. How about you?"

He had to smile. "Much, much better." Of course, he would have liked to have been around when she was reading how to do that. "Were there pictures?"

"Yes, but I didn't look at those." She laughed, and mercy, it was good to hear that.

Roman felt as if he was walking on eggshells around

Mila. On the one hand, it was fun to be with her, but that fun was about to end. He would see her, of course, whenever he came to town, but he didn't want her for a sex-buddy. No. She deserved better than that.

And she'd probably get it.

According to Belle, Mila was definitely looking into the regular dating sites again. The ones that would lead to real dates and not what he'd been giving her. Half sex, sex, sex and a spanking.

He stood, not having a clue what to say, but Mila even took care of that for him.

"Thanks," she said. "You certainly gave me a spring fling to remember."

Spring fling. So, that's what it was. A better label than three-fucks.

Roman went to her, kissed her, and he might have lingered longer if she hadn't stepped back. And she smiled again. The smile didn't look as if she'd had to scrounge it up, either, like the one he gave her in return.

"I need to freshen up," she added. "I'm having dinner with my mom. Pray for me."

It didn't have a "don't let the door hit you in the butt on your way out" ring to it, but it was close. No more kisses. No more sex. And Mila seemed just fine with that. He supposed he'd dodged a bullet by not breaking her heart.

She unlocked the door for him and closed it just as soon as he was out. He didn't hear her lock it, but he did hear her footsteps so maybe she was heading to the bathroom to freshen up. Roman didn't want to stand around on Main Street in a suit so he started for his truck that he'd left in the small side parking lot of the bookstore. The second he rounded the corner of the building, though, he saw someone.

Tate.

He was leaning against Roman's truck, his backpack at his feet, and his son was sporting a scowl that was even scowl-ier than usual.

"Anything go wrong at school?" Roman immediately asked him.

He shook his head. "I didn't have class. I only had to get the stuff out of my locker."

Hell, he hoped Chrissy hadn't left a parting *gift*, one that had put Tate in his mood. Of course, Tate was a master at bad moods, but just lately things had gotten a lot better.

"Get in and I'll give you a ride to the ranch," Roman said, unlocking the truck with his remote key.

But Tate didn't budge. "You were with Mila, weren't you?"

Roman glanced down at the suit, and judging from the fact that Tate had probably seen the blinds down and the closed sign, his son hadn't had any trouble coming up with the obvious.

"Yeah," Roman admitted.

Tate mumbled something Roman didn't catch, but it sounded like cussing, and Tate started to walk away. Roman stepped in front of him.

"Why the attitude?" Roman asked. But then it occurred to him that Tate might have some kind of crush on Mila. Weird, though, because he always seemed to think of her as an aunt.

"You know why." Tate did more of that cussing-mumbling. "You'll hurt her. She's not used to guys like you."

Roman felt as if Tate had slugged him. "And what type of guy is that?"

"You hook up with women, and then you walk away from them. Just like you're doing now. Some of those women want you to walk away, but Mila's not like that. She doesn't leave you dirty messages on the phone or put love bites on your neck."

If this hadn't been such a serious conversation, Roman would have pointed out that Mila was very capable of both those things. But Tate was right.

She wouldn't do that.

Because Mila knew that he wouldn't want to have a flashing neon sign that they'd been together. Not just for the sake of minimizing gossip but because of Tate. She loved his son and cared what happened to him.

"Mila told you she was in love with you," Tate went on. "I heard it that day we were at the grocery store when Mr. Beaumont was being so mean to her."

"I don't think she meant it. I think she was trying to make a point." And stop him from punching Waylon.

"She meant it," Tate insisted. "And you should have stayed away from her so it'd be easier for her to get over you. But you didn't. You dressed up like that and came here to have sex with her."

"A fantasy date," Roman corrected. If it hadn't been for the blow job, he could have told Tate that nothing had happened. But it would be a lie by anyone's standards. "It's just something Mila wanted to do before I left."

"She wanted to do it because it was with you. Sheez, are you an idiot or something?"

That didn't feel so much like a punch as it did a slap meant to piss him off. And it worked. Roman got pissed.

"Mila is fine," he told Tate, though his jaw was tight, making it hard to speak. "She's the one who told me to leave."

Speaking of jaws, Tate's tightened, too. "I don't believe you."

"Fine, then I'll show you." Roman took him by the arm and marched him to the front of the bookstore. Of course, they were drawing attention, and now there'd be more gossip, but Roman didn't give a flying fig about that. He only wanted to show Tate that he wasn't the asshole that his son apparently thought he was.

Roman threw open the door before he considered that Mila might be changing out of the halter dress. But she was fully clothed. Clothed and sitting at her desk. When she lifted her head, though, Roman saw something he definitely hadn't wanted to see.

Tears.

Mila wasn't just crying. She was sobbing.

"Told you," Tate snarled. "I knew you'd break her heart." He bolted out of Roman's grip and started running.

"Go get him," she insisted. She stood and motioned for him to go. "I'm fine."

He didn't believe her, but Tate wasn't fine, either. Right now, his son needed him more than Mila did so Roman took off after him. Even over the sound of his own footsteps, Roman heard her lock the door behind him.

CHAPTER TWENTY-ONE

ROMAN HAD THREE piles of work again on his desk. Stuff from his business, the ranch and Granger Western. If he dug right in, he might be finished by the end of the day, but he wasn't digging. Not into business, anyway.

Instead, he was looking at the email from Tate.

If an email could have shrugged, that's what this one would be doing.

It was a response to a lengthy conversation and follow-up email where Roman had said he was sorry that Tate was upset over seeing Mila cry. Hell, Roman was upset, too. But he'd tried to make sense of it for Tate by explaining that Mila was just sad because she was going to miss them once they left Wrangler's Creek and moved back to San Antonio. It was possibly true.

Possibly an out-and-out lie.

Either way, Roman had gone on for a half hour or more talking to Tate, trying to smooth things over. When Tate had given him only shrugs and the silent treatment, Roman had written the email. Unlike the conversation, he stuck to fun stuff. Like the bronco riding lessons Tate was going to get and the cruise idea. Roman had even tossed in the possibility of Tate spending a week or two of his summer break at the ranch. The email had gone on for multiple paragraphs, had included some smiley faces, and Tate had sent back a two-word response.

Okay. Whatever.

Maybe that meant Tate was no longer so crazy about being at the ranch. Or those riding lessons. Heck, maybe Roman had undone all the good things that had been starting to happen for Tate while they'd been in Wrangler's Creek.

"You've got a visitor," Joe said, sticking his head through the doorway of Roman's office. "It's a strange little woman who said you were expecting her. She put an egg on my desk. Is that some kind of weird hippie business card, or is she just crazy?"

"Both," Roman answered. "Her name is Vita and show her in." And even though he hadn't been expecting her today, he'd expected her. Eventually. By now, Vita had no doubt talked to Mila and wanted a word with Roman about that.

Joe disappeared, and several moments later in walked Vita.

"There's an ill wind blowing," Vita greeted him.

Yes, and it was coming from her. Vita smelled like a bad mix of herbs and stuff that people usually avoided. That was an improvement, though. Sometimes, she smelled like Limburger cheese.

"I'm here because of Mila," she said.

Of course she was, and Roman tried to steel himself up for Vita to curse him—maybe literally—for breaking Mila's heart.

"She's not nearly sad enough," Vita added.

Roman was certain he hadn't heard that right. "Who's not nearly sad enough?"

"Mila, of course. Boy, you need to get your ears cleaned out. Maybe you also need to rethink this whole notion of winning her heart."

Roman didn't have a whole notion about that, but even if he had, it wouldn't have been something he wanted to discuss with Vita. "Isn't it a good thing that Mila's not sad?" Though he was certain he was going to regret the question.

"No. She should be missing you right about now, and she's not. She's not moping or anything."

Well, that was…good. Roman hadn't wanted her to do that. Of course, he hadn't wanted to mope, either, but that's all he'd been doing in the week since he'd left the ranch.

"She bought a bunch of new clothes," Vita went on. "Not fantasy clothes junk, either. Real dresses and shoes. I was all for that, thought maybe she was just trying to cover up her moping, but then she says she's going on a date. A real one."

That was…good, too. Mila was moving on with her life and maybe trying to find Mr. Right. She deserved that.

Vita put her hands on his desk and leaned in. Maybe so he wouldn't miss getting an extra whiff of the herbal cloud that surrounded her. "The date's with your cousin Dylan."

Well, shit. That wasn't good. Dylan could be trying to pump her for information for Lucian to use in a future lawsuit. Yes, Lucian had said he would back off on that, but Roman didn't trust him, and he could have sent Dylan to do his bidding.

"One more thing," Vita said. "Condoms."

Apparently, Vita thought Roman had been blessed with ESP because she didn't add anything to that until Roman made a circling motion for her to continue.

"Mila bought some. A big-assed box of them." Vita's eyes narrowed. "Roman Granger, what kind of dark magic have you spun on her? You've made my daughter hot to trot, and it's not you she's trotting after. Now, what are you going to do about that, huh?"

MILA FIGURED NEARLY everyone in the Longhorn Bar was watching her and her date, Dylan Granger. The few who weren't—one of the Busby boys and Mary Ellen Fletcher—were making out in the back booth, and the bartender, another Busby boy, was having a heated phone conversation with someone. But other than those three, Mila and Dylan had everyone else's attention.

"And then a rat bit off the horse's nuts," Dylan said.

She frowned, her gaze zooming back to him. Not that it had to zoom far because he was seated directly across from her.

He flashed her that panty-dropping smile. "Just checking to see if you were listening."

"Sorry." She ran her finger around her margarita glass, gathering up some of the salt that she licked. "I'm not used to being watched like this."

He leaned in. "Any time you show up with me, that'll happen. Not because people can't take their eyeballs off me but because I'm the sworn enemy of your best friend."

At least Dylan hadn't said that he was the sworn enemy of her ex-boyfriend. Of course, Roman would have had to be a boyfriend for him to become her ex.

They hadn't exactly reached that status. Yes, they'd had sex and then things had gone to heck and back a week ago when Tate had seen her crying. Since then she'd called Tate several times to assure him that she was okay, but she didn't think he believed her.

That was probably because it wasn't true.

On the surface, she was all right, and she'd told that to Sophie and her mom. But something felt off. The kind of feeling that she was forgetting something really important.

"And then the rat chewed off the horse's butt," Dylan said.

"Sorry," Mila repeated, and she forced herself to look just at him.

Looking at him wasn't a chore. Like all the Grangers, Dylan was drop-dead hot, and she should be drooling. Thankful, too, since he'd called her to go out for a drink. She hadn't had to use the dating sites, after all.

"You know, I'm a good listener," Dylan added.

"I'm just a little worried about my cousin Tate," she admitted. "He got the wrong idea about me and his dad."

Dylan had a sip of his beer. "He wanted Roman and you to get together?"

"No," she quickly answered, but then Mila rethought that. "Maybe, but I think he was more concerned that I was in over my head."

"Because you're a virgin." Dylan studied her. "*Were* a virgin." He blew out a breath of relief. "It's probably not a good thing for a man to tell a woman that he's glad she finally had sex. Especially when that sex wasn't with him. But going out with a virgin seems a little…"

"Daunting?" she supplied. "As if you might have to propose marriage just to kiss me?"

He smiled. "Something like that."

"Yet you went out with me, anyway." She paused. "Why?"

Dylan huffed. "Because you're beautiful. Smart. Funny." Now, he paused when she stared at him. "Sophie called and said you were down."

Sophie? Mila would have a chat with her best friend later. Even if Sophie felt sorry for her, which she clearly did, Mila didn't want Sophie setting her up on any more dates. Especially dates with a Granger.

"If you hadn't been beautiful, smart and funny, I wouldn't have listened to Sophie," he went on. "After all, Sophie and I aren't exactly pals. But I listened to her because I wanted to go out with you."

Maybe, but since it was obvious she wasn't having a great time, Dylan would not want a repeat. And that was okay with her. What wasn't okay was the man who came through the front door.

Waylon.

Like she had with Roman, she'd managed to avoid him and vice versa, but he wasn't avoiding her now. He made a beeline for the booth where Dylan and she were sitting.

"I hope you're happy now," Waylon greeted her. "Because this is all your fault."

Mila had to shrug. In addition to avoiding her sorry excuse for a biological father, she'd avoided the gossips, too. She hadn't wanted to hear a rehashing of why Roman had been wearing a suit or having an argument with Tate outside her bookstore.

"What's my fault?" she asked.

"Bernadette left me, and she took Chrissy with her. She moved back in with her folks in San Antonio. She'll probably try to take me for half of everything I have."

Normally, Mila wouldn't have bothered to waste her breath to ask about that, but there was another person involved in this. "What about Arwen?"

"She'll be around," Waylon spat out. "Bernadette worked out something with another family so she can stay in Wrangler's Creek. The O'Malleys."

Mila knew them, and they were good people, but she had to shake her head. "Why isn't Arwen going with her mother?"

"Because Arwen wants to stay here so she won't have to change schools, and Bernadette's going to let her. She always caters to that girl's every whim."

Maybe Bernadette did that because Waylon was so awful to Arwen. Still, this seemed extreme. "Won't Arwen miss seeing her mother?"

Waylon huffed. "No. Because the O'Malleys plan to take Arwen to Bernadette every weekend." Another huff. "Bernadette takes my Chrissy and leaves me a juvenile delinquent in the making, and it's all your fault."

That got Dylan moving out of the booth. He stood, facing Waylon, which meant Mila had to stand, too, because she didn't want her date slugging this moron. Waylon wasn't worth the sore fist that Dylan would get with the punch he was about to throw.

"I'll bite," Mila said. "How is this my fault?"

"Because you're the one who brought up all of that old shit. Bernadette heard you, and she felt sorry for you."

"Maybe your wife didn't feel sorry for Mila," Dylan said. "Maybe she left you because you're a dick."

Mila groaned and stepped between them. Of course, they were drawing a crowd. Not that they didn't have a crowd already, but even Mary Ellen and her Busby date were looking now. That's why Mila tried to keep down her voice.

"Why did Bernadette leave Arwen behind?" Mila asked.

"Who knows? Who gives a shit?" Waylon certainly didn't whisper, and now that she was close enough to him, she could smell the liquor on his breath. Obviously, he'd been trying to drown his sorrows. "All I know is that brat will be right under my nose."

"She'll be under mine, too, and that's where I want her," Mila informed him. "I'll be keeping an eye on her to make sure you don't make her life as miserable as you've made your own."

"Want me to kick his ass?" Dylan asked her.

"Like you could," Waylon challenged.

"Yes, he can," Mila assured Waylon, and she put her hand on Waylon's chest to move him back.

"Don't you touch me!" Waylon slurred. "Don't you even think about sassing me, either."

She hadn't been thinking about it until he said that. Mila couldn't think of a fast sass so she shot him the bird. Not very mature, but it made his eyes narrow.

"That's something Roman taught you," Waylon went on. "Because he did that to me, too."

Good for Roman. And since it'd felt so good to do it the first time, Mila did it again. Then she moved closer and met Waylon eye-to-eye.

"If you don't leave, I'll announce to everyone here that you're my father. And that means they'll know you had sex with Vita. Is that what you want?"

"They won't believe you," he assured her.

"Oh, yes, they will. Because of the way you're act-ing right now."

The bits and pieces of the conversation that people had overheard wouldn't help, either. Truth was, this would get out, and people would fill in the bits they hadn't managed to hear. Mila was just trying to stop the gossip from including a blow-by-blow account of how Dylan had wiped the floor with her birth father, who would clearly never be anything but a sperm donor.

Maybe her words found intelligent life in his head. Or maybe the booze was wearing off. Whatever the rea-son, Waylon glanced around as if seeing the bar, and the other customers, for the first time. Seeing Dylan for the first time, too. All those muscles must have looked a little intimidating because Waylon dropped back a step.

"You stay away from me, bitch, and I'll stay away from you," Waylon declared, and he turned to leave.

Unfortunately, he ran smack-dab into Roman.

Mila hadn't even known he was there. Or how much of this he'd heard. Enough apparently because he was no longer Roman Granger, single dad and business owner. He was badass Roman from Wrangler's Creek.

Waylon tried to step around Roman, but Roman just blocked his path. "If you have balls," Roman said to him, "and if you want to keep them, you will never speak to Mila like that again. Nod if you understand."

In that moment, there was nothing on the planet that was more intimidating than Roman. That's why it didn't really surprise Mila when Waylon nodded. The man probably would have agreed to a lobotomy.

Despite the nod and the intimidation, Waylon wasn't

letting go of this. "Mila's a bitch and this is her fault," he grumbled on his way toward the door.

Dylan, however, didn't look as if he was going to give in so easily to Roman's scowl. "Mila and I are on a date," he told Roman.

"I can see that, and I'm sorry to interrupt." Roman glanced around as if trying to figure out what to do. "Excuse me a second," he said to Mila. "I've decided I'm not going to let Waylon get away with calling you a bitch, after all. I'll be right back."

And Roman stormed off after the man.

It DIDN'T TAKE Roman but a few seconds to catch up with Waylon. The idiot was in the parking lot pointing his keys at somebody else's car. Judging from the confused look on his shit-faced face, he was probably trying to figure out why it wouldn't open.

Roman took out his phone and texted Clay to come so he could make sure Waylon didn't a) locate his vehicle and b) attempt to drive. While they were waiting, if the man did try to get behind the wheel, Roman would stop him.

Gladly.

In fact, it seemed a little like shooting fish in an itty bitty barrel, but he was going to pick a fight with him. Just as Waylon had done with Mila. And speaking of Mila, she hurried out the door of the Longhorn and ran after him.

"Just let it go," she said to Roman. "Treat him like animal poop you might see on the side of the road. It stinks, but it's best to leave it alone."

Roman glanced at her, certain that he had a funny

look because that wasn't a good analogy. "Animal poop doesn't walk into a bar and call you a bitch."

He went toward the man just as Waylon spun around. "What the hell did you do with my car?"

"I vaporized it with my ray gun, you miserable son of a bitch."

"There, you're even," Mila insisted. "He called me a bitch, and you called him an SOB."

That didn't make it even since Waylon had started it, but when the man staggered again and dropped his keys, then fell face-first trying to pick up those keys, Roman knew he couldn't bust the guy's ass. Not until Waylon had sobered up, anyway.

They'd drawn an audience. Everyone who'd been inside the bar was now outside, and if there was anyone left, the sound of the approaching police cruiser would draw them out.

"He's drunk," Roman said to Clay the moment he stepped from his cruiser. "And he called Mila a name."

Clay hadn't frowned or looked disgusted until Roman added that last part. Good. They were on the same page. Now, exactly what page that was, Roman didn't know. That's what he'd come to find out. He hadn't counted on getting caught up in a ruckus with a drunk turd.

Clay hauled Waylon to his feet, and Waylon made a serious mistake of swinging a punch. Probably at Clay. But it came within a breath of hitting Mila. Roman balled up his fist to hit the guy, but Mila caught on to him and pulled Roman into her arms.

"I'm in love with you. Now, stop it," she snarled.

And yeah, everybody heard it. In fact, Mila said it in such a loud voice that maybe people in Canada had heard it. She didn't mean it, of course. This was just her way of stopping him again. Because if Roman had punched Waylon, Clay would have had to arrest him, too.

"You're in love with him?" someone asked.

Roman didn't have to glance back to know it was his cousin Dylan. That probably wasn't something a guy wanted to hear his date say to another man. Roman nearly explained why she'd done that. Nearly. But then he had come here to talk to Mila, and this might be the fastest way to do it.

"Yes," Roman answered. "And I'm in love with her."

A pancake couldn't have given him a flatter look than Mila gave him. Roman just smiled at her. Two could play this dumb game. Obviously, though, it was a game with consequences. In the next thirty seconds, it would be all over town that Mila and he were in love. Someone would call Belle and/or Sophie, and they would start planning the wedding.

One that wasn't going to happen.

"Now, if you don't mind, I need to borrow Mila for a while," Roman added to Dylan. He hooked his arm around her waist and got her moving. Not to his truck because the cruiser and a crowd of gawkers were there. He headed up the sidewalk with her. "Don't worry," he added to Dylan. "I'll bring her back so she can finish that margarita."

Roman expected Dylan to be pissed, but he shook his head and smiled as if he knew something that Roman didn't. It was probably because Dylan might think Mila was really in love with him and vice versa, but his cousin would soon figure out the truth when Mila and he didn't send out any "save the date" cards.

"Your mother came to visit me," Roman said to her once they were out of earshot of the others. "She's pissed at me." Best not to say why unless Mila asked. He especially didn't want to have to use phrases like *hot to trot* and *big-assed box of condoms*. "Tate's also pissed at me," he added.

"*I'm* pissed at you." But she immediately waved that off. "Actually, I'm just mildly inconvenienced. The date wasn't going that well." She huffed. "Dylan seemed turned on that I wasn't a virgin anymore, and that was a turnoff for me."

Hell. Now, he wanted to go back and kick Dylan's butt. "How'd the subject of your virginity, or lack thereof, even come up?" And he hoped it hadn't involved big-assed condoms.

She also waved that off. "Tell me about Tate. I think he's mad at me, too."

There had been a lot of confusing things happening in his life, and that comment was one of them. "Why would he be mad at you? He believes I'm the bad guy in this."

"I don't know. Maybe he's disappointed that I would fall for your *charm*. Maybe he thinks I'm lying about not having a broken heart."

"Well, he did see you crying," Roman reminded her. Which brought him to one of the main reasons for this visit. "Are you sad about what happened between us? Because your mom didn't think you were sad enough."

Mila stopped, stared at him. "Maybe you should tell me what my mother and you talked about."

"Clothes. Your date with Dylan. The condoms you bought. Your lack of moping."

He could tell from the way her stare intensified that

there was one thing in that laundry list that had especially caught her attention. "Condoms?"

Best to get walking again so he didn't have to look
at her while he continued. Her stare had turned to a bit
of a glare, and the fact she'd folded her arms over her
chest wasn't a good sign.

"Vita was concerned that I'd…awakened you."
Awakened? *Fuck*. He never used words like that so he
went with something he'd sworn he wouldn't say to her.
"Vita thought you might be hot to trot."

Mila didn't stop this time. In fact, she picked up the
pace and yanked her phone from her purse. No doubt
to call her mom.

"That would be a surefire way to get her to put a
curse on me," Roman reminded her. Not that he believed in actual curses, but Vita could make his life a
living hell by showing up with daily egg deliveries and
chanting outside his office. "Besides, I told her she was
probably mistaken, that you hadn't bought the condoms
for you and that you weren't hotting or trotting."

She looked at him again when she put back her phone
and took her keys from her purse. That's when he realized they were in front of her bookstore, and she was
unlocking the door.

"I did buy condoms," she said. "For me. Well, for
guys who want to have sex with me."

Shit in a handbasket. Vita was right.

Roman wasn't sure if the tightness in his chest was
because Vita had hit the nail on the head or if it was
because he was feeling as if he'd done a very bad thing
by changing Mila.

"Have you had sex with those guys since I've been

gone?" Clearly, he should have given that question more thought. Because if he had, he wouldn't have asked it.

She dropped her purse and keys on the counter and shut the door. "Have you had sex with women since you've been gone?"

Touché.

This time, Roman did think before he spoke, and he spoke the truth. "No. In fact, I haven't even thought about being with another woman."

"Is that a record for you?" It wasn't a joke, either.

"Possibly," he admitted. "But I have been thinking about sex a lot." He paused, thought and rethought, and even though he knew he shouldn't say it, he did, anyway. "With you."

Her mouth quivered a little. Maybe fighting back a smile. "Well, I've been thinking a lot about sex, too. With you."

She went to her desk, opened the bottom drawer and took out a box of condoms.

Unopened.

His mouth quivered a little. Definitely fighting back a smile.

"But the problem is that rule of yours," she quickly added. "We've had our three times. Anything now would stray into commitment territory."

Yeah, it would.

The moments crawled by with them standing there staring at each other. With a jumbo box of condoms between them.

"So, I guess we could go about this one of two ways," Mila went on. "One option would be for you to rethink your rule, maybe make it four times—"

"Five," he bargained.

Mila nodded, and she made a sound of agreement and approval. "Or a second option could be—"

Roman snapped her to him and kissed her. Hard and long. So that she couldn't finish that sentence. Because he was certain of two things—that he wanted Mila more than his next breath.

And he didn't want any other options.

CHAPTER TWENTY-TWO

OPTIONS SOMETIMES HAPPENED whether you wanted them to or not. For Roman, this was one of those times.

"Well?" Sophie asked.

His sister was on the love seat in her office at the ranch. She had one baby, Katelyn, on her lap and was changing the diaper of the other baby, Kyle, while he lay in a bassinet next to her.

"You'll want to stand back for this," she warned Roman.

The moment Sophie pulled back the wet diaper, Kyle pissed enough to put out a small forest fire. Roman stepped back in the nick of time, and Sophie somehow managed to dodge the stream.

"Here's a tip," Roman said. "When you're taking off the dirty diaper, lift the front of it just an inch or two and wait a couple of seconds until he finishes doing his business. It's the cool air that makes him go off like that."

She stared at him as if he'd just unveiled the secrets of the universe. Roman shrugged. "Hey, I changed Tate enough times to become an expert."

Her mouth quivered a little. Maybe because "diapering expert" didn't go with his bad-boy image. It didn't. But he was a bad boy with layers. And he'd enjoyed fatherhood as much as his sister was obviously enjoying being a mother.

"Now, back to my *well*," Sophie said, putting the fresh diaper on Kyle. "I need help at Granger Western, or I'm going to go bat-poop crazy."

Yes, she'd mentioned that. She had also mentioned that Garrett could step up to help since he had actually run the company for a decade before Sophie. But for Garrett to do that, he would need help at the ranch.

And Sophie was looking at Roman to step up and do that.

"All I'm asking is two months, until it's time for Tate to go back to school," she went on. "By then I should have managed to take at least one nap without help and fit back into my work clothes. And it's not as if you can't take care of your business from here at the ranch. Plus, you know it would make Tate happy since he'd get to ride every day. It's not as if you'd have to deal with Mom, either, since she's wrapped up in Billy Lee and the twins these days."

There it all was in a nutshell. All the reasons why he should come back and help.

The only thing Sophie hadn't mentioned was Mila.

So, Roman decided to get that out of the way, and it might help for Sophie to have the big picture. If she got it, maybe she could help him understand it, too, since he was having a little trouble wrapping his mind around it.

"When Waylon was arrested last night at the Longhorn, Mila did say she was in love with me," Roman confessed. "I said it to her, too, but it's a game we play."

Her eyebrow lifted. "A game that involves a jumbo box of condoms?"

He gave her a stare that only an older brother could manage. "Not that kind of game. Mila said that so I wouldn't punch Waylon, and I said it so she'd leave with me. I needed to talk to her."

Sophie's stare made him feel like an idiot in a way that only a sister could manage. "So, you're not in love with her?"

Roman huffed. "That's not the point. The point is we didn't say it because we meant it. It just diffused a bad situation. I was about to turn Waylon into a greasy spot on the pavement because he'd called her an ugly name."

He hadn't used the actual word because Sophie had been scolding him about cursing in front of the babies. Yes, the very baby who'd just tried to piss on them.

"I know all about what Waylon did," Sophie said. "I got three calls and eleven texts before Mila and you were even out of the parking lot. After that, I know you two argued all the way to the bookstore, that you went inside with her and didn't come out until nearly midnight."

Sheez, there were a lot of nosy people with too much time on their hands.

"I assume your long stay at the bookstore wasn't because you were browsing the new release section," she went on. "I'm also assuming you broke that stupid three f-word rule."

He had. And he'd reached the max on the new rule amendment, as well.

"I love Mila," Sophie said after a sigh. "And I don't want her hurt."

"I don't want her hurt, either," he settled for saying. Roman took a deep breath. "Let me talk to Tate about it, and if he says it's okay, we'll move back for a couple of months."

She smiled. Not a normal smile, either. That was her

victory grin. Probably because she thought if she could get him back to Wrangler's Creek for two months, that he'd stay for good.

Depending on what Tate said about that, she might be right.

No way was he going to admit that to Sophie, though.

Roman kissed Kyle and Katelyn and headed out to the barn where he knew his son would be. He was. Tate was brushing down a horse that he'd just ridden. He spared Roman a glance before he went back to his task.

It had been this way for a while, since Tate had seen Mila crying. Tate shrugged instead of talking and he glanced instead of looking.

"Sophie wants us to stay here for the summer," Roman told him. "Are you okay with that?"

Tate shrugged.

In this case, it might be a legit response because Tate was already practically living at the ranch. He'd been talking the housekeeper into bringing him nearly every day, and when she couldn't, he had called Garrett or Belle to do it. Of course, Tate had ended up staying overnight plenty of times, too.

"Being here at the ranch will make it easier for you to see Arwen," Roman went on. "I noticed she was here earlier."

Another shrug. "She likes to go horseback riding with me."

Actual words. Good words, too. Roman was glad Tate and she were friends. Arwen had just gone through a tough upheaval, but since she was no longer under the same roof with Waylon and Chrissy, she would probably have a better life. Tate could help with that. So would Roman because he'd keep an eye on her as well.

Since that got that particular topic of conversation out of the way, Roman moved on to the next one. The big one. "I screwed up with Mila," he said. "And I don't know how to fix it."

Now, Tate looked at him, and it was more than just a glance. Even though Tate didn't say anything, that look was enough for Roman to keep on talking.

"You know I had sex with her. She had never been with a man before so I knew it was possible that she would fall for me." Roman paused. "I just didn't think I'd be the one falling."

Tate dropped the brush and faced him. "You told people you were in love with her."

So, Tate had gotten texts about that, too. Roman nodded. Tried to put this in such a way that a thirteen-year-old would understand. "I suck at relationships."

"Uh, have you ever had one?" Tate asked.

Roman frowned and started to say—well, hell, yes—but he rethought that. He hadn't had a romantic relationship since he was a teenager. "It's been a while."

"So, you don't know if you suck at them or not."

True. But Roman had a feeling that he would. Of course, that feeling might be based on the three-fuck rule that he'd now squashed. Oh, and based on him not wanting to get his heart stomped on again. There was that.

"It's hard to get over feelings from the past," Roman explained. "Hard to get beyond hurt and stuff."

Tate nodded, paused. "And you think Mila would hurt you the way Mom did?"

Now, it was Roman who froze. No. He was absolutely sure that she wouldn't. Why? Because Mila was Mila.

And right now at this moment, she might be moving on with her life. Without him.

"Shit," Roman mumbled.

"Can I have my own horse?" Tate asked.

Roman was still repeating that "shit" to himself, and he looked at Tate to see him shrug. "Seemed like a good time to ask."

Even though Roman couldn't be sure, he thought Tate smiled. That sneaky kind of smile that Sophie did when she'd just gotten her way.

"You can work for me this summer on the ranch and earn enough money for a horse," Roman said.

That still didn't get rid of the trace of a smile. Probably because Tate had just been given everything he wanted. Well, everything he wanted on this particular day, anyway.

Roman hugged him, knowing that was something a teenage boy didn't want his dad to do. Like that trace of a smile, there was a trace of a hug on Tate's part, causing Roman to break into a full-blown smile of his own.

Tate wasn't the only one who'd gotten a lot today.

Now, Roman needed to see just how much more he could get.

MILA KNEW FOR certain that there were no advantages to being a single woman in Wrangler's Creek. Especially when nearly every single guy in town wanted to get in her pants. There were four of them in the bookstore. The Busby brothers and one of their friends. All vying for her attention.

All idiots.

She suspected their combined IQ wouldn't be enough to get them to triple digits. She also suspected none of them had read a book—ever. They were plucking them from shelves all willy nilly and bringing them to her to get her "opinion." Actually, what they wanted to do was stand shoulder-to-shoulder with her and try to peek down her shirt.

"I don't have an opinion on zombie apocalypses," she told the one making his way to her. "Nor *The Texas Chainsaw Massacre*," she added to another.

"How about this one?" the Busby friend held up a copy of *Fifty Shades of Grey*.

She ignored him and decided to ignore "the customer is always right" rule, too. "If you boys don't plan to buy anything, then leave. I have work to do."

"Boys?" one of them howled. "We're men."

They couldn't prove it by her.

"We are," one of them argued as if she'd verbally disagreed with them instead of just rolling her eyes.

Apparently, the eye roll wasn't a good thing to do because it caused all four of them to come her way. She wasn't actually afraid of them since she knew how to kick a guy in the balls, but eight balls would mean a lot of kicking.

Just as the brainless wonders reached the counter, the door flew open and Roman came in. Now, there were ten balls in the room, and the air was suddenly thick with testosterone.

The Busby boys and their friend went into the man postures, pulling back their shoulders, lifting their chins, wobbling their heads a little as if trying to seem cocky.

"Get the fuck out of here," Roman snarled after taking one look at them. He didn't wait even a second before he turned to Mila. "I'm in love with you."

The first thing Roman said got the boys inching toward the door. The second part got them running. Probably because it sounded like some declaration of war.

Mila just smiled at Roman and gave him a chaste "welcome home, honey" kiss on the cheek. "Thanks," she added. "I've been trying to get rid of them for a half hour."

She started to move away from him, but Roman turned the closed sign around, locked the door. "That's how you get rid of them."

He didn't stop there. Roman took hold of her, pulled her to him and kissed her. It was definitely not a kiss of the *welcome home* variety. It was deep, French and was possibly illegal in a couple of states.

It left her breathless and smiling. "Are we going to amend your rule again?" She slid her hand over the front of his jeans.

His eyes crossed, but he moved her hand away. "Fuck the rule."

She winked at him. "Am I the *rule* now?"

Obviously, he wasn't in as playful a mood as she was. Obviously, not as aroused, either, but that kiss had worked up some heat inside her.

"You're the exception," he said.

He looked at her. Eye-to-eye. While he still had his arm around her waist. And that's when it hit her. Her mouth went dry because it had dropped open and stayed that way.

"You're in love with me?" she asked, and wished that she hadn't sounded, well, stunned beyond belief.

Roman nodded. "I know, I had some trouble wrapping my mind around it, too. Now, here's the deal—you don't have to love me back, but you can't text me any more smiley faces or use the word *peachy*. Especially *peachy* when it comes to anything sexual that's happened between us."

He kept on talking, and Mila heard most of what he said. He was giving her an out, telling her that he'd like to take her on dates and have sex with her on the hood of his truck while it was raining. He mentioned other sex things, too, that all sounded incredibly interesting, but none was as attention-grabbing as the other response he'd given to her.

"You nodded," she said. He looked a little confused by that so she clarified. "When I asked if you were in love with me, you nodded."

He lifted his shoulder. "Yeah. And I also told you that you didn't have to feel the same way about me—"

"But I do. Roman Granger, every memory I have of us involves me being in love with you. Except for nearly getting in a fight in the parking lot of the bar. Oh, and when you put that gerbil down the back of my shirt when I was seven. Other than those two times, I have loved you every minute of my life."

He blew out a breath, kissed the top of her head. Then his mouth made it down to her lips where he did some more damage. Oh, mercy. The man was a handful. Literally. She slid her fingers into his jeans and found pay dirt.

Roman, in turn, slid his hand over her butt. "I think we should start with a spanking." He didn't let go of her while he used his other hand to lower the blinds.

Yes, with her spanking him. They kissed their way to the sofa and fell onto it in a tangled heap. A rather nice heap since she ended up on top of him.

Mila pinned his hands to the sofa. "How many times do we get to have sex with the new rule?"

He hauled her down to him for a kiss and gave her a swat on the butt to go along with it. "We'll start with three hundred and go up if needed."

"Oh, it will be needed," Mila promised him.

Roman smiled. Not a full-blown one because he was still, after all, a badass.

Her badass.

* * * * *

JUST LIKE A COWBOY

CHAPTER ONE

CARLENE SANDERS WAS well aware of the two great weaknesses in her life: premium chocolate and Wynn Beck.

Too bad it appeared this morning she was on a collision course with both.

Just ahead by the barn, she saw Wynn with two huge take-out cups that no doubt contained the hot chocolate that he drank as if it were the cure for all ills. He was walking straight toward her, which meant one of those cups was probably for her.

For once the gossip mill was falling down on the job, because Carlene hadn't heard a peep about Wynn coming home for a visit to Wrangler's Creek, Texas. Too bad. Because whenever her life collided with Wynn, which thankfully these days wasn't very often, she always needed to prepare for it in advance. She usually did that by steeling herself, girding her loins or running for the hills.

Today, she was choosing the third option. It would give her a couple of moments to accomplish the first two.

Carlene skirted the corral and ducked into the cluster of sugarberry trees that was at the back of the ranch house she called home. The running, though, was all for nothing since Wynn saw her anyway and just kept coming toward her.

"Morning, Carlene," he drawled. "On the way over

here, I stopped by the diner and picked us up something to drink. Double dark chocolate with whipped cream and sprinkles. It's a peace offering, of sorts."

Well, he hadn't lost any of that charm, and he knew her Achilles' heel was that chocolate. "What do you want?" she grumbled.

Wynn took a leisurely sip from one of the cups. He also tried to hand her the other one, but she shook her head and scowled at him.

"Now, is that any way to say hello to an old friend?" he teased. He even winked at her.

"Yes, when that friend is an ex-husband, it is."

An ex-husband who could still make her feel too many things. Not just the old attraction, either, but the heartache that came along with it. She didn't need it. And she didn't need him.

"What do you want?" she repeated. "Because your uncle Joe's not here. He moved to Florida shortly after Christmas." That was over two months ago, and Carlene had figured that if Wynn hadn't come home to say goodbye to the uncle he loved, then he had no intention of returning.

"I know. I talked to Uncle Joe just this morning." And then Wynn smiled, all lazy and slow. That Wynning smile was so potent that many women in their hometown of Wrangler's Creek had classified it as foreplay.

He took a step toward her.

"Don't come any closer," Carlene warned him, fearing that he might try to give her a welcome hug. Or worse—a welcome kiss. She didn't want to get any closer to Wynn's mouth or that highly caloric brew.

He didn't listen. What else was new? Wynn never listened when it benefited him to do otherwise. He not only came closer, he also kept on smiling that heat-generating smile.

"Carlene, Carlene, Carlene." He *tsk-tsk*ed her. "That's the best greeting you can manage? And here we haven't seen each other in, what? Two years?"

"Three," she corrected.

Too bad she hadn't even had to think about it for a second. That told Carlene loads about this potentially explosive situation. Like premium chocolate, Wynn was all too often on her mind. Worse, like chocolate, the taste of him was embedded in her memory and her mouth. And it was a taste that she craved much too often.

But he was way off-limits.

They'd divorced nearly three years ago, and he'd left Wrangler's Creek and his uncle Joe's small ranch to go full-time on the bull-riding circuit. Wynn had wanted to make a name for himself. And from everything she'd heard, he had done just that. Maybe he'd leave and keep on making that name so she wouldn't have to see him.

Carlene didn't want to notice, she really didn't, but darn it, he looked good. Of course, looking good wasn't much of a stretch for a guy like Wynn. Good genes poured into great-fitting jeans complete with one of those prize rodeo buckles that was only slightly smaller than a truck hubcap.

He had butterscotch hair that drizzled around the collar of his buckskin jacket. Warm caramel eyes. There was just a touch of milk toffee tint to his skin, a DNA contribution from his Comanche grandmother.

All in all, Wynn looked downright edible.

And that's why Carlene backed up even more when

he ambled toward her. Unfortunately, the freezing-cold sugarberry tree stopped her from backing up any farther.

As if he owned the space between them, Wynn closed in on her. Knowing she had to do something, Carlene made a cross with her fingers and held them up in front of her. The way someone might try to ward off a vampire.

Wynn chuckled. "I just brought you some hot chocolate, that's all, and I'm trying to give it to you. I know how much you love it."

"I'm dieting," Carlene said. Not exactly a lie. She was always dieting. Or at least thinking about it.

Wynn took that as an engraved invitation to give her a full body once-over. His gaze skimmed over her bare, no-makeup face. Her chapped lips. And the poop-stained jeans and boots she wore when she was out feeding the calves—which she'd just been doing.

It got worse.

There were unidentifiable stains on the lime-colored down jacket, a ragged duct-taped rip on the left sleeve and lint bumps everywhere. The thrift store would have rejected the getup, even as a donation for dust rags.

He shifted his stance a little, and she caught a full whiff of his chocolate and of him. The steamy musky-male-and-cocoa scent went straight to the center of her hypothalamus.

And to other parts of her, as well.

"Dieting," he repeated, adding a husky, manly sound of disagreement. "Not necessary. You look pretty good, if you ask me."

He took another sip of the hot chocolate. Lazy. Slow.

Carlene reminded herself that Wynn was only temporarily in Wrangler's Creek and at his uncle's ranch. She wasn't. So, in order to save herself from another round of serious heartache, she needed to keep some distance between him and her.

"It's good to see you, Carlene," he whispered, all low and sexy.

That famous Texas drawl was in full working order. Wynn didn't just speak. He French kissed the words, and they sounded a little lust crazed by the time they made it to her ears.

His gaze dipped a fraction until he got to her lips. His chocolate-scented breath brushed over her mouth. She took in a deep breath, hoping the smell alone would satisfy the sudden craving she had for something hot and sweet.

It didn't.

Nor did it satisfy the sudden urge she had for other hot and sweet things. Specifically, Wynn. And that meant she was in a mountain of trouble.

Carlene tried to move, she really did, but her jeans were caught on something. She struggled, squirmed and otherwise wiggled way too close to a man she shouldn't have been struggling, squirming and wiggling near.

Wynn glanced behind her and chuckled. "Darling, it appears your butt's frozen to the sugarberry."

Carlene got her own verification of that, but it came at a cost. When she turned her head, her boob swiped his hand and her mouth grazed his chin. Definitely not good. A warm boob and tingling mouth were not ways to distance herself from Wynn—especially since he'd noticed that boob swipe. He grinned at her.

But that wasn't all.

With only a micrometer of space now separating

them, Wynn looked deeply into her eyes. "You need some heat," he informed her.

Carlene gulped in a huge chunk of the freezing air. Why, oh why, did this man have her hormonal number?

"And I suppose you think you're the man for the job?" she complained.

He fought with a smile, and somehow all that lip twitching was just as drool inducing as his full-blown foreplay smile. "Yeah, I do. After all, I'm the one with the hot chocolate."

Of all the things she'd thought he might say, Carlene hadn't expected that. She just stared at him. "Huh?"

"Hot chocolate," he said again.

Wynn set one of the cups on the ground and maneuvered himself even closer. He pressed his hips against hers and reached behind her. He drizzled a little of the hot chocolate on the butt of her jeans.

Pinching, pulling and otherwise touching, he unthawed her from the sugarberry.

"Uh, thanks," Carlene mumbled. She craned her neck and caught a glimpse of the residue. Wonderful. Now, she had a saucer-size brown splotch on her rear end.

She started to move again, but Carlene realized she was imprisoned by some pokey tree limbs. Wynn stood between her and much-needed freedom.

He grinned again. And in that grin, Carlene saw the next few moments of her life flash before her eyes. He planned to kiss her. No doubt about it. She'd spent much of her free time since age sixteen either kissing Wynn Beck or daydreaming about kissing him, so she knew exactly how to interpret that expression on his face.

"I've missed you," he said, dropping that voice down yet another octave.

Carlene shook her head. "This won't work."

He nodded. "I know. We've grown miles and miles apart, what with you being here in Wrangler's Creek and me on the rodeo circuit."

"Absolutely. Glad you see things my way—"

He leaned in. "And you're still riled that I left town the way I did."

"I haven't given it a moment's thought."

He brushed his mouth against hers. No more. No less. But, just like that, her body went from the frostbite stage to a raging inferno. The air around them warmed at least a full twenty-five degrees.

Carlene's body suddenly wanted to give in to the moment. Stupid parts of her wanted to wrap themselves around Wynn, haul his mouth to hers and see if he tasted as good as he smelled. She wanted to drag him against that sugarberry and have her way—

But there was no way any part of her could do any of that.

She forced herself to remember that Wynn was off-limits. Ditto for his hot chocolate. One would expand her thighs. The other would break her heart—again. It was time to turn her back on both of these particular temptations before they ruined her life.

She ducked under his arm, pulled back her shoulders and started toward the house. Her exit would have been far more effective if she hadn't had to dodge a frozen cow patty and a couple of surprised squirrels. She staggered and nearly head butted another tree before Wynn caught her arm.

"Careful there," he mumbled.

"Too late for that." Cursing herself for her near slipup and her sudden bout of clumsiness, Carlene extracted herself from his grip and got moving again toward the house.

"Doesn't it get lonely out here all by yourself?" he asked, picking up the second cup of hot chocolate and following her.

"No. I date Birch Davidson now, and we spend a lot of time together."

That was a total lie. She had gone on a few dates with Birch, one of the horse trainers at the nearby Granger Ranch, but Birch was about as interesting as that frozen cow patty she'd just dodged.

"I don't mind being alone here, either," she added. "I've always loved this ranch." Which explained why she'd worked here for the past three years since...

Well, just since.

Running things was hard, sometimes backbreaking, work, but Joe had allowed her to make it into the only ranch in the area that exclusively bred and raised champion-bloodline Santa Gertrudis cattle. People came from miles around to buy the calves and the bulls, and Carlene had plans to expand—to add a small, sustainable farm, too. There was an old cabin in the back that had once belonged to Joe's dad, and she could convert that into a huge chicken coop.

Wynn stopped when they reached the back porch, and he looked out at the pasture. "I've got plans for this place," he said.

That got her attention, and Carlene wondered if she'd said aloud what she had been thinking. She whirled around, frowned. "What?"

"Plans," he verified. He went inside and looked around in there, too. Carlene went after him. "Now I can make it what I've always wanted it to be."

Her heart went to her kneecaps. "What?" she repeated.

Wynn looked back at her, his forehead bunching up. Then he cursed. "You didn't know? Joe didn't tell you?"

Her heart just kept falling, but Carlene managed to shake her head. "Tell me what?"

Well, Wynn wasn't grinning and charming her now. "I thought you knew. I thought that's why you were being so chilly toward me."

"I was being *chilly*..." Carlene stopped. No, best not to get into their past when it appeared there was plenty in their present they needed to clear up. "What did you think Joe had told me?"

Wynn stared at her. The stare of a man trying to figure out how to deliver really bad news. "Uncle Joe signed over the place to me."

Oh, God. No, this couldn't be happening.

"I'm sorry," Wynn went on. "I honestly thought he'd told you."

She managed a headshake. Nothing more. Hard to talk with no breath.

"Joe did have one condition, though," he added a heartbeat later. "I own the ranch. At least, I will soon when the papers are all signed. But don't worry, Joe's condition was that I keep you on so you won't be out of a job. And I agreed. So, I guess that means you work for me now."

CHAPTER TWO

Judging from the gobsmacked expression on Carlene's face, she hadn't had a clue about Uncle Joe's decision to give Wynn the ranch. No wonder she'd been so surprised to see him.

And no wonder there was suddenly fire in her eyes.

This fire was nothing like the heat from the flirting that'd gone on in the back. Nope. She was pissed off.

Without saying another word to him, Carlene marched into the house and yanked her phone from her jeans pocket. No doubt to call Joe. But his uncle was only going to tell her what he'd already told Wynn.

"Joe liked my plans for the place," Wynn told her while Joe's line rang. He set the hot chocolate he'd gotten for Carlene on the coffee table. "And he said it was time for me to be the owner now that I'm giving up bull riding."

Her mouth didn't fall open, but it was close. Clearly, she hadn't known that, either.

Where the heck were the gossips when you needed them?

Wynn hadn't bothered to tell Carlene that little detail about bull riding—or the fact he was returning to Wrangler's Creek—because he'd figured it would be old news by now. Such old news that he'd half expected to find her packed up and moved out since it was obvious she wanted to avoid him.

Even though Carlene didn't put the call on speaker, Wynn was close to her and the house was quiet enough that he could hear Joe's phone ring and ring. While she was waiting for an answer, Wynn had a look around. The place hadn't changed at all in the past three years. Actually, it hadn't changed since he'd moved here as a kid.

There was something comforting about that.

The house itself not only had good bones, the furniture and furnishings were suited for a ranch—saddle-brown leather sofa and chairs, his grandmother's quilt hanging on the wall, the hammered-copper countertops in the adjacent kitchen. While he was continuing to have his look around, he went up the hall to his bedroom, opened the door.

And Wynn frowned.

This was a definite change because it was jammed with boxes and stuff. The bed was still there, but someone had turned it into a junk room.

"What happened here?" he called out.

There was no answer, so he went back into the living room to find Carlene staring at the phone as if she might crush it in her tight fist. "Joe didn't answer," she said. "So I left him a message."

Yeah, he was betting she had. And that it wasn't a friendly *How are you doing?* message, either. Carlene wanted answers, but he hated to tell her that talking to Joe wasn't going to change things.

At least, he hoped not, anyway.

The papers weren't final yet. They were on the way to the lawyer here in Wrangler's Creek, and maybe Carlene wouldn't put up such a fuss. He also hoped that Joe wouldn't back down on this deal.

Because Wynn needed this.

Actually, he needed a life, one where he could manage the pain from his bull riding injuries and deal with the fact that he was a thirty-year-old has-been.

"Why is all that stuff in my room?" he asked.

Her eyes narrowed so he had to guess she didn't want to jump into a change of subject when the other topic of conversation hadn't been resolved yet.

"I'm sure Joe will call you back as soon as he can," Wynn assured her. Of course, that was bull. Joe was enjoying Florida and had been spending his days fishing and reading. "Now about that stuff in my room."

"The boxes belong to me. I moved them here after Joe left. He told me I could live here. I've been sleeping in the guestroom, but your room is bigger and has enough space for all my things."

Wynn was certain he was now the one with a gobsmacked look on his face. "Joe didn't mention that to me. I didn't know you'd moved in."

However, his uncle had said that he wanted Carlene to stay on here. Wynn had figured that meant keeping her job, but maybe in Joe's mind that meant them sharing the ranch, too. That would go over about as well as an erupting volcano in an ice cream parlor.

"What happened to your house?" he asked. Because, last he'd heard, she was still living in town.

"Sold it. Mila Banchini, who owns the bookstore, bought it. She's already moved in."

Hell. That meant she didn't have a place to go. Not an immediate one, anyway. Wynn didn't especially mind her staying there, but Carlene wouldn't put up with that.

Yeah, she'd come close to kissing him when he was flirting with her, but no way would she want him around to jab at the memories of their breakup.

Memories of when they hadn't been broken up, either.

In her mind, the latter was probably worse—since some of those memories had been pretty darn sweet. No matter how bad the problems had gotten between Carlene and him, the sex had been off-the-charts good. There was zero chance she'd want to stir things up with him again.

"Once we talk to Joe," Wynn added, "I'm sure we can get this all straightened out."

She stared at him. "You mean the way you want it." Carlene huffed, muttered some profanity under her breath. "Well, I had plans for this place, too, and Joe said he liked them. *Really* liked them," she emphasized. "Now, I'm pretty sure you and I don't have the same plans, so I smell a rat here."

Wynn nearly played that down. Nearly made a joke. But he gave it some thought and realized she was right.

They cursed in unison.

"Joe's matchmaking," she grumbled.

Yeah, he was. It wouldn't have been the first time, either, but this was taking things too damn far. "He never did want us to divorce. And I can't tell you how many times he would call me and ask me to come home, that both he and *you* would like to see me."

Another huff. "He did the same to me. Always asking if I'd call you because he was feeling *poorly*." She put that last word in air quotes. "He just couldn't accept that you and I are never, never going to get back together."

There'd been no need to double up on the *nevers*.

Wynn knew where he stood with Carlene, and he measured about the same height as hoof grit.

He deserved that measurement.

After all, he'd been the one to leave. The one to push her into marriage, too. A stupid thing to do, since he'd known that Carlene was grounded here in Wrangler's Creek, and it'd been the last place he'd wanted to be. Of course, he had thought he could change her mind.

And she'd probably thought she could change his.

That's how bad marriages were born. How divorces happened. Judging from the narrow-eyed look she was giving him, she remembered all of that, as well.

She snatched up the hot chocolate and took several long sips. Other than great sex, it was the one thing they had in common. An addiction to chocolate. Clearly, Carlene still had that addiction because she made a sound of pure pleasure as she drank, and her eyelids lowered a little.

Those were the same reactions she had during sex.

Something he wished he hadn't remembered.

After she made a few more of the groin-tightening sounds, she took out her phone. "I'll try to call Joe again."

Wynn would have tried, too, but there was a knock at the front door. When he opened it, he almost expected to see Joe standing there with a stupid "gotcha" grin.

But it was Roman Granger.

Not only did Roman own one of the biggest ranches in the area, he'd also been Wynn's boss for the past three years. Well, until twenty-four hours ago, when Wynn had officially retired from the rodeo promotion circuit that Roman owned.

"I didn't expect to see you here," Roman greeted him.

Wynn had already opened his mouth to ask why Roman was there, but that caused him to pause. Because if Roman hadn't expected to see him, then that meant he'd come to see Carlene. Wynn got verification of that when Carlene came to the door. She smiled and automatically pulled Roman into a hug.

That got Wynn's stomach in a knot. Gave him a hefty dose of jealousy, too. And for a good reason. Roman was the love-'em-and-leave-'em type. He was rich and had the looks of a cowboy rock star—women usually took one glance at Roman and wanted to have sex with him.

At the moment, Wynn wanted to punch him in the face.

Hell.

Was that what was going on here? Had Roman come over for some morning sex?

"You smell like chocolate," Roman said to her.

It sounded intimate, and so was the smile he doled out to her. In all the years he'd worked for Roman, Wynn could count on one hand how many times he'd seen his former boss smile, and every time it'd been in the presence of a woman on his to-bed list.

"You look pissed," Roman added, and Wynn realized Roman wasn't just talking to Carlene but to him, as well.

"Carlene didn't know Joe had left me the place," Wynn explained in a grumble.

Roman flexed his eyebrows in an *ah, that* expression. He certainly didn't seem surprised. "Joe called me last night and asked me to come out and talk to Carlene, to tell her what he was doing and why. Sorry," he added to Carlene, "but I was in Dallas and just got back. I didn't figure Wynn would get here this fast."

"Well, you figured wrong," Wynn informed him. There was nothing pleasant about his tone, and that's why it surprised and riled him when Roman smiled again.

This wasn't his ex-boss's panty-dropping smile. This was more akin to, *You're acting like a jackass, and I know why.*

"Why did Joe ask you to come and tell Carlene?" Wynn pressed.

Roman lifted his shoulder in a shrug so casual that only he and a Greek god could have managed it. "Carlene and I are friends. I guess Joe thought it'd be better coming from me. I told him it wasn't going to be *better*, no matter who she heard it from."

"You're right," she said. "And now Joe's not answering his phone because he probably hopes I'll calm down before he has to talk to me."

Roman made a sound of agreement. "Joe's also trying to get you two back together," he added. "But I'm guessing both of you figured that out. Joe will realize it was a bad idea once he sees what a mess this has made of things."

"A mess?" Wynn repeated. "Carlene and I haven't even had a chance to sit down and talk things out. Yes, we both have plans for the place, but that doesn't mean they can't mesh."

"You want to raise rodeo bulls out here. She wants to add a sustainable farm," Roman explained. "You don't have enough acreage to do both, and there's not any adjacent land you can buy. I know this because I own the adjacent land, and I'm not selling. My brother would smother me in my sleep if I sold any part of the Granger ranch."

Carlene looked at Wynn, no doubt to verify that it was indeed his plan to run bulls. He looked at her to verify the farm thing.

They both nodded.

Well, hell.

If Joe had told them both that he liked their plans, then his uncle was getting senile or else was so bent on this matchmaking that he didn't give a rat's butt whether it was logical or not.

"You want some coffee?" Carlene asked Roman. Obviously, she was past the shock enough to remember her manners. Or maybe Roman was just so important to her that he nullified life-altering shocks and such.

Yeah, Wynn was definitely jealous.

"No, thanks, but if you've got any spare eggs, Anita would appreciate it."

She nodded. "Let me go to the henhouse and get some fresh ones for her." Carlene headed out without so much as an explanation as to who Anita was, why she wanted eggs or why Roman and Carlene were so chummy.

"Anita?" Wynn asked after she'd left.

"My housekeeper at my place in San Antonio. She's allergic to regular eggs because of the antibiotics in them, so whenever I'm near Carlene's, I bring her back some."

"Your house is nearly an hour from here. That's a long way to come for eggs," Wynn grumbled.

Roman chuckled, went to the sofa and sat down, making himself at home by stretching out his legs and tucking his hands behind his head. "I always thought you still had feelings for Carlene, and this proves it. Your brown eyes are turning green."

Wynn started to say he wasn't jealous, but the words sort of stuck there in this throat.

"You're jealous," Roman confirmed a moment later. "But there are good reasons why things didn't work out between Carlene and you."

Yeah, there were, but Wynn didn't appreciate hearing that from Roman. "Did you have sex with Carlene?"

Roman gave him that bad-boy scowl he was famous for. "No. This might surprise you, but I don't have sex with every attractive woman who crosses my path."

"That's not what I heard." But Wynn waved that off. It was definitely the green-eyed monster talking. "Carlene said she was seeing Birch Davidson."

"She was. Don't think Birch has been over here in a while, though." Roman paused. "Personally, I don't think Carlene ever got over you."

That caused some of the jealousy to evaporate, but it didn't make him feel good. Because Wynn had always thought that, as well. He didn't want her sad, though. That said, he didn't want her with a guy like Roman. Or Birch, for that matter.

Wynn sank down on the chair across from Roman. "I don't think she'll ever forgive me for leaving."

"No," Roman agreed—a little too fast for Wynn's liking.

Wynn frowned because it was true. And he didn't want it to be. Hell. He still had feelings for Carlene, as well.

"We got married too young," Wynn continued. Not that he knew why he felt the need to clarify this to Roman, but he did. "Barely twenty-two. And we made it last for five years. But then I had all these dreams of being the best bull rider in the state, and she didn't share that dream." He paused. "I figured she had a lot of bad things to say about me after I left on the bull-riding circuit."

"Not really. Well, she did, but Carlene didn't spread it all over town. No way would she want folks to hear just how bad she was hurting." Roman looked at him. "Have you talked to her about all of this? I mean, have you two had a real heart-to-heart chat?"

Wynn replayed that question, and he sensed Roman meant more than the obvious. "You don't mean a discussion about the ranch."

Roman shook his head, but then stopped as if he'd said too much. He hadn't. Roman hadn't said nearly enough.

"Did Carlene actually come and tell you how she felt about me or something?" Wynn came out and asked.

"No." Roman scowled. "Just talk to her, and maybe you'll finally have a clue what she's been going through for the past three years."

Wynn intended to do that, and he was ready to start that chat right now.

Carlene came back inside. She had a basket of eggs under her arm, and she was talking on the phone. "No, I'll tell him," she said. "Thanks, Joe."

So, his uncle had finally returned her call, and only a few seconds after Carlene hit the end call button, Wynn's phone dinged with a text message.

Call me. Joe had texted. We gotta talk.

Heck, that didn't sound good, especially when it was coupled with a surprising expression on Carlene's face.

It was almost a smirk. She wasn't aiming it at Roman, either. It seemed to be all for Wynn.

"Joe apologized," she said. "He's sorry things have turned out the way they did, and he wants to come up with a new plan for the ranch. Wynn, you're no longer the owner."

CHAPTER THREE

THE SMELL REACHED her nose before Carlene had even opened her eyes. A scent she shouldn't have been smelling.

Chocolate.

She stirred, forcing herself to sit up, and checked the clock on the nightstand. It was 6:00 a.m., the usual time she got out of bed, but her body felt as if it hadn't had nearly enough sleep. Probably because it hadn't. She'd lain there, wide awake, most of the night, thinking about the person who was no doubt responsible for that chocolate smell.

Wynn.

To say he'd been upset over Joe's reversal was like saying a Texas summer was a little warm. Wynn had been furious, and she was betting Joe had known that would happen, because, after a very short conversation, Wynn had hung up, saying Joe wanted him to call him back after Wynn had cooled off. Carlene hadn't heard Joe's end of that discussion, but whatever he'd told his nephew, Wynn hadn't liked it one bit. And he hadn't cooled off. Wynn had said a crisp goodbye to Roman and stormed off to check the fences in the back pasture, he'd said. Wynn hadn't come back until well after dinner.

Which he'd fixed and then eaten in silence.

Carlene had hoped that Wynn would be riled enough to move into the inn in town or else stay with friends. But, apparently, no such luck. That chocolate smell was a dead giveaway that he was not only still there, he was making himself at home.

Of course, it had been his home since his uncle Joe had raised him after his folks were killed in a car wreck when he was barely twelve. But it felt like her home, too. Always had. And she wasn't about to give that up—especially now that Joe had given her the green light to stay. Unfortunately, that green light put Wynn and her on course for a head-on collision.

Carlene didn't especially want to face Wynn or his hot chocolate, but she had chores to do, so she forced herself out of bed and headed for the bathroom. The old house didn't have en suites, but there were two full baths off the hall. Since she figured Wynn had slept in Joe's room and used the one nearest to it, she went into the other one.

She'd been wrong.

Wynn opened the bathroom door just as she reached for the knob, and she ended up with her hand on the front of his boxers—the only thing he was wearing.

Good grief. This was way too much of a jolt so early in the morning. Actually, it was too much anytime of day. Because she looked in the wrong direction.

Specifically, the direction of his boxer shorts.

Suddenly, the last three years just flew out the window, and she was his wife and lover again. Emphasis on the lover part. If it had indeed been three years ago, they would have dragged each other to the floor and had a morning quickie right there.

And it would have been really good.

Her body wasn't going to let her forget that, because she got all warm and tingly in places that shouldn't be tingling. But it wasn't three years ago—the hurt was still there—and that's why she stepped back.

The corner of his mouth lifted in that damnable smile, and he had a sip from the cup he held in his left hand. Wynn and hot chocolate. The perfect storm.

Thankfully, she thought of the one thing she could ask that would not only get that smile off his face, but would also rebuild some barriers. Hopefully, ones that warded off tingling.

"Has Joe called you back yet?" she asked.

Wynn's mouth tightened, but it wasn't in a smile. Bingo—her question had worked.

"No. He said he was still trying to figure out what to do. He wanted to sleep on it."

Obviously, that bothered Wynn. He'd counted on having his name on the deed to the ranch. And his uncle had apparently promised him that, too. Part of her felt guilty for pleading her case directly to Joe, but she couldn't lose this place. Not after everything she'd been through.

"It looks as if you're having some regrets," he commented. "Or…something."

She wasn't sure what he saw in her expression that prompted that, but it was too vague an observation for her to start trying to come up with an answer. Especially while he was just inches from her in boxer shorts and drinking that heavenly-smelling brew.

"Why can't you just drink coffee like everybody else?" she snapped.

His smile returned. It was short-lived, though. "Never wanted to be like everybody else."

No, he hadn't. That's what had first attracted her to him. Ironically, though, it was that very quality that had driven them apart. Wynn had wanted to "not be like everybody else" by leaving Wrangler's Creek and becoming a bull-riding star. And in the end, she'd lost him.

"You could have left town and gone on the rodeo circuit with me, you know," he said, as if he knew exactly what she'd been thinking.

No. She couldn't have done that, and it was time to put an end to this tit-for-tat conversation. They were in a narrow hall, too close and barely dressed. Heck, she was just wearing one of his old T-shirts and a pair of skimpy panties. That was it. If he managed to keep spinning this heated web, clothing removal wouldn't take nearly long enough for her to think and rethink this.

"Guess you never got around to buying any PJs," Wynn commented. "When we were together, you always preferred wearing my T-shirt to bed."

She still did. Best not to mention that having something of his next to her body had helped her sleep better. No. She definitely wouldn't admit that.

She started to step around him, but Wynn blocked her path. "I was a little surprised yesterday when Roman showed up," he said.

Carlene waited for him to say more, but he was apparently finished. This seemed to be yet another of his fishing expeditions, and she thought maybe she knew what he was after.

"Roman's a friend," she explained. "I've never slept with him, if that's what you're asking. Not that it's any of your business."

She expected to see some kind of spark of relief. Or

anger that she'd tacked on that last bit. But he just kept staring at her.

Oh, mercy.

What had Roman told Wynn? If Roman had spilled *that*, then she was going to have a serious word with her friend about keeping secrets.

"I'd like to get in the shower now," she insisted. And then she could give Roman a call.

This time, Wynn got out of her way, but before she could go into the bathroom, there was a knock at the door. "For Pete's sake," she grumbled. "Who the heck is that this time of morning?"

"I'll check." With cocoa in his hand and his boxers fitting his butt like a glove, he headed in that direction.

"You might want to put on some pants."

"Anybody inconsiderate enough to come calling at this hour doesn't deserve pants."

She partly agreed with that, though she hoped whoever it was didn't think Wynn had climbed out of her bed that way. No need to help Joe's matchmaking by letting the gossips think that she and Wynn were back together.

Carlene went into the bathroom, took a quick shower and got dressed. She made that quick, too, since she didn't want to linger with barely any clothes on. Not with Wynn in the house. Plus, she wanted to find out who their visitor was. Once she stepped out of the bathroom, though, she had no trouble figuring that out. Because she could hear his voice.

Birch.

Oh, man. Not this.

She doubted it was a coincidence that Birch had come over so soon after Wynn's return. That was more than a simple guess, because in all the years she'd known Birch, he'd never visited her here. Once he'd brought her home from a party, but he'd stayed in the car. Having him walk her to the door hadn't seemed like a good thing to do, since he might have thought it was an invitation to come inside.

And spend the night.

Something Birch had never done.

As usual, Birch was dressed for work in his jeans, boots and cowboy hat. A hat he was now holding in front of him like a shield. There always seemed to be something downtrodden about him, as if he'd just lost something or expected to lose it. Hardly a ray of sunshine and definitely not a people charmer like Wynn.

Carlene made her way to the living room, and she didn't have to listen hard to hear the anger in Birch's voice. And his specific words. Words that weren't exactly true.

"I was working things out with Carlene," Birch insisted.

"So you've said," Wynn answered, not sounding angry at all. It was more like he was bored. "But I'm not sure she plans to work out things with you—"

"Sure she does. I don't want you getting in my way, either. Especially not in my way while wearing just your underwear."

That stopped her from going to the front door, and Carlene decided to head into the kitchen where she could listen a moment longer without Birch seeing her. Or Wynn. Judging from Wynn's tone, he probably wanted her to come in and put an end to this visit, but it wouldn't hurt to let him suffer a little longer.

"Carlene was warming up to me," Birch added.

Another lie, but she kept listening anyway.

"Just a couple months ago, we had a really long talk," Birch went on. "She got drunk at Sophie Granger's engagement party, so I drove her home. Carlene told me what happened."

Crap on a cracker. Carlene had enough fuzzy memories of that night to know that Birch was about to blurt out something she preferred not to be blurted.

"Birch, why are you here so early?" she asked. Carlene didn't exactly run to the front door, but she didn't poke along, either.

Birch blinked, as if surprised to see her. Or maybe he was just surprised that her eyes were narrowed in the warning stare she was giving him. A warning that she hoped he got, so he would stay quiet.

"Uh, I stopped by on my way into work. I just wanted to make sure you were okay," Birch said. He paused between each word. Apparently, he hadn't understood her warning, after all, and was trying to figure it out.

Birch went to her, took her by the shoulders and cast a frown back at Wynn. "Are you getting back together with Wynn?" he whispered. But he didn't give her a chance to answer. "Because you gotta remember how bad he hurt you last time."

Oh, she remembered, all right. And now, thanks to too much booze at Sophie's party, apparently Birch knew it, as well.

"Wynn and I aren't back together," she assured him.

Birch shot Wynn another frown. "But he slept here last night, and now he's wearing just his underwear."

"Because it's early and he hasn't dressed yet. Don't read anything into it, Birch. And don't tattle to anyone in town or at the Granger Ranch about it. People will get the wrong idea."

His mouth twisted. "I don't *tattle*. Besides, folks will get the wrong idea on their own if he's walking around the house in just his underwear." Birch paused. "Wynn said he kissed you yesterday."

Now she frowned at Wynn. There was no good reason to tell Birch that. But Wynn probably thought of it as marking his territory, even though she wasn't his territory to mark.

Wynn lifted his shoulder. "Well, we did kiss."

They had. A little bitty brush of the lips that was still more of a kiss than she'd ever gotten from Birch. Since she couldn't deny that except by lying, Carlene went with a diversionary tactic. "Are you going to be late for work?" she asked Birch.

He checked his watch. "I got a minute or two to talk."

"Well, I don't. I'm sorry," Carlene added, because she'd sounded harsh. With Birch, though, you had to spell things out. "I need some coffee and then I have to check on the calves."

"Fine," Birch sputtered out, "but I'll be by later to make sure you're okay."

She was shaking her head before he even finished. "No need. I have a full day."

There were no signs that what she'd said had sunk in. "Then I'll be by tonight. Maybe by then Wynn will have found his pants," Birch added, walking away.

"One can only hope." Carlene shut the door and headed for the kitchen.

"There was a time when you liked me without pants," Wynn joked.

There was a time when she liked him without boxers, too, but she kept that to herself. Carlene was more than ready to start a pot of coffee, but Wynn had obviously already made it. She poured herself a cup, had a sip and frowned.

"It's chocolate flavored," she said.

He came toward her then, much as he'd done outside the day before. And he had that look in his eye. The naughty one that seemed to ask if she wanted to fool around. Apparently, Wynn had a way of pushing aside unwanted visits, calf chores and unresolved issues. Especially the unresolved stuff, since they had plenty of that.

Some heat, too.

She got a reminder of that when he reached around her for a piece of toast and ended up grazing her stomach with his hand. He noticed, too. Probably because she sucked in her breath before she could stop herself. Their gazes connected, and for one body-tingling moment, she thought he was going to try to kiss her again.

And he did.

He leaned in and brushed his mouth over hers. Mercy, it packed a wallop, and a wise woman would have just stepped back. Carlene wasn't feeling so wise right then, though. In addition to the scalding-hot attraction, she was feeling as if she needed to set some boundaries with him. If she didn't, she would be in a perpetual pattern of stepping back or avoiding him.

"I don't know what you think is going to happen between us—" she started. And it was a darn good start, too. Her jaw was tight. She was semiglaring. Both good facial expressions to convey she wasn't happy about this. But Wynn conveyed some things, too, by interrupting her.

"Sex," he said. "That's not much of a guess, though.

Can you name a single time since adulthood, or even near adulthood, when we were together and didn't have sex?"

No. But she wasn't going to let that spoil her chance to make a point here. "I know you think sex is going to happen, and you're basing that assumption on past behavior, but I do have a fully functioning brain. One that has memories of why sex can't happen."

He seemed to have been expecting the answer, because he made a suit-yourself sound and went back to eating his toast. Some women might have thought that meant Wynn was giving up on the notion, but Carlene knew differently. Wynn was eyeing her and ready to say something she probably didn't want to hear.

"All right," he said. "No sex."

She pulled back her shoulders, and now she was the one eyeing him. And she was doing that with plenty of suspicion. She hadn't really expected him to give up so easily. After all, they did have that history of not being able to keep their clothes on whenever they were around each other. But she had changed in the past three years, and maybe Wynn had, too.

Carlene didn't want to think about why that made her a little sad.

But she thought about it anyway. It had been that throw-caution-to-the-wind spontaneity that had caused her to fall so hard for him. When the spontaneity wasn't annoying, it was like a breath of air. Not the breath-of-fresh-air kind, either. The kind she needed to feel, well, as if she was alive.

They kept eyeing each other, and just when Carlene thought she'd won this particular dispute, Wynn spoke. "What did you tell Birch that time when he brought you home when you were drunk?" he asked.

She nearly got choked on the sip of coffee she'd just taken, and Carlene wished she'd taken that step back from him, after all. A big step, as in one that would have put her in the barn doing those chores she should be doing.

"I don't remember," she said. It was the truth. "I told him drunk stuff, I'm sure."

And that was her cue to get moving. No breakfast for her. She threw down some more coffee and grabbed her coat, ready to head outside to start work. Since Wynn wasn't dressed, that would assure her at least a few minutes to compose herself before he came outside to try to get a real answer to his question. Or to lure her back to his mouth.

Carlene had already opened the back door when her phone rang, and she saw Joe's name on the screen. She'd expected him to call today, just not so soon.

"Is Wynn there?" Joe asked the moment she answered.

"Yes." In fact, he was literally right there. Wynn had already walked over to her.

"Good. Put the call on speaker so you can both hear what I have to say."

Suddenly, there was a butterfly swarm in her stomach. In the next few seconds, Joe could crush her hopes and dreams if he'd flip-flopped again on who was getting the ranch.

Carlene closed the back door, and because she didn't feel too steady on her feet, she sank down at the kitchen table before she put the call on speaker. Wynn continued to stand, and she didn't think it was her imagination that he seemed to be trying to brace himself for bad news, as well.

"First of all, I'm very sorry about all of this," Joe started. "When Wynn told me he was finally quitting the bull riding and settling down, I got all excited and spoke before I could think this through. I'd forgotten to take into account that Carlene loves the ranch, too."

"Are you taking back the place?" Wynn came out and asked him.

"No. But I'm afraid there's been a change of plans. I'm signing over the ranch to both of you. Half to Carlene. Half to you."

Both Wynn and she groaned. Obviously, this was a compromise, Joe's attempt to make them both happy, but this wasn't the way to go about it.

"Now, I know what you're thinking, Wynn," Joe went on. "That Carlene isn't actual kin and probably shouldn't be part owner."

She flinched. Of course, Carlene had known she wasn't blood kin, but she hadn't realized that would be a sore point for Wynn if Joe did, indeed, give her half. Wynn probably thought that, as Joe's only living relative, he shouldn't have to share it with anyone.

"But Carlene worked the place just like it was hers," Joe added. "I'm hoping you can both call it home."

"You're matchmaking," Wynn spat out.

"I was. At first," Joe readily admitted. "But I've been thinking on this all night, and it's not about getting the two of you back together. I don't believe that'll happen. There's been too much hurt, too much water under the bridge, but that shouldn't stop you from making the ranch the place it should be."

But it could.

After looking at Wynn, she was almost certain he felt the same. Which meant they had to find a way around this. Maybe she could even scrape together enough money to buy Wynn out.

"Carlene, I figure you're already trying to find a way to run the ranch by yourself," Joe went on a moment later. "Well, don't. Because when my granddaddy left the place to me, I told him I wouldn't sell off the land like other folks were doing."

"I wouldn't want to parcel it out," she assured him.

"No, but you're probably trying to come up with a way to get rid of Wynn. Again, don't do that."

Joe had just put her in an impossible place. One with a man she still wanted, but who'd crushed her heart.

Joe had never been exactly, well, focused. Carlene had seen it time and time again when he'd bought too much of one thing and too little of another. He'd often missed appointments or gotten so involved with reading a book that he'd forgotten about the chores. Simply put, he was a dreamer, but right now, Joe was dreaming the wrong dream.

"Here are the only two conditions I have," Joe continued a moment later. "You can't sell your halves, not even to each other. And you have to live there together." Joe paused before he delivered the final blow. "If one of you moves off the ranch, then you forfeit your half to the other."

CHAPTER FOUR

WYNN USUALLY CONSIDERED himself a happy man, but he damn sure didn't fall into that particular category right now. Nope. He was mad at his uncle Joe for reneging on the deal for him to have the ranch. He was mad at the cold weather, with those blasted iron-gray clouds that were spitting down sleet on him.

And, yep, he was mad at Carlene, too.

Unlike him, she didn't seem to be seething, though, and hadn't been since Joe delivered his verdict. Her lack of a reaction was probably because, unlike yesterday, she was now half owner of something she'd thought she'd lost. Still, she was just *half*.

No way would the place actually be hers, but she was sure as heck acting as if it was. She'd gotten on with her chores as if nothing had changed.

Along with ignoring him.

He guessed that was her plan—just pretend he wasn't there for the next fifty years or so. Well, Wynn had done that, too. He'd spent a good chunk of the cold-ass day fixing fences. Normally, it was something he liked to do—the solitude, working with his hands—but it hadn't given him much solace today.

Plus, there were the aches and pains. Too many of them, considering he was only thirty. Riding bulls had definitely taken a toll on his body, what with two concussions, four broken bones and a dislocated shoulder. The pain wouldn't interfere with the work he had to do, but each twinge was a reminder that being a bull rider had cost him more than just Carlene.

Wynn finished up a fence repair and rode his horse back through the pasture so he could check on the herd. There were plenty of hay bales all around. Plenty of water from the creek, too. In other words, the Santa Gertrudises had everything they needed to thrive, even in the winter.

But Roman had been right. There was enough land for these cows, but not for the bulls Wynn had wanted to bring in. For Wynn to get what he wanted, he'd have to upset a good balance that Carlene had obviously managed to work out with the cattle-to-land ratio. He'd have to screw up her plan. Since he'd already done that once, he wasn't so inclined to do it again.

Well, if her plan had truly been to be married to him, that was.

At the time, it'd sure seemed that way. His plan, too. Now, though, she was much wiser, and she almost certainly didn't have him on her "dream" list. He might make her crap list, though, if he didn't talk this out with her and let her know that things could stay as is. He wasn't sure how he would fit into "as is," which was another reason for them to have a chat.

When Wynn rode back to the house, he didn't have any trouble finding her. She was in the log cabin behind the main house. It was his grandpa's old place that was now being used as a storage shed. Or, at least, it had been. But, like the boxes in his room, there was stuff out here, too.

Judging from the cobwebs in her hair and the dust

on her work clothes, Carlene had been cleaning. She also had a fire going, and the flames were snapping in the rough stone hearth. The place wasn't exactly toasty warm, but it was a heck of a lot better than being outside. That's how Wynn justified going inside with her, but he really did want to know what she was up to now.

"Let me guess. You're turning this into a B and B or a dude ranch," he joked.

She didn't scowl, didn't look at him as if he were toenail fungus. Carlene actually smiled, put her hands on her hips and glanced around the place as if admiring her work. And she had certainly worked. All the boxes and old tools had been shoved to a corner, and she'd cleared the living room and the area that led to the kitchen. The last time he'd been out here, he could barely get the toe of his boot through the door.

"I'm turning this into a home again," she said. "Joe didn't say anything about one of us not being able to move out here. The electricity's still on, and the plumbing works, so I can live here."

Wynn frowned, and he wasn't sure why he was frowning because it wasn't a bad idea. The place wasn't huge, two bedrooms and a small bath, but it would be plenty of room for Carlene.

"Anyway, I thought I'd finish cleaning today and get my things moved in tomorrow," she continued. "After that, you won't have to see me."

His frown deepened, and this time he knew why. "What if I want to see you?" he threw out there.

She dismissed that with an idle chuckle and went to the massive window just over the sofa. From here, they had a wide-angle view of the pastures.

"I was going to make this into a chicken coop, but I

can build a new one out there." She pointed to the left side of the pasture. "Or there." She motioned to the other side. "I guess it all depends on how we divvy up the land. I was thinking about taking the east half and you could take the west."

He was frowning again. Again, he knew why. "I hadn't thought to divvy it up at all."

"Well, we'll need to do that. How else are we going to fit in all our plans? I figure you'll want to bring in those bulls, and I want to raise some goats."

Now, he was really frowning. "Texas ranchers don't raise goats."

"No, but Texas *farmers* do. I took this class on cheese making, and I need goat's milk for that. I won't have any trouble selling it at the farmer's market."

Well, hell in a handbasket. Now they were getting into the cheese business. Maybe they could build a cracker factory to go with it.

"Garrett called earlier," she continued, still looking out the window. "Apparently, Birch left here this morning and went straight to talk to him. Garrett thinks I'm miserable and offered me a job. A place to live, too. He said I could use the guesthouse on the ranch."

It took Wynn a moment to process that, and something jumped right out at him. Obviously Garrett, and maybe plenty of other people in Wrangler's Creek, thought this living arrangement wasn't a good idea.

It wasn't.

But why were they so sure of it?

"Are you miserable?" Wynn asked.

She snapped toward him, and when she looked at him, he could almost see the regret she had about spilling that. Again, he wanted to know why.

He gently took hold of her arm and turned her so they were fully facing each other. "Roman hinted that something had happened after I left. There are enough people worried about you that I know something's wrong."

Carlene huffed. "Well, what's wrong is my ex-husband breezed back into my life and keeps trying to put the moves on me."

That was true, but there was something else. "What the hell happened after I left three years ago?" It was time he got some answers, too.

She huffed even louder than the last time and would have dodged his gaze if he hadn't kept a grip on her arm.

"I'm not leaving this cabin until I find out what went wrong," Wynn added.

Carlene stared at him. And stared. Then she muttered a few words of profanity. Wynn stared at her, as well, waiting. Because there was nothing that was going to make him back down from getting an answer.

Or so he thought.

But he'd been wrong.

Carlene caught onto the front of his shirt, wadding it up in her hands, and she yanked him to her. In that same yanking motion, she managed to land her mouth right on his. And she kissed him. Really kissed him. She made it hot and deep right from the start. Not many places to go from there, except maybe straight to bed.

She tasted like birthday cake. Always had. Something sweet and fun. It was a taste that filled him with expectations. And lust. Especially lust. He went from surprised to rock hard in seconds.

Of course, Wynn knew this was a ploy so that he wouldn't press her on the question, and that riled him.

But it didn't rile him enough to put an end to the kissing. He wanted this for just a little while longer.

Carlene gave him *longer*.

She kept kissing, and she lifted her hands, sliding them around the back of his neck until there was nothing between their bodies.

He expected her to protest, but that wasn't a protesting sound she made. It was a purr. Soft and silky. Just like the woman herself.

His chest was already pressing against her breasts, and he moved his hand to the front of her shirt to do some touching and playing. She made another of those purrs, and he could tell that both the kisses and the touches were heating her up. Since he was well past the heated-up stage, he forced himself to think of what to do next. He could just go with the flow, but that would land them on the floor for some crazy, fast sex. Or he could consider that this maybe wasn't the best idea.

His erection didn't want him to consider it. Actually, no part of his body wanted it, but he had to look beyond the moment. Something he wasn't always good at doing. Still, Wynn tried, and what he saw was that this could seriously screw up the tenuous relationship they had. And if it didn't screw it up, it might give Carlene expectations that he wasn't sure she should have.

Not right now, anyway.

And that's why Wynn pulled back and looked her straight in the eyes. "We'll have sex after you tell me what happened."

Man, it was hard for him to do that. Having a hot, willing Carlene in his arms was pure fantasy material. But there was a price here that Carlene might not want to pay.

"Did you have a miscarriage or something?" he pressed. Because that was the bad thing that kept coming to mind—that she'd lost a baby, their baby, and he hadn't been there with her when it happened.

"Fine," she snapped.

But Carlene didn't say anything else. She stepped away from him, folded her arms over her chest. Her bottom lip began to tremble a little while the seconds just crawled by.

"I had a breakdown, all right?" she finally said.

So, no miscarriage, but Wynn had to shake his head. "What do you mean?"

"I mean, I went crazy, and they had to put me in a place for crazy people. There. Are you happy now?" Unlike him, she didn't wait for an answer. Carlene grabbed her coat and stormed out.

"What are you going to do?"

Carlene stared down into her beer. The answer wasn't in the mug of Lone Star, so she looked at her friend who'd asked the question.

Mila Banchini.

She was seated across from Carlene in a booth at the Longhorn Bar. When Mila arrived about an hour earlier, she'd been in a fairly good mood. After all, with their busy schedules, they didn't get together that often for drinks anymore. But Carlene had clearly managed to spread her doom and gloom mood to her friend. Mila's forehead was bunched up, and there was concern in her eyes.

Carlene was certain there was a Texas-sized amount of concern in her own eyes, too. It coordinated well with the doom and gloom.

"I never wanted Wynn to know what happened to

me," Carlene said. Since there still weren't any answers in the beer, she had a sip of it.

Mila lifted her shoulder. "It's hard to keep secrets in Wrangler's Creek."

Carlene made a sound of agreement. "True. But in this case, I thought it was okay because only Roman and you knew."

And they knew because Mila had been the one to drive Carlene to the hospital in San Antonio. Mila had called Roman shortly thereafter so he could wait with her while the doctors had been evaluating Carlene.

Carlene groaned softly. Not exactly sugarplum memories. "I might have told Birch, too, when I had too much to drink at Sophie's party."

"No." Mila immediately shook her head. "You told him you were still in love with Wynn and that Wynn had broken your heart."

Carlene stared at her and was about to ask how Mila could possibly know that. Then she remembered that Mila had been in the car with them that night. Well, it was something, at least, that Carlene hadn't blabbered to Birch, but that didn't undo the bottom line here.

Mila and Roman had kept her secret.

It had been Carlene who'd ratted herself out to Wynn.

Or, rather, she'd told him just enough to let him know that, because of him, she had crumbled like a dry autumn leaf under the heel of a boot.

"So, what are you going to do?" Mila repeated. She had a sip of her own drink. Not beer. It was pink and had a skewer of cherries and pineapple chunks spearing out of it.

"Murder is illegal in Texas." It was Carlene's attempt at a joke.

Mila patted her hand. "You don't want to murder

Wynn. And that's the problem. You've always wanted him. Still do."

Yes. And Carlene didn't even attempt to lie about it. A lie that big might have sent a lightning bolt right at her. And speaking of lightning bolts, one did come into the bar.

Wynn.

He stepped in, looking around, and the moment he laid eyes on her, he started her way. Carlene so wished she'd found answers in her beer or in this chat with Mila. No such luck, though. She was completely clueless about how to handle this.

Wynn, however, seemed to have given this some thought.

He set aside her beer, hauled Carlene out of the booth and kissed the living daylights out of her. It happened so fast that she didn't even see it coming. But, mercy, she felt it all right. The tingling came, and it didn't seem to matter that she was answerless or that this was going on in the middle of a crowded bar. For a few seconds, everything vanished but the heat that the kiss was generating.

Wynn kept kissing her until they'd die if they didn't break for air. That's when Wynn stopped kissing her and grabbed her coat from the booth.

"Carlene and I have to…uh, talk," Wynn said to Mila.

Mila smiled. "With you two, sometimes kissing works better than talking."

Carlene agreed, but then again, that was because she was under the influence of the blistering attraction. That's why she didn't stop Wynn when he helped her into her coat and took her outside.

His truck was parked right by the door, and he'd left

the engine on. It was warm when he pulled her inside and he got behind the wheel. It became even warmer when he kissed her again. Not just her mouth, either.

Oh, man.

He went after her neck, tonguing her in the most sensitive spot she had above the waist. She cursed him for remembering the location of that spot—just below her ear. And she cursed him again when he reminded her that he knew how to use that spot to make her want a whole lot more of him than just his mouth and tongue.

His hands, for a start.

And he gave her that, as well.

Those nimble fingers worked their way beneath her top, found her bra and pushed down the cups so he could pinch her nipples. Again, they were hot spots, and Wynn knew it. Coupled with the neck kisses and his other hand sliding up her thigh, Carlene was ready to get him naked right there.

And then someone tapped on the window.

Wynn and she flew apart as if they'd just been caught doing something they shouldn't have been doing. Which was the truth. At least, they shouldn't have been doing it in front of the Longhorn.

Carlene had to wipe off the condensation on the window before she could see the tapper. It was Roman. He was scowling and smiling at the same time, something that only Roman could have accomplished.

She lowered the window when Roman motioned for her to do that. "Busy?" Roman asked.

There was definitely no smiley part in her scowl. "I know I'm playing with fire," Carlene said. She kept her voice at a whisper, but Wynn probably heard her anyway.

"Well, as long as you know what you're doing," Roman said. His scowl was gone now, and he was back to his usual badass expression.

Oh, Carlene knew what she was doing, all right, but she had no idea what the consequences would be. At best, there'd be a lot of confused feelings. At worst, well, she didn't even want to go there.

Roman took something from his pocket and tossed it into the truck. A condom. "Be safe. And if you find a lull when Wynn's tongue isn't in your mouth, maybe you should tell him what happened to you after he left."

"I did tell him," she said. At least, she'd given Wynn the big picture. Not the details, though.

Wynn leaned forward so he could make eye contact with Roman. "You're not going to threaten to kick my ass if I hurt Carlene again?"

"Oh, that's a given. But only Carlene can decide if she's going to let you do that to her. And only you can decide if you want to avoid the ass whipping by doing the right thing."

With that annoying advice, Roman strolled away and into the Longhorn. It was annoying because it was true. On her part, anyway. She held her own destiny in her hands. She could put an end to the kissing and not risk another broken heart. Another meltdown.

Or she could do something that would prove she was no longer going to fall apart without him.

She picked up the condom and showed it to Wynn. "Let's put this to good use right now."

CHAPTER FIVE

RIGHT NOW WOULD have to wait a few minutes. Those kisses and touches with Carlene had made Wynn crazy, but he wasn't so far gone that he thought it would be a good idea to get Carlene naked in a public place where another window-tapping incident could happen. That's why Wynn started driving.

"Hurry," Carlene insisted.

That reminder wasn't necessary, and it was barely recognizable as a word since Carlene—along with her mouth and tongue—were making their way down into his shirt and onto his chest. This was the problem with being with his ex, who knew every inch of his body. And she knew plenty about how to make him crazy.

Wynn risked kissing her once they'd made it out of town, but it was a quick one so he could focus on the road. Despite the raging inferno in his body, it was best if they arrived at the ranch in one piece.

Carlene, however, didn't seem to have those same concerns. Nope. She kept unbuttoning his shirt and continued to French kiss her way down his chest to his stomach. Most women would have probably stopped there and waited for less cramped maneuvering space, but not Carlene. He'd learned a long time ago that she didn't fall into the "most women" category. She dipped down her head and kissed his erection through his jeans.

Wynn cursed her, which made her laugh and kiss him harder. He wanted to tell her to slow down, but he no longer seemed capable of something as complex as human speech. That's why he just said to hell with it and pulled off onto a ranch trail. They were off the road where they wouldn't get hit or land in a ditch, and once he had the engine in Park, he could go after her with both hands. And his erection.

But Wynn froze.

Even though he hadn't thought himself capable of human speech, some human thoughts popped into his mind. He still wasn't sure exactly what Carlene had gone through after he'd left, but it had no doubt been bad. Bad enough for Roman to threaten him with the butt kicking if he did it again. Wynn definitely didn't want to send her into another tailspin.

"I don't want to hurt you," he managed to say.

Carlene was in the process of unzipping him, but her head whipped up. Thanks to the headlights and a full moon, he had no trouble seeing her eyes. And the surprise in them.

She stared at him for several snail-crawling moments. "Good. The best way for you not to hurt me is to have sex with me right now."

Wynn knew his mind was fuzzy from the heat, but he wasn't sure if it was the fuzziness or if Carlene just wasn't making much sense. He wanted to give that some thought. Wanted to do the right thing. But the only thought Carlene seemed to have was getting him unzipped.

Which she managed just fine.

With their eyes still connected, she freed him from his boxers. The corner of her mouth lifted into a smile, and she lowered her head. After she took him into her mouth, Wynn gave up on the notion of making sense. Hell, it was possible he no longer knew the meaning of the word *notion*.

However, he did know a lot about pleasure because Carlene was giving him a big-ass dose of that. It was amazing. And brought back so many memories of the times they'd done this when they were teenagers.

It brought back another memory, too.

That he didn't want her to finish him off this way. He wanted to be inside her for that; he could make good use of the condom Roman had given him.

Wynn took hold of her shoulders, pulling her back up. In the same motion, he lowered her to the seat. She struggled a little at first, no doubt trying to get back to what would be a fast undoing for him. But when he kissed her, she slid right back into it. Wynn did some sliding, too. He pushed up her top, unhooking her bra so he could kiss her breasts. The fire was making them very needy, very fast, but that didn't mean he was ready to give up all foreplay. Especially when this foreplay was something he'd really missed.

It wasn't just the way she tasted. Or the soft feel of her skin. It was that silky sound of pleasure Carlene made when he took her nipple into his mouth. The sounds went on for only a couple of seconds, though, before she apparently reached her threshold for foreplay.

The battle began to get her out of her jeans. It wasn't pretty. Wynn cursed when he banged his funny bone against the dash. Carlene didn't fare much better when her foot got tangled up in the steering wheel. Wynn nearly jumped out of his own jeans when she accidentally blew the horn. But he didn't let blaring horns or bruises deter him.

He finally shimmied her out of her jeans. Out of her panties, too. And he took another moment to admire the view. It was a painful moment because his erection was aching now. That could possibly be because during the jeans battle, Carlene had elbowed him in the groin.

Pushing the pain aside, Wynn got the condom on and then pulled Carlene onto his lap. This was his favorite way of having sex with her. Maybe because they'd had so much practice at it. Body to body and face to face where he could kiss her when he pushed right into all that tight heat.

Kissing her mouth might be like birthday cake, but being inside her was like every holiday rolled into one. Unforgettable. And just plain fun.

She moved the right way, sliding back and forth in just the perfect rhythm. Slow at first. Then, faster. Then, much, much faster. He needed that pace, that friction, but he knew what Carlene needed, too, so he slipped his hand lower. Between her legs. He touched her in a spot that he knew would send her soaring. Of course, the added benefit to that was Carlene would cause him to soar right along with her.

So, he touched. Kissed. And took the fun to the last, final stage. Carlene did, indeed, send him soaring.

HER BUTT WAS jammed against the steering wheel. Normally, Carlene would have done something about it. Like move, for instance. But she wasn't sure she could move just yet.

The climax was still rippling through her. The first big jolt was over, of course, but she was getting some nice aftershocks. Plus, she was in Wynn's arms, pressed against his body, so there were perks to that, too. Kissing him was one of them, so that was what she did. She kissed him and let the dreamy feel of pleasure wash over her from head to toe.

Wynn didn't seem to be in a hurry for her to move so she lingered a while. What she wanted to do was linger more than a while, but the butt cramp she suddenly got upped the urgency for her to get off his lap.

"I guess I've let those muscles get out of shape," she grumbled.

"Nothing wrong with your muscles or your shape."

He kissed her, bringing back the dreamy feel, but when she pulled back and their eyes met, Carlene knew that *dreamy* was going to go on the back burner for a bit. Wynn wanted to talk now. Or, rather, he wanted to listen while she told him what had happened to her. That didn't seem like a conversation they should have while she was naked, so she started to dress. That had a twofold purpose. She really did need to put her pants on, and if she was dressing she wouldn't have to look him in the eyes when she told him.

"Do you remember the day you left?" she asked, but didn't wait for an answer. "I was at the ranch and watched you drive away."

"You waved to me," he said.

Carlene nodded. She had cursed him, too, but he probably hadn't been enough of a lip reader to know that.

"Anyway, I was okay for a day or two," she went on, "but then I started crying and couldn't seem to stop. Joe got worried and called Mila. She came over, took one look at me and got me into her car. She told Joe that she and I were going on a girls' trip. Where we went was to a hospital in San Antonio."

"I'm so sorry," he said, and that definitely wasn't his charmer tone. She could hear the sadness, the regret. Not exactly a good finish to the best round of sex ever had in a truck.

"We should finish this conversation at the ranch," she suggested.

He stared at her as if he might challenge that, but he zipped up and got them moving. It didn't take them long, especially now that there wasn't a raging, hungry heat inside them. It was only at the dormant raging stage right now, although she figured a kiss would ignite it again. But she doubted Wynn was going to kiss her until she finished airing her dirty laundry.

Once they were back at the house, Wynn disappeared into the bathroom for several minutes. Enough time for Carlene to fix them cups of hot chocolate. She considered adding some tequila to hers, but admitted the booze would be just a crutch. No, it was best to get through the rest of this while sober. And, besides, tequila and hot chocolate would probably taste disgusting.

"Do you hate me?" Wynn asked when he came back into the living room.

"No." That was the truth. Carlene sat down on the sofa and patted the spot next to her. After pausing, Wynn joined her.

She waited until he'd had a sip of his hot chocolate before she continued. "I saw some doctors at the hospital in San Antonio, and I mentioned that I was having some very depressing thoughts." It hadn't helped that she'd still been crying nonstop. "Anyway, I believe they thought I was suicidal. I wasn't. At that point I was just really sad and congested from all the crying."

"The doctors thought it was more serious?" he asked.

Carlene hated the look on his face, and she knew he was blaming himself. Back then, she'd blamed him, too, but she knew now that it wasn't his fault. Since she could have, indeed, gone with him on the rodeo circuit, this was on her shoulders.

She nodded. "The doctors sent me to what they called a mental health resort. Sort of a spa with counselors. I was there for a month."

Now, the profanity didn't just stay in his eyes. It traveled to his mouth, and to stop him from giving her an apology she didn't want, Carlene kissed him. She didn't make it a long one, though. No French involved. That would only lead to sex, and she needed to finish this chat first.

"I got the help I needed there," she assured him. "And the counselors helped me work through what I was feeling." Carlene took a deep breath. "Now you know. I wasn't woman enough to go on without you."

"That's BS." He added a bunch of other curse words, too. "You did go on. You rebuilt the ranch."

"Yes, but only after I went crazy."

No more cursing, but he did make a soft grunt that sounded as if he was agreeing with her. "After I left you," he said, "I purposely rode bulls named Ball Buster and Lucifer. That was my version of having a breakdown. I paid for it, too, by getting one concussion too many."

Sheez. That didn't sound like a breakdown. It sounded crazy. "Were you hurt bad?" He shrugged which meant the answer was yes. "How bad?" Carlene pressed.

He dragged in a long breath. "Bad enough that I had to stop riding. But I was ready to stop," Wynn quickly added. "I'd made it to the top and still had enough of a brain left to know that the top wasn't where I wanted to be. Maybe it was never where I wanted to be."

Carlene frowned. "But you're the one who left," she pointed out.

"Yeah, because I thought I'd lose it if I stayed here, if I didn't give my dreams a shot. And I knew if I lost it, that I'd take you down with me. I thought if I left, that would be the best thing for you."

So, that's what had been going through his mind. It was possible Wynn had even told her those things, but Carlene had been too heartbroken to hear them. She sure as heck heard it now, though. Heard it and understood it.

"You should hate me," Wynn said.

She huffed. "Already tried that. Didn't work. In fact, the only thing that's worked is this."

And she slid her hand around the back of his neck, pulled him to her and kissed him. There was one thing better than truck sex and that was couch sex. They could save the bed for later, if they had enough condoms.

Carlene was about to ask him about the condom count, but Wynn took over the kiss and reminded her that talk was sometimes overrated. He kept kissing her and started to get her naked.

But a sound stopped them.

Someone was tapping on the door.

As they'd done in the truck, Wynn and she flew apart, their attention going to the small glass panels on the front door. The glass was plenty clear enough for Carlene to see who was doing the tapping.

Not Roman this time.

But Joe.

"Interrupting anything?" Joe asked, when he opened the door and stuck his head inside.

Yes, he had definitely interrupted, but if Joe noticed, he didn't seem concerned. He came in almost sheepishly, holding his cowboy hat in both hands and looking like a man on the verge of maybe doing some groveling.

Yep, it was groveling, all right, because it started almost immediately.

"I owe you both a big *I'm sorry*, and that comes from the bottom of my heart," Joe said.

Carlene had never understood that expression and wondered if apologies from the top of the heart would be any less sincere. Either way, Joe seemed to mean it.

"You came all this way to say you're sorry?" Wynn asked.

"That, and I had a little business to take care of. I've been trying to fix things, you see. I just came from talking with Garrett Granger, but he and Roman won't sell any land. They will, however, lease us enough acres for you to raise those rodeo bulls."

Wow, she hadn't expected that, but she was certain that Wynn was grateful. So was she, because this meant there'd be enough land for both Wynn and her to carry out their plans.

"There's more," Joe went on. He took an envelope from his coat pocket and put it on the coffee table between the two cups of hot chocolate. "That's the deed to the place. It's in both your names. But there's also a check so that you can build a second house. I suggest you put the second one all the way at the back of the property line."

The line was nearly a half mile away from the ranch house.

"That way, you and Wynn will never have to see each other," Joe added. "You can run the front part of the ranch with your cows, chickens and goats." He made a face, though, when he mentioned that last part. Once a cowboy, always a cowboy. "And Wynn can run the back half of the ranch with his bulls."

Obviously, Joe had given this a lot of thought. Maybe more thought than Carlene had been giving it in the last couple of hours.

She looked at Wynn to see what his feelings were about this, but he was looking a little sad or something.

"I don't want your money," Wynn told his uncle.

Joe nodded. "I figured you'd say that, but it's not my money. It's yours. I've decided to give you your inheritance early. And it's not as if I'll miss it. My daddy left me a pretty good chunk of cash, and I've got plenty to live the way I want. Now I want the same for you two. I know this doesn't make up for what I did. But maybe it'll fix things the right way."

He gathered them both in his arms, kissed them on their foreheads and then turned and headed for the door.

"Wait." Wynn stepped in front of him. "You're just leaving?"

Joe blushed a little. "Got a hot date tomorrow, and I don't want to miss it. Besides, I'd imagine you've got plenty of details to start working out. Building that house, buying those bulls." He smiled at Carlene. "And you can get started on those goats. I'm expecting you to send me some of that cheese you learned how to make."

"I will," she assured him, and gave him a kiss on

the cheek. "You're sure you have to go? I could fix you some hot chocolate..."

"Thanks, but no thanks. Gladys—that's the name of my hot date—won't like it if I miss my flight. I need to be at the airport in an hour. And no, don't offer to drive me because I got a rental car. Stay put, get those plans done and then you two can start your lives far apart from each other. Just the way you want," he added.

They stood there, watching him leave, his final words practically echoing through the room.

Just the way you want.

Yes, two days ago Carlene had wanted just that. To be far away from Wynn. And while this new plan wouldn't exactly put them "far" apart, they would have plenty of space between them.

Plenty.

The wave of doom and gloom came, but unlike the last time, Carlene knew she wouldn't just give into it. Nope. She could stand on her own two feet.

She snapped toward Wynn. "It's all right if you go. I swear, I won't fall apart."

He frowned. Really frowned. He glanced at the envelope Joe had left before his attention settled on her.

"I could probably say a lot of things." His voice was tight, like that frowny expression on his face. "Some of those things would be right, some could be wrong."

She steeled herself for the wrong things, although she hoped they would be right. But Wynn didn't say anything. He pulled her to him and kissed her.

He made it openmouthed.

And long. And really hot.

He made that kiss exactly the way Carlene wanted it to be, and he pulled back just short of breath-gasping time.

"Was that the right thing to say?" he drawled.

She nodded. "Perfect."

He kissed her again. And again. The next one, though, involved him maneuvering her to the couch. Not for that envelope, though. He went after her top. She went after his jeans.

"I don't want a second house," he said through the kisses. "I don't want a life apart from you."

"Good," she managed to say. "Because that's exactly what I don't want, too."

"Perfect," Wynn repeated, and he proceeded to show Carlene that her memories of couch sex with him had definitely not been exaggerated.

* * * * *

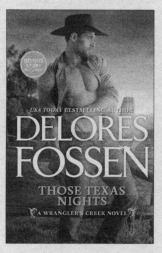

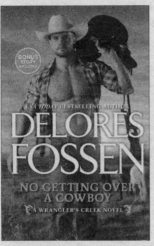

When it comes to sweet and sexy
romance, no one does it like
New York Times bestselling author

MAISEY YATES

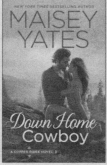
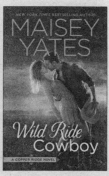

Available June 27   Available August 29

*Come home to Copper Ridge, where sexy cowboys
and breathtaking kisses are just around the corner!*

Get your copies today!

"Fans of Robyn Carr and RaeAnne Thayne
will enjoy [Yates's] small-town romance."
—*Booklist* on *Part Time Cowboy*

www.HQNBooks.com

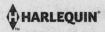

INTRIGUE

EDGE-OF-YOUR-SEAT INTRIGUE, FEARLESS ROMANCE.

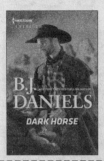

Save **$1.00**

on the purchase of ANY Harlequin® Intrigue book.

Available wherever books are sold, including most bookstores, supermarkets, drugstores and discount stores.

✂

Save $1.00

on the purchase of any Harlequin® Intrigue book.

Coupon valid until October 31, 2017.
Redeemable at participating outlets in the U.S. and Canada only. Not redeemable at Barnes & Noble stores. Limit one coupon per customer.

52614848

Canadian Retailers: Harlequin Enterprises Limited will pay the face value of this coupon plus 10.25¢ if submitted by customer for this product only. Any other use constitutes fraud. Coupon is nonassignable. Void if taxed, prohibited or restricted by law. Consumer must pay any government taxes. Void if copied. Inmar Promotional Services ("IPS") customers submit coupons and proof of sales to Harlequin Enterprises Limited, P.O. Box 3000, Saint John, NB E2L 4L3, Canada. Non-IPS retailer—for reimbursement submit coupons and proof of sales directly to Harlequin Enterprises Limited, Retail Marketing Department, 225 Duncan Mill Rd., Don Mills, ON M3B 3K9, Canada.

U.S. Retailers: Harlequin Enterprises Limited will pay the face value of this coupon plus 8¢ if submitted by customer for this product only. Any other use constitutes fraud. Coupon is nonassignable. Void if taxed, prohibited or restricted by law. Consumer must pay any government taxes. Void if copied. For reimbursement submit coupons and proof of sales directly to Harlequin Enterprises, Ltd 482, NCH Marketing Services, P.O. Box 880001, El Paso, TX 88588-0001, U.S.A. Cash value 1/100 cents.

5 65373 00076 2   (8100)0 12281

HICOUPBJD0617

"I want to ask you about your babies," Nikki said. "Oakley and
Jesse Rose?" Was it her imagination or did the woman clutch
the dolls even harder to her thin chest?

"What happened the night they disappeared?" Did Nikki
really expect an answer? She could hope, couldn't she? Mostly,
she needed to hear the sound of her voice in this claustrophobic
room. The rocking had a hypnotic effect, like being pulled
down a rabbit hole.

"Everyone outside this room believes you had something to
do with it. You and Nate Corwin." No response, no reaction to
the name. "Was he your lover?"

She moved closer, catching the decaying scent that rose from
the rocking chair as if the woman was already dead. "I don't
believe it's true. But I think you might know who kidnapped
your babies," she whispered.

The speculation at the time was that the kidnapping had been
an inside job. Marianne had been suffering from postpartum
depression. The nanny had said that Mrs. McGraw was having
trouble bonding with the babies and that she'd been afraid to
leave Marianne alone with them.

And, of course, there'd been Marianne's secret lover—the man everyone believed had helped her kidnap her own children. He'd been implicated because of a shovel found in the stables with his bloody fingerprints on it—along with fresh soil—even though no fresh graves had been found.

"Was Nate Corwin involved, Marianne?" The court had decided that Marianne McGraw couldn't have acted alone. To get both babies out the second-story window, she would have needed an accomplice.

"Did my father help you?"

There was no sign that the woman even heard her, let alone recognized her alleged lover's name. And if the woman had answered, Nikki knew she would have jumped out of her skin.

She checked to make sure Tess wasn't watching as she snapped a photo of the woman in the rocker. The flash lit the room for an instant and made a snap sound. As she started to take another, she thought she heard a low growling sound coming from the rocker.

She hurriedly took another photo, though hesitantly, as the growling sound seemed to grow louder. Her eye on the viewfinder, she was still focused on the woman in the rocker when Marianne McGraw seemed to rock forward as if lurching from her chair.

A shriek escaped her before she could pull down the camera. She had closed her eyes and thrown herself back, slamming into the wall. Pain raced up one shoulder. She stifled a scream as she waited for the feel of the woman's clawlike fingers on her throat.

But Marianne McGraw hadn't moved. It had only been a trick of the light. And yet, Nikki noticed something different about the woman.

Marianne was smiling.

Don't miss
DARK HORSE by B.J. Daniels,
available August 2017 wherever
Harlequin® Intrigue books and ebooks are sold.

www.Harlequin.com

HIEXP0717

Get 2 Free Books,
Plus 2 Free Gifts -
just for trying the *Reader Service!*